Swimming
to Ithaca

Also by Simon Mawer

FICTION

Mendel's Dwarf
A Jealous God
The Bitter Cross
Chimera
The Gospel of Judas
The Fall

NON-FICTION

A Place in Italy

Swimming to Ithaca

Simon Mawer

LITTLE, BROWN

My thanks to Phaedon Stamatop̶̶̶̶̶̶̶̶̶̶ance with the Greek.

LITTLE, BROWN

First published in Great Britain in May 2006 by Little, Brown

Copyright © Simon Mawer 2006

A CIP catalogue record for this book is available from the British Library.

ISBN 0 316 73099 8

Typeset in Garamond by M Rules
Printed and bound in Great Britain by
Clays Ltd, St Ives plc

Little, Brown
An imprint of
Time Warner Book Group UK
Brettenham House
Lancaster Place
London WC2E 7EN

www.twbg.co.uk

For Charles Walker

One

Thomas Denham watched his mother dying.

The historian in him had expected the event to have a significance of some kind. It surprised him to find none. Oh, there was tragedy of course. Agony, misery, fear, all those things, for him and his sister – but above all, presumably, for their mother. But at the time, in time, there was no *significance*. Nothing he could get hold of, understand, absorb into his personal world. There was no meaning. Deirdre Denham, née Boltby, had lived. Now she was dying. The fabric of time and space that had opened for a few years to allow her existence was now closing. She would vanish. That was it.

A young doctor came and examined her, and afterwards took him aside. 'Not long now,' she said. She might have been talking about a train they were waiting for. 'She seems unconscious, but that doesn't mean she can't hear what's going on around her. So.'

So? So what? What was he meant to do with that piece of knowledge? The doctor strode away to her next appointment with death. She looked about sixteen. He thought of asking whether she was fully qualified yet, but didn't. Two types of person you daren't antagonize: the waiter in a restaurant and the staff in a hospital.

The terminal ward was a warren of rooms linked together by the meanderings of a long corridor – it was euphemistically called the Simpson Ward, but all the patients knew what 'Simpson' meant. 'I don't want to go into the Simpson Ward,' his mother had said during the early days of her treatment. Irony stalked the corridors of the hospital: Simpson was the inventor of anaesthetic, the man who had first tried to take the pain out of sickness.

Thomas rang his sister. They had visited in shifts during the later stages of the illness, changing places like soldiers on sentry duty. Paula had been there most of the previous night, when their mother was still more or less awake, and had gone home in the early morning when Thomas appeared. But now it seemed that the moment had come for double turn. 'You'd better come now, Paula.'

There was a silence on the other end of the line. Not silence in the abstract, but *a* silence; something positive.

'See you soon,' he said, and replaced the receiver.

He went back to his mother's room and sat by her bedside and watched the slow rise and fall of her chest beneath the covers. She wasn't old, but the illness had made her so. She had become thin and haggard and wrinkled, wasted by both the disease and its treatment, with a scrub of grey hair that had regrown after they had abandoned the chemicals that had made it fall out in the first place. 'Mother?' he called softly, but there was no reply.

There are easy deaths – something short and sharp, like his

father's – but his mother's had not been like that. It had taken eighteen months. Or four years. Or a lifetime. Like any piece of history, it all depends where you want to draw the start line – eighteen months earlier when they had detected metastasis in bone and brain? Or two years earlier when breast cancer had been diagnosed? Or you might date it all from the moment when that first cell somewhere in the pliant tissue of her left breast had mutated from the benign to the malignant. When would that have been? Undatable, so not historical? Or you might go further back, to an unperceived moment when sperm first nuzzled into egg within the claustrophobic fallopian tube of a Sheffield college teacher's wife one rainy October day in 1923. Death begins from the moment of conception. A life is the history of a death.

At one point during her illness his mother had told him, with something approaching pride, that she had finally returned to the weight that she had been at her wedding; as though there were an upside to the disease after all, a hidden benefit. Later, much later, just a week or so ago, she had said something else. Lying in her bed in the hospital, cold despite the heat, her hand lying on the sheet like the claw of a bird, she had said to him: 'This is a punishment.'

'What on earth do you mean, Mother?'

'I believe that we are punished for what we have done. This is my punishment.'

He had been dismissive. 'Don't be silly. What do you have to be punished for?'

For a moment she had seemed about to answer. But then she had just closed her eyes and he hadn't pursued the matter. Why, he wondered, had she cause to fear punishment? The idea of punishment as a reason for this suffering revolted him, yet later he thought, Why not? Medical science could not give a reason, aside from the obvious organic ones – this mutation, that carcinoma, those metastases – so why not invoke the callous judgement of some irascible and inhuman god?

He met Paula in the waiting room. Her face was strangely mask-like, as though the skin had been pulled taut against the gale that was blowing through their lives. 'She's unconscious now,' he told her as they embraced.

Paula pushed him away. 'Unconscious? Oh God. Since when? Why didn't you tell me?'

'I did, just now. The doctor says that she still might be able to hear what's said to her.'

'Hear? Oh my God.' She seemed to find unconsciousness a disaster, but surely it would be a blessing, wouldn't it? She hurried into the room and sat down beside the bed, holding the claw of her mother's hand, whispering to the figure beneath the blankets. What was she saying? They weren't in the habit of opening their hearts to one another, not this family. They talked, oh yes, but they never talked about what was at the heart of things, possibly because the implicit assumption was that there was nothing there, really, no heart of things at all to have anything at it. Just life and you got on with it. Or death, and you got on with that too. Matter-of-fact, be it the Yorkshire plainness of his mother's side or the London pragmatism of his father's. 'I'm not a man of very deep emotion,' his father had told him once. And, on another occasion: 'Never get yourself on the wrong side of an unequal relationship. I badgered your mother into marrying me and it's not been an easy relationship ever since.'

Had that been a joke? But no, it was serious – one of the few bits of advice his father had ever given him, apart from an awkward little lecture on sex when Thomas was about twelve. 'I know all about it, Dad,' he'd wanted to say during that agonizing conversation, but of course the truth was quite otherwise: he had known nothing about it, nothing beyond the basic mechanics, gleaned from an encyclopaedia, of penis and vagina.Notthat his father's dissertation did much good – everything that Thomas knew he had learned from Gilda.

Thomas watched his mother die, accompanied to the brink by her daughter. At around two o'clock – morning or afternoon? – the faint rise and fall of her chest stopped and she was dead.

Paula wept. This was unusual. She was an efficient woman, in matters of the heart as in matters of career. She had a husband and two children, a house in Kent and a flat in London, and a successful career in journalism. She wrote a column giving advice to people on how to conduct their emotional lives. Weeping didn't seem to come into it; and yet there she was, weeping.

Thomas watched his mother die, and found that he couldn't weep.

There were things to do, the undertakers to ring, the registrar and the solicitor to contact – phone calls to make and letters to write. Paula was busy, what with deadlines to meet and the children to organize, and an interview to do with a footballer who spent more time in the gossip columns than he did in the sports pages. She would try to get down in the afternoon.

So he cancelled a lecture and two tutorials and drove out through the city towards Essex, that forgotten lump of England tucked away behind London's arse – a landscape of estuaries and inlets, of salt marsh and clay fields lying slack beneath a pewter sky. You could smell the sea on the air, see it in the bloom that lit up the sky from beneath. The house where his mother had spent the last few years of her life was in the middle of the town, tucked into a line of what were once fishermen's cottages. Presumably the houses had then been squalid hovels, reeking of fish and shit, the object of bourgeois disapproval and philanthropy, and the threat of condemnation as unfit for human habitation. Now they were subject to preservation orders, and painted in pastel shades that no fishwife could ever have envisaged.

Lace curtains twitched as he unlocked the front door. He wondered whether the neighbours knew. He wasn't even sure who they were, old ladies with Zimmer frames replacing the fishwives of yesteryear. He'd never been sure what had led her to this final stop in her journey; some vague idea that living near the sea was good for you?

Inside the house there was something of his mother's presence, like the potter's thumbprint in clay. She had sat there, in *that* armchair, walked over *there* to *those* bottles (most of them near-empty) to pour herself a gin and it, which is what she always drank, a little too much of late. Chemotherapy, she used to say, when she was in her cups. There were Staffordshire pottery pieces, and a painting of a Mediterranean hillside, and a portrait of her done in pastels by a friend. It was a strange likeness that grasped many of her features – her nose, the set of her chin, the slightly impatient compression of her lips – without capturing any real sense of her presence.

On the mantelpiece was a picture of his parents at their wedding. Spring 1947, at a hotel on the edge of the moors above Sheffield, the two of them cutting the tiered cake. There was something touching about her slender fragility, and the shadows in her face and behind her smile, a smile that Thomas knew from memory as one thing (warm, motherly) and saw now, frozen in that photo, as something else (remote, guarded, sad). He had been to that hotel as a child, and to the church. Both buildings were remarkably similar for their Gothic pretences and their grey, soot-stained stone. He had gone with his grandparents and their curious Yorkshire accents and comfortable manners. They had taken afternoon tea in the hotel and paid a hushed visit to the shadows of the church, which seemed a secretive and unknowable place, like the sexuality that it had licensed that had, in its turn, engendered Thomas. Was he perverse to find sex in a church? At the time (twelve, thirteen years old, not long after that embarrassing conversation with his father) he had thought so. It had shamed him. He had knelt in one of the pews and prayed for forgiveness. Now he considered it a remarkable percipience, a sign of the historical insight that was to dog his adult life. *With my body I thee worship, with all my worldly goods I thee endow.* Sex and economics – a heady cocktail.

Where, he wondered vaguely as he examined the photograph, was his mother now? The thought was a childhood relic, a leftover from his innocent past when the ceremonies of religion had half convinced him. 'Nowhere, Mother,' he said out loud.

Unsure where to begin, he went upstairs to the room that she had used as a study. It faced the back of the house, overlooking the narrow garden that she had cultivated assiduously until her illness. There was a cupboard and a chest of drawers, a bureau and a filing cabinet. He opened the bureau and found letters, a whole drawer full of them, a mosaic of various sheets, of differing colours and textures, differing hands, differing sizes, different salutations.

Dear Deirdre . . .
My Dearest Dee . . .
Dee darling . . .
Dear Mrs Denham . . .

One or two were in his own childish handwriting, the weekly letters he had been constrained to write from boarding school.

Dear Mummy,

It is raining here and we can't go out. I'm not very happy because 7/6 isn't really enough. Can you please send me a postal order, please. Not much. 5/- ~~is enough~~ *would be* ~~all right~~ *alright. Yesterday (Sat) we played St Anthony's. I didn't score but Maloney did.*

There were similar offerings in Paula's childish hand and, in contrast, one or two from their grandfather, composed with a certain quaintness, like missives from a previous century: *My Dearest Deirdre . . . with great affection, your loving father.*

Time passed, signalled by the sound of a carriage clock that she had bought at an antique shop in York and which beat like a pulse on the shelf above her desk. The speed of time disturbed. How do you measure it? Seconds, hours, days, years, centuries of course – but that's not how it is. Time isn't a scalar dimension like distance or mass; it's a vector, like acceleration. It can vary, speed up, slow down, deviate. At times it can be like struggling uphill – a boring afternoon, a visit to the dentist – while at others it's like freewheeling and the wind is in your hair and you haven't noticed the ditch that lies ahead. The problem with time is that in order to measure it you need to have somewhere to stand outside it. Give me a fulcrum and a place to stand and I will move the Earth. Archimedes, of course. Thomas felt the need for something similar, a place outside time from which to observe and measure its passage.

Another letter.

My darling Dee,
May I, after all these years? Perhaps I shouldn't. Dear D, then. Γειά σου. Ya sou. Do you remember how I tried to teach you

some Greek? And how we laughed? Or perhaps you have put all
that behind you, stuffed it into the part of your memory that is
reserved for painful things.

The reason I am writing is that time has passed, and time,
surely, is the great healer. But not only healer. Emasculator.
Whatever is the female equivalent of that, I wonder? Effeminator
doesn't sound right, does it? Anyway, it was all so long ago and
now I fancy that you might not be too appalled to recognize my
writing again and perhaps reply. No obligation on your part, I
assure you.

Με πολύ αγάπη
Geoffrey

Geoffrey Crozier: a small, dark man with an uproarious laugh
and something of the attitude of a market trader. 'Always
sounds as though he's about to try and sell you something,'
that's what Thomas' father used to say.

Attitude. There was this man walking along the street, and
the wind blew his hat off. Well, off he goes running after it, but
just as he's about to reach it, there's this dog, grabs the hat and
eats it. The man shouts to the dog's owner: 'Oi! Your dog's just
eaten my hat.'

'Oh yeah?' the dog's owner says. 'Well that's *your* problem,
mate. In this wind, you should have held it on.'

'Oh,' the man with the hat says. 'That's your attitude, is it?'

'No, mate,' the dog's owner replies, 'it's not *my* 'at 'e chewed,
it's *your* 'at 'e chewed.'

Paula shrieking with laughter. She didn't really understand
the joke, but Geoffrey was laughing uproariously, and so was
their mother, so Paula laughed too. 'Attitude!' Geoff would cry
from then on, and Paula would double up in laughter. Attitude!
Attitude!

There were other words in the vocabulary of laughter:

'pellucid' was one, and 'anemone'. 'Pellucid,' Paula would say eagerly, and Geoffrey would wince. 'Rude,' he'd cry. 'Rude.'

Thomas took the pen and a blank sheet of paper and wrote out a transliteration of Geoffrey's Greek salutation, and discovered meaning hidden beneath the unfamiliar letters: *Me poli agapi*: with much love.

And what would she have written in reply? *My darling Geoffrey?*

He put the letter aside. Ideas were crawling through the undergrowth of his mind, memories circling behind him, tantalizingly just out of sight, but always there, like threatening shapes in the shadows. From a photograph on the top of the bureau, she looked back at him from thirty-five years ago, with that tired, unhappy smile that had been her trademark. The expression seemed almost derisive now that he was reading her mail.

'What are you looking for, Tom?'

'Unpaid bills, that kind of thing.'

'You know how organized I was. You'll not find anything out of place.'

'What about letters from Geoffrey Crozier?'

'What about them?'

'Who was he, Mother?'

'A dear old friend. What's wrong with that?'

'You tell me.'

But she didn't. Just the smile.

He got up from the desk and went to the bookshelf. The book wasn't there, but eventually he found it downstairs in the sitting room, a narrow volume with the title in faded gold lettering down the spine: *Aphrodite Died Here*. He recalled flicking through it as a child and seeing the author's name on the title page, being told by his mother that this was what Geoffrey did when he was being serious, which wasn't very often as far as Thomas could see. 'Geoffrey is a very clever man,' she always told her son.

Now for the first time he glanced through the pages with adult eyes. The date of publication was, in Faber's rather pretentious style, mcmlvi. Inscribed in ink on the inside of the cover – the same hand as the letter – there was this epigram:

> Priceless is the measure of your glance
> But worthless is my gaze.
> Treasure are the words you spoke
> But paltry is my praise.

Shelley? Byron? *To Dee, with great affection, Geoffrey*, it said beneath. The poems themselves were very different in style, free verse, full of allusions to things Levantine and sexual and classical, the kind of stuff that Lawrence Durrell might have written. He read over a few of them, and then returned the book to the shelf.

'Mother?' he said out loud.

The silence in the house was complete. She wasn't there. There was no one there, not even Thomas. He was merely a watcher, standing out of time, while in his memory his mother and his father flickered between what they had been when he was three and thirteen and twenty-three; and all the time they were ageless. He held their hands and swung, three years old, across the lawn outside the block of flats where they once lived in Oxford. He refused her hand and walked, thirteen and solitary beside her, down a street in Gütersloh in West Germany. He sat across a squalid student room and argued with her about politics or morals or music, and was twenty-three. And then, abruptly, memory released her and she aged, rapidly, fearfully – and became grey and thin, wasted by the disease, lying in her hospital bed, about to be pulled out of time and into eternity.

'Mother?'

No answer.

He got up from the desk and wandered into her bedroom. In the wardrobes her dresses and suits hung like flayed skins in the shadows, scented with the perfume that she wore for as long as he could remember, always the same perfume. *Scent*. 'Women wear perfume, ladies wear *scent*,' she always used to say.

Paula would have to go through the clothes. She'd have to get out of her bloody deadlines and commitments and things. She'd have to do her bit.

The phone rang just as he returned to the study; almost as though his thoughts had conjured her up, it was Paula: 'What are you doing?'

'I'm going through her stuff. Someone has to do it.'

'Can't we deal with it after the funeral?'

'There are letters to write, people to contact. Can I send you a list of people to call? I can't do it all myself. And someone has to go through the papers—'

'Just make a bonfire and burn them.'

'Share certificates and all? And the deeds to the house? There's the solicitor and the will and things like that. You don't seem to understand. There's her clothes, but you'll have to do them. I'm not going through her knickers and petticoats.'

'I told you – after the funeral. Incidentally, I'll have to bring the children. Will Phil be there?'

'Probably.'

'Good. Send me that list. Can you fax it?'

'I suppose so.' He put the phone down. As he turned back to the task in hand the doorbell rang. The sound startled him, as though he had been caught doing something illicit.

He went down to open the front door and found a woman standing outside. 'Yes?'

She looked as though she might just have stepped off a boat:

unkempt hair, a shapeless sweater and trousers that were too short; boat shoes on her feet, those canvas things with leather thongs for laces (although 'thong' meant something else nowadays). Ought he to know her? Her face was vaguely familiar, lined and tanned even though it was spring and the weather lousy. Fiftyish. Lean, almost masculine. 'You're Thomas,' she said, holding out her hand. She blinked as she spoke, as though things were flying in her face.

He took the proffered hand. 'I'm afraid . . .'

'I have you at a disadvantage? That's what they say, isn't it? I'm afraid I have you at a disadvantage. I've seen pictures, you see. I'm Janet. Janet Burford. Maybe Dee mentioned me? How is she? That's what I called to ask. I know how ill she is and I was just passing by and I saw that someone was here, and . . .' She shrugged, looking over his shoulder into the hall. Perhaps she was checking to see if he was up to anything suspicious. Perhaps she wasn't sure that he was Thomas after all. Maybe she had just guessed. Maybe she was the local Neighbourhood Watch.

'I'm afraid she's not here,' he said. 'She died.'

She put her hand to her mouth, blinking again. 'Oh God.'

'Yesterday afternoon . . .'

'Oh God, I'm so sorry.'

'Yes, well, there you are . . .' What a stupid thing to say. As though remarking on the fact that this woman, Janet Whatever-she-called-herself, was indeed there, and not, like his mother, no longer there. Or anywhere else, come to that. He cast around for something to say. The word 'say' rang in his mind. He lived by saying, talking, standing there in front of dozens of bored students, pontificating, mouthing, declaiming, a whole thesaurus of utterance. Why do people always have to say things? Why couldn't they just keep silent? 'Look, I . . .'

'No, I . . .' The woman hesitated, shifting her feet on the doorstep, blinking. 'I used to come round and have, you know, coffee with her. We chatted. I'm so sorry. I'd better go. I'm sorry, awfully sorry. I . . .' And she turned and went, hurrying across the road to the far side where there was a pub called the Fisherman's Catch. She walked quickly past the pub windows, leaning slightly forward. Not bad-looking; but that bloody blinking.

There were two manifestations of Thomas at the funeral. One was focused only on the misery, on the vastness of loss and the exquisite lack of hope; the other watched the sorry procession of coffin and bearers, the heaped flowers, the hieratic gestures of the priest, with something like satisfaction at the sight of ancient ritual being enacted under the dead elms of the country graveyard. That aspect of him regarded the mourners dispassionately. There were about a hundred of them, emerging from all corners of the British Isles. Cousins and aunts and uncles, of course, but also others, distant friends coming forward out of childhood memory, as though characters in a play had suddenly stepped down off the stage and mingled with the audience, where they were now revealed without the make-up that had made them seem so young during the performance.

'We never realized she was so ill . . .'

'We're so awfully sorry . . .'

'She was so wonderful a friend. And your father as well . . .'

'What a shame we lost touch . . .'

After everything, after the coffin had been lowered into its pit and a handful of earth scattered on top, and the undertaker's men had got down to work like navvies, they all went back to the house, crowding into the sitting room and the kitchen, spilling out into the narrow garden at the back, commenting on the lovely flowers dear Dee had planted, and look, how clever the way she's done that trellis and put in those climbing roses – the present tense stumbling awkwardly back into the past.

Janet Burford came and embraced him and gave him a hesitant kiss. She was red-eyed. Was it so peculiar to be red-eyed at a funeral? And why had he even remembered the woman and her name?

'Who's she?' Paula asked later.

'A friend.'

She raised her eyebrows. 'My God, she's years older than you. I thought you went for the younger ones.'

'Not mine, you ass. Mother's.' They laughed at the misunderstanding. 'She's called Janet. She came round the day after Mother's death. She rang the bell and stood there blinking like a bloody lighthouse. "You must be Thomas," she said. Don't know how she knew.'

Janet was frowning at them from across the room.

Paula said, 'I hope she can't lip-read', and their laughter threatened to run out of control, like giggling in church. They used to be like that as children, united in giggles against the solemnities of the adult world.

As they struggled with self-control, a woman emerged from the crush of mourners and advanced on the two of them. 'Tom, dear! And Paula. Oh, how sad it all is.'

Thomas smiled distractedly, not knowing who the woman was, but knowing that he ought to know. 'It's Binty,' she said. 'Binty Paxton.'

'Of course. How kind of you to come.'

Binty was small and rotund. He remembered the rotundity but not the smallness, nor the hints of chocolate-box prettiness that lay there beneath the slack flesh and blemished features. Her husband loomed behind her, as disproportionately tall as she was short. 'Shame it has to be under such sad circumstances,' he said, reaching out a gaunt hand.

His wife was talking over him as she had done for decades: 'Dee was such a wonderful person. She was such fun, and so natural. She came into our lives like a breath of fresh air. So long ago, those days. A different world.' Exactly which days was she referring to? 'And you two? Both married, aren't you? Dee always wrote a little note with her Christmas cards. Hand-written, not one of those dreadful circular things. Kept us up to date.'

'Actually, I'm divorced. But Paula has managed to stick it out.'

'Oh dear. How sad.'

'No, quite happy. Happily divorced.'

And then suddenly, like crows moving off a carcass and leaving only debris behind, the people had gone, leaving Thomas and Paula, and the children and her husband in solemn alliance, to clear things away. With the help of Janet Burford.

'I was awfully fond of her,' Janet explained, as though to justify her presence. 'We . . . we spent a lot of time together. We talked,' she added, with emphasis, as though there might be some dispute about what precisely went on.

'I think she's after you,' Paula whispered. The giggling resumed. Children again, without the controlling influence of a parent to admonish them.

For dinner that evening they took a large table in the restaurant of the Ship Hotel, across the road from the house. The room was called The Bo'sun's Cabin and had the look of a maritime museum, cluttered with sextants and quadrants, compasses, chronometers and binnacles. Brass glinted in the shadows. The ceiling was low and beamed, the windows were portholes and the bar was fashioned out of a capstan. Mine Host, sporting a yachting cap, presented diners with menus that resembled, approximately, a ship's logbook. 'As long as we don't get leg of Long John Silver we'll be all right,' Paula's husband Graham remarked.

'Dead man's leg,' said Paula's son. He was thirteen and at boarding school, and knew suet pudding.

'Dead parrot,' was Thomas' own suggestion. The giggling began, edged with hysteria. The fact of being able to laugh at a moment like this seemed imbued with blame. You should be mourning; you *were* mourning, and it shouldn't manifest itself like this, not with silly laughter.

'Chicken cutlass,' said Paula. 'Sprinkled . . .' she added, spluttering with laughter, '. . . sprinkled with . . . with . . .'

'Go on,' her children cried, nudging each other. 'Go on, spit it out.'

'Sprinkled with . . .' Paula was red in the face, her laughter smothering everything. Mine Host watched, trying to use a smile to hide the suspicion that he was the butt of the joke. Even Philip laughed at the sight of his aunt in distress. 'Go on, Aunt Paula. Spit it out!' His voice was raised as high as the others'. A pleasing sign, this. Ever since the divorce he had been a sullen child. Thomas felt that rare emotion: paternal warmth. 'What, Aunt Paula? Sprinkled with what?'

Finally Paula managed it: 'With old salt!'

When the laughter had subsided Mine Host approached the table to take their orders. 'Sorry to hear about your bereavement,' he said.

After dinner Phil and Thomas walked back to the house. 'Why are we staying at Grandma's?' the boy asked. 'Why can't we stay in the hotel like Aunt Paula and everyone?'

'Why throw money away?'

'They're throwing money away, so why shouldn't we?'

'Because it's *my* money.' It was intended as a joke, but it fell flat in the way that most of Thomas' jokes did fall flat with Philip. It seemed that his son had never forgiven him for letting Gilda walk out. The evidence of Thomas' culpability was plain enough in the boy's eyes: Phil and his mother now lived happily with her second husband, while Thomas remained alone with, occasionally, an unsuitable young woman to share his bed and his breakfast. Only once, a few years before, had the two of them ever tried to discuss these things. 'I want you and I want Mummy,' was all Philip said on that occasion. 'Both together.' As soon as Thomas attempted any kind of explanation, that had been Philip's reply. He had repeated the words over and over: 'I want you and I want Mummy, both together. I want you and I want Mummy, both together. I want you and I want Mummy, both together.' The mantra of a disturbed child. That evening had ended with convulsive tears until eventually sleep overcame him.

Thomas had rung Gilda to confide in her. 'I think Phil's got problems.'

'I should think he has, when he sees his father fucking girls who are young enough to be his sister.'

'I think maybe we should get help for him.'

'What do you mean, "help"?'

'A shrink perhaps.'

'Oh, for God's sake grow up. All Phil needs is the comforts of a father – something that you seem unable to provide. If you can't handle it just send him home early. Norman understands him, Norman's just like a father to him. Norman'll deal with him.'

They reached the front door of the house. 'Sad about Grandma, isn't it?' Philip said as Thomas turned the key in the lock.

Father put his hand on son's shoulder. 'It happens, Phil, it

happens. Lots of things happen in life, not all of them good.'
Brave, male words.

'Too right,' Philip said, making his way upstairs to the spare room.

Next morning they saw the children off to the seaside with Graham. 'Frinton,' Paula had insisted. 'Not Clacton. You'll hate Clacton.' There was a feeling of relief to see the Volvo draw away. There were things to do that only she and Thomas could manage – organization, certainly; expiation, perhaps. She stepped across the threshold into the hallway. 'God, isn't it strange?'

'What?'

'Her not being here.'

'I've got used to it. I've been here much of the last ten days.'

'Stop trying to score points.'

'I'm not.'

Always rivals, rivals and friends at the same time, an exquisite kind of relationship that is perhaps reserved for siblings; they could say cruel things to each other that didn't seem to hurt. Maybe that was the way they showed their affection. He watched her looking round the place, picking things up to examine them, then replacing them carefully where they were, as though she was in an antique shop or something. 'Working out how we're going to split the booty?'

'Oh, shut up.'

'Well, we've got to decide. That's why we're here. That's why we've dumped poor old Graham with the kids. It's what you do. In circumstances like this.'

She had picked up a porcelain piece, a shepherd and a

shepherdess that may have been – their mother had never had the piece valued, preferring fantasy over dull fact – early Meissen, and when she looked round at him her eyes were bright with tears. 'I'd rather have her back.'

'Of course.'

'I find myself talking to her, d'you know that? Sounds silly and sentimental, doesn't it? But I do nevertheless. I was doing an interview two days ago and I found myself thinking, That's a good question, isn't it, Mummy? And when I was writing it up: "Hey, read this," I said to her. "Isn't that good?" I almost expected her to reply.'

'But she didn't.'

'Of course she bloody didn't.'

'The question is, which her do you talk to? Her as she was when she was ill, or her when she was healthy, or when she was young, or what?'

'It's just her. Like it always was.'

He shook his head. 'No it's not. It's not at all like it always was. When she was alive, then there was just *her*. But now she's dead you've got a choice. Which memory do you choose? Which version of her, at what age?'

'What is this, a history lesson or something?'

'You haven't answered my question.'

'There's no choice involved. It's just her.'

He smiled, that aggravating expression he used with students when they said something stupid that he wasn't going to grace with further discussion. 'Let me show you what I've found.'

'What is it?'

'Just wait.'

He ran upstairs to the study and returned with three plastic slide boxes. Paula watched while he fiddled around with a projector in a corner of the sitting room. 'What's this? Holiday snaps? You know what the two most boring things in the world are? Other people's holiday snaps and other people's dreams.'

'These are *your* holiday snaps. Maybe your dreams as well. I found them last night when I was poking around after Phil had gone to sleep.'

He moved a corner table aside, took pictures down. Then he drew the curtains and plunged the room into a sudden, untimely darkness. A white shaft of light snapped through the shadows, spotlighting the far wall. Paula had turned in her armchair, putting her legs up and over one of the arms in a manner that her mother would never have allowed.

'Are you sitting comfortably? Then I'll begin.'

He pressed the button on the remote control. A second's blackness, a whirr and click from the slide tray, and then, abruptly, there she was, projected almost life-size on the far side of the room, blanketed by shadows and framed by light, leaning against the wing of a car.

Paula gave a small gasp of surprise.

Dee was wearing shorts. The detail is important. She was wearing something like a T-shirt – did they have T-shirts in those days? – and a pair of shorts. The shorts were high-waisted but strikingly brief for the times. And the legs were strong and suntanned. A tennis player's legs. And you could see the rise of her breasts beneath her T-shirt, and the shadow of her nipples where, Thomas realized with the force of revelation, he had once sucked.

'Crumbs,' Paula murmured thoughtfully. 'I've never seen her in this light before.'

'No.'

The car had the swollen lines and chrome trim of the fifties, the paintwork the colour of sun-faded grass. Behind the car was the plastered wall of a house, brilliant white in the sunlight, with shuttered windows. Above the roof there was a sky of impossible turquoise.

'Where did you find these?'

'In the bottom drawer of the filing cabinet. There's a whole box of them. Evidence.'

'Evidence of what?'

He didn't reply. His mother looked back at him: but his mother at thirty-three years old, and so in a sense not his mother, not the woman who had died, not even the woman he recalled in his memories of decades ago when he was a mere ten years old, but someone else: Deirdre Denham, known then and always as Dee. '*Deirdre*,' she used to lament. 'What an awful name. It sounds like an anagram of "dreary".' But she assuredly was not dreary, standing there at the far end of the room beside the fireplace, leaning against the car and looking back at her two children with a slight smile. Was her expression underlain with the faint brush-strokes of sadness? Her hair was waved and brushed back. She had a marked widow's peak and her face was almost heart-shaped, almost symmetrical.

She was beautiful. Thomas had never realized that before. She was his mother – many other things, but always that – and therefore sexless because so profoundly sexual: the flesh that had conceived and borne him and nurtured him. His creator. And she had been beautiful, alluring, replete with sexuality.

Paula's voice came from the shadows: 'Look at that smile. Ironical, or what?'

'I don't think things were ironical in those days.'

Laughter in the dark. 'And those *legs*. Blimey.'

'She was always proud of her legs.'

'I'm not surprised. Wish I'd inherited them. Do you remember the car?'

'Of course.' He could remember the choosing of it, the question of its colour. What would be appropriate to export from the drizzle of England to the sun of the Mediterranean? The family had argued about red, and decided that it would look too hot. So it was green.

'And the house?'

He clicked the remote control, to move woman and car aside to reveal a house behind her, a single-storey building with a shallow, tiled roof and white walls. To either side of the doorway there were palm trees with trunks shaped like pineapples. On the veranda were two people – the same woman, wearing a cotton dress now, and a small girl. The little girl almost moved. She almost ran down the steps and down the concrete path to where the man with the camera stood. But of course she didn't. She just stayed there, almost moving.

'That's me.' Paula's voice was quiet, as though they had just trespassed on to forbidden territory and didn't want to alert the guards.

'That's you. At number one hundred and twenty-seven, Sixteenth of June Street, Limassol.'

'How do you remember that?'

'How do you remember anything?'

'It doesn't really look that long ago. Like yesterday. The colours.'

'Kodachrome. Father must have been a bit of an expert. I mean, you didn't get much amateur photography in those days – not of this kind. Box Brownies was the usual—'

'It's not *that* ancient.'

'Isn't it?' He pressed the reverse and there she was again, leaning against the now familiar car. He saw now that she was about to say something. The smile was half a smile, half an opening of the mouth to speak. What was she going to say? What *did* she say on that day more than three decades ago?

'Do you know what she said to me?' Thomas asked.

'*Then?*'

'No, a few weeks ago.'

'I expect she said many things.'

Should he tell her? He had not really made up his mind, even as he uttered the words. He could have made something else of it, could have recalled some childhood moment, fabricated some adolescent incident. But he didn't. 'She said she believed her illness was a punishment.'

Paula was quiet. She no longer shifted in the armchair in the shadows behind him. But her stillness wasn't something negative, an absence of movement; it was active: she held herself in check, as you might hold yourself in against laughter or against tears.

'She say anything like that to you?'

'What did she mean by it?'

'How do I know? But I wonder.'

'What do you wonder?'

'What it was. That made her feel she deserved punishment.'

'Isn't that her business?'

'She's dead now. She's not there to have any business.'

He pressed the advance button and the house slid back into place, and pressed once again to move the house on.

A family group stumped through the cold across the top of some mountain plateau. 'That's Troödos,' Paula cried.

'And that's Geoffrey, isn't it? With Mother.'

He pressed the advance again and there once more were just the two of them, Dee and her little girl, crouching in some field amongst poppies, dozens of poppies around them so that it looked as though they were crouching in a bleeding graze, the kind of thing you get on your knees when you fall on gravel, the blood bubbling up in a dozen little gouts. The pain. 'I remember that,' Paula said. 'That picture, I mean. I remember it being taken . . .'

She paused, watching the figures as though something was about to be enacted there in that distant view of a field bleeding with poppies. But nothing and nobody moved.

They had lunch in the pub across the road, and afterwards went for a walk along the desolate waterfront. The river was flowing against the wind so that the wavelets had their tops blown into smithereens, like smashed glass. There were sailing boats moored in ranks, their rigging vibrating in the wind like the rattling of snare drums. Are they called ratlines because they are always rattlin', or are they called ratlines because rats run up them? One of Geoffrey Crozier's jokes. The riverside path ran along the top of the sea wall. And at the end, below the level of the path and therefore at sea level more or less, there was a house. White-painted weatherboards and a wooden porch. He stood looking down at it for a moment. 'That's the blinking woman's. You know. Janet What's-her-name.'

'You mean the woman who fancies you?'

He ignored the taunt. 'I'll bet she gets in a flap when there's a flood warning out. I'll bet her eyelids go like bloody gnats' wings. She's almost below sea level.'

'So's most of the town.'

As they watched, the side door of the house opened and someone came out. Her brown woollen skirt and loose-fitting shirt were visible from where they stood. There was a brief altercation with what appeared to be a dog, and then the woman went back inside. 'That's her. Blinking Janet.'

'She's a potter,' Paula said. 'That's what she told me.'

'Obviously she's a potter.'

'What do you mean, obviously?'

'Looking like that. Obviously she's a potter. She's probably a vegan as well. And a firm believer in homoeopathic medicine. And practises Zen Buddhism.'

'You're a bigot.'

'I'm a historian. Historians see the patterns in things.'

They turned and made their way back along the path towards the town. 'Perhaps it was Geoffrey Crozier,' he suggested.

'What do you mean? What was Geoffrey Crozier?'

'That made her feel guilty. Perhaps they had an affair.'

'Don't be daft.' She looked round at him. 'For goodness' sake, Tommo, what's the matter with you? On no evidence whatever you're accusing Mummy of having a sneaky fuck with a friend of the family forty years ago. I mean, what's your problem?' Her anger was real.

'He was always around, wasn't he? And she always talked about him. And that letter, you've read that letter.'

'That's bugger all. You need facts, hard facts.'

'But there's no such thing. Facts die, just like people. All that remains are scraps – and we have to do our best with those.'

'This is the historian speaking again, is it?'

He smiled at her anger. 'Never anything else.'

They paused at the far end of the main street, looking down the row of houses towards the clocktower and the Ship Hotel and the row of one-time fishermen's cottages. Graham's Volvo had just drawn up and the children were piling out. They could hear Linda's laughter, and even Philip was shouting something in excitement. Graham caught sight of them and waved.

'At least they've had a good time. Are you sure about taking Phil back to Gilda's?'

'Of course I'm sure. It's not out of the way.'

Surprisingly Paula took his hand and squeezed it. 'It's us now, isn't it, Tommo?'

'What do you mean, "us"?'

'In the firing line. And in thirty years' time it'll be them.' She laughed. 'That's what history teaches us.'

*

Dear Thomas,

I was most awfully sad to hear of your mother's death. It was kind of you to write and let me know. I am very sorry that Bill and I were unable to be at the funeral but a long-standing and important appointment in London meant that we couldn't make it. Although we exchanged Christmas cards, I had not seen Deirdre for many years, but I recall our days in Cyprus with great happiness – they were wonderful times, although often tinged with sadness. My best wishes to both you and your sister, whom I remember with particular fondness on the voyage out.

Yours ever,

    Jennifer Powell

Two

They embarked at Southampton Docks. Gulls laughed and jeered at the scene. There were families gathered on the quayside and soldiers drawn up in ranks, and a regimental band played 'A Life on the Ocean Wave'. The troopship gleamed white against the dockyard buildings and the grey water.

'When do we see Daddy?' Paula asked.

'Soon.'

'Tomorrow?'

'A few days. Twelve days, they say.'

'Twelve days is for ever.'

Dee's parents had come down to see them off. There was a restrained parting, the pecking of cheeks, the assurance of mutual care and concern, the impatience of Paula to be off. 'You look after your mummy now,' said Dee's father to his granddaughter, and Paula, who seemed happy to play the games of adults, agreed that she would.

Soldiers humped kitbags on to their shoulders and filed up the gangways, turning and waving to the crowd. 'A Life on the Ocean Wave' changed to 'Will Ye No Come Back Again?'. Women wept.

'Why are they crying?' asked Paula, who had never before seen adults in tears.

'They're crying because their husbands are going away. Like when Daddy went away.'

'But you didn't cry.'

'I tried not to. But I was very sad.'

'And now you're not sad. Because we're going to see him.'

'That's right.'

Officers and their families boarded by a different entry port from the men: different gangway, different cabins, different decks, different worlds. Dee and Paula climbed up to where a sailor and a white-coated steward stood at the port. They might have been entering a hotel: inside it was all wooden panelling and mirrors and brass fittings, and a desk with uniformed receptionists. Only the plan on the wall – the various decks, the muster stations marked in green, the restricted areas in red – betrayed the fact that this was, in fact, a ship. That and the plaque that showed the vessel in bas-relief sailing into a bronze sunset. Apparently, she had once been the *Königin Luise* of Bremen, launched in 1925 as part of the Norddeutsche Lloyd passenger fleet. But now she was the *Empire Bude*, and British voices were raised loudly beneath her ornate plaster ceilings, the voices of the victors.

The purser was magnificent in navy blue and gold braid. He checked their names against a list, and presented Dee with the keys of the cabin as though she had won some kind of trophy. 'Welcome aboard, Mrs Denham,' he said. A steward led them along the deck and up a companionway, down a narrow corridor, past rows of doors almost like cells in a prison.

'Here we are, ma'am.' He opened a door with more of a flourish than the cabin deserved. It was narrow and claustrophobic, little bigger than a sleeper compartment in a railway carriage. A window looked out on to the promenade deck and the davits and underside of a lifeboat.

'Will we go rowing?' Paula asked.

'I hope not.'

They unpacked excitedly, finding neatly hidden cupboards to stow clothes, putting out their washing things neatly round the sink, folding nightclothes under pillows and hanging Dee's dresses – few and cheap – in the narrow wardrobe. The bathroom was next door. 'I expect we have to share it with other cabins,' she told her daughter.

'Will there be other girls for me to play with?'

'Perhaps. Now let's go up and watch while we set sail.'

'Is it a sailing ship?'

'It's a steam ship, but that's what you say – set sail – even if it's a steam ship. You say different things in a ship. The floor' – she tapped with the toe of one shoe – 'is the deck. And this' – she pointed to the ceiling (she could actually touch it, if she stretched), and her tone was less certain on the point – 'is the deckhead.'

A voice came from the Tannoy in the corridor outside, calling all visitors to return to shore. 'Now come on, let's go and see. We can wave to Grandpapa and Grandmamma.'

They hurried on deck. Her parents waved from among the crowd, where families of officers and other ranks were muddled together, because the quayside was the territory of civilian democracy rather than military rank. The moorings – great hawsers of woven steel – were cast off. The distant, submarine rumble of engines rose in pitch and volume and made the deck shiver beneath their feet. Around the stern, where the soldiers were lined up, seawater was churned into the whiteness of dirty washing, while above their heads, from the side of the yellow smokestack, a siren blew like a call for the dead to awaken.

'Wave!' she cried to Paula. 'Wave at Grandpapa and Grandmamma! Goodbye, Grandmamma! Goodbye, Grandpapa!' And Goodbye, England, she might have added. Goodbye many things. She felt a childlike excitement, an emotion that quite matched anything Paula might be feeling. There were two kinds of foreign travel, and until this moment she had experienced neither. There was 'abroad' and there was 'overseas', and the latter was much the more exciting of the two. 'Abroad' could be nothing more than a day trip to Calais, but 'overseas' was Empire. What they were doing now was supremely overseas.

'Wave!' she cried, waving herself, and making out the diminutive spots of her parents' faces, the two of them stripped of feature by distance and yet, like out-of-focus photos in a newspaper, incontrovertibly those of her mother and father. Faces that she had known and loved and that had always been there when she needed them. Almost always.

'Where are they?' Paula cried, as though seeing them was somehow important, vital even. 'I can't see them. I can't see! I can't see!'

Dee pointed. 'There. Over there.' And then, quite suddenly, she couldn't make them out either. Maybe they had turned away. No, surely not. Surely they would still be waving as, to the trumpeting of its own and other invisible sirens ashore, the *Empire Bude* edged out into the Solent. Somewhere a band still played. 'Rule Britannia', that absurd and bumptious tune.

'I can't see Grandpapa and Grandmamma,' Paula said. 'They've gone.'

Clouds hung above the docks like damp, grey blankets over

basins of dirty suds. Gulls wheeled and tilted behind the ship and the quayside where they had embarked diminished as though they were looking at it through the wrong end of a telescope, until it was no longer dry land inhabited by waving, weeping people, but had become a mere underscoring of warehouses and cranes, a boundary between the grey sky above and the grey water below.

She held Paula's hand tightly. Her eyes stung with tears, but whether they were tears for the parting with her parents, or tears at the absence of Tom, or tears of sadness that she did not feel quite guilty, wasn't at all clear.

They stood at the rails to watch the coast slide past, the oil refinery at Fawley, the Isle of Wight away to the left, which was, Dee pointed out to Paula, 'port'.

'What's port? The port's what we've just left.'

'That's right. *Left* is *port*.' Dee laughed. It seemed absurd. Paula laughed too, perhaps at the sight of her mother laughing. 'On a ship,' Dee explained, 'you *leave* the port, and *left* is port. Maybe that's how you can remember. Left is port and right is "starboard".'

'Starboard's silly,' Paula said bluntly. The engines drummed beneath their feet, a percussion that was to accompany their very existence throughout the voyage. The water slipped past like oil and their whole world shifted very slightly, as though to remind them that nothing was secure from now on.

'Where are the waves?'

'The waves will come.'

The waves came. The ship passed through the narrows between Hurst Castle and Sconce Point, out of the Solent and into the Channel, and the waves came. The vessel began to pitch into the water, shuddering slightly at each impact, like a genteel lady at some repeated solecism. The Needles were away to port. There was a breath of spray in the air. 'It's lovely, Mummy!' cried Paula; while Dee felt the tremor of the ship transfer itself organically to her stomach, and quite suddenly the excitement was not so wonderful, the day not so thrilling, the sensation of guilt at the idea of Tom, abandoned in his prep school, not so acute. Quite suddenly what mattered was the feeling of nausea that spread from her abdomen throughout the channels of her body to her joints.

The subsequent two days were spent in a kind of limbo, confined to the cabin for hours on end, relieved with occasional walks along the promenade deck and rare visits to the dining saloon for toast and tea and mashed potato, which were Binty's recommendation for treating seasickness. Binty and Douglas she already knew vaguely, but it was inevitable that now they would become close friends. Acquaintances became friends quickly in this world of enforced company. Binty was small and vivacious and Douglas was tall enough to make the matter of their physical coupling seem a bit of a mystery. 'Laurel and Hardy' was what Edward called them, which wasn't fair because Binty was quite pretty and hadn't got a moustache, and Douglas was anything but lugubrious – rather a dry wit in fact. There were others on board, the Powells, and a meek little man called Nissing, and Marjorie Onslow. Marjorie was large and jolly, and she mothered everyone. She mothered Paula and Dee, she mothered Binty and she would have mothered Jennifer Powell if she had been allowed; she was going to mother soldiers and airmen because she worked for SSAFA, the Soldiers', Sailors' and Airmen's Families Association, whose role was to mother those who were far from home. She claimed that an ancestor of hers had given his name to Onslow Gardens. 'I thought that was the Earl of Onslow,' said Jennifer, who knew that kind of thing. Marjorie rolled her eyes. 'My lips are sealed.'

'I don't expect they're alone in that,' Jennifer said. Her husband was a colonel on the Governor's staff in Cyprus, a man who seemed to be constructed out of mahogany and patent leather, buffed and polished until he shone. Jennifer possessed a kind of superior vulgarity that Dee had never before encountered. She was a large woman within the boundaries of whose body you could glimpse the outline of a once slender young girl. She described herself in equine terms. 'Once upon a time I was a pretty foal, then a fairly successful hunter and later a good brood mare. Now I'm afraid I'm just a hack: a safe ride, but no longer very exciting.'

Nissing was in the Ministry of Public Buildings and Works. 'Works and Bricks, are you?' Jennifer said. 'Should think so with a name like that. Call you Hut, do they?'

The man smiled. He'd learned to smile. It was a full two days before it was revealed that his Christian name was Rudolf.

And apart from those passengers, there were also the officers of the two embarked battalions, young subalterns doing their National Service, and more senior officers who had the air of men grown old beyond their years because they had seen action in Suez, in Palestine, in Korea, in the war. The CO of one of the battalions was accompanied by his wife, and she became the doyenne of the civilian passengers, seated regally at the captain's table while lesser beings were invited to dine there on a rotation whose precise details seemed as arcane as the rankings of the British peerage.

Dee hid behind her seasickness and her faint Yorkshire accent and watched all this whenever she could. Paula was often somewhere else, playing with children from the other families on board, and for much of the time Dee lay in her bunk while the world of their cabin twisted and turned around her, and her stomach with it. Binty referred to Dee's complaint as *mal de mer*, as though you needed to be French to feel pukey. 'You'll be over it in a while,' she assured her. But for the moment it appeared a permanent state, like being a semi-invalid.

Three

Thomas is giving a class at the university. The class is on the historical method: Historiography, Module 101, worth twenty credits towards History, Modern, Single Honours. It consists of a dozen youths – eight girls and four boys. In a strange way he thinks of his students as more or less his contemporaries. Objectively that has long since ceased to be the case, but he has always suffered from a curious illusion: that whenever he is with a group of people he is always the youngest in the room. This is still plausible enough at meetings of the Academic Liaison Committee, chaired by the Vice-Chancellor and presided over by half a dozen bores who remember when the place was still a polytechnic; but sustaining the idea in the present company amounts to some kind of minor delusion. Nothing to awaken the interest of a psychiatrist, but definitely bizarre.

'Never forget,' Thomas says, 'that the word "history" is cognate with the word "story". What I mean to say by this is that history is, essentially, a narrative. Just like a novelist, the historian is creating a narrative intended to explain something.'

A hand goes up. 'What does "cognate" mean?'

'Related to.'

'So why didn't you say that?'

'Eh?'

'Why use complicated words when a simple one will do?' The speaker is a youth of about twenty (they are all youths of about twenty) with a prominent Adam's apple. This, more than the length of his hair or the structure of his body, defines him as male.

'Sorry, I didn't get your name.'

'Eric.' Eric cocks his head to one side, as though saying his name is some kind of challenge. His black T-shirt has TUNC written across the front.

'Well, Eric, do you like Indian food? Curry, stuff like that?'

'Yeah.' He draws the word out into at least three distinct phonemes. Clearly he feels that this has suddenly become an interrogation; he is reluctant to admit anything.

'But when you were a kid, I'll bet you preferred burgers. Well, words are like that. Grown-ups can usually manage rather more demanding fare than kids.'

The class laughs, all except Eric. Thomas has won, but it is a temporary victory, a mere skirmish. Eric will counter-attack later on, and every week throughout the life of the class. He will counter-attack and eventually he will destroy any group feeling that the class may acquire, and thereby he will win.

Thomas continues: 'The fictional narrative is created out of ideas in the novelist's mind; so too the historical narrative. The difference is that the historical narrative is expected to operate within certain bounds: it has to pay attention to the various bits of evidence that exist – documents in archives, pieces of physical evidence, archaeological artefacts, maybe first-hand eye-witness accounts. Yet these are just relics, things left over and endowed with a significance by the mere fact of their survival. We cling to them like survivors of a shipwreck clinging to flotsam – a broken chair, a piece of railing, a lifebelt.' He smiles as he elaborates his analogy: 'And while we grab for these chance relics, we must always remember that the ship itself, the wreckage of the past, is slowly sinking into the depths below us.'

One of the girls giggles. 'Like the *Titanic*?'

'Just like the *Titanic*,' Thomas agrees. 'The *Titanic* exists in our minds as a historical icon, a piece of narrative – film, book or whatever – while the remains are actually there on the bottom of the seabed . . .'

The girls are remarkably similar to the boys, most of them. Almost all wear jeans, all wear T-shirts, most have pieces of cupro-nickel embedded in various parts of their faces – a ring in this eyebrow, a stud in that nose, a cannabis leaf impaled in an earlobe. Thomas wonders about other, gender-specific possibilities. Does that girl, seated next to Eric and fidgeting all the time, perhaps have a gleaming ring through the nub of her clitoris? Does the one with the orange brush on her head maybe have a stud through a pink and perky nipple? But then, he wonders, does Eric?

Only one of the women really stands out from the rest. She is wearing a silk shalwar-kameez and, among the funereal blacks and greys, glows as brilliantly as a gemstone. What is her name? Sharaya? Something like that. Inviolate, he guesses. Inviolable as well, in all probability. She too has something stuck through her nostril: a fragment of ruby gleaming like a bead of fresh blood. Next to her is the only girl wearing a skirt. She may be older than the others, but it's difficult to tell. That's what fashion does these days – reduces everyone to the pubertal. Thomas catches her eye and, gratifyingly, she smiles back at him.

'And then there's another problem,' he says, addressing this girl alone. 'That is the whole question of narrative. Did people in the past live out a narrative? Do we ourselves live out a narrative? I think the answer is no. Events just happen. No one is writing a story.' He pauses, smiles acerbically. 'You might walk out of here and get hit by a bus. A purely contingent event. It wouldn't be part of any story, and no self-respecting author would allow it to happen halfway through a novel and just finish the thing there and then. But it might happen in reality. And in reality other people might make a story out of your life, with the bus as a dramatic and tragic conclusion.'

The slide projector has been set up ready, pointing at the screen on the wall. He switches it on. 'Can someone turn out the lights?'

They are plunged into a sultry darkness. 'Where's the pop-corn?' Eric's voice asks.

'Look,' says Thomas, and there she is, suddenly on the screen, thirty-three years old, standing against the car in the bright sunlight of decades ago.

'Take this, for example. A photograph, a relic, one of those pieces of flotsam. What do you make of it?'

There's an uneven silence, a scuffling of feet and a few inarticulate whispers:

'Who is she?'

'Where is it?'

'That's what I want to know,' Thomas says. 'Answers to all those questions.'

'*When* is it?' asks the skirted girl.

'The car'll give it you,' says Eric, who is, apparently, something of a connoisseur. 'Nineteen-fifties, isn't it? Ford Consul, or summink. Vauxhall, it's a Vauxhall. Victor.' It is unclear whether he is claiming victory or whether that is the name of the model.

'And it's not England, is it?' someone else says. 'The architecture.'

'And that sky. Maybe you could identify the plants.'

'And what about her? Hockey player is she? Strong legs.'

'Trust you to notice that.'

'Who is she?'

'She's class, isn't she?' says a male voice. 'Posh. Somehow you can tell that.'

Eric puts in another word. He appears to be enjoying this. 'Surely the point is this: does it matter?'

'What do you mean by "matter"?' asks the girl in the skirt. Wondering what her name is, Thomas glances at the list in front of him. He can barely read the names in the backwash of light from the projector. Kale? Can it be Kale? Have they named her after a *cabbage*?

'Well, is she of any historical significance?' Eric asks. 'That's the *point*, isn't it? It's historians that decide. That's what Tom here is trying to say, isn't it? So, who is this woman? Does she *matter*, historically speaking?'

'She certainly mattered to my personal history,' says Thomas. 'She's my mother. Was. Was my mother.'

After the class the girl in the skirt – Kale, it *is* Kale – lingers behind. Clearing up her books, or something. The others push out of the room and head off down the corridor leaving her alone.

'Is it really Kale?' he asks.

She looks up with a quick smile. 'Cognate with cabbage, you're thinking.'

He feels his stomach lurch, the sensation you get in a fairground, on the big dipper or something. 'You don't look much like a cabbage.'

'It's Kay*ley*, actually. Cognate with Kelly. That's what my mother always told me. Irish.'

'And you believed her?'

'Don't you always believe your mother? Didn't you believe yours?'

'I didn't always know what she was telling me.'

She stands there looking at him. She has short hair and thinly pencilled eyebrows and wide-open eyes. Her lips glisten. They form a complex piece of topography, a recurved bow, something convolute and secretive. She's wearing a black leather jacket and a blue denim skirt and her legs are bare. He has already noticed them, of course. White and smooth, as though she has just waxed them. A slight sheen. 'How about some lunch . . .?'

She looks at him thoughtfully. What is she seeing in his expression? A bit unnerving, really, that kind of collected, composed look in an undergraduate. 'I'm sorry,' she says. 'I'm meeting my boyfriend.'

'Oh. Right. Maybe another time?'

A shrug. 'Why not?'

It was W. H. Auden. He remembers that as he watches the girl leave the room. W. H. Auden claimed to suffer from the same illusion, that in any group of people he always felt that he was the youngest present. Mind you, Auden wouldn't have entertained the other illusion that Thomas has, the one about the girl called Kale, the one where she's standing in the middle of the seminar room with her skirt round her waist and her knickers round her ankles.

Thomas creeps through his mother's house like a spy. He searches through the darkened rooms like a thief. Time passes. There are the letters he has already seen, neatly piled besides some household bills. On the top, the one from Geoffrey

Crozier. Crozier never came to the funeral, despite Thomas writing to tell him. When was that? Two weeks ago? Two days? Time is a malleable dimension. Historians struggle with dating, with calendars and chronologies, but the human brain treats time in cavalier fashion. Her death seems months ago, and only yesterday.

He opens drawers. More papers, letters, photos. He leafs through them without method, cursing himself for being so unprofessional, for stirring up the archive, for destroying those subtle matters of placement and orientation that may themselves provide fleeting, ephemeral information. Later, fearfully, he goes into her bedroom where there is the wardrobe painted with flowers, and the dressing table with its clutter of potions and creams, the chest of drawers and the queen-size bed, covered still with its eiderdown. He can taste the smell of her in the air, the last exhalation of her presence. The drawers of her dressing table reveal a froth of silk and cotton, things that had once lain close to her flesh, but never as close as he. He plunges his hands into the drawer and lifts a muddle of clothes to his face and breathes her in. For a moment she is there in his brain, conjured up by her smell, her scent, the haunting effects of some portion of the brain – the limbic system, maybe – to evoke a whole presence. Redolence is close to recollection. Why is that? Where is the history of smell?

'Tom, what on earth *are you doing?'*

A flash of heat in his face. He shoves the things back in the drawer, his hands shaking. 'Just looking, Mummy.'

She crosses the room, glances at him curiously, closes the drawer. 'Well, you mustn't look without asking,' she says, and crouches beside him to take him in her arms; and her smell is there, infusing his brain, muddled up with the whole of him. Her breasts large

and soft. He wants to see them. He wants, for a shameful, sup-
pressed moment, to suck at them.

He opens other drawers and inside the last, lifting aside some woollens, he discovers a manila envelope. The word *Oddments* is scrawled across the flap in her handwriting – he remembers the characteristic flourishes, the slant and attack, the style that once brought breathless excitement whenever he received a letter from her. Her handwriting is as redolent of its creator as her features and her voice, and her smell.

Oddments.

Thomas takes the folder through into the study. He can't deny a certain quickening of the pulse, a certain tremor in the bowels as he sits at her desk and slides the contents out on to the polished wood. There are a couple of newspaper cuttings, a photo, a crumpled, faded bill from a restaurant, a typewritten menu and, in a folded sheet of plain paper, a pressed flower – a cyclamen. He unfolds the newspaper cuttings. The first one includes a poem, one of Geoffrey Crozier's, entitled 'Swimming to Ithaca'. And there's a sheet of plain paper, brown with age, with another poem on it, typewritten and dedicated. *For Dee, with affection, Geoffrey.* This one's called 'Persephone'. Something about Lethe, the river of forgetfulness that guards the entrance to the underworld. He puts both poems aside. The second cutting is altogether more interesting to the historian. It has the name of the newspaper – the *Times of Cyprus* – pencilled across the top in her handwriting, along with the date: *15th May 1958.* At the head of the story is a portrait photograph of a man wearing a uniform cap. His features are smoothed by the morbid hand of a photographic studio and his smile is hopeful, the kind of smile you wear when you are putting a brave face on things before going off to war. The story below reads:

BRITISH OFFICER SHOT

A British military spokesman reported yesterday that Major Damien Braudel, of the Second Battalion of the Ox and Bucks Light Infantry, died in Limassol on Wednesday of gunshot wounds. The precise nature of the incident is not yet clear, but Army sources said that the probability is that it was an E.O.K.A. action. Major Braudel had been on Cyprus for one year with his regiment, during which he had been involved in operations against E.O.K.A. bands in the Troödos Mountains. He leaves behind his wife and two children. Next of kin have been informed.

A vague recollection stirs, like the elusive image of a dream that remains with you after waking. Damien. And Braudel, a name that memory suddenly and surprisingly gives him as Brawdle. Even that is evidence of a kind, the fact that the misspelled name has lain in his mind all those years, to be lifted out of memory and compared with the actual spelling in print before him. He tries not to pursue the recollection lest it fade away entirely. Instead he turns to the photograph that lies tantalizingly face-down on the desk, with that crisp concavity that is caused by shrinkage of the emulsion. Two inches by three, with deckle edging. Written on the blank back – again, her handwriting – is the name *Nick*.

It's like playing pelmanism, that childhood game where all the cards of a pack are placed face-down and you have to pick them up in pairs, recalling where the failures were so that others may be matched. He turns the photograph over and reveals a black and white snap of a car. It isn't a car that he recognizes – it's some kind of 1950s model, possibly American, with a wide band down the whole length of the body just below the windows.

Yellow stripe for taxis, white stripe for hire cars. Why does he remember that? What random bits of circuitry bring that kind of fact floating out of the depths? And which was this – yellow or white? The stripe appears darker than the ground beneath the wheels or the blinding white wall behind. A taxi, then, in bright sunlight. With the driver standing by the door – a young man in white shirt and dark trousers and dusty shoes with pointed toes. His black hair is swept back in a cowlick, his eyes and mouth are smiling. And Thomas' mother is standing beside him, her face composed, her hands clasped in front of her, her eyes hidden by dark sunglasses with thick plastic frames. She is wearing that full cotton frock, decorated with fruit – oranges and lemons. Her waist is narrow, clinched by a wide belt. But there is nothing else, no other hint from the past, no faint footprint to mark the passage of something or someone. Just the photograph of a young man – in his twenties? – and Thomas' mother – in her thirties – and a taxi parked outside a garage. And the only significance that it carries is that it is here, preserved for over forty years in an envelope marked *Oddments*. Mere survival is evidence.

He picks up the menu card. This is easy. The lettering across the top announces HMT EMPIRE BUDE, and the date is typed below: 17th May 1957. The meal is of passing interest, an elaborate confection of Frenchified names that come down to brown soup, meat and two veg, apple pie, cheese and coffee. But in a ragged frame around the typed words there are nine signatures, scrawled in a variety of pens and at a variety of angles. One he makes out immediately because it is his mother's. Another, written in a looped, convent-school script, is naively readable: *Araminta Paxton*. Araminta, he knows, is Binty. And there is Douglas' beside it. Douglas and Binty.

The other signatures mean little. Something that may be

Jennifer, another that may be *Roger*. *Nissey?* Does such a surname exist? Another name begins with M and O. And there's a DB.

Turning the menu over, he smiles to find that there is more writing on the back: *To the Hidden Dreamer, from one who's rude and able, DB.* The same rabbit-eared B in the same handwriting as the signature. There is a quickening, the foetus of an idea stirring in the womb of his mind. He counts the possible letters in this signature and comes to something between eleven and fourteen. That will do. It is within the limits of historical probability, that malleable border that historians instinctively draw around their little islands of fact.

He grabs a piece of scrap paper and finds a ballpoint pen in one of the cubby-holes in the desk.

'Let's play anagrams,' she used to say. 'Try "Thomas Denham".'

Me sad hot man.

'Do you know what I am? I'm the Hidden Dreamer.'

The sad hot man considers the phrase on the back of the menu: 'one who's rude and able'. He finds it quickly enough, *rude able* transforming into *Braudel* beneath his pen, leaving only a superfluous E. A small tug of excitement. He scribbles down the remaining letters in a rough circle – *ONE WHOS AND E* – but he can't make anything out of them. It's like the final clue of the crossword, the one that won't work out whatever you do with it, however you bend the meanings and the words.

But if *ONE* signifies "I"? I WHOS AND E.

Which gives him the letters for 'Damien', all except a missing M. And leaves him with *SHOW*. Is there some hidden message in that? Show what?

I'm.

Where do answers come from? How does the brain work, the hidden circuitry of memory and reason and association? I'm rude and able, that's what the original anagram had been. He writes it out and it works exactly: *Damien Braudel – I'm rude and able.*

Thomas laughs. He can almost see them, in the wood-panelled main dining room of the *Empire Bude*, at the captain's table perhaps, passing their menus round for signing – the last dinner of the voyage? – the women in cotton frocks with wide skirts and starched petticoats, the officers resplendent in mess kit, like peacocks. The band would be playing, and the major would be turning to Deirdre to say: 'You may be a hidden dreamer, but I'm afraid I'm rude and able,' and everyone would be laughing.

Or.

Or maybe it was just a secret between the two of them, the hidden dreamer and her rude and able swain.

He rings Paula. 'I'm at the house. I saw the solicitor and everything seems to be more or less in order. Now I'm going through her papers.'

'What for?'

'Looking for bills, that kind of thing. Hey, what do you remember of the journey out to Cyprus?'

'What's that got to do with it?'

'Something I found. A ship's menu, actually. The *Empire Bude.*'

'I was little more than a baby. Five? Six? I just have impressions of the ship – wood and plastic and rather dark in the cabin. Like a railway sleeping compartment, I think. And being woken up when we went through the Straits of Gibraltar. And women crying.'

'In the Straits of Gibraltar?'

'No, you idiot, that must have been before. When we were

leaving. I remember a crowd and the sound of the ship's siren, and women crying. I'd never seen adults cry before.'

'You don't often see it now.'

'In my line of work you do.'

'And what about Damien Braudel? Do you remember him?'

She is silent for a moment. 'What's this all about, Tommo?'

'I just asked if you remember him. He was there on board, you see. You remember Mum and Dad talking about him?'

'Vaguely. Didn't something happen to him?'

'Right. You see, you *do* know. He was murdered by EOKA. But he was one of your fellow passengers on the *Empire Bude*. I've got his signature on a menu. And I'm rude and able—'

'I wouldn't put it as strongly as that, although you do tend to go after young women—'

'—is an anagram. They played anagrams. Don't you remember? Hidden dreamer? Don't you remember her saying that? She was the hidden dreamer. Don't you remember?'

'No.'

'Well, she used to. And this is where it came from, I guess. They were playing anagrams at dinner one evening.'

'Sounds innocent enough.'

'Who said anything about guilt?'

'You did.'

A hot, dark room, ransacked by shadows. In the room there is a bed, strewn with sheets. Among the sheets, on the bed, two figures, naked, glazed with sweat, limbs locked together. Their movement is violent and staccato, with no beauty to it. There is sound, a rough grunting, neither male nor female, barely even human. And then abruptly all is over and the two figures part, and lie for a moment side by side among the ruin of the sheets. She sits up, running her fingers through her hair so that she is lifting it up in a cloud – an uncharacteristic gesture he has never seen before. Her breasts hang loose, each tipped with a dark disc. One of her legs hangs off the bed; the other is up, the knee bent. Her lap is a deep shadow that crawls part way up her belly.

She turns and speaks to the man, but the words are not distinct. Just the tone.

Then she looks towards the door.

Four

'It's all psychological,' said Major Braudel.

They stood at the railings of the stern promenade deck, watching the wake and the gulls swooping down for garbage. They were somewhere in the Bay of Biscay and the weather was warmer although the sea was the same, long Atlantic rollers meeting the ship on the starboard quarter, rolling and pitching her at the same time, the very worst sort of motion. But somehow her body was beginning to accept it and she was starting to feel better. It was rather like recovering from a bout of flu: she felt weak and elated at the same time.

'How does saying it's psychological help?'

'It doesn't help at all, really. But it's an interesting point.'

'Not if you're seasick, it isn't.'

There was a squad of soldiers doing physical training on the deck below. The soldiers had undernourished figures and pale skin that looked as though it was being exposed to the sun for the first time ever. A drill sergeant shouted commands and the men made Xs and Ys of themselves, and bent to touch their toes.

'What are those men doing?' Paula asked.

'They're making themselves big and strong,' Major Braudel told her.

'They look weedy to me.'

'That's the problem.'

Braudel was an officer of one of the two battalions aboard. He was tall and slender, with pale hair. Perhaps his hair colour made him seem young, as well as his symmetrical features and smooth complexion. Certainly he seemed more youthful, more enthusiastic than Edward. The evening before, he had come over to their table and tried to persuade Dee to dance. The band had been playing and there were one or two couples attempting a wayward foxtrot. But she had claimed that she was still unsteady on her feet, and still a little queasy, so instead he had gone off to the bar and returned with a glass of some murky concoction that he presented to her with comic solemnity. 'What you need is a brandy and milk. Does wonders for a hangover.'

'But I haven't got a hangover.'

'You soon will have, if you drink all that brandy and milk.'

That had made her laugh. It had been the first laugh since leaving the Needles astern. He introduced himself to the others at the table. His Christian name, he confessed with some embarrassment, was Damien. 'After the apostle to the lepers.'

They hadn't understood the reference.

'A Belgian priest who went to Hawaii to look after lepers. My father was Belgian, you see. And a devout Catholic. He came to England during the Great War, married my mother and never went back.' He looked at Dee thoughtfully, almost embarrassingly. 'Where's the accent from?'

'Can you hear it?'

He grinned. 'Ee ba gum.'

'Sheffield,' she admitted; she *admitted* it. It annoyed her, that she should not be proud of the fact.

'I know Sheffield well,' he said. 'I've spent hours lying in wet heather on the moors. Bang, bang, you're dead, that kind of thing. The natives were quite friendly. They'd come out and bring us cups of hot tea. But they looked at us strangely when we didn't drink it from the saucers.'

Somehow that conversation had signalled the end of her sickness. And now it was morning and they were approaching the Portuguese coast and she had woken up to a new world of possibility. For the first time she had felt genuine hunger, and on their way to breakfast she and Paula had encountered Braudel again. 'You need a turn round the deck,' he informed them. 'You must get up an appetite before you eat.'

'I've already got an appetite,' Paula told him.

Braudel laughed, and took her hand. 'We have to think of Mummy, don't we?' They walked together towards the dining room, with the land gleaming away to port and the waves sparkling in between, and the sun coming up, cool at first but on a trajectory that would take it high and hot. Damien had, he explained, been this way before.

'What, on the promenade deck?'

'No, you chump. This bit of sea. Last year, bound for the Canal Zone.'

Dee was amused by the way he called her 'chump', as though he was the brother she had never had. 'Chump' seemed the kind of term used between brothers and sisters.

'You were at Suez?'

'Just about. We'd just landed and deployed towards Port Fuad and then they pulled us out. Bloody farce. Betrayed by the Yanks. And after all we've done for them.'

'Jolly good, I'd say.'

He looked at her in surprise and some amusement. 'Jolly good what?'

'The withdrawal.'

'You think so?'

'I think Suez was a terrible mistake. And Eden a fool.'

'Good God, you'd better not say that kind of thing here. They'll keelhaul you.'

'Don't you agree?'

'I'm a soldier. It's not my job to think.' He smiled and looked away to the horizon and the smudge of land that was, so he told them, La Coruña. '"The burial of Sir John Moore", you know? He played a big part in the history of our regiment. "Not a drum was heard, not a funeral note/As his corpse to the rampart we hurried."'

'Actually it's "corse".'

'What?'

'Corse, not corpse. Sort of poetic. Means the same thing.'

'Is that so? Gosh, I bet *you* don't saucer your tea. Where did you learn that?'

She made a face, an expression of regret. 'I was at college for a while, studying English. Then I left to join the ATS and wasted two years, really. After the war all the places at college were taken up by men who had just been demobbed and there didn't seem any room for me.' It was sunny now. The sea had had the grey brushed out of it, to be replaced with a blue that you never saw in Britain. The waves seemed teasing rather than threatening. 'And anyway I met my husband. He sort of swept me away from all that . . .'

Beneath the sun the British had undergone a metamorphosis, like imagos easing their way out of the grey chrysalis of life at home. There was colour, there was laughter, there was a subtle shedding of old clothes in favour of new – tropical drill for khaki battledress; white cotton for brown wool. Pallid flesh took on shades of pink and tan. They indulged in novel games – quoits and deck hockey, and a shooting competition off the stern of the ship with balloons as targets. Dee partnered Braudel in a deck-tennis mixed-doubles competition while Paula laughed and shrieked from the sidelines. They got through to the final before being beaten by Binty and Douglas, who took the whole thing very seriously and became quite cross when Braudel and Dee laughed at their own mistakes. 'There's no point in playing if you don't take it seriously,' was what Binty said. But away from competition she was very sweet and had become quite a friend. 'I can see that fellow's got quite a pash on you,' she remarked as they went to shower and change. 'Edward would be jealous.'

'Well, he's no reason to be.'

'Of course not, my dear. Everyone knows that shipboard romances are just a game. And he *is* a bit of a dish.'

Did that mean that Binty gave her seal of approval to their mild flirtation? She and Douglas had promised Edward that they would look after Dee during the voyage. Did that, Dee wondered, extend to guarding her marital virtue?

That evening at dinner they played a ridiculous game of Damien's invention. It was called anagrams. The object was to compose phrases out of the letters of each other's names. He won comprehensively. 'I'm rude and able', he made out of his own name, and 'hidden dreamer' from Dee's. 'Are you?' he asked.

'No,' she replied tartly.

The ship's orchestra played songs from *My Fair Lady*, and she and Braudel danced together on the small apron of parquet that was the dance floor. It wasn't milk and brandy in her glass now, but gin and it, a mixture that Damien persuaded her was rather superior to gin and tonic. 'It's stronger,' she said, sipping it warily.

'That's why it's superior.' He had this mocking tone which amused her, as though he found everything faintly ridiculous – the ship, the reason for his journey, Dee herself. He was a soldier because he enjoyed soldiering, he told her. Nothing better. Certainly not working in some bloody office for a few pounds a year more than he was getting now. See the sand and flies of the world, he said. He was married, but his wife was staying in their house near Aldershot until it became clear how long his battalion was going to be abroad. He had two daughters, of nine and twelve.

'I'd like to meet your family,' Dee said. 'What's your wife's name?'

He smiled. 'Sarah. She's not like you,' he added.

'What does that mean?'

'Unspoiled.'

'She is?'

'You are.'

The band played 'I Could Have Danced All Night' and they found themselves dancing rather close, his face against her hair, her own cheek against his chest. 'Damien,' she whispered. 'I don't think so.'

He moved perceptibly away. 'No, I suppose not.'

Binty was watching, she knew that. Paula was in the cabin, being babysat by the ever-willing Marjorie, Tom was a thousand miles away at his boarding school and Edward was a thousand miles in the other direction, but Binty was watching. When the band finished, she and Damien went out on deck for a breath of fresh air. He held her hand. She felt bewildered and slightly light-headed. 'I must go and relieve Marjorie,' she told him. 'Really, I must go.'

'Of course,' he agreed, and gave her a chaste kiss on the cheek before releasing her.

*

55

The next day the ship hove to in a flat calm. There was a church service on deck, with the chaplain of one of the battalions officiating. The headland away to port in the heat haze was Cape Trafalgar. Flags fluttered overhead, the famous signal that the *Victory* had flown on that October day in 1805 – England Expects That Every Man Will Do His Duty – while the band played 'Eternal Father, Strong to Save' and hundreds of voices, male voices, were raised up to the enamelled turquoise sky:

Eternal Father, strong to save
Whose arm hath bound the restless wave,
Who bids the mighty ocean deep
Its own appointed limits keep

Wreaths were dropped overboard for the dead, and Dee felt ridiculously proud as she watched them float away on the gelatinous surface, proud that figures out of history – Lord Nelson pale and sensitive, Hardy tall and noble, hundreds of ordinary seamen with their tarred pigtails – could be real to men and women one hundred and fifty years later. This was the glory of the British, she felt. There were things that were disgraceful, things that her father quite rightly railed against; but not this. She saw Damien down on the lower deck with his men, looking fine in the uniform of his regiment, and she felt proud for him and a little guilty.

During the night they passed through the Straits of Gibraltar. Dee woke Paula so that they could look out across the black sea to the lights of Tangiers on one side and Algeciras on the other. By the next morning they were in the open sea once more, and memory of that narrow passage was no more than a half-remembered dream. While Paula squealed with delight they watched dolphins sliding through the water like knives and flying fish darting like thrown daggers. The soldiers had rifle practice down on their deck, firing at targets thrown astern of the ship. The sound of gunfire was flat and abrupt, puny against the huge space of sky and sea.

Heat came gradually, in the ship's stately progress eastwards down the Mediterranean. The heat increases going south and going east, that's what Damien told her. It seemed obvious about going south, but why should heat increase going east? 'Because you're heading towards the Orient,' had been his reply.

'But that's no answer. It's just a word.'

'Typical Sheffield, always wanting literal reasons. Doesn't Orient *sound* hot? Isn't that good enough? Doesn't it sound hot and exotic, full of rich scents and strange flavours? But don't ask me why.'

So she expected the heat, even if she couldn't explain it – but not quite the oppression of it, the damp beneath her arms, the insidious trickle of sweat between her breasts, the thin layer of moisture that developed between her palm and the small starfish of a hand that was Paula's.

'Do you know the poem "Sailing to Byzantium"?' she asked him. They were standing at the rail, watching. He was close enough for her to feel his hip against hers.

He didn't.

'That's what we're doing. We're sailing to Byzantium.'

Five

Thomas attends a faculty meeting, a tedium of discussion and deliberation in which they argue about labels on office doors. Should the department, in the pursuit of equality and the denial of hierarchy, abandon academic titles? Should the élitist 'Dr T. Denham' become the egalitarian 'Thomas Denham'? The arguments circle, like the flies circling aimlessly in the centre of the room. 'Why shouldn't you be able to distinguish me from the caretaker?' one of Thomas' colleagues, a man of great personal courage, asks. 'Did I spend years acquiring letters after my name in order to be reduced by your absurd principles from a *fellow* to a *bloke*?'

There's laughter – after all, the joke was quite good – but Thomas fails to join in because he is not paying attention. With all the eagerness of the hunter for the quarry, he is thinking of the next class of Historiography Module 101.

As so often with hunting, waiting is rewarded: once again

Kale is the last to leave at the end of the class. She has that calm air of method, a taking of her time instead of rushing for the door like an adolescent. Today she looks older than previously. Perhaps it is her make-up, the blood red of today's lips. It is so difficult to tell these days. Fashion gives little clue, manner gives less. She is, perhaps, in her late twenties. His heart lifts and sinks, both at the same time: a safer prospect, but at the same time less impressionable.

'How about today?'

She glances up, puzzled. 'Today?'

'My offer of lunch.'

'Oh.' She looks round as though for an excuse, but doesn't find one in the now empty seminar room with its disordered rows of chairs, its fire extinguisher and evacuation notices, its framed pictures of political posters from the Soviet Union – Trotsky like a glaring demon, Lenin pointing into the sunrise. Is it a good sign that she hasn't come equipped with a get-out line? Or maybe she has completely forgotten his previous invitation and isn't clever enough to invent an excuse on the spur of the moment.

She shrugs. 'All right.'

'Good,' he says. 'Great.'

They leave the building together, talking history, which is fine as far as Thomas is concerned. History is life; life history. He talks, she listens, and anyone overhearing might conclude that they are simply teacher and pupil discussing academic issues of mutual interest. They walk along the plate-glass flanks of the building, past a noticeboard that exhorts people to come to a disco, a demonstration, a festival of alternative film. It is a delight to have this girl walking by his side. Her presence confirms what he always feels, that he is as young as she; younger, in fact. Perhaps her height helps. She is quite tall, as tall as his mother.

Discussing Eric's absurdities, they go out through the gates and pause on the pavement, on the edge of the traffic. 'He's a laugh,' Kale says.

'He's the face of barbarism. Did you hear his comment when I gave you *What is History?* to read? He asked whether it was available on video.'

'That was a joke.'

'It was the truth dressed up as a joke.'

'Whatever.' She moves to cross the road and Thomas grabs her as a bus sweeps past, mere inches away. 'It's a one-way street.' He points. The words are there, at her feet: LOOK LEFT. 'For a second I thought you were going to bring the narrative to an abrupt halt.' She gives a nervous laugh as he takes her arm and ushers her across the road in safety.

For lunch he has decided on a pub that isn't usually frequented by members of the department. You have to know these things if you want a modicum of privacy. The Spigot and Firkin, it's called, a place of noise and crush, populated by office workers on their lunch break. Thomas orders a pint of beer for himself and lager and lime for her and they stand side by side to examine the menu chalked on a blackboard behind the bar. Simultaneously they decide on the same thing: chicken tikka masala. That provides some amusement, a further fragile bond. Shared danger overcome, shared taste expressed.

'Is Britain the only country in the world where you are expected to pay for your food and drink before you actually get them?' he wonders aloud as he hands over the money.

The barman appears unmoved by comparison with other nations, other cultures. 'What name's that, mate?'

'Thomas.'

He writes *Tom* on the order slip.

'It's Thomas,' Thomas insists, and watches while the man

makes a correction: *Tomass*. Is that a joke? Kale seems to find it all funny, this expedition to the pub in his company, this choosing of the same lunch, this complaint about the way the bill works, this insistence on his full name. It is as though he is the student and she the teacher, and she is patronizing him – or maybe that is just the Auden illusion at work.

They edge away from the bar and find a fortuitously empty table with two low stools where she perches awkwardly, her knees together, her skirt as tight as a drum, a glimpse of white visible in the shadows. She sips her drink and looks at Thomas. 'So tell me, why did you show us that picture last week? The one of your mum. I mean, Freudian or what?'

He tries to shrug it off. The truth is, he doesn't really know himself. 'I was looking through family photos, trying to understand my own history. The idea just occurred to me.'

She sniffs and sips. 'Mid-life crisis or something?'

'Thank you. Actually, she just died. A fortnight ago.'

'I'm sorry. You didn't say that bit.'

'I didn't think it mattered.'

'Doesn't it? Did you love her?'

'I adored her.'

'That's different.'

'How is it different?'

'Adore is worship? Love is between equals?' Her speech has an upward, interrogative lilt.

'Very philosophical.'

'So which is it? Love or adore?'

Summoned by a voice from the bar calling 'Tom!', he goes over and collects their food. 'Adore *and* love,' he says on his return, putting her plate in front of her. 'Both those things.'

'That's nice then, isn't it?'

'Very nice,' he agrees.

She eats, and talks. Thomas watches her mouth, its complex of movement. How could one be skilled enough to apply colour to that compound shape, those curves, that arabesque? He pictures her doing just that, with a pencil of lipstick, pouting her lips at the mirror. Her jaw seems delicate, like a cat's. He imagines the touch of her teeth – small, white, sharp – and the contrasting pliancy of that fugitive tongue. She explains why she has joined the history course, why she didn't go directly to college when she left school, what she does and doesn't do. She has worked in an office, works in the local library at the moment, worked as a tourist guide for a while. 'Hidden London and stuff like that. That's the history, I guess. I had to learn it all, like a taxi driver almost. But I loved it.'

'And so you signed up to the course?'

'More or less.' She lives south of the river and she is, it is no surprise to discover, a mother herself. 'Emma. Six. She's at school – in fact I mustn't be late 'cause I've got to go and pick her up. Actually, that's why I joined the course. I found this kind of grant? For single mothers who've never been to university? I thought perhaps, I don't know, I might become a teacher or something.'

'And Emma's father?'

She shrugs, a neat little lift of those narrow shoulders, but says nothing.

'And what about the boyfriend? The one last week?'

Another shrug. 'Steve.'

'Are you . . . together?' Is his probing getting too obvious? But you need to reconnoitre the battlefield, see where the enemy lies in wait. She chews, swallows, takes a further mouthful, picks delicately from her mouth a piece of chicken tendon and places it on the side of her plate, looks up at him.

'Sometimes. What about you?'

'I've got a son, called Philip. Phil. He's thirteen.'

Is there a flicker of concern in her expression, a narrowing of the eyes, a subtle shift of attitude? 'You're married?'

'We split up. One of those amicable divorces.'

A nod. 'That's what happens with marriage.'

'Not my parents'. Till death them did part.'

'It's a generation thing, isn't it?'

'Perhaps.'

'I read somewhere that nowadays marriages last about the same time as they used to in Tudor times; only then they were finished by the death of one of the partners. Sorry, that's a bit nerdy.'

'Tell me,' he says encouragingly.

She shrugs again, embarrassed. 'It's just that most times the survivor got married again. But now it's divorce that finishes them. If you see what I mean. So actually people have the same number of partners, more or less, whatever era.'

'That might be right.' The noise of the bar intrudes. Someone pushes past, heading towards the lavatory. 'I think she had a love affair,' he tells her. 'My mother. About the time of that picture.' It surprises him to say it out loud like that, to a complete stranger, but Kale merely sniffs.

'I expect she did. What's the big deal about that? I expect she had lots of offers.'

'Do you get lots of offers?'

She looks at him thoughtfully. 'Some.'

'And you think my mother would have had lots, even in the nineteen-fifties?'

'Was it any different then? Didn't people fuck, just like they do these days?'

The word 'fuck' brings its little tremor of shock, even now. Someone at the next table glances round to see who has spoken.

'Perhaps not quite as often. Not with different people at any rate.'

'Isn't there a report? That'd tell you. Masters and Johnson, isn't it?'

'Kinsey. Masters and Johnson was the sixties.'

'Kinsey, then. Anyway, good luck to her, if she did. Why should you worry?'

Why indeed? But it is his mother they are talking about. It was she who lavished (the word has a wonderful, expansive feel about it) her love on him, who made him who he is, and who he is not. And there is also the disturbing fact that when he looks at the photos of her as she was then, he sees her through the sphinx-like eyes of an adult, the riddled gaze of Oedipus.

They order coffee. 'I'd love a ciggy,' Kale confesses. 'But I'm trying to give it up. For Emma's sake, really.'

'Perhaps we can do this again?' he asks when her cappuccino has been drunk and it's time to go.

'Do what?'

'Have lunch.'

'P'raps.' She's looking for her bag underneath the table, rummaging among her things. 'Sorry, I must go to the toilet.'

He watches her make her way through to the back of the bar. 'Toilet' was one of his mother's hates. She insisted on 'lavatory', the rationale being that 'toilet' is a genteel euphemism. But so is 'lavatory'. So is everything, really, except shit-pit. One generation's euphemism is another's vulgarity. One generation's 'making love' is another's 'fuck'. What would his mother have thought of Kale? The word 'fuck' expressed with no more import than if she had said 'eat'; and speaking with food in her mouth; and going to the toilet; and showing the line of her knickers beneath her skirt. And being called Kayley. 'No, Mother, it's spelled K-A-L-E.'

'Well, I don't see why. It's just a vulgarism. Might as well call her Kylie and be done with it.'

'People can't help their names. It's the parents you've got to blame.'

'It's not the parents, it's the social climate. Nowadays there's no pressure to have good taste. Vulgarity has become fashionable.'

Kale returns, glancing at her watch. 'Going to miss my bus,' she says. 'Thanks ever so for the lunch. Really nice.'

Thomas helps her into her coat and follows her towards the daylight. Has she forgotten his question? Will he have to broach the subject all over again? 'Next week?'

'OK. If you like.'

His heart pauses. 'Or . . .' Don't push your luck, he thinks, and then pushes it: 'How about sooner?'

'All right by me. I'm in college most mornings.' She goes out through the door. It has started raining and she stops to rummage in her bag for an umbrella.

'How about an evening? What do you like? Theatre? Music?'

'*Evening?*' She looks up with an expression of faint surprise. Does evening make it different? 'S'not easy, is it? Babysitters and stuff?' She steps out into the drizzle, a slick fish escaping Thomas' clumsy grasp. But at least she hasn't mentioned Steve.

'Bring Emma along too.'

The umbrella erects itself, a complex of levers and hinges. 'To the *theatre?* In the *evening?* She's only six for God's sake.'

'*Cats,*' he calls after her. 'We'll go to *Cats.* A matinée.'

On the brink she stops. A bus sweeps by, throwing spray out of the gutter and across her legs. 'Fucking bastard!' she shouts. Then she looks back at him and grins. 'If you can get tickets.'

'When?'

'Whenever. Thanks again for the lunch. See you.'

*

Dear Tom,

How unhappy I was at the news about your mother. Darling, darling Dee was one of the people I loved the most – she has been coming to see me at least once a month, and make me laugh, and was such a faithful and reliable friend. I don't really know how I'm going to get by without her. Sorry this is short, but typing is not very easy. I have to use some silly little gadget in the only hand I can still move. Did she tell you about me? Anyway, I'm wheelchair-bound and that's why I won't be able to get to the funeral. I would love to have been able to say goodbye to her properly, but I will certainly say a prayer, and one for you and dear little Paula. I don't expect she is any longer, is she?! Little, I mean.

With love and all my sympathy,

Marjorie

Six

At Cyprus, the ship dropped anchor offshore. Apparently the port at Limassol wasn't deep enough for large ships and they all had to do this, wait in the roads for lighters to come out. Dee stood with Paula on the deck, much as they had stood to wave goodbye to her parents at Southampton, except now the view across the water was smudged with heat, and coloured ochre and white and buff. She could see sheds and warehouses, a line of concrete buildings, houses with shallow-pitched tiled roofs, palm trees, dust. And the domes of churches, and the pencil points of minarets. Byzantium, she thought. The young in one another's arms. There was a heat haze beyond the town, but somewhere there – fifty miles away – were the mountains. She heard someone say the name, pointing as though they could be seen through the blur of heat: Troödos. She slipped her daughter's grip and patted her hand against the thin cotton of her dress. Might the cloth become transparent with the sweat?

Might she be revealed, standing there at the rail, as though in her underwear?

'Where's Daddy?' Paula asked.

Dee pointed to the quayside, where you could see people waiting at the water's edge. 'Over there somewhere.'

'I can't see him.'

'You will soon. We must be patient.'

'We've been patient for weeks.'

'Twelve days.'

The smell of the land reached her, a whole complex of scents, mingled, grappling with each other, some of them identifiable – dung, sewage – others quite beyond her experience. What were they? The putrefaction of the Orient. That's what Damien said. She thought of him with something like shame, how he had walked with her along the deck after dinner last night – after they had all signed each other's menus and promised to meet up again once they had landed. He had put his arm round her waist and she hadn't stopped him. It had been warm in the night air, with a cool breeze that only came with the way of the ship. The water rustled like silk along the sides of the hull and there was a moon, of course there was a moon, hanging low in the night sky and burnishing the surface of the sea. They had stopped in the shadow of a lifeboat and he had pulled her towards him and bent to kiss her on the mouth.

'Damien! What are you doing?' The papery touch of his lips. Very fragile they had seemed, while he was big and strong and smelling faintly of cologne and cigarettes. 'Damien, please.'

He had released her. 'I'm sorry. I really don't know . . .' Apologies and embarrassment. 'I thought perhaps you—'

'I what?' She hadn't been angry. Flattered slightly, but also something else: ashamed.

He had regained his composure, taken out a cigarette case from inside his jacket and offered her one before lighting up himself and staring out into the darkness. 'I thought perhaps you liked me. I'm sorry that I was mistaken.'

'But I do like you, of course. Just not in that way.'

'You must think me a cad.'

And she had laughed. She couldn't help it. The word 'cad'. She'd never heard it outside the cinema. 'I'm sorry, I don't mean to be rude.' But the laughter was still there, bubbling up inside her breast.

'Don't you have cads in Sheffield? I'll bet there are lots. Yorkshire cads.'

'It's not that.' She had looked away into the night, at the phosphorescent wake streaming out behind the ship, at the faint brush-strokes of silver cloud lit by the moon. It was almost impossibly beautiful, more beautiful than the moonlight on Ladybower Reservoir, more beautiful than anything she had known. She had so few reference points. The bloody Pennines. She'd never *say* that, 'bloody'. Instead she said, 'I'm thirty-three years old; I've got a daughter asleep in our cabin, a son away at boarding school and a husband waiting for me in Cyprus. It's all that. And you've got a wife and children as well.'

'You mean if it weren't for all that—'

'It *is* rather a lot.'

He laughed. She watched the glow of his cigarette as he inhaled. 'But still, I'd have had a chance. I think I'm falling in love with you, you see.'

Her laughter was sympathetic now, under control. 'You don't *know* me. You don't know what you'd be letting yourself in for. It's just a silly shipboard infatuation.'

'That's the literal Yorkshirewoman speaking, is it?'

'Don't keep going on about that.'

'But it's there in your voice. I love it.'

'Don't be daft.'

'There you are. "Daft", not "darft".'

'Well, I wish it weren't.'

'Why?'

'Because it labels me.'

'There are other things that label you.'

'What are those?'

'Your beauty.'

'Flattery.'

'Your Yorkshire prudery.'

'There you go again.'

'Your legs.'

'You can't tell much by the shape of a woman's legs.'

'Oh yes, you can.'

She was not quite sure on what terms they had parted. He'd bent to kiss her chastely on the cheek, and squeeze her hand, and whisper 'Good-night,' and then they'd gone to their separate cabins – Paula was still fast asleep, Marjorie was nodding over her book – and that had been that. Dee had undressed and lain in her narrow bunk for a long time awake, thinking. Of Edward, of Damien, but of other things, too. The excitement of the coming morning. The heat. The plain fact of her body, damp with sweat; her daughter in the bunk across the tiny box of a cabin; and her son, all those miles away in some anonymous prep-school dormitory. And Charteris. Before Edward there had only been Charteris. Charteris had gone away to the war, on the Russian convoys, and had not returned. She had only been eighteen years old at the time but his memory lingered, and shamed her: often, when her husband lay on top of her, it was not his penis but that of her dead sailor that slid inside her.

The cabin trembled with the drumming of the engines, a submarine stirring that filled the whole vessel. Her forefinger was there, among the rough hair and the soft, slick folds of what Charteris had called her purse. Paula stirred in the other bunk.

Dee tensed the muscles of her thighs and thought of Damien and Edward and Charteris, her finger moving gently with the motion of the ship, waves of guilt and delight filling the basin of her body like a great swell of fluid that finally, rapturously burst.

Damien had barely glanced at her during breakfast, and throughout that last morning he scrupulously avoided her, so much so that she felt constrained to send him a note: *I hope that goodbye yesterday evening was not goodbye for ever. I am fond of you, Damien. D.* And immediately regretted it.

'Where's Daddy?' Paula asked.

'You've already asked that. And I've already told you.'

'When are we going to see him? I want to see him.'

'So do I.'

An announcement came over the Tannoy, a metallic voice – 'Is it a frog?' Paula asked – inviting families with children to make their way down to the disembarkation deck. There was a crowd on the stairs, people wishing each other goodbye and making plans to meet again – all the people she had met, had dined with, talked to, played deck quoits with and all the silly things you did at sea, rather like those games you played at the seaside yet never played again during the remainder of the year.

'Darling, how wonderful it's been.'

'Oh, Binty, we must keep in touch.'

'Of course, my dear.'

It was when they were near the entry port that Damien appeared. He looked absurdly handsome in his uniform, and so young. She blushed as he approached through the crowd.

'I got your note.'

'I shouldn't have sent it.'

'But you did.'

'It was a gesture. A stupid one.'

They edged towards the companionway. It was like an emergency, women and children first. She felt his hand hold her arm, invisible in the crush. 'I'll see you again?'

'Won't you be chasing EOKA?'

'Not all the time.'

'We'll see.'

They were at the entry port, looking out of the shadows into the blinding sunlight. It was like being on the edge of a diving board, the great open space below. 'Hold my hand tight,' she said to Paula, and stepped out on to the platform. A sailor took her arm and turned her towards the gangway that went down the side of the ship to where the lighter was moored. 'Easy now, ma'am,' he said, as though she had been making things difficult. And then to Paula, 'Goodbye, miss. Have a safe journey.'

'I'm going to see my daddy.'

'Lucky him,' the sailor said. They descended the iron steps cautiously, the sea visible below through the gratings, and the upturned faces of the sailors at the side of the lighter. Dee hoped they couldn't see up her skirt. And then, guiltily, she hoped they could. You can tell a lot by the shape of a woman's legs. What could they tell from hers? 'All aboard the Skylark!' a sailor shouted, handing her across the gunwales. The engine puttered and the lighter cut a smooth curve through the septic water. Behind them the *Empire Bude* fell back while ahead the quayside came nearer, the crowd of people waiting at the barriers, the soldiers, the godowns behind.

Shock. That was the word. The shock of sensation: of noise, of smells, of sights, the uneasy sensation of tripping across the gangway, clasping Paula's hand. The shock of sunlight on hot stone. Dust, fine and yellow. And Edward there, looking good in his khaki uniform, suntanned and somehow exotic, waving across the barricades as they went forward into the shadows of the customs house to find their bags; and then he was hugging her to him, holding her waist against him so that she felt very fragile for a moment. 'God, I've missed you,' he was saying into her ear, and it was true enough that she had missed him, familiarity being a strong emotion and denial of familiarity a stronger one still. He let her go and crouched to pick up Paula, who was hiding her face in Dee's skirt. She screamed and laughed together as he hoisted her up into the hot and dusty air. And above all this there was the noise of the quayside and the stevedores, dark with sweat and oil.

They cleared customs and recovered the trunks that had not been wanted on voyage, loaded all this into the boot of the car and set off to what Edward called 'home'. How could it be home? As yet she had only seen it in a photo he had mailed to her in England. The road led away from the harbour buildings, past low houses with tiled roofs and a dried streambed where eucalyptus trees grew. There was a mosque over on the right, and another one just ahead, their minarets pointed at the hot sky. There were oleander and carob trees along the road, and that smell coming through the open windows of the car, the smell that was undeniably exotic and strange: the smell of the Levant. It was a word that had meant little until now – Levantine, Levant. And the other one: Byzantine. She had sailed to Byzantium. She was here.

'That's the Turkish Quarter,' Edward said. The word 'Turk' carried semantic power. She knew nothing much about the Turks, but still the word meant something. It signified a darkness, a strangeness, a violence hidden behind silk and brass. The people by the roadside were draped in black: an old woman with a scarf over her head, a man with grey moustache and baggy black breeches, leading a donkey.

'You know what they say?' Edward asked, seeing her glance. 'About those breeches, I mean. They say that the Muslims believe the next time the Prophet comes he will be born of man.'

'Who says?'

'And those trousers are to catch him if he should pop out.'

'Who says that? That's ridiculous. Who says that?'

'Geoffrey.'

'Who's he?'

'Geoffrey? Geoffrey Crozier. You'll meet him.'

Beyond the Turkish Quarter was a modern suburb where, in a kind of geological convulsion, concrete was just beginning to establish itself over the scrub and stone of the Mediterranean landscape. Among bungalows and apartment blocks a flock of sheep grazed under the eye of an ancient shepherd. The house came into view, one of a long line of new, concrete buildings, each with its parched garden, each with its tilted, red-tiled roof, each approximately whitewashed. A mirage of English suburbia refracted through the prism of Mediterranean air. A sign said 16TH OF JUNE STREET.

How can you name a street for a date? Dee wondered. The house had a pair of palm trees on either side of the front door and a veranda across the front. Edward seemed eager that it should be all right. 'Not exactly Broomhill,' he said as he parked the car, 'but home sweet home.'

Paula ran up the steps on to the veranda, calling excitedly. She wanted to see her room, she wanted to see her room. Edward held Dee's hand as they followed her. They went inside, out of the glare of the sun – that presence that dominated the day in a manner that she had never imagined. The rooms were bare and shadowy, their green shutters barricaded against the heat. Ceiling fans rotated in the stillness like dark bats circling overhead. While Paula ran from one room to the other in excitement Edward took Dee into his arms. 'How do you like it?'

'It's fine,' she said. The hot air hammered on her skin. She thought she might not be able to breathe. 'It's lovely.' She longed for cool and rain, for the mist draped over the rim of the Pennines, and the city below, cool and damp. 'It's lovely.'

That evening, once Paula had been persuaded to sleep, they made love in the heat, beneath the circling ceiling fan, their bodies slick with shared sweat.

Seven

They meet outside the tube station. Kale is dressed up – black velvet trousers and jacket beneath her overcoat. And she's done her lips in a dark, venous red. Venous or vinous? Either will do. Or Venus, come to that. Her eyelids are the colour of wet slate. It's rather touching that she has gone to this trouble; makes him wish that he had done something better than jeans and a jacket. Her daughter is a sharp, half-shy, half-bold little girl, with blond hair and her mother's suspicious glance. 'Emma, this is Dr Denham. He's one of Mum's teachers.'

'You can call me Thomas if you like,' he says.

Emma thinks about this offer. 'You're a *man*,' she says.

'Good guess.'

This amuses her. 'I guessed, I guessed,' she cries, jumping up and down. 'He's a man. I guessed!'

They walk round to the theatre, almost like a family, the little girl skipping along between the two adults, pulling at

Kale's hand and grabbing at Thomas' to try and swing between them. 'Stop it, Emms,' Kale snaps. 'Otherwise we'll go home.'

Yellow cat's eyes watch them as they approach the theatre. 'Is it about Fritz?' asks Emma, whose own cat, Kale explains, is called Fritz.

'Sort of,' Thomas tells her. 'Lots of different cats. Mystery cats and Jellicle cats and all sorts.'

Emma loves cats, and she loves *Cats*. Small and golden and animated, she sits between the two of them in the centre of the stalls, and sighs and gasps and squeals and giggles and finally, at the death of Grizabella, has to be consoled. 'She didn't *really* die,' Kale explains. 'She's got to be there for all the boys and girls tomorrow.'

They leave the theatre into a surprising real world that has turned dark and wet in the meantime, lit by shop windows and headlights and streetlamps. Traffic wades down Long Acre. 'Let's go back to the flat and make some tea,' Thomas suggests.

There is a moment's hesitation while Kale hitches up her coat tails and crouches to explain yet again to Emma that Grizabella is not really dead. 'Really, Emms. Mum promises.'

He wants to see Kale in the context of his flat. He wants to be with her. The feeling, growing within him over the last few days, has metamorphosed from mere thought to something physical inside his chest. He wants to be able to touch her, to have her touch him just as she is now touching Emma, stroking her cheek and tapping her on the nose and laughing to get her laughing as well. 'Come on, Emms. It's just a *play*?' The upward lilt, hopeful and anxious.

'Does that mean it's a game?'

'Sort of. A complicated game that you watch other people playing?'

'I want to play it. With Fritz.'

'You can. We'll soon be home and then you can play with

Fritz.' Kale looks up with an apologetic smile. 'I think we'd better be going.'

He repeats his invitation: the flat, the cups of tea, domestic bliss, but she shakes her head. 'You're very kind. Isn't Thomas kind, Emms? But I think we'd better be getting back to Fritz, don't you?' It is the first time she has ever used his first name. As a prelude to departure.

'Are you sure?'

She's sure. The tube station is just there, shoppers and office workers disappearing into its maw like water sluiced down a drain. 'Thanks ever so for taking us,' she says, and gives him a quick, neutral smile and a quick, neutral kiss – her cheek is cool and damp – and turns away. As the two of them disappear into the station entrance he calls, 'I'll give you a ring,' but whether she has heard, or cares, he isn't sure. Persephone returning to the underworld, he thinks, and feels an absurd sense of bereavement.

Next day Kale isn't there in the class. All the others are, but not Kale.

'Anyone any idea?'

Eric shakes his head. 'Probably 'ooked it. She did tell me she wasn't sure about doing this course. It's a free world, isn't'it?'

The class gets under way and Thomas pretends not to care that next to the Pakistani girl – Sharaya, Shanaya? – there is an empty chair. They consider various interpretations of history, and argue about whether you can ever be truly objective. 'Of course you can,' Eric insists. 'I mean, it's just what happened, isn't'it? There are just the facts. All the rest is bullshit. Isn't that what someone once said? History is bullshit.'

'Henry Ford. It was "bunk". History is bunk.'

'Same difference.'

At the end of the class Thomas goes to his office and looks up

Kale's number. There is no reply when he calls. He imagines a terraced house divided into single-bedroom flats, the communal telephone ringing in the communal hallway – lino floor, a pram under the stairs, some litter, the smell of damp and drains – and no one there to lift the phone. Back home later that evening he tries the number again and this time there is an answer, a man's voice that says, 'Yeah?'

Is this the faceless Steve? 'Kale?' Thomas asks. 'Kale Macintosh? Is she there?'

'Dunno. I en't seen 'er.'

'Could you find out?'

'S'pose.'

There is a pause, a scuffling of the receiver and a voice shouting somewhere far away, then footsteps and, thankfully, her voice right in his ear. 'Who is it?'

'It's Thomas.'

'Oh.'

'We missed you in the class today.'

'I had things to do.'

He adds, in a burst of honesty: '*I* missed you.'

A silence.

'I've got a present for Emma, you see. And I wanted to give it to you.' He hasn't any present. This is a complete fabrication, the ad-libbing of the practised philanderer. But already he knows what the present will be.

'Look,' Kale's voice says, 'what's all this about?'

'What?'

'You going on like this?'

'It's not *about* anything. I just want to see you. And give you a present for Emma.'

There is a silence, as though she is reckoning this answer, turning it over, considering it in various lights. Like examining a banknote under one of those ultraviolet scanners to see if it's counterfeit. 'I'll be in college tomorrow,' she says finally, and puts the phone down.

Before arriving at work next morning, he goes into the bookshop just round the corner. It used to call itself The College Bookshop and stocked a wide variety of obscure academic texts, but that was before profit became an issue. Now it is Books 'n' Stuff and only stocks big sellers, but will happily order anything that you may want and blame any delay on the distributors. That morning there is no problem, however: Thomas doesn't want an academic text, he wants *Old Possum's Book of Practical Cats*, which is a book they do have, stacked high and selling fast in a new edition, along with CDs and tapes and the book of the musical, and posters.

He counts out the money, and there and then, on the cash desk, writes a dedication on the flyleaf: *To Emma – Grizabella lives! – love Thomas.*

'Seen the musical, have you?' asks the girl at the till.

'As a matter of fact, I have.'

'I love "Memory", don't you?'

He does. He admits as much. 'Memory's all we've got, isn't it?'

'We've got T-shirts as well,' she reassures him.

Grabbing his purchase, he hurries across to the college, where he is late for a meeting of the ad hoc committee appointed to draw up guidelines for a departmental policy on gender and ethnicity in the study of history – known as COGESH – where he sits for an hour at a table with five other colleagues, arguing about whether all departmental literature should be edited to remove gender-specific pronouns, and if so what should be substituted. It is a matter of 's/he' or 'he or she' or that weasel compromise 'they'. The argument goes round and round in circles, like Thomas' bowels.

'What's that you're reading?' one of his colleagues asks when they break for coffee.

'Present. For a child.'

The colleague glances at the book, scowls and puts it down as though it is tainted. 'Anti-Semite,' s/he says.

When finally he gets to his office he finds the door ajar. Cautiously he pushes it wide open to discover Kale sitting there, looking thin and pale. Her legs stick out like oars from a beached boat. She gives him a fleeting smile. 'I told the secretary I had an appointment with you? She was suspicious, but I sort of persuaded her? And I found the door open.'

'That's because there's nothing worth stealing.' He holds out the book towards her. 'Here it is. Emma's present.'

She takes it, flicks the pages over, finds the dedication and looks up. Her smile is lopsided, perhaps guarded, as though she wants a line of escape to be kept open. 'Emms will love it.'

'I thought of getting the CD and then I thought, better get the words, so you can read it to her.'

'It's great.' She nods, and puts the book aside. 'Can you close the door?'

'And lock it?'

That is a mistake. There is no answering smile. He looks round for somewhere to sit, somewhere other than behind the desk. But it isn't that big an office and there is nowhere else. He pulls the chair round to face her. 'So, what happened on Tuesday?'

Kale doesn't look at him any longer. She is playing with her fingers – slender fingers, each tipped with a nail of gleaming pearl – examining them as though they are recent acquisitions and she isn't sure how they work. She coils them experimentally round each other. 'I want to know what this is all about,' she says, as though referring to some pattern her fingers have made.

'What?'

'Oh, come off it. You've been kind. Kind to Emma and me and all that. Taking us to *Cats*, buying me lunch, this book, all that crap. But I want to know what you're after.'

He shrugs, although she isn't looking. 'You make it sound wrong.'

'You've got a reputation, you know that? You've been with a load of students, haven't you? That's what they say. And I just want to know whether you are just lining me up for a quick fuck.' A thoughtful glance up at him, mouth delicately twisted. She is biting the inside of her lip, small sharp teeth nipping flesh. 'I'm not concerned about me. I can look after myself. I'm thinking of Emma.'

'Of course—'

'Of course nothing. Just tell it me straight. I'm pissed off with being lied to. Just tell me.'

'I haven't lied to you.'

'So don't lie now.'

'I wasn't intending to.' Thomas laughs humourlessly, aware of the serious import of things he might say, trying to find the right combination of words. 'It's not easy—'

'To tell the truth?'

'That's not what I meant. It's not easy to answer your question.'

'That's an answer.'

'No, it's not. The question's unfair. It's one of those "Have you stopped beating your wife?" sort of questions. It doesn't give me any room to move. No, I'm not after a quick fuck, so yes, I must be after a slow one. You know what I mean.'

'You tell me.'

'I want to get to know you. Christ, how can you say anything witty and original in a conversation like this? I want to get to know you. I find you attractive – it'd be ridiculous to pretend I don't – and I enjoy your company. If you don't mind mine . . .' She doesn't avail herself of the opportunity that he has given her, so he blunders on: 'As to the other students you mentioned, well, yes, there have been a few. Probably fewer than rumour has it. The historical narrative often differs from reality. And there haven't been any hard feelings – well, nothing more than normal. OK, I've exploited my position, but they've enjoyed the exploitation. Mostly. Anyway, no one ever complained.' He shrugs helplessly, aware that she has given him rope and he is busily tying it round his neck. A mere shrug is never going to be sufficient to dislodge it, and might even throttle him. 'That's all I can say, really. No pressure, no promises, no quick fuck. Maybe a slow one. If that's what you want. Unless Steve's in the way.' And then he falls silent, wondering if he has just kicked the chair away from under him.

She looks up. Her eyes are tired, as though she has been kept up half the night looking after Emma. He wants to kiss them, just touch his lips on to those blue-grey lids. Will he ever be able to do so?

'Usually they run a mile,' she says, 'when they discover I've got a kid.'

'Not me,' he says. 'I've had practice.'

Eight

The house was a hiring. There was something quaint about the term 'hiring'. It sounded as though you might find it in a Thomas Hardy novel. Sixteenth of June Street. What had happened in Cyprus on 16 June that merited immortalization in the naming of a long, straight suburban street lined with new concrete bungalows? Dee never found out. It was the date of the Orthodox Feast of the Holy Spirit. Geoffrey told her that. Perhaps that was it.

Her weekends were circumscribed – Saturday meant a trip to the beach with a picnic; Sunday meant the garrison church, and afterwards lunch in the Club – but every weekday morning a car came to take Edward to work and Paula to the primary school, and Dee was left alone with the maid. Voula was a young girl of impossible shyness and no English. Dee experimented with Greek phrases. The girl laughed. After some days and much misunderstanding, Dee discovered that her real name was Paraskevi, Friday. 'Is there really a name Friday?' It seemed absurd, but the girl nodded, giggling with embarrassment. Girl Friday, Dee christened her. It seemed a fitting name.

Like a female Crusoe examining jetsam on the beach, Dee scoured the previous day's editions of *The Times* and the *Daily Telegraph* for news of home. She wrote letters to Tom, to her parents, to friends back in Sheffield, and waited hungrily for their replies. Only after a while, cautiously, sniffing the air and listening for sounds, did she begin to explore the world in which she found herself marooned.

At the back of the house there was a wide open space of rough grass where goats and sheep grazed. On the far side of this area a small shanty town of shacks and lean-tos had been erected. There were people there, ragged children playing in the dust. *Tsigani*, Voula told her, screwing up her face in disgust, gypsies. Dee hadn't expected gypsies. These were nothing like the gypsies she knew from Britain. They were something exotic and oriental. She watched them, and felt that she was standing on the shoreline, looking across to another world entirely, somewhere that had no point of contact with her own. Where had these people come from and where were they going? And more than that, what would happen to her if she went over to them? BRITISH OFFICER'S WIFE KIDNAPPED BY GYPSIES. What a headline that would make! The imagining of it gave her a curious thrill, something deep and organic. She imagined a gypsy man, like something she had read about in a story by D. H. Lawrence: dark and dirty, with flashing eyes and a lean, hairless body, coming into the caravan where she lay waiting, his figure blocking the light from the door as he loomed over her. Except there were no caravans here, and when she did finally get a sight of one of the adults he was ragged and dirty all right, but bowed and ill-shaven and repulsive, more like someone you might see on a city street back home, mumbling along the pavement, sodden with meths.

The other side of the house was different: here there was a deserted suburban street, roughly made of concrete and rock, edged with weeds. Tentatively, taking Paula with her for support, she ventured down as far as a small grocery shop that advertised Keo beer and Kean orange juice. There were boxes of unfamiliar vegetables outside on the pavement – purple aubergines and sweet peppers that looked as if they were made of red and yellow plastic – and, in the shadowy interior, tins of things that you did not find in England: *hummus* and *tahina* and *taramasalata*. Flat loaves of pitta lay in a glass-fronted cabinet, like religious offerings. There was the smell of cumin and fennel.

In this shop they were greeted with surprising ceremony. A chair was put out for her. Orange juice was brought for Paula and thick, black coffee for Dee, along with a glass of water. *Glyki*, she learned: sweet. *Efharistó*: thank you. The owner – his name was Demetris – beamed at them. Dee only had to ask – *parakaló*: please – and things were brought, and packed into a brown paper bag. The youngest child would be dispatched with her to carry the purchases home, and she learned to give him a piastre tip, but learned also to keep it secret, for his father would have been cross. She discovered his birthday and bought him a small present, a plastic aeroplane. His name was Evangelos, which seemed too much for a young child to bear.

'How d'you get on today?' Edward would ask when he got back in the evening. If she had been out with some of the wives – perhaps Binty had picked her up to take her to a coffee morning or swimming at Lady's Mile – then she would tell him all; but if she had spent the day alone then she would say little, because somehow it was her experience and no one else's. Edward spent the day in the company of his colleagues in the offices of the Headquarters up on the cliffs at Episkopi. He lunched in the mess and talked and laughed and drank with his own kind, immersed in a world that she visited almost like a foreigner whenever there was a party at someone's house or a ladies' night at the mess. It was on occasions like that, with the men decked out in mess kit, their chests gleaming with the medals they had won in Italy or the desert or Burma, that she wondered about Damien Braudel.

She first met Geoffrey Crozier at a party given by Binty and Douglas. He was rather older than Edward, a short, dapper man with Brylcreemed hair and a toothbrush moustache. 'Crozier, as in bishop,' he said, shaking her hand solemnly. There was an incongruous London edge to his voice, half-breathed aitches, glottal stops. He was a civilian among the military, a banker of some kind, although exactly what he did was not clear.

'Can I open an account with you?' Dee asked him.

'It's not quite that kind of bank, I'm afraid. The Levant Investment Bank. We're a merchant bank.'

She was not familiar with the term. It had a raffish sound to it, as though it dealt with argosies and camel trains, traded in silk and spices. Geoffrey had, so he said when she asked about his family, managed to keep his wife in England. 'The problem with Guppy is that she can't stand too great a contrast between her body temperature and the surrounding air . . .'

'But that's daft. She must have a temperature of ninety-eight-point-four like any human being. So Cyprus would be better for her than England.'

Geoffrey laughed. His laugh was infectious, as sharp as a costermonger's. 'Guppy's blood's as cold as a fish's. That's why she's called Guppy.' The name conjured up an overweight and slatternly woman, wearing carpet slippers perhaps.

'What's her real name?'

He looked puzzled. 'D'you know, I forget? Let me see . . . Veronica, that's it.'

'So why "Guppy"?'

'Oh, she's always been Guppy. Ever since she was in nappies.'

They were out on the terrace at the back of the house, a married quarter in Berengaria village. Berengaria was a military enclave outside Limassol, an imitation of an English suburb drawn in strange, foreign colours and alive with animal sounds – crickets, tree frogs, the mournful cry of a scops owl – that you would never hear in England. He asked how she liked the island.

She confessed that she enjoyed the place. And she found the locals very friendly. 'I'd expected . . . oh, I don't know. Indifference, at least. Hostility, maybe. I find them very warm.'

He agreed. 'The Cyps love to have someone be nice to them, that's the truth. They're not bad types really. Bit like the Irish – they want to be loved, but they do reserve the right to shoot you in the back if necessary.'

She laughed. It didn't take long to discover that he was remarkably expert on arcane matters of Greece and the Greeks. He could converse easily with the locals in their own language and evoke smiles and laughter just as he did with the British. And there was the further, surprising fact – she discovered this the next time they met, when he came with her and Edward and Binty and Douglas up into the mountains for a picnic – that he was a poet.

They'd gone to Platres, a village high up among the pine trees, into a cool that you couldn't find down on the coast. The road wound up through olive groves and vineyards, then higher and higher, lifting them out of the heat until the coast was a distant smudge of brown in the haze and the trees had turned from olive to pine, and there was the smell of resin on the air. They drove through the village and on up the road until there was a place they could pull off on to a forestry track. Geoffrey let the others get on with unpacking the cars while he stood looking out over the roofs of the village and the dome of the church. Far beyond, in the haze of distance, was the faint blue wash of the sea and the silver expanse of the Akrotiri salt lake. 'Platres, where is Platres?' he asked of no one in particular. 'And this island, who knows it?'

Binty was spreading a rug on the ground, and finding plates and cutlery, putting out the food, getting things organized. 'Geoffrey, what on earth are you going on about? For goodness' sake shut up and do what you're good at – open that bottle of wine.'

He did as he was told – 'Ah! The old trout's a soak!' he cried – but Dee had understood that his words had been neither casual nor whimsical. When they were settled and they all had a glass of wine and the food was being passed round, she asked, 'That was a quote, wasn't it, that "who knows this island?" business?'

He smiled gratefully. '"The nightingales won't let you sleep in Platres/Tearful bird on sea-kissed Cyprus." Greek poet called Seferis. He was here a few years ago. Yiorgos Seferiades is his real name. He's a diplomat, works for the Greek Foreign Office.'

'I didn't know you liked poetry, Geoffrey.'

He shook his head. 'I don't really. Often I loathe it. But it likes me. You know the kind of thing? Hangs round me like an unwelcome friend. The kid at school that no one gets on with, and I'm too damn kind to tell him to bugger off, and of course everyone judges me by him. Oh, *Geoffrey*, they say: he hangs around with old Poesy. Funny fella.'

'Do you write it as well?'

'I try. That's a very different thing.'

Only later did she come across one of his pieces, published in the *Times of Cyprus*. She kept the cutting on her bedside table. She preferred poems that rhymed, of course, but she thought she understood what he meant. There was much about this island that she had not expected, either. And she fancied herself in the midst of her own particular Odyssey.

Swimming to Ithaca

When I first came ashore on Ithaca
I expected something different.
The grey olives, fingering the wind,
Were predictable enough.
The asphodel, with its cat's piss smell,
Anticipated.
And of course I knew it would be hot and dry.

But when I first came ashore at Ithaca
It was Penelope who surprised me.
Her manner with the suitors,
And her impatience with my stories.
And the relationships she had been weaving
In my absence.

I had hoped to find an ally in Telemachus
But he just shrugged his shoulders
And asked where I had been all this time.

Expedience had become habit, that's the trouble.
I'd been halfway round the world,
And no one cared to listen.

We become our absences.

One day she went into the town on her own. You weren't supposed to do this. You were advised against being on your own, despite the truce that had been declared by EOKA.

'I want a taxi,' Dee said to the owner of the grocery shop.

'My cousin,' was his reply.

And so, half an hour later, his cousin came with the taxi. The vehicle was a large, brash Opel Kapitan, a model that you didn't find in Britain but you saw everywhere on the island – flashy and chrome-trimmed, like an American car. It wore a wide yellow stripe down one side, which signalled its status as a taxi, and scabs of pink undercoat paint all over it, which signalled its owner's status as a driver of flair and masculinity. Cyprus racing colours, the British called the patches of undercoat it bore, or Cyprus blush. He laughed when she told him. The cousin was called Stavros. He was a portly man, with remarkably small feet for so large a body. He emerged from behind the steering wheel of the Opel like a dancer executing some intricate passage, a *paso doble* or something. Taking Dee's hand he bowed over it as though it were the hand of the Queen of the Hellenes, or perhaps Penelope's or even Aphrodite's. 'My lady,' he breathed. 'Please.'

Dee noticed that the nail on the little finger of his right hand was disproportionately long, nurtured and cultivated like a pet. She felt a tremor of disgust. He seemed entirely untrustworthy. Used to Yorkshire plainness, she was suspicious of anything that might be dismissed as flannel, and flannel Stavros certainly possessed. 'More flannel than a haberdasher's,' her Aunt Vera was wont to say.

With great ceremony she was ushered into the back of the car and the door slammed shut. Again that fluid shuffle, and Stavros was behind the steering wheel, peering round with a smile of white and brown and gold. 'Where my lady want to go?'

'Just into town,' she told him.

He looked pained at the idea, at the tragic waste of talent that this would involve. 'But I take you anywhere. *Anywhere*, lady. Nicosia, you want Nicosia? I take you Nicosia. Shops? Bars? I take you. Kyrenia? I have cousin in Kyrenia sells thinks, good thinks, good price. I take you there.'

'Just into town, thank you,' repeated Dee, and there was something in her manner that told Stavros that they would be going no further, at least not today.

That was her first real expedition on her own. She, who was happy enough walking by herself on the moors above her home town, was thrilled with the excitement of being on her own amid the racket of a Mediterranean port, walking beneath palm trees on the seafront, sitting outside a café on a rickety iron chair to drink Turkish coffee and eat drippingly sweet *kadeif*, witness to the noise and anarchy of the town. Edward was flying that morning, and she looked up, squinting against the brilliant sun while a Meteor jet, glinting silver, traced a fine line of white through the sky above the Akrotiri peninsula. Was that him? She imagined him there in the cockpit, his face hidden behind the rubber oxygen mask that smelled the same as condoms, his gloved hand holding the control column with a kind of delicacy while he pulled it back into his belly and sent the jet soaring towards those faint brush-strokes of cirrus cloud that were all the eastern Mediterranean could manage. 'That's my husband,' she wanted to call out to someone. 'There, flying high above us all.'

Later she went and found Marjorie Onslow, at work at her SSAFA canteen near the harbour. 'I've escaped,' Dee confessed. 'Come out on my own.'

Marjorie was delighted to see her. 'Jolly good thing too. If you like you can always give me a hand here.'

*

That afternoon, after Paula had come back from school, Binty picked them both up and they went swimming at Lady's Mile. There were some other women there, camped among the paraphernalia of the beach – deckchairs, umbrellas, rugs and mats. 'What on earth do you do all on your own, Dee?' she was asked. 'You must come out with us more often.'

She smiled at them apologetically. She didn't drive, she explained. And she rather liked being on her own in Limassol. She felt closer to the spirit of the island.

'Limassol?' There was a collective shiver of disgust. 'Ghastly place. Now Kyrenia's all right, and Nicosia's tolerable. But Limassol! Anyway, you'll soon be in married quarters, won't you?'

She supposed so. There was discussion about these, debate about whether one could live in Berengaria village where the Paxtons were, or whether it was better to hold out for something in the military base itself, on the cliffs above the village of Episkopi. Within the base there were various suburbs – Gibraltar, Kensington, Paramali. Paramali was the ideal, a kind of royal court, where the senior officers' houses circled around the mansion of the C-in-C like planets orbiting the sun. But Edward was only a wing commander and would be lucky to get a house there.

The conversation shifted to other matters. She listened to talk of the behaviour of the Cypriot leaders who didn't know what was good for them, and the young hoodlums who were quite happy to grab a pistol and shoot an innocent civilian in the back, of the British politicians and the Governor who was a good chap, being a soldier. He'd sort it all out.

Someone mentioned the EOKA leader, Grivas. The name brought a thrill that was almost sexual, as though he were a rapist on the prowl. The previous year a photograph of him had been published in the newspapers – a snapshot of a mustachioed rogue sitting on a tree stump in a woodland clearing with his merry men around him. He was known as Dighenis after a legendary hero: it was like calling an Englishman Robin Hood. 'They'll get him,' the women said. 'He's a diabetic, needs a constant supply of insulin. So they'll get him that way.' Was this true? A strange banality, to find your enemy through his medical prescription.

The young children ran about in the sand and splashed in the shallows while the women called to them to be careful. Talk drifted easily away from politics, to families and schools. Those who had children at Lancing College and Charterhouse were admired, those who could afford only lesser places were pitied. One family had their children at Eton; but they did not come swimming with this group.

'Where's Tom?' the women asked her. On the seesaw of social acceptability the faint hints of Yorkshire in Dee's voice brought her down, but Tom's preparatory school in Oxford raised her up. She thought of him languishing in the ink-stained shadows, estranged from home and parents, being bullied, perhaps. The thought made her eyes sting. And then came a different, more dreadful thought: that perhaps he didn't miss his family, that he was growing up and away already, callused by separation to a hard indifference.

That evening she spoke to Edward about swimming at Lady's Mile, but she didn't mention her morning expedition into town. It was her experience alone and not a thing to share. And perhaps he might forbid her to do such a foolish thing, and then she would be obliged not to, whereas now, with the matter not even mentioned, no one could gainsay her. She was not a solitary person, but her situation had made her so and to her surprise she enjoyed the new experience.

Geoffrey Crozier came by. He arrived shortly before lunch one day, after the maid had gone, when Paula was at school and Dee was pottering about the house; later she speculated that perhaps he had been watching the house to make sure that this was so. But she was not displeased at the visit. He made her laugh when they met up at parties, and Edward liked him well enough. They'd even gone on an expedition to a monastery with him – a place called Stavrovouni, which, Geoffrey explained, meant the Mount of the Cross – although she and Paula had not been allowed to enter the building itself. 'The poor old priests would get over-excited at the sight of you,' Geoffrey said. 'They'd come over all faint.' He'd taken Edward into the strange and scented shadows and explained about how the services were conducted and how the incense was made and how they painted icons and how the monks never washed because they considered dirt to be a gift of God. That was the thing about Geoffrey, there was always a ridiculous joke lurking just beneath the surface of one of his solemn dissertations. He was fun, aslant from the military world that she found herself living in. So she was not displeased when she peered round the front door and saw him standing there on the veranda. She was not displeased, but she was faintly embarrassed by being caught off guard. She was wearing shorts. She only ever wore them around the house and somehow she felt almost undressed when confronted by him, dressed as he was in a lightweight suit and holding a panama hat across his front. 'Geoffrey, what on earth are you doing here?'

'Do you think I shouldn't be?' He stepped into the cool shadows of the hallway. 'Gawd, do you think Edward would be suspicious if I he knew I was visiting the little woman behind his back?' He made to pick up the phone. 'Tell you what, I'll give him a ring. Edward, I'll say, I'm here alone with your little wife. Is that OK?'

She grabbed his hand to stop him. 'Don't be idiotic.'

'Ah, so there *is* reason for him to feel aggrieved?' He grinned at her discomfiture. 'Don't worry, love, your secret is safe with me.'

She laughed her moment of panic away, tossing her head and leading him through into the sitting room. 'I'm certainly not your love,' she called over her shoulder as she went. She knew he was watching her legs as she walked. She was barefoot, her soles cool on the tiles. She didn't know whether she should go and change. 'What can I get you? A nice cup of tea?'

His cry of repugnance delighted her. 'Isn't it a bit late for that? Breakfast's over long ago, and anyway I only drink coffee. But now it's midday, more or less, so gin, I think. Pink for preference.'

'I don't even know how to do pink gin,' she said, and so, as though he were letting her into a great secret, he showed her, swirling Angostura Bitters round a glass in a solemn ritual. 'This is the blood,' he said, raising the glass to catch the light. Then he poured the gin, and handed the glass to her. 'And this is the Holy Spirit.'

'Don't be blasphemous.' She took the glass and sipped the liquid with care. 'But it's practically neat!'

He nodded sagely. 'Like so many fine things, the secret is in the "practically".'

Out on the veranda – 'See? We're out in the open. No secrets to hide' – she wondered what to talk about. She was aware of her bare legs, and his eyes on them. Her shorts were cutting into her. She shifted to make herself more comfortable, and thought that she must seem awkward, fidgeting self-consciously under his gaze. 'I found one of your poems,' she said. 'In the *Times*. "Swimming to Ithaca".'

'Oh, that.'

'Who's Penelope? How did it go? "But when I came ashore at Ithaca/It was Penelope who surprised me." Is that Guppy?'

'Guppy?' He gave a hoot of amusement. 'Grief, no. Guppy's only ever had limericks written about her. There once was a lady – I'm not really sure about the "lady" bit but that's what you say in limericks – There once was a lady called Guppy/Who suffered severe cynanthruppy—'

'What on earth's that?'

'Cynanthropy? Psychiatric condition: you think you're a dog. Don't you learn nothing at school these days? She tried a relation/With a randy Alsatian/But settled for a fuck with a puppy.'

'Geoffrey!' Dee stood up uncertainly, disconcerted by his smile and his gaze and the shocking obscenity that he had uttered. 'What horrid language.'

He looked genuinely contrite. 'Have I offended you? I'm sorry. I couldn't help it. When the Muse calls . . .'

She felt absurdly prim standing there, schoolmarmish and slightly ridiculous. 'I think I must go and change,' she said, and retreated to the bedroom. There she stood in the middle of the room, looking at her figure in the mirror on the wardrobe. Her legs. Was it true, what Damien had said? She shivered, despite the heat. She could imagine Geoffrey sitting there on the veranda, laughing inwardly at her fright. In something like panic she took a cotton frock out of the wardrobe and pulled it over her head, struggled with the zip at the back, and then looked around as though for some kind of alibi. The newspaper was there on the bedside table, folded to Geoffrey's poem. She picked it up and, still barefoot, went out to confront her guest.

He looked relieved at her reappearance. 'God, I'm sorry to shock you. I thought—'

She tossed the newspaper on to his lap. 'There's the poem. Tell me about it; tell me about your *proper* poetry.'

'My poetry? It's nothing. Just a sideline.'

'But you *do* it.' She was happier now, cooler, her body moving freely beneath the loose cotton.

'It doesn't sit very well with my work, does it?' he said.

'What *is* your work?'

'I've told you. Banking. The Levant Investment Bank, Limassol branch.'

'But what do you *do*?'

'Read miles and miles of tickertape,' he said airily. 'Buy and sell shares in unlikely enterprises in the Lebanon, that kind of thing.'

'And where did you learn your Greek?'

'What is this, an interrogation?'

'Just a question. No one speaks the language here, none of the British. Except you. I've been here a few weeks and already I know as much as most people – *pos íste?* and *sto kaló* and that kind of thing. Why are you so different?'

'Classics at school, my dear, and then at university.'

She couldn't suppress her surprise. '*Classics?*'

'Does it shock you? You don't think of Geoffrey as a man of refined eddication, do you?'

'Well, it does seem a little surprising. And what happened then?'

He laughed and drained his drink. 'This *is* an interrogation! I must be going. I can't spend the whole day being interrogated by a pretty woman, even though that might be more to my taste than sitting at the teleprinter receiving abusive messages from head office.'

'But you haven't answered my question.'

'Don't you know you should never ask about a man's past? He may be forced to tell the truth. After university I went to Greece. I wanted to turn my ancient Greek into demotic or something. Worked for the British Council, and then I got caught there in the war and had a bit of trouble getting out.' He waved the newspaper at her. 'I'll give you a copy of my slim volume.'

'Slim volume? You mean there's a book? You've had your poems *published*?'

He looked gratified. 'Most certainly I have. Foreword by Larry Durrell. Published by Faber & Faber, greeted with indifference, died of neglect.'

'Who's Larry Durrell?'

'Another poet fellow. Left the island only last year. I must show you where he lived. It's in the north. A very beautiful place'

'How wonderful, to be published.'

'Not once you are. Once you *have* been published you crave real recognition – sales, fame, the adulation of beautiful women. What did Oscar say? The only thing worse than being famous is not being famous.'

'I think it was "being talked about".'

'I'm sure it was. Anyone can quote accurately; quoting inaccurately takes skill. That sounds like Oscar as well, doesn't it?'

'Is it?'

'No, it's me. Now, how am I going to get a copy of my deathless poetry to you? Why don't you come to dinner? Next Wednesday? Will that be OK? Don't dress up. Come in shorts if you like.'

Geoffrey lived in Limassol, in an old Levantine house in the centre of town: there was a vaguely ogival arch to the windows, an arabesque ornateness about the exterior decoration, columns that might have come from a mosque. Geoffrey himself opened the ponderous door. 'Come in, come in,' he said. 'Welcome to my 'umble abode.'

The house wasn't humble, and it certainly wasn't ''umble'. The rooms were high-ceilinged and white and almost cool. There were rugs on the floor and the sly gleam of brass in shadowy corners. Hanging on one wall was a Turkish carpet that glowed red and cream in the half light, almost as though it were illuminated from within. 'Hereke,' Geoffrey said as Dee paused to admire it. She put out her hand, and found the touch as soft and cool as skin.

'Is it silk?'

'Certainly it's silk. Worth a couple of hundred quid. Fancy making an offer?'

Worth seemed a very vulgar consideration when confronted with such a treasure. She looked round, feeling foolish, overwhelmed by the place and conscious of the poverty of their own home, the sense of impermanence that she had when she was there. 'It's wonderful. You never said anything about where you live. I imagined – I've no idea what I imagined. Gosh, some of these things must be priceless.'

Geoffrey laughed. 'Funny, isn't it – the difference between priceless and worthless? Has it ever struck you?'

She didn't know how to answer. The puzzle seemed too difficult, like a crossword clue you couldn't solve. He led them through from one room to the next, where there were sofas and armchairs and more carpets on the floor. Doors were open on to the garden. 'However did you find this place, Geoffrey?' she asked. 'How old is it? How long have you had it?'

He shrugged. 'I don't know much about houses. I just live here.'

'What do you mean, you just live here?'

He looked at her with that smile – self-mocking, mocking of other people, mocking of everything: 'Actually that was another quote. But that doesn't mean it's not true. I rent the place. None of this is mine. The owner's a businessman in Istanbul. Runs a chain of brothels.'

'He must be a pimp with very good taste,' Edward said. He had picked up a framed photograph. It was the only piece that seemed out of place in the whole room – a monochrome photograph in a frame of chrome-trimmed Bakelite. 'Is this one of his, Geoff?' He showed it to Dee. It was a portrait of a young woman, her face turned profile to the camera. She was looking down, past her bare left shoulder, towards something on the floor. Or perhaps she was merely averting her grave gaze from the photographer. Her features were sculptured out of shadows and light, the line of her neck moulded into a long, fine arabesque. Dee fancied that her skin would feel just like the Hereke carpet hanging on the wall – cool and silken.

'That's Guppy. It's by Bill Brandt.'

There was a hiatus, like a slight, embarrassed cough. 'That's *Guppy*?' Edward returned the picture to its place. 'My God, no wonder you're keeping her secret.'

'Who's Bill Brandt?' Dee asked.

'Photographer fella. One of her friends.' He pronounced the word with elaborate care, as though 'friend' meant something quite unusual. Edward grinned. Dee frowned. *Don't*, she mouthed at him from behind Geoffrey's back. *It's not fair.* But Edward ignored her. 'Well come on, old fellow, you can't hide her away for ever. Especially if she looks like that. Isn't she coming out to meet us all?'

'Maybe,' Geoffrey said. 'Maybe.' But it was unclear exactly what he was referring to, her coming out or his hiding her away for ever. 'She doesn't like travelling, can't bear it in fact. Now, let me get you both a drink. What will you have? Dee has quite taken to pink gin . . .'

The other guests turned up shortly afterwards, a Greek Cypriot lawyer and his wife and an under-secretary or something from Government House. They ate at the table out in the garden. Dinner was cooked by a Greek woman who smiled and bobbed in the background, and it was served by a young man who was, so Dee presumed, the woman's son. There were peppers and aubergines, and things done with yoghurt and tahina. The conversation was fitful, partly fuelled by their host's laughter, partly halted by an elaborate discourse on politics and economics from the lawyer. While crickets trilled among the vegetation, the question of *enosis* arose, and EOKA. There was talk of the emergency, of nationalism and terrorism. The name of Grivas darted through the shadows of the discourse. Old Grievous, Geoffrey called him. 'Of course, terrorism pays,' he said. 'We've seen that clearly enough in Palestine and India. Why do we try to pretend that it doesn't?'

'Why do you call it terrorism?' asked the lawyer. 'Why not call it a struggle for national identity?'

'You can't make that sort of claim when a quarter of your population is Turkish.'

'A mere eighteen per cent,' the lawyer insisted. It was difficult to interpret his feelings. He spoke perfect English. His manner was balanced and reasonable, but there was an undercurrent of anger beneath his even tones, as though he knew that he was being teased, and, despite knowing about the British habit of teasing, had not learned the ability to shrug it off.

The mollifying words of the under-secretary tried to ease the conversation on to safer ground: 'I see Cyprus as the crossroads of the Mediterranean. A melting pot. If the Cypriots seize the moment they can show us the way to the future. When I was in Lebanon—'

'But it is *not* a melting pot,' the lawyer pointed out. 'In four hundred years of living together there has never been a single mixed marriage between Greek and Turk. Not a single one. There are no mulattos here.'

Geoffrey laughed. 'What about Othello?'

'Othello,' the lawyer pointed out with a triumphant smile, 'was an agent of an imperialist power.'

The dinner party broke up soon after that. The under-secretary had to drive back to Nicosia, and the lawyer and his wife liked to get to bed early. They made their goodbyes and thanks, and Geoffrey watched them out into the darkness of the street. 'For God's sake stay and have a nightcap,' he pleaded when Edward and Dee made a move to follow.

So the three of them settled into the chairs in the sitting room, and there was a feeling of relief at the departure of the others and the possibility of relaxing. Brandy – 'Armagnac, not bloody Cyprus gut-rot,' Geoffrey said – gleamed like amber in their glasses. They talked – or rather, Geoffrey talked. His conversation was alternately funny and serious, revealing and guarded. He talked about his time in Greece, about how he had escaped from Piraeus aboard a leaking tramp steamer in 1940, and how they had been attacked by an Italian aircraft off Crete – 'Bloody great monster with floats. Like Donald Duck flying' – and how they had finally reached Alexandria. 'Met up with Larry Durrell there,' he said. 'Just as he was shedding his first wife.'

'What did you actually do in Egypt, Geoffrey?' Edward asked. 'Surprised we didn't meet – Shepheard's or somewhere. The Gizeh. What were you up to?'

The man laughed and waved an airy hand and poured more brandy. 'This and that. You know the kind of thing. That's where I met Guppy. And where I first read Cavafy.'

'Who the hell's Cavafy?'

Geoffrey made a face. 'You don't know Cavafy? He's impor-tant, dear Edward, important. The poet laureate of the Levant. Which' – he got up from his chair – 'reminds me.' He held up his hand. 'Don't you move. Just stay where you are. I won't be a moment.' He crossed the room, his progress slightly unsteady, as though he were still on the deck of the tramp steamer out of Piraeus. They heard his footsteps on the stairs, and then above their heads.

'Probably not come down again,' Edward suggested. 'Probably flake out on his bed and wake up halfway through tomorrow morning.'

But Geoffrey did return, with a steadier step and a sly smile and in his hand a book that he presented solemnly to Dee. 'With my compliments.'

'Oh, my goodness!' She turned it over delightedly, like a child with a surprise present. It had a plain blue cover and the title *Aphrodite Died Here* and Geoffrey's name on the spine. She had never expected him to remember. Perhaps she had even imagined that he had been teasing her over his claim to have been published.

She opened the book to the title page and there was his handwriting – four lines of verse above a line of dedication:

> Priceless is the measure of your glance
> But worthless is my gaze;
> Treasure are the words you spoke
> But paltry is my praise.

She read the words with something like shock, remembering their conversation earlier. 'How appropriate. Where do these lines come from?'

He smiled and tapped his forehead.

'You made them up?' It seemed astonishing. 'I don't know how to thank you,' she said.

'"Thank you" is quite enough.'

'But can you spare it? I mean, you say it's not in print any longer . . .'

'I've got a whole warehouse full of them back home. And you'll find a copy in every sixpenny tray outside every bookshop in the Charing Cross Road.' He laughed. There didn't seem to be any bitterness in the laugh, just genuine amusement.

'Old Geoff?' said Edward when they were undressing for bed that evening. 'You've certainly made a conquest there.' He was whispering, trying to keep his voice down because Marjorie had been babysitting and now she was in the spare room just next door. 'I think the fellow's a complete fraud.'

'That's just your snobbishness,' Dee said sharply. 'Because he's got a cockney accent.'

'South London, actually. And you've got a Sheffield one and I don't say that about you.' He was laughing at her. She had loved his laughter. The sublime laughter of a pilot, that's what she had thought when they first met.

'Who cares where he comes from? He's a character, and you and your awful air force friends can't abide characters. Particularly characters with talent. How many other people do you know who are published poets?'

'Now you *are* being silly. We adore old Geoff. But you've got to admit he is a bit of a phoney. It wouldn't surprise me if—'

'If what?'

'Oh . . . nothing.' He climbed into bed and beckoned her to join him.

'His poems are lovely—'

'You haven't read them.'

'One of them, I have. And it's wonderful. And now I'm going to read them all.' She slipped in under the sheet. She was always shy of being naked beside him, even after years of marriage and two children.

'And that house of his—'

'Well there's nothing phoney about that. It's a beautiful place—'

'Oh, I'm not denying it. Of course it's beautiful. It just happens to be his, that's all.'

'*His?* You mean all that stuff about the businessman from Istanbul—'

'Is precisely that: stuff and nonsense. Like so much of what he says.'

Suspicion bubbled up to the surface. 'And Guppy?'

Edward shook his head. 'I don't believe Guppy even exists . . .'

O val windows, and the cabin flooded with light. The sensation of flight is strong: the shrill scream of the engines, the cabin bucking in turbulence, pain in the ears. The solemn child seated beside one of the windows knows the technicalities, more or less. It has all been explained to him by his father, who knows these things: the cabin is pressurized – a new enough thing – to five thousand feet, which means that his ears have popped, and are popping still, and buzzing with a sound that isn't the noise of the engines. This sound will remain with him for days after the aircraft has landed, giving a strange slant to his perception of things, as though the soundtrack of real life had been somehow corrupted.

Outside, beyond two layers of Perspex and a rime of ice crystals, is a brilliant landscape of cloud and sky and sunlight, each one a substance of the utmost solidity, so that one might imagine oneself climbing on those clouds, walking on that sky, sliding down that sunlight. The wing flexes and glitters in the cold, while air rages across its narrow aluminium desert, polishing the metal to a mirror. Noise from the engines, a shrill whistle, dominates the cabin, ousts thought. The propellers are arcs of rainbow colours. The engine pods have letters on them: RR in black, mourning the death of Henry Royce. He knows these things. He has a flypaper mind. Facts stick to it. The Honourable Charles Rolls died in an air crash in 1910; his partner, Sir Henry Royce, died in 1933. Ever since the latter's death, the company, manufacturer of the finest cars and the finest aero engines in the world, has been in mourning.

'Look at the pen,' says his neighbour, demonstrating a fountain pen that is leaking ink. 'The low pressure.'

Tom thinks the man ever so clever, to understand this physical phenomenon. Later, he will think him bloody stupid for having brought a filled fountain pen along with him. He turns away to gaze through the window.

Far below, like crumbs of biscuit scattered across a blue plastic tablecloth, are islands. In the pocket in front of him he finds an airline map covered in red lines as though a malicious child has scribbled great diagonal slashes of red ink across the page. From the map he identifies the islands as the Cyclades. He wonders about the name. Something to do with cycling, circling. As though at his command the aircraft tilts and turns, drawing its upper wingtip in an arc across the sky, pointing the lower wing, like a dagger, at one of the islands.

It is afternoon. An entire day has been spent like this: take-off in the early morning from the airport outside London; a long haul above the clouds of Europe to Munich; then on to Athens, where a hot wind battered across the concrete as the passengers made their way to the transit lounge; and then up once more, with the sun westering and the brown islands sliding beneath the fuselage like marine animals on the seabed beneath a boat. Then a final landfall, in the late afternoon, after a stretch of blue sea, the aircraft whining and pitching as it lets down over a dun-coloured plain between the mountains on the one hand and the mountains on the other and Tom's ears popping as though bubbles are exploding inside his head. The machine shudders through the turbulence, with the *engine note rising and falling, then thumps into the concrete, bounces hesitantly, as though uncertain for a moment whether to relinquish its hold on the air, then sets down finally and firmly, shuddering against the brakes and the reversed pitch of the propellers.*

Through the window, concrete and barbed wire pass by, a low line of tattered buildings, and, in the distance, a wall of mountain rising up from the plain like a breaker curling in on a sandy shore. The colour is dun, dust, dried turd.

Eventually, outside concrete sheds, the aircraft comes to rest. The engine noise dies away and the passengers are left in defeating silence. They rise wearily from their seats and begin to sort their things. A brittle, blonde air hostess comes down the aisle and asks him if he has everything. 'Your books? Don't leave anything behind.'

No, he won't. He's boarding-school bred and his world is his possessions.

'Come on, then.'

The two of them – an uneven alliance – advance up the aisle towards the door, gathering a small flotilla of other children as they go. And then there is the open door, and beyond it the heavy hand of heat, like a slap in the face. Tom hesitates on the edge of the stairs, looking down at the dusty concrete apron where soldiers stand with rifles at the port. Barbed wire like candyfloss. 'Go on.'

The steps are steep, the handrail smooth and hot. There are people to direct the stream of passengers towards a line of buses. Like quarantine patients, like prisoners under guard, they are shut into one of the vehicles. Students from Athens University have appeared from an Olympic Airways flight and they join the passive London passengers, two fluids as immiscible as oil and water, the one shouting, calling, pushing and shoving, the other subdued by heat and tiredness and being British. The Lords of Empire. Tom sits where the hostess points, pushed against a window while the vehicle –

crowded, noisy, not clean – moves off, staggering past the soldiers and through the barbed wire. There are people waving from behind the barricades, waving and shouting. Tom stares vacantly out of the grimy window. He watches, isolated in this maelstrom of Greek. Students crowd the aisles, pointing to their relatives on the street outside, laughing, often laughing, shouting, always shouting. Tom locks himself into his private room. He is trained to shut himself away, to find privacy in the midst of the crowd – in the lunch queue, in the muttering nightmare of the dormitory, at the bottom of a rugby scrum. His parents might be a thousand miles away for all he cares. Youths push and shove in the aisle. Tom absorbs sights and sounds and smells, the grime of the window, the dust and dirt beyond the glass, the people running along the street, cars jockeying for position, the police waving, the buildings with signs in Greek lettering.

'Look.' It is the man with the pen, tapping his shoulder from the seat behind and pointing. 'Look. Your parents.'

Tom looks. There is a car in the traffic beside the bus, a green Vauxhall, with his father's face framed in the window, looking up, grinning, waving. Tom raises his hand in salute.

Memory gives instants of remembering, like a night-time landscape lit by a summer storm. The scene at customs and immigration is glimpsed only on the edge of one of those lightning flashes: long benches with portly officials dressed in shabby suits, marking suitcases with chalk like schoolmasters marking prep. And then a barrier, and his parents, smiling and laughing and bending to hug him, and Paula hanging back in the face of someone who has done the impossible – flown thousands of miles all by himself.

Memory is neutral, it records without emotion. There was relief, presumably; love, certainly. But distant love, filial love, a love that has been compromised by absence. We become our absences.

Darkness descends over the landscape of memory, to lift once more at the hotel, the Ledra Palace, set about with Moorish arches, encircled with palm trees, its interior a lake of polished marble. A true palace. In the mirror of their room he glimpses his mother half-naked, her breasts as heavy as fruit, swaying as she bends. He has never seen her fully naked. Does she have pubic hair? He has heard about female pubic hair, but has never seen it: it is mere rumour.

There is nothing else, no memory of the meal that evening, no record of walking through the streets of the walled city. There is just a vague recollection of a car journey the next day, through a sere, alien landscape – a desert, complete with palm trees and discon-solate camels. And then up through the hills, a monastery capping a conical mountain on the left, the road winding through dusty vil-lages where people stand and stare. There are slogans daubed in blue paint on some of the walls – ΕΝΩΣΗ, ENOSIS. A dusty military convoy passes by, Land-Rovers with great metal stanchions nosing forward above their bonnets and ten-tonners with a soldier stand-ing up through a hatch in the roof of each cab. Minarets point admonishing fingers towards the sky. Old men in baggy black breeches struggle with donkeys. The hills to the left disclose a tri-angle of turquoise sea. 'Look,' his mother says, pointing out of the window. 'Olive trees.' For Tom, olive is a colour not a tree. Or a character in a cartoon. His head whistles and pops. The whistling is like the sound of aero engines echoed in the brain. Speech is a dis-tant thing, indulged in by adults. 'My ears hurt.'

'The pressure, old boy,' his father advises him. 'Hold your nose, close your mouth and blow gently.' Later they reach the outskirts of the city, edge among the buildings and traffic, find the ragged street named for a date that seems to carry no significance – the 16th of June. Home, of a kind.

The panic summer, throbbing with cicadas and heat. They go to the beach. They go up into the mountains where the air is scented with pine resin and seeded with coolness, and from where the horizon is a blur of haze that may be the mountains of Anatolia. They go to

Salamis and explore the ruins of the Roman city while the sun hammers down on their heads. They go to Famagusta and to Paphos. They go to Curium, on the south coast, where they creep past the solitary guard in his hut and, hidden from official eyes, scratch at the surface of the baked soil with a trowel, to discover there bones and shards of pottery and, gleaming like opal, fragments of ancient glass. Picking through the wreckage of two thousand years ago, Tom discovers the past. 'I want to be an archaeologist,' he confides to his mother.

'Well, you'll have to work very hard at school,' she tells him.

Polo at Happy Valley, with dust rising around the thundering animals. It was as you might imagine a cavalry action: a milling confusion of men and horses, a rising cloud of dust, the punctuation of sudden charges of excitement. There were tents along the edge of the field and a regimental band played 'Colonel Bogey'. 'Extraordinary performance,' said Edward, who felt that the Air Force had a duty to laugh at the Army and its pretensions. 'Anyone would have thought we were at Poona.'

They were at the bar with Binty and Douglas and others when one of the polo players came over. He was wearing jodhpurs and high boots with knee-guards. His shirt was dark with sweat and the face beneath his helmet was streaked with dust. Dee didn't recognize him at first, even as he took his helmet off and wiped his hand on his jodhpurs and held it out to her. 'I was wondering if I'd meet up with you here,' he said. 'Sorry, I'm in a bit of a muck sweat, but I couldn't let you get away without saying hello. It's Damien Braudel.'

She had expected to bump into him eventually, of course. In the circumscribed world of the military it was inevitable. But even so she felt a tremor of panic, a flush of embarrassment. 'Of course,' she said. 'Damien, of course.' It was a bit of a relief that Binty and Douglas were there to provide distraction, to engage him in conversation, to ask how he was and what he was doing and all that kind of thing. She introduced him to Edward.

'Mrs Denham kept me out of harm's way on the voyage out here,' Damien said as the two men shook hands. 'She plays an impressive game of deck tennis.'

'Far cry from polo. Let me get you a beer. Looks as though you could use one.'

'That's very kind of you, sir.' Edward went away to get the drinks. Damien glanced round.

'Damn it, the next chukka's about to start. We're on a hiding to nothing against the Blues. They take the whole thing so damn seriously.' He touched Dee's wrist. 'Look, I'm afraid I'll have to rush. Apologize to your husband for me, will you? Are you going to be at the do at the mess this evening?'

'I think so,' Dee said.

'Jolly good.' He paused, grinning down at her. 'You look bloody marvellous, Mrs Denham, do you know that? Prettiest girl here.' Binty was laughing at something someone had said. The band parped and farted in the background. He lowered his voice. 'I'd love to give you a kiss, but I don't suppose that'd be a good idea.'

'I don't think so either.'

He smiled. 'Take it as read, then. See you this evening.' And then he had gone, striding away across the hard-baked earth to where a groom was holding his pony.

He looked very different that evening, wearing his scarlet mess kit, a peacock among the drearier RAF pigeons. But Edward seemed to get on well with him, which was a blessing, and Binty thought him ever so wonderful as he regaled them with stories of hunting EOKA in the mountains. 'Some of them are bloody brave chaps, you know, whatever the mandarins at Government House say. Take Afxentiou, for example, holed up in his cave, entirely surrounded, never gave in. Stout fellow, if you ask me.'

'But Afxentiou was a killer with a price on his head,' Douglas protested. 'Anyone will fight to the death if he's facing the death penalty.'

Damien smiled. 'I don't know. I've never been in that position.'

Now that the battle in the hills had been won and lost, more or less, his battalion had been redeployed in the Limassol district. 'Perhaps we'll see something of each other?' he suggested. He addressed the question to the group in general, but Dee knew that it was meant for her. She seemed to know him so much better than the mere week on board the *Empire Bude* merited. He's rude and able, she thought, and I'm the hidden dreamer, and she smiled to herself at the silly nicknames. The fact was that she was absurdly happy to see him again, and frightened of the happiness.

'Perhaps,' she replied.

'Have you heard about Seferis?' Geoffrey asked. They were on their way to Bellapais, to see the abbey and the house of the poet Durrell, to see how beautiful the island could be when it put its mind to it. The road from Nicosia to the north coast led over Pentadaktylos, the 'five-fingered' mountain that had been created, so legend had it, by the hero Dighenis squeezing a lump of mud and throwing it to the ground. The range was a great petrified wave of rock rising out of the Mesoaria plain and hanging over the north coast. It was almost cool up there among the pines, three thousand feet above sea level, with the air coming in through the open window of the car. Tom and Paula were playing in the back, some game they had invented that involved spotting birds in the air and animals on the ground. It was a game that Tom always won.

'Seferis?' She felt close to Geoffrey, at one with him, delighted by both his laughter and his seriousness. Edward was away, on detachment in Jordan, and she was liberated by his absence, and guilty at the thought.

'That poet fellow I spoke about – nightingales in Patres, and all that stuff. He's just been appointed Greek Ambassador to Britain.'

'How strange, for a poet to be an ambassador.'

'Very Greek. The poets are the unacknowledged legislators of the world. Who said it?'

She didn't know, and he did. He was mocking her, making it like a test of some kind. When he caught her out it amused him. 'Shelley, my love. Percy Bysshe.'

'But will it make any difference whether the Ambassador's a poet?'

'It shows that the Greeks have civilized minds, even while they shoot British soldiers in the back.'

It was difficult to decide whether he was joking. Geoffrey was a type she had never met before, or rather he wasn't a type at all, but unique, and daring. He had this sympathy for the Greeks, and yet a loyalty to his own kind. He combined seriousness with reckless laughter.

Up on the crest of the mountains they stopped to explore the ruins of Saint Hilarion Castle. Tom and Paula were running around the broken walls while Dee and Geoffrey clambered up the hillside after them. She stumbled on the path and he held her arm to steady her. The cicadas shrieked and whirred like dervishes; the children shouted and threw stones. They climbed up through the ruins and gained the edge of the precipice, where you could see down on to the north coast and the tiny scar of white limestone that was Kyrenia harbour.

The two children stood on the brink, with the gulf, the great emptiness, the plunging hot air beneath them. 'Be careful, Paula,' Dee cried. 'Tom, look after her!'

'You could fly from here,' Tom said thoughtfully.

'You could fall,' his mother called, in that tone that adults use for children – peremptory, reproving.

'Would I die?' Paula asked.

'You would hurt yourself very much.'

The road led down in steep curves to the coastal plain, to Bellapais village. Villagers watched curiously as the visitors drove into the tiny square in front of the abbey. The abbey was a ruin, like Fountains or Whitby – a far-flung outpost of the Gothic, Latin Church in this Levantine world of Islam and Orthodoxy. They wandered through the cloister. The place was an essay in desolation and corruption, the arches empty, the chambers vacant, the stones broken. This is what happens to outsiders here, Dee thought. Stone stairs led up on to the roof of the church, from where you could look out over the village. A Greek flag flew defiantly, and illegally, in the breeze. Behind the houses the slope rose up, climbing steeper and steeper through terraced vineyards and pine trees to cliffs and the rocky watershed high above.

Geoffrey talked about how this landscape would change, how the whole place would change. 'Invasion' was the word he used.

'By the Turks?'

He shrugged. 'If not by the Turks, by tourists. Hordes of bloody tourists. It'll be destruction, whichever way you look at it. The barbarians will get here soon enough.'

In the narrow alleyways of the village they peered at the

doorway of the writer's house, shuttered now. Two years earlier, as violence erupted in the island, Durrell had abandoned the place and decamped to Nicosia. A year later, after a spell as press officer to the government, he had abandoned the island altogether. 'The trouble with Larry,' Geoffrey said, 'is that he's really just one of those orientalists that the empire produces. He wants things to fit his own personal vision of the Greeks and the Mediterranean – a piece of folk art, really. All poetry and mythology and dreaming of Byzantium.'

'And what's your vision?' she asked him.

He laughed. The laughter was paradoxical: for the moment he was serious. 'I have no vision. I just try and survive.'

'But you write poetry.'

'You mustn't hold it against me.'

In the café outside the abbey the children drank Coca-Cola while Geoffrey ordered a gin for himself and a beer for Dee. Their table was under a mulberry tree. There were no visitors around, no tourists, no one but the four of them and the old men of the village fiddling with their worry beads. A couple of them were playing backgammon, leaning over the board as though gloomily contemplating the future of mankind, slotting the pieces into place with the slickness of someone using an abacus.

Tom and Paula drifted away. When they were out of earshot Dee turned to Geoffrey. 'Tell me about Guppy,' she said. And so he told her. Of her pure, distilled beauty, her loveliness that turned everyone's head. And of the betrayals, the arguments, the exploitation and the unhappiness, the drunkenness and the deceit.

'Yet you haven't divorced.'

'It doesn't suit her to.'

'And you accept that? Can't you do something yourself?'

He was silent. Perhaps she had strayed over the boundaries of what was acceptable. He sipped his gin and drew on his cigarette and smiled. 'Perhaps it suits me too.'

Afterwards they drove on down to the coast, to the town of Kyrenia. The alleyways of the little port were cut through by blades of sunlight. There were tin cans of geraniums on windowsills and beside doorsteps. Cats lay in the shade. The air smelled of hot stone and drains. In the harbour there were a few fishing boats moored against the quay, a squat fisherman mending his nets, a single shop selling trinkets. Geoffrey and Dee walked ahead, with the children following.

For ever, for as long as the neurones and synapses in Tom's brain survive, those figures walk round the harbour of Kyrenia. It is always midday, always midsummer. By some trick of memory, Paula vanishes and there are only the two of them, his mother and Geoffrey, walking ahead along the curving mole that embraces the empty harbour. Tom is not there either, of course; he has no memory of himself – he is the camera, capturing these moments of sun and shadow, the rough bulk of the Castle with the Union Flag flying over it, the minaret of a mosque rising above the roofs, the fisherman mending his nets, toes gripping the netting to hold it tight against his grasp.

Where is Tom's father?

There is a pure white sailing boat moored at the quay, a ketch or a schooner, its ratlines vibrating in the breeze. 'Are they called ratlines because they're always rattlin',' Geoffrey asks, 'or are they called ratlines because rats run up them?'

Tom's mother laughs, and moves in a way that she never ordinarily does – a light, sudden skipping, her hips thrown, her skirt swirling. She catches at the man's hand, holds it and lets it go. He has never seen her hold his father's hand.

Later – you can move through memory like you move through a dream, jumping without effort from place to place, from scene to

scene – later they are in a cellar beneath Clito's Bar, drinking com-
mandaria; *later, earlier, they are climbing the stairs to the dining
room of the Harbour Club, and then laughing over lunch, talking
with people, about people, making jokes, constructing rhymes,
telling absurd stories. The windows are open and the room is wide
and hot, circled by ceiling fans. White linen, white shirts, and his
mother laughing. Has he ever seen her as happy as this?*

Summer dissolved, a draught of cooler air from the north
spreading pockmarks of cloud across the even face of the sky.
There were occasional showers of rain. Never had Dee imagined
that rain could be so welcome, that she could lie in bed and
hear this sound, like the sea, like wind in the trees, and feel
reborn.

She prepared Tom's things for his return to England. In some
intangible way, he seemed to offer protection from whatever
it was that lurked beneath the hard, baked surface of this
Levantine world where she lived now. He watched her and, she
thought eagerly, loved her, and kept her rooted in the England
from which he had come. She held him to her and willed him
not to go.

Edward was too busy to make the journey to the airport.
There was an exercise on, some elaborate game they played –
the Russians moving over the border into Iran, Syria invading
Lebanon, one of those apocalyptic scenarios that they rehearsed
over to themselves at Headquarters, in the hope, perhaps, that
playing it would prevent it. So first thing in the morning, with
Edward's car waiting in the road outside, father and son said
goodbye. They were both in uniform, the one in the grey-blue
of the Air Force, the other in the navy shorts and knee-length

socks and Aertex shirt of prep school. 'Give all our love to Grandmamma and Grandpapa when you see them,' Edward said.

'*All* your love?' asked Tom. 'That means you won't have any left.'

'Well, lots of it anyway. Now I'm afraid I must rush, old chap.'

They didn't kiss, but instead shook hands like grown-ups do. Edward took Paula with him. She was going to Binty's for the morning, the long drive to the airport judged too tiring and difficult for her. So it was just Dee and Tom who were left in the house, with Tom's suitcases ready, waiting for the taxi.

The driver was Stavros' nephew. He was in his mid-twenties and wore crêpe-soled shoes like a Teddy boy's. His hair was black and Brylcreemed and swept back in a quiff; modelled, Dee presumed, on that American film star, the one who had killed himself in a car crash. James Dean. He had an easygoing manner, as though the client relationship didn't quite fit. Perhaps it didn't, really: he had only come to Cyprus to help his uncle out with the driving. 'Are you Greek?' Tom asked him.

'Course I'm Greek.'

'You don't sound Greek. What's your name?'

'It's Nicos. But you can call me Nick, if you like.' He had, he explained, lived in Enfield, in north London. 'Norf London' was how he said it.

The little boy considered him thoughtfully. 'Do you support EOKA?'

'Tom!' Dee cried. 'That's not the kind of question you should ask.'

'But do you?'

The driver didn't answer directly. 'One day,' he said, 'you'll understand.'

'Understand what? What'll I understand?'

'Tom!'

But the driver only smiled. 'It's all right, ma'am. I'm used to it. I get it from my family all the time, only from the other direction. It's just politics.'

They had an armed guard with them, a military policeman in plain clothes. He sat in the front seat beside Nicos. His name was Cox. He had, so he said, another two months to finish his tour in this fleapit and thereby complete his National Service.

'What are you going to do then?' Dee asked.

'Dunno, really. Go to college, maybe. Join the police force, maybe. Be a bloody picnic compared with this.' He glanced suspiciously at the driver. 'At least the natives will be on your side, know what I mean?'

They passed army trucks on the road. In one village an army patrol was searching houses, lining up the inhabitants beside the road while the squaddies went through the houses.

'Why do they do that kind of thing?' Nicos asked plaintively.

'Looking for EOKA, mate,' Cox replied. 'It's your lot's fault.'

There was something of the atmosphere of a hospital about Nicosia Airport, a dirty, overcrowded hospital: the anonymity, the indifference, the same concern with one's own affairs and lack of concern about others, the same isolation and sense of loss. Dee delivered Tom to an air hostess who wore the brittle smile of a nurse. She watched the pair go through the gates as one might watch someone being wheeled into the operating theatre. When the two of them were lost in the crowd beyond the barriers she returned to the car alone.

Cox was leaning against the front wing of the vehicle talking to Nicos. When he saw her approaching he stubbed out a cigarette and stood to some kind of attention, as though he didn't really know how to behave when he was out of uniform and dealing with a civilian. 'Everything all right, ma'am?'

Of course everything was all right. Nicos held the back door open for her, and she stood uncertainly for a moment, looking in at the empty seat. Suddenly everything was not all right. Her eyes stung. The dust, maybe. Out on the concrete, beyond the barbed wire and the airport buildings, an aircraft was manoeuvring for take-off, its engines rising in pitch to what seemed like a cry of anguish. It wasn't a cry of anything, of course. It was mere noise with no meaning at all. But she made it mean something: it was her cry of anguish for the loss of her son. They stood and watched as the aircraft – a Viscount painted in the red and silver of British European Airways – turned at the head of the runway and held itself tensioned against the brakes. There was that pause, the rising pitch of the engines, and then its sudden movement down the runway, gathering pace, trading one element for another, rising up off the tarmac and into the air, climbing up into the blue sky, diminishing.

Nicos bent towards her. 'You OK, Mrs Denham?' His hand was on her arm and there was a sudden and surprising dismantling of the barriers that lay between them. 'Hey, we don't want to spoil a pretty face. Here, you take this.' He produced a white handkerchief from his pocket and handed it to her.

She dabbed at her eyes, and then looked at the handkerchief and saw that it was black with mascara. 'I'm awfully sorry. I—'

'That's quite all right. Part of the service.'

She almost laughed despite the tears. 'Phaedon Taxis at your command?'

'That's right. Difficult customers catered for. Specially pretty ones.' The aircraft was small now, something distant, a crucifix in the sky, turning over the mountains and setting course for England.

'There,' Nicos said. 'He'll be OK, Mrs D, you mark my words. He'll be OK.' He put a protective hand on her head as she ducked into the car, almost as though he was delivering a benediction. 'Mrs D,' he asked when she had settled into the seat, 'why aren't all Englishwomen like you?'

She smiled up at him. 'What on earth do you mean by that?'

He frowned. 'You *feel*. That's Greek.'

'All Englishwomen feel,' she said. 'They just don't always show it. They think it's a sign of weakness.'

The journey back was uneventful. Cox slept, his head weaving from side to side with the motion of the car. Was he thus sleeping on duty, and did this constitute some heinous breach of military discipline? Dee felt dreadfully alone in the back seat, almost as though she were a mourner returning from a funeral. She tried to imagine Tom in the aircraft, flying high over Europe; but she had never flown herself and her imagination failed her: he was merely absent, and she was bereft.

When they reached Limassol, they dropped Cox off at his camp, out in the wasted suburbs of the city, and then continued home. Sixteenth of June Street was deserted. There was something dispiriting about the rows of random concrete houses, the garish blooms of bougainvillaea, the dusty palm trees. Nicos brought the car to a halt outside the gate. 'You all alone here, Mrs Denham?'

'My husband doesn't get back from work until late.' It was like admitting to something shameful.

'Well, how about you come back to our place for a coffee? Meet the family, see that Greek Cypriots aren't all monsters.'

'I never thought they were.'

'That Cox fellow did. Couldn't make me out, the fact that I speak English as good as him.' He paused. 'How about it? We're only just round the corner.'

There was something endearing about his attitude. Living in the circumscribed world of the military, where people knew each other's ranks as though by instinct and each wife acquired a reflected status that mattered every bit as much as her husband's, it was refreshing to discover this London lad who couldn't give a damn. 'Thank you very much,' she said. 'I'd like that.'

They drove a few streets away to where a sign on one of the buildings proclaimed PHAEDON TAXIS. The family apartment was above the garages. It had wide, impersonal rooms and glistening marble floors. There were gilt mirrors on the wall, a sideboard like something from a church sacristy, ornate armchairs of exquisite discomfort. Ancestral faces gazed down from the walls like icons in a church – a grandfather who had been mayor of the city, a great-uncle who had worked for the Health Department in the 1920s, a cousin who was a bishop, a more remote ancestor who, sporting moustache and tarbush, had been in business during the Ottoman period. 'All right, in't it?' said Nicos with pride. 'Darn sight better than Enfield, I can tell you.'

She sat with him at the kitchen table beneath a circling fan, with Archbishop Makarios gazing benevolently down on them from above the cooker. Nicos' aunt made coffee, while his grandmother nodded and grinned toothlessly from a chair in the corner. '*Endaxi*,' she kept saying. '*Endaxi*.' Two little girls came and gazed with wide eyes at the English lady sitting primly on her straight-backed chair.

Where would Tom be now? Dee wondered. Somewhere over Europe. Impossible to imagine, suspended in the air in a steel tube. Alone.

On the stove the coffee seethed and died, seethed and died. The thick black liquid was presented to the English lady along with a glass of water and a bowl of fruit in syrup. '*Glyká*,' said the aunt. 'Eat, eat. This red cherry, this orange. This one' – she pointed to a small, glistening black slug – 'this one *vazanaki*, this one' – a small, dried turd, perhaps from a cat, perhaps from a small dog – '*karydhi*. Very good.'

Dee regarded them with alarm.

'Don't know what you call them,' Nicos admitted. 'Thems are walnuts, I think. Not the sort of thing you get in England, eh?'

She sipped and nibbled, and showed polite enthusiasm. Nicos seemed pleased by her approval. He talked to distract her. His interests were pop music and cinema. Music especially. 'I used to go down the dance halls in Tottenham – the Mecca and the Royal. Y'know what I mean? Jive, and that. D'you know how to jive?'

She didn't. But sometimes people did it in the mess, at parties. What about rock 'n' roll?

Only what she'd seen on the Pathé News, at the cinema. That Bill Haley fellow.

He laughed. 'Bill Haley? He's an old man. Past it. You should listen to Eddie Cochran and Buddy Holly and cats like that.'

Cats?

Again that laugh, a rough, derisive sound. And then, quite suddenly – it was as much a surprise to herself as it was to anyone – she was in tears. Sitting there on one of those wooden chairs with a rush seat, just like Van Gogh had in his room at Arles, and weeping. Tears running down her cheeks.

'*Po, po, po!*' the aunt exclaimed, while Nicos crouched down and dabbed at her cheeks with his handkerchief. 'What's up?' he asked. 'Aren't you feeling well?'

'It's all right.' She shook her head. 'Please don't fuss.'

But they did fuss, of course they fussed, the aunt running round the kitchen for whatever it was that cured tears, the old crone cackling in the corner, the little girls holding their faces. Nicos clapped his hands and said something that made the women disappear, and they were alone, just the two of them in the bare, comfortless kitchen. He brushed an errant strand of hair away from her face, stroked her cheek. He seemed to have metamorphosed into something new – the brother she had

124

never had, perhaps. 'It's just Tom,' she whispered. 'I just thought of him, that's all.'

'He's all right, Tom is. A big, tough lad.'

'He's just a child and he's all on his own and he should be here with me.'

'You'd be surprised how tough they are. Kids on their own, I mean. I should know. Hey, you want to use the bathroom, Mrs D? Wash and make up and stuff? Make yourself look all grown-up again.'

She managed a laugh. 'I'm must seem awfully feeble, crying like this.'

'What's feeble about it? We're not afraid of crying here. That's one of the things we find difficult with the English. I told you, didn't I? They don't show their feelings. But you do and that's all right. Now you go to the bathroom and put yourself to rights, and I'll drive you home when you're ready. OK?'

'OK.'

He touched her cheek again. His fingertips seemed surprisingly delicate, like a woman's. 'Come on, I'll show you where.'

Like everything else in this apartment, the bathroom was vast, as though it belonged to some institution, a boarding school or a clinic. There was a glass shelf with a bar of Lifebuoy soap and a tin of shaving cream and a shaving brush just like the ones her father used. Badger's hair. Did Nicos use things like that? Or perhaps Stavros. She closed the door, thankful to be alone, fearful of stepping back outside into an alien world where people watched her and noted things and judged. A strained and flushed face stared back at her from the mirror. She ran some water and splashed her eyes, then patted her skin dry and tried to fix her make-up. The misery had subsided. She didn't look too bad. Slightly aggressive now, making a face at herself in the glass. Tough and Yorkshire. Cautiously she opened the door and ventured out.

'You look wonderful, Mrs D,' Nicos exclaimed when she appeared at the kitchen door. The aunt was there beaming, and the two little girls, and the old grandmother, all of them waiting as though they had been set up as the chorus in some ghastly Greek comedy, to provide assurance and agreement. *Kaló*, they said. *Kaló*. Or something like that. 'I'm sorry,' she said, and the old crone said '*Po, po, po!*' and the girls laughed and the aunt said that it didn't matter, it was nothing, what can you expect when a mother says goodbye to her son on an aircraft, an *aircraft* of all things? *Aeroplano*. And then the door opened and Dee looked round, and Stavros of the large belly and small feet came in. He paused in surprise, seeing a British woman sitting there. 'My lady!' he exclaimed. 'You are welcome beneath my roof. I hope they have looked after you.'

'They've been wonderful,' she said, and at that moment she felt an affection for them, a genuine, familial affection which was, a small part of her whispered, quite unwarranted.

It was when she was going, when they were just about to get into the car, that the camera was produced. She stood awkwardly beside Nicos in front of the car, while his uncle manipulated shutter speed and aperture. 'Photography is Greek word,' he said proudly. '*Photo-grapho*. Light-write. That is what it mean.'

The shutter clicked.

Nine

Thomas emerges from the tube on to the concourse of the mainline station, and there she is, standing beneath the departures board. A tide of passengers ebbs and flows past her but she remains still, a pale and steady flame emitting the faint smoke of a cigarette.

'Hi,' he calls.

She turns. The flash of relief that lights her face is extinguished so rapidly that Thomas isn't sure whether it was even there in the first place. 'Oh, it's you.' She tosses her cigarette on the ground and treads on it. 'The train's in five minutes. I thought you were going to be late.'

'I thought you'd given up smoking.'

'Not when I'm nervous.'

It's an awkward moment. They don't quite know how to do this. He takes her hands and leans forward to kiss her on the cheek, which is the first contact they have had since that hastily snatched kiss on the pavement outside Covent Garden tube station after the matinée of *Cats*. Overhead, the station names and train times whirr and clatter like dominoes.

'How's Emma?'

'She's fine. She likes going with her gran.'

Gran. His mother used to assess the whole gamut of abbreviations: Grandmamma, Grandma, Granny – a dying fall of social acceptability. Gran was almost at the bottom. Holding hands for the first time and self-consciously, they set off for the platform.

The train traipses eastwards out of the city. Stepney and West Ham give way to Barking and Romford, drab terraces and tower blocks making room for housing estates and factories and, finally, grey fields of clay. Kale sits opposite him with her legs drawn up under her and her body half turned so that she can look out at the Essex flatland. 'When I was a kid we came to the seaside this way,' she says.

'Clacton?'

'Frinton. My Mum said it has more class than Clacton.' She smiles suddenly. An epiphany, when she smiles. 'I should take Emms. She'd love it.'

'We'll do that then. Next time, when the weather's decent. Frinton, with Emma.'

'That'd be nice.' And then the smile goes and she is looking out again and not saying much, just biting at the inside of her lip while passengers push past up the aisle. Two rows away a couple are bickering, the fracture lines of a relationship open to public view.

'What's up?' Thomas asks.

Kale turns. 'Just thinking.'

'What about?'

'Things.' Her words might be evasive but her eyes have a

remarkable candour. They catch his gaze and throw it back. Her pupils are wide, almost to the limits of her irises.

'You aren't having second thoughts, are you?'

'What d'you mean?'

'About coming.'

'It's strange, that's all. You know what I mean? Going with you.'

'Why strange?'

'Different.'

'From what? From Steve?'

'I don't want to talk about him.'

'And if I want to?'

She shrugs and looks out of the window. 'He's my business.'

'And me? Am I your business as well?'

'Not really business, is it?' She smiles fleetingly. 'Contingency.'

'Like being hit by a bus?'

The smile flickers again. At him or with him? Her upper lip has a curve to it, a strange vulnerability, as though it is bending under pressure. It is almost painful to sit like this, opposite her. He wants to touch her, that's the ridiculous thing, just touch her. He would be happy to kiss her as well of course, on the mouth, on the eyes, wherever her body is open to the world, wherever the devil can get in. If he kisses her on the mouth, he wonders, will he be able to feel the places she has nibbled, the small shreds of torn and clipped membrane on the inner surface of that lip? But just a touch of her hand would be enough.

The train, the bickering of the couple near by, time itself, go on.

From the railway station it is a short walk into town, down the main road that passes the public library, the cinema (closed), a video-rental shop, a pub and a DIY centre. There's a scrawl of paint on one wall. *NINJA*, it says. 'Just like Brixton,' Kale remarks. But along the riverfront it isn't a bit like Brixton, and even Kale admits as much. 'Pretty,' she judges it. She doesn't hit the Ts – pri'y, she says. 'Reelly pri'y.' And it is pretty enough, the houses made of old red brick and fronted with white weatherboard. Quaint, certainly. There are bay windows with bric-à-brac for sale, there is the lounge bar of the Ship, an ice-cream parlour called Swallows and Amazons, a small restaurant advertising fresh crab, a shop selling disposable cameras and souvenirs, a tourist information kiosk. Over the sea wall the tide is out, leaving a glistening stretch of mud where sailing boats lie despondently on their sides, like beached whales. Gulls dip and swoop over them, laughing and jeering as though they are responsible for this practical joke. In the stream beyond the flats, a gleaming cabin cruiser escapes towards the sea.

Kale laughs with delight. 'It's all right,' she decides, as though there was the looming possibility that it might not be. They buy a pint of winkles at Shipton's Shellfish and Kale remembers how you use a pin to uncurl the flesh out of the shell. She eats and laughs and squeezes his arm for a moment, then lifts herself up to kiss him on the cheek. There's the faint scent of fish. 'We should buy funny hats. And what about postcards?' And then: 'We should have brought Emms, shouldn't we?'

'Next time,' Thomas agrees. 'Next time.'

The plan is to have a look over the house after lunch. Arrangements are vague. Are they going to stay the night? Is that understood? 'For the weekend', that was what they discussed on the phone, so of course it means they'll stay the night. Saturday night and Sunday morning. So what are the contents of that bag that she has slung over her shoulder, the same one she brings to college? A change of underwear? A washbag? A clean T-shirt? Impossible to tell. The inscrutable arrangements of women.

They have lunch in the lounge bar of the Ship – the Binnacle Bar, distinguished by a large, phallic binnacle that occupies pride of place beside the electronic pinball and the Exterminator console. The landlord greets Thomas by name and asks how it's going, how his sister is, are they going to put the house on the market?, all that kind of thing. He eyes Kale curiously, trying to work out whether this is Thomas' wife. But surely this one is too young. A niece? A girlfriend? 'Just down for the day, are you, dear?' he asks, trying to find some way to interrogate her. She smiles a flat smile that may be yes, may be no, probably is 'Mind your own fucking business.'

They take their drinks over to a far corner. 'I don't want much,' she says, glancing at the menu. 'Perhaps the Dover sole.' She looks at him thoughtfully. 'It used to be easy when you were a kid, didn't it? You know, going out and that. But it gets more difficult as you get older.'

'I suppose it does. But it needn't be difficult. Just be happy.'

'Happy?' She considers the idea for a bit. Thomas feels daunted by her silences. 'Your mum?' she asks. 'Was she a happy person?'

'Not really.'

'I'm not surprised. Not many people are.'

'I am. Sometimes.' He hesitates, on the edge of confession. 'Now,' he admits. 'I'm happy now. With you. I'm completely and pathetically happy. There, I've said it.' It's a late-twentieth-century version of a confession of love. Love is spelled L-U-R-V-E and only happens in pop songs.

Kale smiles. 'That's nice then.'

After the meal they go out of the other door, on to the High Street. Thomas points across the road to the row of houses on the far side, red brick and weatherboard, the doors picked out in blue and yellow. 'There it is. The yellow door.'

Just as they are about to cross the street, someone calls out his name. He stops and turns. It's the blinking woman, Janet What's-her-name, advancing on them down the street. 'Thomas!' she's calling. 'Thomas!'

'They all seem to know you here,' Kale remarks.

'Hardly anyone knows me.'

Janet comes up to them with outstretched hands. For a moment it seems that an exchange of kisses is expected. 'I haven't seen you since the funeral. How have you been? Are you getting over it?' Her blinking eyes pass quickly over Kale, down to her narrow feet, up to her face.

'This isn't . . .?'

'Kale,' Kale says, holding out a narrow hand. 'Pleased to meet you.'

'A friend,' Thomas explains.

'I knew it wasn't your wife—'

'Well, it wouldn't be, would it? I mean, we're not married any longer, are we? So she wouldn't be my wife even if it was her, which it isn't.'

Janet smiles. 'No, of course not. Dee showed me photos.'

'What of? The divorce?'

She blinks, as well she might. 'The wedding. Gilda, wasn't it?'

'Was. Very much past tense.'

'And your son? Philip, isn't it?'

Is she doing it deliberately? Thomas agrees that Phil's name is, indeed, Philip, and he's fine, just fine. And, yes, they are planning to put the house on the market, once they've sorted things out. And Janet tells them both how much she misses Dee. She was such a good *friend*. They had such good *talks* together; they got on so *well*.

Is she, Thomas wonders, about to ask for something? It's then that he decides to make an offer. Perhaps one could call it hush money. 'Is there anything you would like, to remember her by?'

Janet blushes. 'Oh.' She blinks, and considers. Her eyes seem to brim with tears. 'Well, yes, maybe there is. There's a shepherd and shepherdess. Meissen, she always said—'

'Then you may have it.'

'That'd be kind of you.'

'It'll save Paula and me arguing over it.'

'How wonderful. Look, are you staying?' She glances at Kale once again, as though assessing the relationship, trying to work out whether they fuck yet, or whether this is an affair at its very infancy, or worse, whether this young woman, a mere girl with a coarse London accent, is nothing more than a pick-up. 'Why don't you drop by? For a cup of tea or something? This afternoon? Later, if you like. A drink?'

He shrugs, not finding it in him to refuse.

'About six? You know where I live, don't you?'

He admits that he does. They watch her walk away. 'How bloody awful,' Thomas says.

'Who is she?'

'Some woman my mother befriended. Local potter or something.'

Hand temporarily in hand – her fingers are cold to the touch – they cross the road to advance on number 37. He turns the key in the lock and pushes the front door open, on to the silence and shadows of the hallway. 'Here we are then.'

Inside, the air is still, almost as though the place is holding its breath and waiting. 'Sort of spooky,' Kale says. They step over a scattering of letters on the doormat. Bills, circulars, missives to the dead. Floorboards creak and flex under their feet. He opens the first door on to the gloom of the sitting room. Nothing has changed since he was last here. The armchairs are untouched, the Chesterfield sofa, the side tables, the odds and ends that cluttered up her life, all these things are unmoved. Only dust has settled. And memory. He draws the curtains to let daylight in. The room is made manifest by daylight.

'Nice place,' Kale says.

He can hear his mother's voice: 'nice' is small and precise. It's a good word for distinction and discrimination. It is not a synonym for pleasant or attractive or good. 'It's all right. But there's a lot of maintenance to do. The roof, the guttering, the bloody weatherboards.'

'Wish I could live in a place like this.'

'It'd be a long drag into college.'

She looks at him. This is a moment of strange freedom, each assessing the other, neither knowing what the other is thinking, each trying to work it out. It occurs to him that this is the first time they have ever been truly alone together, unless you count his office in college. Every other encounter has been in a public place.

Kale takes her denim jacket off – GLAMOUR, it announces in glittering imitation diamonds across the shoulder panel – and hesitates a moment before tossing it on to one of the armchairs. Her shoulders seem fragile; on her right arm, just visible below the sleeve of her T-shirt, there is a smoky blue tattoo of a butterfly. 'That's her, isn't it?' she says, taking the wedding photo from the mantelpiece. 'I recognize her from that slide you showed us. So this is your dad.'

It is, indeed, Thomas' father. Was. *Was* Thomas' father: Flight Lieutenant Edward Denham, DFC, AFC, as he was then, young, hopeful, uncertain of what he should do after the end of the war, finding nothing else but to continue flying. He has stepped down a rank in the post-war reduction in forces, but at least it's a job.

'What happened to him? You never talk about him. Always your mother.'

'He died in a plane crash, shortly after his retirement. A lifetime flying and he gets killed in a private aircraft.'

'How terrible.'

'The contingent event again, like being hit by a bus. As though someone suddenly tore up the script and cancelled the performance.'

She looks at the photograph thoughtfully. 'I could have fancied him.'

'What about his son?'

There is a smile somewhere behind the curve of her mouth; but she doesn't say anything, doesn't rise to the bait, just puts the picture back where it belongs and picks up something else, the shepherd and shepherdess that his mother always thought might be Meissen, original Meissen, whatever that means. She turns the piece over in her hands. The shepherdess' expression makes it clear what she is after: she may be laughing and pulling away from the shepherd, but it is plain enough that she's expecting him to follow. 'This what you offered to that woman?'

'That's it.'

'Pretty.' Carefully she replaces the figurine where she found it. 'You know, there's something weird about all this? As though it's still her house? And she's just gone out for a while?'

'It's not hers any longer, it's mine. Ours. Paula's and mine.'

'But that's not what it feels. She's all around, isn't she? Don't you feel that? You know, once when I was a kid I went into a neighbour's house when they'd all gone out. Me and my boyfriend. I mean, we were fifteen or something, not a big deal. We got in round the back and through the kitchen door. This feels a bit like that. Somehow you could sense that they were still there, even though we'd seen them leave.'

'What happened?'

'Nothing really. It was doing it rather than anything else. The excitement. We looked round a bit, and then we were, you know, fooling around—'

'Fooling around?'

She makes a face, lips pinched. 'You know what I mean. And

we heard their car stopping out the front so we had to get out the back door quick. It was a laugh. No harm done.'

Does this visit feel like that to her? he wonders – are they like children on a dare, evading the adults, fooling around? She is looking at the portrait of his mother hanging on the wall above the fireplace. 'What was she like, your mum? Nice old lady? Kind to kittens?'

'She didn't like animals, and she was never old. And she could be quite cutting when she wanted.'

'You're a bit obsessed, aren't you?'

'I don't think so. Just honest. When you lose your mother . . .' He is at a loss for words. Unusual for him who lives by words, lives by explanation and exposition, by lies. 'It does something,' he says finally. 'Something inside breaks.'

'Your heart?'

'Not that. Some much more fundamental part of the machinery.'

She crosses the room and peers out of the window on to the street, as though looking to see if the owners are coming back unexpectedly. When she turns and leans against the windowsill all he can see is her silhouette against the daylight, the shape of her. 'What would she have thought of me, then?'

Now there's a question. He has practised it over and over: What do you think of her, Mother? he asks. She says 'nice' and 'toilet' and 'Gran' and all those words that you despised. She's got an illegitimate child, which isn't a term we use any more but one that you wouldn't give up, would you? That fact alone would condemn her in your eyes. And yet . . . she's sharp, isn't she? And disturbingly honest. In yer face; up front; characteristics that you used to claim for your Yorkshire background. No flannel. What do you think?

'She'd have thought me a common little tart, wouldn't she?' Kale says.

He can't really see her expression against the light. Is there some quality of anxiety that he hasn't seen before? Does she look vulnerable for the first time? 'Don't be bloody silly. You mustn't think anything like that.'

'But would she have thought it?'

'She'd have found you . . . interesting. She'd have liked your style, your guts.'

'And how do you feel about me, Professor Denham?'

'Doctor. Professors are even older. I feel a bit as though I've been hit by a bus.'

'A contingent event?'

'Something like that.'

She laughs. That's something. Laughter is not bad, he thinks, although the innocent laughter of amusement and anticipation would be preferable to this laughter with its cynical edge. Nevertheless, this must be the right moment. Right moments have featured much in his life, the instant of weakness, the second of vulnerability. He goes over to her and puts his hands on her shoulders and at least she doesn't resist when he draws her gently towards him. In fact she even complies, turning her face slightly to look at him. He examines the small details of her features: the edge of her lips where the glossy membrane merges into downy skin; the eyes that are wide in the diffuse light, with the irises reduced to mere circles of blue around her obsidian pupils. How do you get pupils that large? Has she been taking something? Belladonna, that's what they used in Victorian times. Deadly nightshade. Atropine, after one of the Fates. Nowadays it's probably ecstasy or GHB. She has attempted to pluck her eyebrows into something resembling Hogarth's curve of beauty, but it's the failure to achieve any theoretical beauty that moves him, the imperfections and blemishes that stir him. She has a small, angry spot beside her nose, covered with a dab of cream. Her mouth is half open and there is the faint bitterness of cigarettes on her breath. He touches his lips on to hers and feels, for an instant, the wetness of her tongue and the sourness of her saliva, the unfamiliarity of taste and touch.

'What do you want to do?' he asks.

She shrugs. 'Don't mind.'

Is that compliance? What would the Committee on Staff–Student Relations say? 'Shall we go upstairs?'

'OK.' She follows him into the hall. At the foot of the stairs he stands aside to let her go first. She pauses for an instant, and then, accepting the challenge, goes ahead up the narrow stairs to the landing. The floorboards flex beneath her feet, as though making small mutterings of protest.

'Where's the toilet?' she asks at the top. He shows her. The door is thin and he can hear her moving about beyond it, sliding the lock across, lifting the lid of the lavatory. It is impossible not to imagine her dropping her jeans and squatting with her knickers round her ankles, impossible not to give an image to the sound of the rivulet running out of her and splashing into the bowl. Looking for distraction, he opens the door opposite. The curtains are drawn, the whole room perfused by a watery light. There is just the bare mattress on the bed now, but all the other things are still there – the photos, the ornaments, the pictures, a small collection of shells that she must have picked up on one of her walks along the foreshore, a photograph of his father, a watercolour of a village nestled in the moors above Sheffield. Hope village, that was the name. He remembers her telling him. She went there with a boyfriend, long ago, in the days before she knew his father, impossibly distant. They'd climbed one of the hills behind the village, Win Hill, and the next day he'd gone away to sea and never come back. Charteris, that was what she called him. Charteris.

On a whim, he opens one of the wardrobes. The door releases a faint exhalation of perfume. Dresses hang there in the shadows. He leafs through them as one might turn the pages of a book: the ones she wore recently, but also the relics, the left-overs from the past, kept through some kind of nostalgia. She never wanted to let go, of her past any more than her life. Behind him he can hear the lavatory flush and the bathroom door open and close. Floorboards creak. He doesn't turn, but he senses Kale there behind him. 'These are hers,' he tells her. 'My sister must come and do something about them or I'll throw the whole lot out, give them to Oxfam, whatever it is that you do.'

'That'd be a shame.' She reaches past him and takes one of the dresses off the rail, one of the old ones, a summer frock that he actually remembers his mother wearing. It has narrow blue and white stripes. He can't link it to any specific moment in the past, but simply with her presence – her smell, her touch.

Kale holds the dress against herself to show him. 'How's that? It's real fifties stuff, isn't it? What do you think?'

'It looks all right.'

'Did she look good in it?'

There is a sudden quickening of the memory. 'Wait there.'

'Where're you going?'

'You can see for yourself,' he calls. He finds it immediately among the slides that he discovered. There's an old slide viewer that he found as well. Equipped with new batteries, it still works. He slips the slide into the slot and holds the viewer out to her.

It is indeed the same dress. There is the past, glowing inside its plastic box as though somehow it is preserved there in minia-ture; and there is the real thing in Kale's hands. Paradoxically, the photo seems imbued with life and significance, while the relic – the dress itself – is limp and dead and devoid of context, like a costume left in the dressing room of a theatre after the production has closed. Just a length of cotton.

'How fifties is that?' Kale exclaims. 'And look at those flowers. Where is it?'

'Cyprus. That must be, I don't know, nineteen-fifty-seven.'

'And the little girl?'

'My sister, Paula.'

Kale holds the dress up and looks from it to the photo and back again. 'It's sort of creepy, really, to have it in your hands.' She is about to return the dress to the wardrobe when Thomas stops her.

'Put it on,' he says.

'What?'

'Try it on.' He laughs, to encourage her. 'You'd look good in it.'

She cocks her head on one side. 'Like your mother?'

'We'll see.'

'You serious?'

'Why not?'

She's biting the inside of her cheek, as she does when she is puzzled. 'You'll have to turn round. I'm not having you watching.'

This manifestation of prudery amuses him, but he turns away just the same, and listens to the movements behind him, the sweep of denim against skin as she drops her jeans round her feet. He's alert to every whisper. He can hear her easing the dress up over her hips, straightening it where it clings round the waist, shrugging her way into the bodice. He knows the moment when she reaches awkwardly round the back for the zip. There is the insect sound of the zipper being pulled up. Like a cicada.

'OK, you can look now.'

He turns.

Kale has been snatched back into the past. Her own clothes lie like a shadow on the floor, and from forty years ago her heart-shaped face looks back at him. 'How's that?' She turns her hips, letting the skirt swing. With one hand she pushes her hair up at the back.

'Wonderful.'

She pirouettes. The skirt billows out and the whole room seems to turn with her, the walls shifting, the floor tilting and swirling as though it were a cabin in a ship. 'Is that like her, then? Mrs Denham, at your service?'

Thomas watches with a mixture of wonder and delight. 'Your shoes.' He goes down on his knees.

'What's wrong with them?'

'Anachronistic.'

She sits down on the edge of the bed while Thomas unlaces her shoes with fumbling fingers. There is the scent of hot leather as he pulls them off. Her toes are narrow, the second longer than the big toe and slightly webbed with its smaller neighbour, so that the two form a V. There is something infinitely endearing about this anatomical quirk. He lifts one foot and bends to kiss the forked toes while Kale laughs uncertainly, as though this is some kind of game the rules of which she has not quite understood. 'You got a foot fetish or something?'

'They're lovely,' he assures her, resting her foot back down on the floor.

'They're deformed.'

'Beautiful.'

'I used to be shy about it when I was a kid. Used to get teased.'

'On the beach at Frinton?'

'At the local pool.'

He is still kneeling before her, like a swain before his love. 'There's a mend here.' He takes up a piece of the skirt to show her. 'It must have been torn.' Gently he lifts the fabric to bare her knees. She makes a vague attempt to push the skirt back down but he holds her hand to stop her. Her legs are pale and narrow. A ghost's legs. He leans forward to kiss the hourglass of her right kneecap where the skin is rough and the hairs have been rubbed into a stubble by wearing trousers.

'Hey!' she cries uncertainly, as though kissing knees were some kind of mild aberration; which perhaps it is. He pushes the skirt further, up over her thighs.

'Hey, what are you up to?' But she doesn't resist, just lies back, propping herself on her elbows and looking down at him with those wide, black pupils. How far, he wonders, will he be allowed? The skirt slides up over the top of her thighs, until it unmasks a sudden, sharp triangle of white nylon. Tendrils of hair are visible through the thin mist of the material. The skin of her belly is white and smooth, brushed with down.

She bites at her lower lip – a row of pearls are just visible against the soft red pulp. 'What are you up to, Thomas?'

'Do you mind?'

'You make me shy.'

He reaches out to take the waistband of her briefs. Still she doesn't stop him, and when he pulls she even lifts her hips slightly to let the scrap of material pass; but at the vital moment she twists, bringing her left leg over her right and shutting herself off from his gaze. He manoeuvres the briefs over her knees and down to her ankles. The gusset bears a brush-stroke of yellow, like the reflection of a buttercup beneath a child's chin. 'You're lovely,' he whispers.

'No different from anyone else.'

'You're you.'

It's a tautologous proposition, and thus incontrovertible. But still she argues the point. 'Am I me? Or' – she twists her mouth, nibbles her lip – 'am I your mum?'

He takes hold of her left knee and tries to straighten her.

'Don't be stupid,' he says, and she laughs, half struggling against his grip – 'Hey!' – and then the struggle ceases and her muscles slacken, and quite gently he can open her, like a book.

Thomas looks. Kale shifts nervously, telling him again that he is making her shy; but still he looks – at the contours of her stomach and hips, at the hillock with its scrub of hair and its secretive, half-hidden curl of inner lip. He imagines that mouth parting to admit her various lovers, or gaping in a scream in order to expel the wet head and slippery shoulders of her child.

'Thomas,' she says, but what she intends isn't clear. He moves closer and her secret smell rises to meet him, a warm amalgam of perfumes – sharp citrus, a hint of ammonia, a suggestion of musk, the scents of life and decay, of the cradle and the grave. Damp strands of hair brush against his nose. 'Thomas,' she repeats. Her hand is on his head, as though in benediction. Her lips open to the pressure of his tongue. Somewhere far away a child screams. From a great distance a woman calls his name: 'Tom,' she cries. 'Tom.'

Janet Burford's house seems to have been furnished from a car boot sale. There are worn carpets on the floor and old and damaged furniture in the rooms – a broken-backed sofa, chairs whose raffia seats need repairing, a dining table with marks and cigarette burns on its top. Many of the horizontal surfaces are taken up with her pottery. The colours are ochre and blue, aquamarine and sand. Abstract paintings on the walls betray the same hand. Somehow the place manages to combine an air of impermanence with the sense that it has been like this for decades.

A dog barks. 'That's Barbara,' Janet explains. 'I've shut her in her kennel so she won't bother you, but she's quite all right.' She is wearing baggy trousers that would look fine on a rapper, and a woollen sweater that would look good on a fisherman, and shoes that must have come from an army-surplus store. She blinks and smiles and shows her visitors through into the kitchen, where the smells of cats and mould merge seamlessly one into the other. It's difficult to imagine Thomas' mother here, exchanging confidences over the bin bags.

'I'm so glad you came. What can I get you? Wine, would you like wine? I've got a bottle in the fridge.'

The bottle is already open. It's clear that little else is on offer. 'Wine will do fine.'

She hands Thomas a glass just as he holds out the hastily wrapped package that he has brought for her. There's a moment of awkward laughter as they almost spill the wine, almost drop the package, and finally make the exchange safely.

'Just like Christmas,' she says, unwrapping the figurine. With a small cry of delight, she holds it out to see. Among her modernist stuff the Meissen piece looks absurdly delicate and fragile – a small, intricate thing of light and laughter. She turns it round and over in competent potter's hands. 'Oh, it's wonderful.' And there are tears in her eyes, so much so that Kale puts out a hand and touches her on the forearm, and evokes a self-deprecating smile. 'It means so much,' Janet explains. 'So much.' She puts the piece down and gives Thomas a quick, clumsy kiss on the cheek, and then she turns to Kale and does the same. She is blinking away tears and apologizing, and using the back of her wrist to wipe her eyes – the gesture of someone who is used to working with grimy hands. 'Look.' She turns the piece over to show them the base. 'Look.' There, blurred in the glaze, are the crossed swords of Meissen. 'See the dot? That's about seventeen-sixty. If it's genuine.' Her eyes are glistening. 'Always supposing it's genuine. There were many fakes, many of them very fine. Like this one, if it is a fake.'

'Or even if it isn't,' Thomas points out, which makes her laugh. There is a lightness in her face when she laughs, almost a glimpse of beauty. But sun and wind have done their worst and her complexion is lean and leathery, like a sailor's.

'I know! Let me show you my studio,' she says, as though the idea has just occurred to her and is brilliant and original. 'Would you like to see it? Would you?'

Of course they would.

'It's out at the back. Bring your wine if you like. No rules in this house.'

They follow her out. The dog barks loudly from her kennel near the back door. The garden is a scrappy piece of lawn, with herbaceous borders down the sides and, along the far wall, a concrete shed. Janet opens the door and they look in on a workshop that combines the qualities of an art studio with those of a factory. There is an industrial kiln at one end, two potter's wheels, trestle tables and shelves full of pottery in grey clay and biscuit. Some are vases and bowls, others mere organic shapes – penises and wombs, it seems to Thomas, but then he is in a particular state of mind. The earthen smell of clay dominates the place. Kale walks round asking intelligent questions about firing temperatures and slips and glazes that suggest that she has done pottery at some time. This revelation brings home how little he knows about her, how much he has to learn.

'Let me give you something in return,' Janet suggests. Her eyes are bright, as though this is also a new and exciting idea. 'Do I give you something each, or one for both?'

It's a clever question, evoking a revealing hesitation, a glance between the two of them that Janet watches with bright attention. She is probing: despite the rushed voice, the anxious blinking, the nervousness, she is probing the subtle matter of their relationship, and finding pressure points of discomfort.

'I reckon one each would be far too generous,' Kale says, which is as neutral a reply as anyone could give. It is she who chooses their present – a sinuous vase in sand and blue – and then Janet kisses both of them again and squeezes Thomas' arm and wishes them well. Not 'happiness' – just 'well'. The words are chosen with care. There are tears in her eyes once again as she stands at the door to her house and watches them walk away.

'She's on the edge,' Kale remarks when they are out of earshot.

'On the edge of what?'

'You know what I mean. She's damaged.'

'Oh, come on. Just blinks a bit.'

'And cries.'

'She was fond of my mother, apparently.'

'Sure she was. Notice her wrists?'

'Not especially.'

'Scarred. She's tried to top herself sometime in the past. And if they've tried once, they usually succeed.'

'What are you? Some kind of psychologist?'

'I just know, that's all.'

Except for the lights in the window of the pub and the accompanying noise that spills out on to the pavement, the town is shuttered and empty. Back in the house Kale puts the vase on a table in the sitting room. 'It's yours really,' she remarks. 'Nothing to do with me.'

'It's ours,' Thomas says. 'She gave it to the two of us.'

'*We* don't have anywhere to put it.'

Thomas prepares supper. There are eggs in the fridge and a bottle of wine, carefully placed there on his last visit. As he fixes omelettes he can't get Janet out of his mind, her nervous chatter, her bloody blinking – the sensation she gives that she is wobbling on the edge of a precipice that cannot be seen. He remembers her grip on his arm and the smell of her as she came to give him a kiss – something dry and dusty, like clay.

'Where are we sleeping?' Kale asks when they have cleared up.

'In the spare room. I'll have to make the bed up.'

'We're sharing, are we?'

'Not if you don't want to.'

She shrugs. 'Not your mother's room?'

'No.'

'I thought that was your bag.' She's good at that little smile. It's a disturbingly alluring expression, carrying with it both detachment and desire.

'You're my bag,' he tells her.

Her smile stays there, but metamorphoses into something else, something softer and less cynical. Perhaps, he thinks, he is starting to tiptoe through the defences that she has erected around the soft, vulnerable core of her; perhaps she is letting him in.

Floorboards creak as they climb the stairs again, like the footsteps of his mother watching their every move. But the spare bedroom has no relics, no other presence – just a room with a double bed and a chest of drawers. Gilda and he used it, but their exertions there have left no impression. It is filled with Kale's presence now, a spare figure undressing without shyness, letting him watch her, coming to him with a sudden startling tenderness. She folds herself against him. 'You're all right,' she whispers. There is the smell of mint on her breath, and the already familiar taste of her skin. Her breasts are soft and loose, older than the rest of her, sucked.

'So are you.'

Her voice breathes in his ear. 'Are you nervous?'

'Very,' he replies.

'You weren't before.'

'Now's different.'

'How different?'

'Then I thought I might be able to survive you. Now I'm afraid that I won't.'

Ten

The Denhams gave a party. The problem had not been whom to invite, but whom to exclude. Guests crowded into the house on 16th of June Street and filled much of the garden. Their cars lined the road outside. The Powells came all the way from Nicosia, Jennifer exclaiming how charming it all was down here in the Deep South; Binty and Douglas were there, along with Betty and Johnny Frindle and others from Akrotiri and Episkopi. Even Nissing came, with his slightly surprised expression and his awkward heartiness; and Marjorie, who seemed to find Nissing so attractive that she spent much of the evening with him.

It was Edward who had suggested they invite Damien: 'That polo-playing fellow, what about him?' he asked when they were making up the guest list. 'A good chap, I thought. Interested in sailing. Is his wife over here?'

'I don't know.' She made a counterfeit hesitation. 'I don't

think so. Anyway, I'll put him down and maybe ring and ask. I think I've got a phone number somewhere.'

And now she was standing in the garden awaiting Damien's arrival with apprehension. She told herself this was foolish, because she knew that she had nothing to fear and nothing to expect. He was an acquaintance; someone who had occupied a particular moment in her recent life and now was abstracted from it. But she understood something else: that while there may be a natural and often predictable progression from acquaintance to friendship, you may pass from acquaintance to intimacy in a single, perilous step.

He arrived late, when the party was in full swing. It was Jennifer who spotted him first. 'It's that lovely Major Bordello!' she cried and, taking charge, paraded him round the garden to meet people. Damien seemed startled at such celebrity. He smiled awkwardly and shook hands and exchanged names and views on the political situation and the weather and how to fight EOKA, and when he finally managed to reach Dee he had the manner of a drowning man who has reached the shore just in time. He kissed her on each cheek. 'It's lovely to see you again.'

Was it? Was 'lovely' the right word? Disturbing, perhaps; discomfiting, disquieting, a whole thesaurus of unease. They were away from the noise of the party, over by one of the palm trees. Did it look as though they were trying to escape notice?

'Jennifer Powell's rather a handful, isn't she?'

'Jennifer? She means well.'

He smiled. 'As far as I recall she means "elfin porn jewel". Isn't that right? She was delighted with the elfin bit, however inaccurate. She didn't mind porn jewel either.'

Dee laughed, the kind of laugh that threatens to run out of control, the type that is evoked as much by excitement and suppressed fear as by anything particularly funny. 'How on earth did you remember that?'

'I never forget a good anagram.' He paused, smiled at her, *into* her, into her eyes, remembering what he had said to her on the promenade deck of the *Empire Bude* in the hot, Mediterranean evening, and knowing that she remembered. 'And you – are you still the hidden dreamer?'

She slipped out of that as though evading his grasp. 'What about "Bill Powell"? Do you remember him?'

He glanced across at the ponderous figure of Jennifer's husband and thought for a moment. 'Low ill pleb,' he said triumphantly. 'Bill Powell: low, ill pleb. Except that he wasn't ill, really. That was you.'

'Seasick,' she corrected him. 'Not ill.'

'Whatever you call it, it took three days away from us.'

There was a sudden silence between them, filled by the word 'us'. She put her hand on his arm. 'Damien,' she said. Just that, just his name. No warning, no admonishment, no particular emphasis. Just his name.

'Can we meet?' he asked. 'Please.'

'We *are* meeting. Here. Now.'

'I don't mean that. I want to see you alone. I want to talk.'

'You *are* talking to me.'

'I haven't stopped thinking of you, d'you realize that? Ever since the bloody boat.'

Like a bomb going off, laughter erupted from the table where the drinks were. Were they being laughed at? She looked up anxiously, but it was just Geoffrey making a joke.

'I know.'

'And you?'

'And me,' she said quietly, and regretted the words as soon as they were spoken, because they could never be unsaid. Denied, yes, but never expunged from memory. She moved her hand to his elbow, to steer him back towards the crowd. 'Come on, we can't stay alone like this—'

'Yes we can. People talk to each other at parties.' There was a hint of anger in his tone, an edge of desperation.

'Come and meet Edward again. He took to you, you know that? He said you wanted to get some sailing.'

She led him over and got the two of them in conversation, then moved away among her guests. She felt strangely detached from the talk and the movement and the laughter. She could only watch from outside, see the gathering for the ugly thing it was, a strange, amoeboid organism, swelling, dividing, contracting, sliding from focus to focus – from drink to food to music – giving voice to its desires and its discomforts. On the terrace some couples began to dance to music from a gramophone. She wandered past them, smiling at people, exchanging a word with one group, laughing at a joke here, listening to part of an argument there, distracted all the while by the presence of the man who was talking with her husband and who glanced over the heads every now and again to catch her eye.

What might happen? She toyed with ideas and possibilities, some of them credible and dull, others improbable and frightening. There was a part of her – a romantic, emotional part – that believed that there was a unitary thing called love, and that you might fall victim to it, and it would overcome willpower. One of her secrets was that she had never experienced this force with Edward; another was that, as an eighteen-year-old girl, she *had* experienced it with Charteris. And now she feared that this emotion lay in wait just ahead, and might ambush her at any moment, bringing with it fear and destruction. The party went on and people came and went, and there grew inside her this deep, invisible core of fear. The presence of all these guests around her, their noise and their laughter, their watching eyes, suddenly terrified her. Never before had she lived her life so publicly; never had she had so many acquaintances, and so few friends.

Marjorie's canteen was housed in two old storerooms down by the harbour. There was about it the smell of the things that had once lain there – rope and sailcloth and stuff like that. Marjorie dominated the place from the far end, where there was a counter and a large brass and steel tea urn. There was usually a couple of squaddies from the castle garrison, sitting at the Formica-topped tables, drinking tea and playing cards. They were National Servicemen, here by compulsion rather than choice. 'This is what they want, poor dears,' Marjorie would say: 'Home from home.' The canteen was saving up to get a dartboard. They already had chess and draughts and shove-ha'penny, and a small library with ragged paperbacks and copies of *Titbits* and *Lilliput*.

Dee helped out twice a week, making flapjacks and scones – recipes she had from her mother – and serving the soldiers, just like a waitress at the ABC. She would call the taxi to drive her down early in the morning and pick her up at midday to take her back. She could have taken the bus, of course, but that would have been difficult and embarrassing, crowded in among all those Greek women going in to market, the object of stares and comments in a language that she didn't understand. It was an obvious solution to call for Nicos and his flashy, battered Opel Kapitan. Sometimes he'd come into the canteen for a cup of tea, and have a chat with any soldiers who had fetched up there. They found him strange, with his knowledge of Greek and his undeniable London accent. Nick, they called him, or Nick the Greek. If the place wasn't too busy, Dee would sit with him and get him to teach her useful phrases, greetings and questions, words she could use in the shops or with the maid.

'Worked at Belling's for a while, din' I?' he told her when she asked about his life in London. 'Assembling water heaters and cookers and the like. But it's a dead-end thing, working on a bloody production line all the time, 'scuse my language. And anyway, they were laying people off . . .'

'You lost the job?'

'More or less. There was a foreman, had it in for me. I reckon he did it.'

'And your uncle offered you a job here in Cyprus?'

'Needed another driver, see.'

'And how does it compare?'

He shrugged. 'I wanted to go to America. That's where the future is, in't it?'

'Is it?'

'Course it is.' He snapped his fingers. 'You can get a job easy as that in America. And earn good money, too. I got a cousin in the States – mill worker, something like that. He's got a Cadillac, swimming pool, the lot.'

'And he's only a mill worker?'

'No. That's the *name* of the place. Mill Worker.'

'Maybe that's Milwaukee.'

'Yeah, that's right. Milwaukee. Weird name, in't it? Indian, they reckon.'

She laughed, and he laughed with her. Something about him reminded her of Charteris, something in his look, in the cast of his face, the way he looked up and smiled at her, the manner in which he laughed.

'I reckon they want to find me a wife,' he said. 'You know what Greek families are like. Trouble is . . .'

'What's the trouble?'

'All the girls here have got moustaches.'

She laughed at the joke, loudly enough for Marjorie to look up from behind the counter. 'And then there was this business here in Cyprus.' He lowered his voice. 'You know what I mean . . .'

'No, what do you mean?'

'The political thing.'

'Union with Greece? Enosis?'

He shrugged, flipped his hair back. 'We're Greek, aren't we? Why not?'

The door opened. Nicos glanced round as half a dozen soldiers came into the canteen, laughing and joking about something. Dee recognized the shoulder flashes of Damien's regiment. One of them had the chevrons of a corporal on his arm. 'I'd better leave you to your work,' Nicos said, pushing his chair back. 'Oh, there's this.' He tossed something on to the table, a small card. She turned it over. It was a snapshot of him and her, standing in front of the Opel Kapitan. 'Souvenir,' he said as she slipped it into the pocket of her apron. 'See you later.'

There was a moment of pushing and shoving near the doorway as he tried to get through. 'Hey Nick, where you going?' one of the soldiers said. 'Off to report to your EOKA friends?' Dee saw him look round, his expression somewhere between fear and anger. 'Hey!' she cried out. 'Stop that.' She leaped up and went over to them, pushing her way between the men and Nicos, her figure a sudden, fragile barrier. From behind the counter Marjorie's voice was surprisingly sharp, almost military. 'Corporal! I will report you as responsible for any misbehaviour.'

The corporal said something – 'Let it go,' or something like that – and the scuffling died away. With a backward glance at Dee, Nicos went out into the sunlight, while the men sat down.

'I'll have no nonsense in here, you mark my words,' Marjorie told them. 'If you can't be hospitable to others, then we won't be hospitable to you.' She had the tone of a headmistress talking to her prefects. The soldiers shifted on their chairs and grinned sheepishly. Dee and Marjorie set to work, taking orders, making sandwiches and pots of tea. A couple of the squaddies ordered sausage and mash.

'They're just kids, bless them,' said Marjorie as she and Dee worked. 'They wouldn't really hurt a fly.'

'I thought that was their job, to hurt flies and things.'

'Don't be silly. They're just kids away from home wanting a bit of fun. You're rather fond of him, aren't you?'

'Who? Nicos?'

'Who do you think? You were up there like a terrier to defend him.'

Dee smiled. 'He reminds me of someone I once knew. Years ago, during the war. I don't know what it is, exactly.'

Marjorie smiled slyly. 'An old flame?'

'My only flame before Edward. It didn't burn for very long: extinguished by the Arctic Ocean, actually. He was in the Merchant Navy. He . . .' She stopped. She didn't want to say any more. In fact she was uncertain why she had even told Marjorie as much as she had. 'Nothing, really. Just a childhood romance. I was only seventeen.'

Marjorie was dishing out sausages on to plates, slapping mashed potatoes beside them. 'Well poor old Nick's certainly soft on you.'

'Marjorie, you're being daft. I'm old enough to be his mother.'

'I don't think so. Older sister maybe. But that's not how he sees it. I can recognize the signs well enough, my dear. Look at all these lads. Young boys, away from home just like your Nick—'

'He is *not* "my" Nick.'

The older woman laughed. 'The trouble is, he thinks he is.

When you bring him in here, he never takes his eyes off you. You be careful, that's all I'm saying.'

'You sound like my Aunt Vera.'

'She's probably a very wise woman.'

When she was out of sight of Marjorie she took the photo out of her apron pocket and looked at it. My Nick, she thought with a smile. That faint smile, part amused, part questioning. Charteris.

Winter came, with cold winds from the Anatolian Mountains and a scattering of snow on the heights of Troödos. Throughout the summer the mountains had been hidden from the city by a haze of heat but now they were plainly there, shouldering up into the cold air, their flanks draped with forest, the tops painted with white. Now, when the Denhams drove up the winding road to Platres with Binty and Douglas and Geoffrey, they took coats and woollen hats and gloves. The children threw snowballs at each other and cried for the pain of cold fingers while the wind battered their ears and soughed through the girders of the radio masts that crowned the summit. There was a cold that Dee hadn't felt since arriving on the island eight months earlier: cold as a substance, a fluid permeating the bones. It reminded her of the Peaks in the first snows, Kinder Scout and Bleaklow. When she told Geoffrey he laughed. He'd never been north of Peterborough, so he claimed.

'Kinder Scout was where they had the mass trespass in the nineteen-thirties,' she told him. 'You must know about that.' Surely he knew, surely he had heard about it. He was just being obtuse. She felt almost cross about it. He was a typical bloody southerner! 'Workers demanded access to the moors and the landlords denied them. The gamekeepers fought to keep them out.'

'Workers against landlords? Sounds like a piece of socialist mythology.'

'My father was part of the Sheffield contingent. They took the train up to Hope—'

'Hope?'

'It's a village. Pretty name, isn't it? The hills above it are called Win and Lose. Northern humour, I suppose. The Sheffield party walked over the hills to meet the group from Manchester but they were late and they had to watch the battle with the game-keepers from the top of Jacob's Ladder. Father always says that he was disappointed not to be in the fight; Mother says he was well out of it.'

'Sounds quite a character, your old man.'

'He's a typical Yorkshireman. Loves cricket and rugby league and a political argument.'

'Is he Communist?' The aerials overhead moaned in the wind, as though they were straining with the effort of listening. They *were* listening, of course. They were peering over the far horizon, over the Taurus Mountains and the Anatolian Plains, gazing across the Black Sea into the heart of the Soviet empire.

'Am I being vetted, Geoffrey?'

He laughed. 'D'you know, the only Greek Cypriots I feel really sorry for are the Communists? They're the only ones who want to throw out all this factional nonsense and join forces with the Turks, and EOKA has killed more of them than it has us. Did you know that?'

'You haven't answered my question.'

'I'm just trying to find out where you stand.'

'What's it to do with my father, then? He's just an old-fashioned socialist.'

'And you?'

'Well, I've always voted Labour, if that's what you mean. My whole family has.' She paused. 'I *am* being vetted.'

'Get a move on!' Edward called. 'What the hell's keeping you?' He had gone on ahead and was fiddling with his camera, adjusting the aperture, pointing it at them as they came across the summit.

'Dee's giving me her family history,' Geoffrey called back.

'Her father can argue the hind legs off a pit pony. Has she told you that?'

'More or less.'

'And he thinks Anthony Eden is the embodiment of evil.'

The picture was taken and they followed Edward down to where the cars were parked. In the relative warmth of Platres they found a café that served tea and cakes. It was just like coming off the moors and discovering a place where you could get a large stoneware pot of tea, and home-made scones and jam. The children fought and bickered, while Geoffrey expounded his views on the island. And she thought of Charteris, of how one Sunday he'd borrowed a car and they'd driven up to Hope village. 'Which do we climb?' he had asked as they stood on the road and looked up at the twin hills to the north of the village. 'Win or Lose?'

Of course they chose Win, and when they had slogged up to the top they stood there clinging to each other in the wind, looking down on to the Ladybower reservoir, laughing and crying at the same time. It had been a day like this, more or less – cold and clear, with a view for miles and miles, and the wind battering them. The last weekend, before he went away.

The last time she ever saw him, in fact.

In the café in Platres she laughed along with the others; but no one understood that she was not laughing at Geoffrey's outrageous jokes. She was laughing at the name of the hill. Win, indeed. They had surely climbed Lose.

Persephone

The goddess of the world has crossed Lethe.
Her scent, of myrtle and jessamine,
Is long gone; and with her passage
All memory of spring's effulgent blooming
Vanishes:
Hyacinth is drowned,
Myosotis is forgotten,
Anemone, the wind flower,
Is blown away by gales.
Dog rose and dog violet
Are thrown to the dogs.

Now candles gutter in the wind
And Olympos stands against the sky
Draped in a winding sheet –
Like an old man at his own funeral.

If Zeus is still king, he doesn't show it;
Hades rules now.

Geoffrey wrote it for her, typed it on a sheet of paper and dedicated it across the top in his own hand: *For Dee, with affection.* Edward laughed. 'Going about with one of his poems tucked down your front? He'll make a fool of you if you're not careful.'

'What do you mean?'

'Poor old Geoff's a bit starved of female company these days. He's got his eye on you, my dear.'

She felt a surge of anger. 'Can't you understand friendship?' she said.

'I can,' he said, 'but can he?'

In those winter days Dee felt herself drifting away from Edward, the slow, tidal drift of flotsam in the stream. Partly it was his work that was to blame, of course; but it was more than that. Difficult to put your finger on. Perhaps secrets had something to do with it. Perhaps he had secrets; certainly she did, a whole population of thoughts and ideas whispering to her, hinting, accusing, such a world of things inside her head. Hidden dreams, and none of them known to anyone else; sometimes, not even to herself.

Tom can hear his parents arguing. Argument has become part of their life together; probably – he's unsure of this – part of everyone's shared life. But if this is what sharing your life is like, he doesn't want to join in. 'Stop arguing!' he shouts at them, and sometimes that works and the row fades away to a sullen resentment; but often, all too often nowadays, his imprecation gets thrown back at him. By her. 'Just mind your own business,' she tells him. 'This is nothing to do with you. This is grown-ups.'

It is, he thinks, she who initiates the arguments. His father is passive in the face of his mother's anger, ergo *he is not guilty. His mother started the row. She is to blame. Tom lives in a blame world and it seems only logical to apportion blame. That is how school works. 'Who did it?' is the great, accusatory question. He has, on occasion, owned up to things he did not do, so overwhelming is the sense of guilt. Once or twice he has even been beaten for what he has not done, the cane cutting across his backside through the thin stuff of his pyjamas with a shock that is electric in its intensity. In the dormitory afterwards they compare strokes of blue and mauve scored across pale, fragile buttocks.*

Fragments of memory, pieces that once made a whole incident complete with cause, effect, conclusion, but are now just dissociated splinters, like shards of brightly coloured glass: she shouts at him about something – answering back? Not tidying his room? Teasing Paula? What else could it be? – and emerges from the bathroom to berate him. She has been getting ready to go out and his offence is grave enough to interrupt this preparation.

'Do what you're told! Don't argue with me, just do as you're damn well told!'

She's standing there in the corridor, wrapped in a towel, her legs and feet white, the tattoo blue of veins visible through fine skin. She has the towel draped across her front, propped against her breasts, hiding her belly, dropping down to her knees. 'Don't argue! Just do it!'

She turns to her toilet, and there is a moment – a mere microsecond trapped for ever like a fly in the amber of his memory – when the tail of the towel sways outwards and he has a glimpse of the front of her thighs and her loose belly.

Has she noticed? She returns to her room, rearranging her grip on the towel to hold it together across her backside. She grabs and misses and the towel is open, and he can see her buttocks, uncrossed by cane strokes, soft and white and vulnerable, moving with her stride, and the tapering pillars of her thighs, and the tendons at the back of her knees where the skin is folded awkwardly and the veins run smoky blue. And the cleft between the buttocks which curves round to the other side and makes a fold like Paula's. But he knows now that, unlike Paula's, there is hair. Rumour has become fact. He has seen it. That's where he came from.

Beating retreat on the parade ground at the garrison at Dhekelia, in the east of the island. The Powells had invited them. Apparently it was a celebration of the Battle of Isandlwana in the Zulu War, when Bill's regiment had been cut down to a man. There were buglers and the regimental colours paraded, and soldiers stamping their feet and marching and wheeling like machines. The band played 'Rule Britannia' and 'Land of Hope and Glory', and the Union Jack flew over the scene and made you feel quite emotional. General Kendrew took the salute as the battalion doubled past the podium to the sound of 'The Keel Row'. 'Anyone can celebrate a victory,' Bill explained proudly. 'It takes real art to celebrate a defeat.'

Afterwards there was a reception in the mess. Stewards cruised among the guests with trays of glasses. Regimental silver gleamed behind the buffet – a gilt tiger stalking an ebony sepoy through the jungle, a silver palm tree shading dying silver infantrymen, sconces and plates inscribed with names of for-gotten battles like Savandroog and Khulamba. Dee wondered whether Damien would be there, and what would happen if he was, and how she would feel and how he would react. She hadn't seen him since the party they had given at the end of summer, hadn't even heard from him, except to receive a note of thanks. Perhaps he had been posted away. Perhaps he was not even on the island any longer. Would he, she wondered, have contacted her to tell her that?

And then, amidst the crush of people at the buffet, she found herself standing beside him, mere inches away. He was in mess kit – tight red jacket and narrow blue trousers, like a toy solider in a playroom.

'We're bloody piggy in the middle,' he was complaining to someone out of sight beyond him. 'It's not proper soldiering at all. One side throws rocks at the other and the other throws them back, we get it all in the neck.'

'Are you talking about the buffet?' Dee asked.

He turned. For a palpable moment he seemed shocked to discover her there beside him. Then he laughed, almost with relief. 'Politics, I'm afraid. How wonderful to see you. How are you? How are the children? And Edward? Is he around?'

'We're over there with the Powells.'

'I thought I heard Jennifer's voice. Can't really mistake it.'

There was a woman at his shoulder, watching this little exchange. Her hair was cut short and her face was without make-up, as though she was determined not to look pretty. But she *was* pretty. She was sleek and blonde and there was something expensive about her, in the way that simple, well-made things seem expensive. 'Aren't you going to introduce us?' she asked.

'Of course I am.' He hesitated as though confused, as though he couldn't quite recall her name. 'This is Deirdre. Deirdre Denham. She's called Dee, actually. She came out with me on the troopship.'

The woman composed a smile. Her handshake was cool and sharp. 'Oh, yes. Damien mentioned you. Deck tennis, wasn't it? I'm Sarah.'

'Sarah?'

'Sarah Braudel. Damien's wife.'

The encounter was a shock. His wife – mentioned so casually, referred to only to be dismissed – had seemed an insubstantial presence in his background, a mere shadow. Yet here she was, in flesh and blood, amused by Dee's discomfiture and curious to know what on earth she did here on this bloody island. Her tone suggested that everyone should have something to do, some overriding passion that put all else in the shade. Hers centred round horses – three-day eventing, point-to-point, that kind of thing. What was Dee's enthusiasm?

'I don't have one, really. My family, I suppose.'

Sarah laughed. 'The dutiful wife following her husband round the world, is that it?'

'You make it sound worse than it is.'

'I make most things sound worse than they are. That way it's a pleasant surprise when you find it otherwise. Like this island. I always tell people that it's just sand, flies and boredom. Makes it so much better when you're lucky enough to find something different. Do you have the children out here with you?'

'Tom's boarding. Of course he's home for the holidays at the moment, but—'

'He's not at Ampleforth, is he? It *is* Yorkshire, isn't it? Your accent, I mean. To tell you the truth, I can never tell Yorkshire from Lancashire. I get into the most awful trouble sometimes. My brothers went to Ampleforth. That's how Damien and I met up.'

'Yes, the accent's Yorkshire—'

'Damien did say. He said you had lots of fun on the boat.'

'I suppose we did. It certainly wasn't sand and flies. Sick and wind, perhaps.' She laughed, and Sarah laughed as well, which created a fragile, momentary bond between the two of them. They moved away from the crowd, nursing plates of food. Damien hovered anxiously.

'Tom's at prep school, in Oxford,' Dee told her. 'But our little girl is here. She's far too young to board. You've got daughters, haven't you?'

Sarah seemed surprised that she should know, as though details of her family might be confidential information. 'They're nine and twelve. I don't think I could bear to let them go to boarding school. They're at a convent near Godalming.'

'You haven't put them into school here then?'

'Good God, no! I wouldn't risk the army school.'

Dee felt foolish, not quite sure of what was being explained to her. 'Have you left them with relatives?'

'Gracious, no. I'm only out here for the holidays, to see that Damien's on the straight and narrow and give the girls a look at the Med. We've kept the house in England and the girls and I are off back home as soon as poss. The point-to-point season starts next month.' Her smile was larded with disdain. 'So nice to meet you, Deirdre. Perhaps . . .' But she never said what perhaps. Someone else was talking to her and she turned away.

Later in the evening Damien came over and asked Dee to dance. The band played 'Singin' the Blues' and 'See You Later Alligator' and they did a sort of jive, imitating one or two of the younger couples. 'I'm sorry,' he said when they came together for a moment.

'For what?'

'For Sarah. She gets nervous, and when she's nervous she snaps.'

'If *she's* nervous, what do you think I am?'

'Why should you be nervous?'

She didn't answer. The jive came to an end and a soldier who had pretensions as a crooner came to the microphone and sang 'Stardust'. Damien drew her close, closer than he should have, just like it had been on the *Empire Bude*. It was late by now and the lights were low and there was a crowd on the dance floor and no one seemed to notice. The song had that awful, facile appositeness, like so much popular music. That was the trick, wasn't it? Words that would evoke easy associations. *Sometimes she wondered how she spent the lonely nights dreaming of* . . . what, exactly? The hidden dreamer, hidden even to herself. 'We shouldn't be dancing like this,' she said, but she didn't back away. Other dancers milled around them.

'Safety in numbers,' he said, his mouth close to her ear. And then, 'I'll ring you, when Sarah's gone. Is that OK? I'll ring you and we'll fix something up. Is that what you want, Dee?'

The music was coming to an end, and she knew that she was about to say something she might regret.

'I don't know, Damien. I really don't know.'

*

166

'You seem to get on well with that Braudel fellow,' Edward remarked on the drive home. 'Danced with him a lot.'

'Once, just once.'

'Three numbers.'

'Were you counting?'

'Not specially. You're in danger of getting a reputation, you know?'

'What on earth do you mean?'

'As a flirt.'

'Oh, for God's sake!' She sat in the passenger seat, staring ahead through the windscreen. The beams from the headlights were like smudges of chalk across a grimy blackboard. There was a bit of drystone wall, roadside olive trees and, for a moment, a dead cat lying in the middle of the tarmac. 'I was going to tell you that his wife's over for the holidays. Maybe we should have them to dinner or something.'

'So you can roll your eyes at him? What's she like?'

'Horsy.'

He laughed. 'Looks horsy or sounds horsy?'

'You know what I mean.'

'Looks horsy, from what I saw. No wonder he keeps her hidden away in England and goes after you.'

'He's not hiding her away and he's not going after me. You're getting paranoid, Edward. They've made a choice, for the sake of the children. At least she's doing that, refusing to send them away to boarding school.'

'Is that a dig at me?'

'It's just a fact. Take it as you like.'

The phone rang. She knew it was him, even as she lifted the receiver. 'Where are you?' she asked.

'In a bar somewhere in Limassol.'

'Doing what?'

'Just mooching around really. Is Edward there? Can I talk?'

'He's at work. It was lovely meeting Sarah at that do. Is she still here?'

'She left last week. Can I see you?'

There was a pause, one of those awkward moments on the telephone which, in a face-to-face encounter, would have been filled with expression and gesture.

'Dee, are you there?'

'Yes, I'm still here.'

'How about it?'

'I was thinking of going down to Marjorie's later. Perhaps I could drop by.'

'Who the hell's Marjorie?'

'You must remember her from the *Empire Bude*.'

'I don't remember much from the *Empire Bude* except you.'

'Don't be silly. She runs a SSAFA canteen down near the Castle.'

'Oh, I know. Where the men go for tea and sympathy. Well, that's more or less where I am. Café Aphrodite, although Aphrodite herself seems a more likely candidate for Circus Fat Woman than Goddess of Love. And she could always double as the bearded lady if they were strapped for cash.'

'I can find it.'

'My dear thing, you can't *miss* it.'

Nicos drove her. They went past the fire station and the hospital and the police headquarters. He glanced at her in the mirror, his eyes sliced out of the context of his face, devoid of expression. 'Miss Marjorie's canteen?' he asked.

'Actually, I'm going to a place on the seafront first – the Café Aphrodite or something.'

'A bar?'

'What's wrong with that? I'm meeting a friend.'

The car edged its way through the narrow streets of the old town, round parked trucks and pedestrians. The minaret of a mosque could be seen rising like a missile above the roofs.

'Not a good area,' Nicos said. 'Zig-Zag Street and that. Not the sort of place you should be going.'

'It's perfectly all right. We've been here many times.'

'Over there's the Turkish Quarter.' He gestured towards the invisible boundary where dark figures watched from across the divide of religion and culture. 'Bastards,' he added.

'What a stupid thing to say, from someone who has lived in England.'

'What's England got to do with it? You English don't under-stand. Turks kill Greeks, you know that? For thousands of years they've been killing Greeks.'

'And now the Greeks are killing the British,' she said. 'What's the difference?'

'Not now, they're not. Not when Dighenis calls a truce.'

'But they will be, when the truce is called off. And then you'll be just as bad as the Turks.'

The road led past workshops where fires burned in the shad-ows and blacksmiths hammered at iron like Hephaestus at the forge. Hephaestus was the husband of Aphrodite – a poor crip-pled consort for the unfaithful goddess. Geoffrey had told her that. And then there was the massive bulwark of the Castle, with soldiers on guard outside and the Union Jack flying above. Beyond were the warehouses and the tiny harbour. The car turned along the waterfront, with its promenade of old, salt-corroded houses. There were one or two run-down hotels, the offices of a couple of shipping companies, a few cafés. At the

Aphrodite tables and chairs spilled out on the pavement, but only one customer was sitting there. Nicos pulled in to the side of the road to let her out. 'Shall I wait?'

'No, don't. Come and pick me up from Miss Marjorie's canteen in an hour's time.'

But he didn't pull away from the kerb. As she walked towards the tables, she was conscious of his watching her from behind the reflected sky of the windscreen.

Damien rose from his chair. He was wearing a pale suit and his hat was on the chair next to him, almost as though he were saving a place for her. He bent to give her a discreet kiss on the cheek. 'How are you? It seems ages since the party.' He pulled the chair out for her to sit. 'Is it too chilly out here? What'll you have? How about a brandy sour? That's what I'm drinking – it's the only way I've discovered to make the local hooch palatable. Or you can have it with whisky, if you'd prefer.'

'That's fine.'

'Whisky or brandy?'

'Either.'

She sat at the table, wondering why she was here, why he had invited her and why she had accepted. You could disguise it as an innocent encounter if you wished, but she knew it for what it was: an assignation.

'Brandy, then. Didn't you pay that taxi off? He's still waiting.'

'He's meant to pick me up at Marjorie's, but he's probably checking you out. Marjorie thinks he's in love with me.'

Damien laughed. 'A taxi driver? That's a bit *infra dig*, isn't it?'

'It's not something you can help.'

'Don't I know it. I'll tell him his services are not needed.'

'Let me,' she said, but he'd risen from his chair and was walking away towards the taxi before she could stop him. She watched anxiously as he talked at the window of the Opel. After a few seconds the car drew away from the kerb and roared off down the seafront. When Damien came back he was laughing. 'The fellow's a London Teddy boy, for God's sake. I thought he might knife me when I told him.'

'What on earth did you say?'

'I told him to bugger off, that's what.'

'Damien!'

'Well, more or less. First I asked him why he was hanging around, and he told me that he wanted to make sure Mrs Denham was all right. And I said that I was an officer and a gentleman and besides that I was Mrs Denham's favourite poodle, so he could push off. What is he, your bodyguard?'

'I told you. He's got a crush on me, poor soul.'

'He's not the only one.'

'Don't be silly. One's enough. You shouldn't have done that. It's not fair, pulling rank on him.'

'Rank? He's not a bloody soldier, is he?'

'Of course he's not a bloody soldier. And don't speak like that. He's not a bloody anything, not a bloody Cyp, not a bloody wop. He's just a taxi driver.' She felt angry and bewildered, defensive about Nicos. That Damien could be so crass. There was an awkward pause.

'Hey, I've bought a new car,' he said. 'Did I tell you?'

'Of course you didn't tell me.'

'Isabella, she's called.' He pointed. The vehicle was parked near by. Isabella wasn't a nickname he'd given it, but the name of the model. It was a white convertible two-seater, a flashy roadster with a long bonnet and lots of chrome and the maker's name – *Borgward* – in script along the front wing. 'Isabella' seemed to suit it; a blowsy, tart's name, he suggested. 'You wouldn't believe that Germans could be so imaginative, would you?'

She laughed nervously, hoping that the encounter had been

put back on an even keel. Their drinks came. 'To us,' he said, raising his glass.

'Us?'

'Why not?' Damien looked at her. She sweated in the pale sunshine. He smiled and held her gaze and she felt the sweat trickle insidiously from her armpits and run down her flanks. She knew that it glistened in the valley between her breasts, and saw his eyes flicker down to see it. And suddenly he wasn't chatting any longer, but was leaning slightly forward across the table and talking quietly to her and watching her closely for the slightest hint of evasion or pain or guilt or whatever it was. Love, he was talking of love. 'From the moment I first set eyes on you – and you looked like death warmed up at the time, so it must be real.' He had taken her hand, and held it, shaking it slightly as though to emphasize his words, the weight of them, the import.

'Damien, you're being daft.'

'No I'm not.'

'People might hear.'

'There aren't any people to hear. I almost said all this at your party but I didn't quite have the guts, and I wanted to say it at that bloody do at the mess, but I couldn't. And Sarah was there anyway, which made it difficult. But now I *am* saying it, so bloody well listen, hidden dreamer. I love you and I want to take you away from your husband and I want to divorce my wife. And I want to marry you and be with you for the rest of my life. There, I've said it. And you might tell me to piss off, but still I've said it and now I can die a happy man.'

She took her hand back carefully, in case he might crush it. Hers was light and fragile; his was strong, the fingers and the back brushed with hair, the nails cut short and square. And she wondered what that hand had done, where it had been. She saw it hooked around the trigger of some ugly weapon, a Lee-

Enfield or whatever it was they used nowadays. A Bren gun, a Webley pistol, a Sterling. She saw it touching his wife's body, going down over her belly and into the dense thicket of pale hair. She felt it touch her own body, inside her, just as she had imagined it that night on the *Empire Bude*. She shivered, as though he had actually done it, touched something at the quick of her. 'I thought you were a Catholic,' she said. 'I thought Catholics couldn't get divorced.'

'They can get a civil divorce.'

'It doesn't sound very civil to me.'

'Is that all you've got to say?'

'It's taken me aback, really. I could hardly have expected all this, could I?'

'Well, what *were* you expecting? Deep in your cold, cold heart, you love me too. Don't you?'

She felt a tremor inside her. It was something beyond control, something contingent, like a disease. 'I don't know what I think,' she said. 'I think you're being daft, and I don't think it would help if I were to be daft as well.'

'But you'd like to be?'

'I didn't say that.'

Damien made a small exhalation of breath that may have been a sarcastic laugh, may have been an expression of pain. He sipped his drink and shifted in his chair to look out towards the sea where a ship was waiting in the roads, just as the *Empire Bude* had waited to disembark her passengers all that time ago. Further out a naval frigate was steaming past, its white ensign clipped by the breeze, its black guns fingering the air fore and aft. It was on patrol for smugglers, looking for the caiques that brought in arms and ammunition to EOKA, and Grivas' insulin. 'I've discussed it with Sarah,' he said.

'You've discussed what with Sarah?'

'I told her. About my feeling for you.'

'You've *what*?'

'Oh, not by name, but in principle. Actually, I think she guessed. "Have I met her?" she asked. I admitted that she had. Briefly, I said, and she smiled and said, "Pretty little wifey." I'm not sure whether it was a question or a statement.'

'It sounds patronizing, whichever it was.'

'She is patronizing. So what do we do about it?'

Dee shook her head. 'Nothing. You've done enough as it is, merely by saying what you've said. You aren't really going to abandon your family, are you? I certainly couldn't love you if I thought you might. It wouldn't be a lovable thing, would it, for me to abandon Tom or Paula, or you to abandon your daughters? It's not the kind of thing either of us would do.'

'So what *is* the kind of thing we do?'

'Right now the kind of thing we do is, we have our drink and then I go on to Marjorie's,' she said quietly.

'I'll take you in the car.'

'Don't be silly. Marjorie's is only just along the front.'

'Let me take you for a spin.'

'Damien, please.'

'I need to be alone with you.'

She closed her eyes. 'Damien, please,' she repeated quietly. 'Don't you see how impossible it all is?'

Eleven

Kale has no history. She has a present, but no past. No father, no aunts, no uncles, no cousins. There was a man who lived with them for a while, when they were in Tottenham. 'I called him Uncle, but he wasn't. It's always Uncle, isn't it? Uncle Ronald. Then he pushed off and we were on our own, apart from my mum's boyfriends. Quite a few of those,' she adds with a small sting of irony. She has no past, no roots. 'We never really belonged nowhere. Anywhere. Never belonged anywhere. I mean, London, yes. But what's that mean these days? And we moved a lot – Walthamstow, Tottenham, a couple of years in Wood Green, and then south of the river. Mum's not a Londoner herself, though. She was born in Birmingham. Came to London when she was sixteen. But when I ask her about family, well, she just sort of avoids the question. Know what I mean?'

He doesn't, really. He and Paula have family – their mother's relations in Yorkshire, cousins of his father in Hampshire. They don't see them much, but they're there to provide some kind of reference, some sense of being knitted into the warp and weft of Britain in the twentieth century. Is Kale's type the future? Freedom from history. You just are. You have no reason and no context.

'What about your father?'

She shrugs. 'He pushed off when I was three. That's what Mum says. I don't remember.' Her look seems to ambush him, a hard light of intelligence shining through the stunted education. 'Family history's a bit of a luxury, isn't it?'

'I suppose it is.'

Their disparate present lives barely overlap, like circles in a Venn diagram describing some logical but unsolved puzzle. How to increase the degree of intersection? How to pull her closer? And what other unperceived circles intersect with hers? There's one marked 'Steve', and another with her mother's name, and one with Emma's, of course. But what others? He doesn't know. He has slept with her and yet all he knows is the detail of her, the curves and interstices. She will be standing there beside him, wearing jeans and a scrap of T-shirt, and he knows all the things you can't see – the curl of her strange, bifurcate toes, the precise shape of her kneecaps, the rough nest of her body hair, the hang of her breasts and the dark shadows in her axillae; all these things, but not her, the surface, but not the substance.

They have lunch together on the days when Kale is in college. Sometimes she is amused by him, sometimes evasive and distracted. When she is amused it makes him happy: it suggests a degree of intimacy, something shared. On the other occasions Thomas wonders whether she is thinking of the boyfriend.

'Tell me about him.'

'I don't want to.'

'Are you still with him?'

'I told you, we've broken up. Shall we talk about something else?'

One Saturday they meet in Hyde Park and take Emma to the Natural History Museum. Emma holds their hands and swings between them as she did when they went to the theatre. 'Stop it, Emms,' her mother snaps. But Thomas loves this illusion of paternity, of being a family, possessing and being possessed. They pass through the great doors into the nave of the building, almost like entering a cathedral. Dinosaur skeletons, not saints, peer down at them from the shadows. Emma squints up at the monsters and asks, 'Are we frightened, Mum?' and Kale decides that no, we aren't really frightened; but we are just a bit nervous.

'What's nervous?'

'Nervous is being afraid without really knowing it.'

Thomas is afraid without knowing it. He's afraid of loss. He's afraid that she may decide, on a whim, that that's it, it's all over, whatever has barely started is now finished. Emma watches the dinosaurs, Kale watches Emma, he watches her, loving the sight of her, the articulate movements of her body, the set of her head, the thoughtful frown as she concentrates to read one of the information cards to her daughter.

After the museum they have a meal – Kale calls it 'tea' – at a hamburger place that is all red neon and yellow plastic flowers. 'Why don't you come back with us?' Emma asks Thomas when the meal is over and it is time to go. He smiles on her as an ally in his covert, urgent battle.

'Thomas has his own home,' her mother explains.

'Let's go to his home, then.'

' 'Fraid we can't, Emms. We got to get back.' *Go' uh ge' ba'* – a dance of glottal stops. What she has to get back for, Thomas doesn't know. She answers the phone in some office for single mothers; she works part-time at the Brixton Library, cataloguing;

she helps out in a café of some kind. Those little bits of others' lives that intersect with hers. They walk together as far as the tube station and she gives him a quick, tantalizing kiss before vanishing with her daughter down into the bowels of the underground once more. Persephone.

Two days later he is standing at the window of his office high up in the Arts block when he catches sight of her far below on the concourse of the university: a tiny figure that is yet instantly recognizable. She is with a man. At least, the man is talking to her. From on high Thomas watches. They are talking, urgently, even argumentatively. He can tell by the gestures, the insistent pointing of the man's finger, the set of her feet, the way she turns away and he grabs her by the arm and twists her back to face him. For a second he wonders whether there is going to be violence, and he will be forced to watch, helplessly, from seven storeys up. And then she has shaken herself free and walked towards the entrance of the building below his viewpoint. The man stands watching.

Thomas hurries to the lift and descends to the ground floor. There is no sign of Kale in the reception area. He goes out to the concourse. Two students are handing out leaflets protesting against the poll tax. A couple of tourists are seated on a bench, consulting a map that is folded to the wrong page. People come and go. One of them – a colleague in the Department of Philosophy – greets him as he passes. But there is no sign of Kale, and no man who might have been talking to her, no man called Steve. He returns to the seventh floor and as he passes the offices the secretary calls out to him. 'That Kale Macintosh left this for you.' She is holding out some handwritten sheets of paper: an essay, due in two days ago.

'Where did she go?'

'She just handed it to me and went back down.'

'The lifts must have crossed.'

The woman regards him with dry amusement. She is an ally of sorts. 'Ships in the night,' she says.

Back in his office he glances through the essay. Her handwriting is naive and laborious, with painstakingly looped characters. The letter T is frequently capitalized; in place of a dot, the i always bears a small circle like a little o of surprise. *History should be Telling iT like iT was,* she writes. *This is whaT The German historian Ranke meanT when he said,* Wie es eigentlich gewesen – *we must show It like It was. Some people Think This is wrong, but iT seems To me quiTe righT.*

He feels a surge of affection. And fear. Suddenly she no longer appears the assured, confident woman that he has taken her to be: quite unexpectedly she seems like a vulnerable child.

Of course, Telling iT like iT was is also understanding iT like iT was, and This may be very difficult . . .

*

Dear Dr Denham

Thank you for your enquiry regarding
Major D. Braudel of the 2nd battalion,
the Oxfordshire and Buckinghamshire
Light Infantry. I have looked through the
regimental diary for the period you mention,
and although the diary does not as a rule
mention individuals by name, I do find a
reference to this officer in the entry for
Wednesday 14th May, 1958. I quote it, in
its entirety, below:

'Major Braudel, CO D Coy, murdered, probably
by Eoka, while off duty in Limassol.'

If you wish for further details of this
officer's career I suggest you get in touch
with the Army Records Office which holds all
individual records of service. I must warn
you, however, that such information is usually
only released to the individual in question or
to immediate relatives.

Yours sincerely,

Trotter, J. Lt Col. (retd).
Curator, Museum of Ox & Bucks L.I.

'What do you want?' Kale asks. She stands in the middle of his office, biting the inside of her lip. Today she looks about sixteen. Sometimes she looks tough and grown-up, a good thirty or more. Other times she seems little more than an adolescent. She even changes her gait, her way of standing. Today it's a short, sharp skirt and heavy shoes and her knees turned inwards. Pigeon-toed. She's wearing one of those shirts that looks crumpled even when it's not.

'I just want to return your essay,' Thomas explains. 'And to see you alone for a bit.'

'People'll get suspicious if you call me in like this. Eric already says I won't have any problem with my grades, if I play my cards right.'

'Eric's a silly prat.'

She takes the essay from him and glances over it. He has scribbled a few comments in the margin, and marked it at the end. 'What's that mean? Fifteen out of twenty-five. What's that?'

'It means it's not bad, for a first attempt.'

'What do you mean, not bad? I can't do any better than that. I can't help it if I can't write. It's not my fault.'

'You'll get better. With practice.'

'I haven't got time for practice.'

'I want to see more of you,' he says. 'I want a bit of practice as well.'

She shrugs. 'It's not easy, is it? There's Emma. There's my work. There's other stuff.'

What other stuff, he wonders? 'Who was it you were arguing with the other day? I was looking out of the window and I saw you on the concourse. With a man. Was that him?'

She shrugs. 'Maybe. Maybe it was.'

'I thought you'd finished with him.'

'He wants me back, doesn't he?' Her tone suggests that Thomas ought to know, that it's obvious.

'And what about you?'

'I want to be left in peace, don't I?'

'By me as well?'

'Maybe . . . maybe not.'

He takes her hand. He expects her to snatch it away, but she doesn't. She lets it lie there, fragile and cool, like a small mammal lying passive in a cage. And then he notices the bruise. It's on her wrist, a luminous grey-blue mark like a tattoo, a pretty enough thing really, an abstract shape curling cleverly round the narrow bones.

'What's this?'

She looks, almost with surprise. 'I fell. Bashed it against a cupboard.'

'Come on, Kale, I'm not naive.'

'I fell. Why don't you believe me?'

He takes her other hand and examines that, but the skin is unblemished. 'Was it him?'

She doesn't stop him when he unbuttons her cuff and pushes the sleeve up. There are other marks, blue marks, on her upper arm. Bile yellow and a hint of rust. 'What you going to do? Examine me all over?'

'You haven't answered the question.'

She is silent, like a child caught out in some misdemeanour and unable to concoct an excuse or an alibi.

'That's enough of an answer, isn't it?'

'It's nothing.'

'What did he do?'

'Pushed me about a bit. The usual stuff.'

'Usual stuff? Has he done this before?'

'Sometimes. He gets carried away. Angry. He gets angry.'

'Why don't you do something about it? Go to the police or something.'

That brings dry, sarcastic laughter. 'For this? Fuck all they'd do. Probably just use it as an excuse to send the social workers round and take Emma away. Look, we're all right, OK? Me and Emma, we've moved in with my mum and now we're all right.'

'Where were you before?'

She hesitates, evades his look, bites her lip. 'With Steve, of course. I was living with him.'

'You never said that.'

'Why should I? I didn't leave him because of you, if that's what you're thinking. We were breaking up anyway, and you came along, and that's OK. But I didn't walk out on him because of you.'

He has a thought. More than one thought in fact; a dozen, all fighting for his attention, like a roomful of students all clamouring their questions at the same time. Focus, he tells them. Reason calmly. Work from premises to conclusions, taking one line of argument at a time. He chooses the first thought that floats to the surface: 'How long had you been with him?'

'Couple of years.'

'How long is a couple?'

She shifts evasively. 'Four.'

'*Four?*'

'Four or five, something like that.'

'Five years living with him? I thought he was just a casual boyfriend.'

She shrugs and looks away but he takes her chin and turns her head towards him. She's pale, and her eyebrows have that ill-plucked look about them. Her mouth is twisted as she bites the inside of her lower lip. For the first time her eyes don't hold his.

'Kale, is Steve Emma's father?'

'Steve? You're joking.'

'I'm just doing a bit of maths, that's all.'

'Well, you're a better historian than a mathematician. She's six years old. It doesn't add up, does it?'

'In history the maths often doesn't quite add up. That's because the witnesses are often inaccurate.'

There's a flash of anger. 'Are you saying I'm lying?'

'Approximating, maybe.'

'If you're interested, I don't even know who her father is. I was having a bad time then, seeing a lot of guys, in a bit of a mess. Know what I mean? And Steve sort of got me out of that, gave me something to rely on. Look, can I go now?'

'If that's what you want.' But he's still holding her hand and she doesn't make a move. Cautiously he draws her towards him. There's even a faint response as he kisses her, an offering of her mouth. He can smell the sweetness of something she has been sucking – strawberry, perhaps – and the sourness of tobacco behind it. She moves against him, faintly at first, then with a strange insistence. Anger has done something, opened the door to reconciliation. He can feel her hip bone nudged against his thighs. She backs against the desk and papers cascade on to the floor with the sound of snow sliding from a roof. He lifts her on to the desk, pushes her skirt up, opens her legs.

At that moment there's a knock on the door.

They pause, suddenly silent. 'Who is it?' she whispers in his ear. 'Shh.'

A second knock. Is it possible to hear someone listening? There is a sensation of sound inverted, like a vacuum sucking the faintest noise from the room into the funnel of an ear on the other side of the door. Kale laughs softly, pressed close to him, her mouth by his ear. 'Is it locked?'

'Shh.'

They wait for the tap of footsteps retreating along the corridor. 'I'm sorry,' he says. 'God, how bloody awful.'

She's still laughing. 'Is it locked?'

'Of course it's locked.'

'You dirty old bugger. You were planning to fuck me, weren't you?'

'The idea had crossed my mind.'

'I'll bet.' The moment of possibility has gone. She jumps off the desk and turns away to find her bag. 'Well, I think I'd better be going before they come back with an axe and break the door down.'

'Come away with me,' he suggests. 'Next weekend. I've got to look someone up in Brighton. Brighton's just as good as Frinton. Better. Better than Frinton.'

She hesitates at the door. 'What about Emms?'

'Bring her as well. Of course.'

She bites her lip, considering. 'All right,' she says. 'Why not?'

'Are you in a relationship with Ms Macintosh?' asks one of his colleagues. They are in the canteen, bathed in bright, fluorescent light like in an operating theatre. There is the clash of metal on metal, as though someone is doing battle in the stainless-steel kitchens beyond the serving counter. Other colleagues – friends, sympathizers – carefully avoid their table, as though the subject of the interrogation is already known to all. Was this, Thomas wonders, the prowler in the corridor, knocking while he and Kale were about to knock?

'That all depends.'

'On what?'

'On why you are asking me. On what you mean by a relationship.'

'It's not really a semantic issue, is it? Nothing to do with COGESH. It's rather more than that. An issue for Staff–Student Relations.'

'It's not an issue of any kind. Kale is twenty-eight years old and a mother. She doesn't need a watchdog to look after her.'

There is an academic shake of the head. A prim smile. 'Neither her age nor her maternity is the point. The new code of conduct expressly prohibits associations of an intimate nature between junior and senior members of the college when a direct mentorial or pedagogic relationship already exists. We are attempting to establish the same kind of professional relationship that you might expect between doctors and their patients.'

Thomas smiles back. He's feeling the exultation of conquest, daring and dangerous. 'Then you'll just have to catch us at it, won't you?'

Geoffrey Crozier lives in that no man's land between the celebrated Brighton and the unknown Hove. He has a flat in a building called Tatham House, a Regency confection of white plasterwork on the seafront. In the town itself there are souvenir shops selling trinkets to tourists and language schools selling English to ravenous packs of Italian and Spanish kids; but here, on Regent's Square, it is all pillars and Corinthian capitals and swags of florid vegetation: Brighton Rock has given way to Wedding Cake.

A rickety cage of *fin de siècle* ironwork edges Thomas upwards from the ground floor towards the penthouse. It gives the curious illusion that the cage is stationary while the stairs and landings are sliding downwards past him, potted palms and closed doors descending into the depths. A resident, caught at the moment of watering, watches this apotheosis suspiciously. The lift comes to a halt in the manner of machinery breaking down rather than something reaching its programmed destination. The gate folds back, like an umbrella collapsing.

There are two doors here on the topmost floor but only one of them is open, and there – it's a shock – is Geoffrey Crozier himself, standing in the opening with his arms held out as though Thomas might throw himself into them like a prodigal son. 'Tom!' he cries. 'Tom, me old shiner, come in, come in!'

There is something immaculate about Geoffrey's appearance, something cultured and perfect. *Dapper*, Thomas' mother used to say; a word that he didn't really understand in those days but which, he felt even then, bore within its twin plosives a hint of criticism. Nowadays 'dapper' is out of date, but may be usefully replaced by 'smooth'. Geoffrey is smooth. His white hair is of the evenness of freshly fallen snow on a rooftop, the moustache a narrow cornice of snow on the façade. He is wearing beautifully creased white slacks and a crocodile-leather belt. His shoes gleam. His dark blue shirt looks as though it must be silk. Only his skin is flawed, with patches of pale pigmentation on cheeks and forehead and on the hand that grasps a Malacca cane. But his grip when he shakes Thomas' hand is strong. 'It's good to see you again, Tom. Come on in! Come on in! What a bugger I couldn't make it to your darling mother's funeral. But you'll understand. You know what they say about hip replacement? Bend over with care, don't kick the cat, and keep away from magnets.' The voice is quite unchanged. There is exactly the same timbre, hint of cockney, hint of laughter that Thomas recalls from childhood.

They pass through a hallway into an expansive sitting room lit by wide windows. Chairs and sofas in chrome and white leather stand on the black floorboards like exhibits in a gallery. One entire wall is covered by a mural. It shows a long, *trompe l'oeil* balustrade on which a *trompe l'oeil* cat sits looking out over the swimming-pool blue of a fictive Mediterranean. Tendrils of vine and wisteria writhe around the edges of the scene. Gauze curtains fly in the false breeze. In the middle distance there is a smoking island that might be Stromboli.

'What do you think?' Geoffrey's tone is part apologetic, part proud. 'The previous owner had it done so you mustn't blame it on me. I think he used the place to keep his several mistresses. You must have a look at the bathroom.'

Thomas follows him down a short corridor to a marble bathroom with a view over the Bay of Naples. A purple Vesuvius smoulders in the haemorrhage from a bloody sunset. 'What do you think?'

'It's amazing.'

'Just what I thought when I first saw it, my dear. Amazing. Camp meets kitsch. I couldn't possibly have had it painted over. Gordon thinks that all English houses are like this, so I took him round the Pavilion just to show him that they can be a lot worse.'

Who, Thomas wonders, is Gordon?

They return to the sitting room. 'What'll you have? Is it too early for gin? Of course not. Your mother always drank gin and it, didn't she? Medicinal, she used to say. I tried to educate her towards pink gin, but it was always gin and it for her. You'll stay to lunch, won't you? I've sent Gordon out to do his magic round the delis, with strict instructions to bring back things Greek. How about that? Taramasalata and hummus and other outlandish things. Once upon a time the Brits had never heard of them. Nowadays it's hard to find anything else.'

Thomas takes his gin and circles the room cautiously, trying contexts and settings, endeavouring to work things out, spot clues, sense hints: a Persian carpet here, a Rennie Mackintosh chair there, a bookshelf with an eclectic collection that includes *Aphrodite Died Here* and *Fortune's Hostage*, both slim volumes by Geoffrey Crozier. He is surprised to discover, on one shelf, a silver-framed photograph of a nude woman. It shows her from the waist up, strongly lit, her head turned profile and tilted down as though she is looking at something on the floor. There is a sculptural beauty to the photograph, the curves and convexities of a piece by Barbara Hepworth or Henry Moore. One of the woman's breasts is in dark silhouette; the other, a perfect teardrop, is bisected by shadow. Its nipple is a wrinkled nub, the only surface in the whole photograph that is not satin-smooth.

'That's Guppy,' Geoffrey says. '*Was* Guppy. My wife. Taken in 1947 by Bill Brandt.'

'Bill Brandt? Really?'

'Do you know him?'

'Of course I know him.'

'More than your mother did. I used to have a censored version around the house in Cyprus. It wasn't the kind of picture you could show off in its entirety, not in those days, not in polite society anyway.'

Guppy. The nickname seemed absurd, slightly derisory. Thomas has always imagined someone lardy and lumpen, and now he is presented with this – a sculptural beauty photographed by one of the masters of the twentieth century. 'She was very beautiful' is all he can manage as a comment.

Geoffrey laughs. 'Weren't we all, once? Your mother was beautiful, and now she's dead. You were a beautiful little boy, and now look at you. And as for me—'

'What happened to her?'

'Who, Guppy?' Leaning on his cane, Geoffrey leads the way out through french windows on to a small roof terrace. 'We split up years ago. Before Cyprus, during Cyprus. These things take time, don't they?' They look out over the promenade and the silver sheen of the Channel. Away to the left, the gaunt, skeletal finger of the West Pier points hopelessly towards France. There is that pearly bloom in the air that you find near the sea, the gleam of salt. Geoffrey lowers himself cautiously into a wicker armchair while talking of his beautiful, mad wife. 'The poor dear died only a few years ago. Mad as a hatter by then, poor old thing. She drank. Sounds old-fashioned nowadays, doesn't it? The demon drink.'

'People still do it.'

'Few of them like Guppy, I fear. Drank like a fish, in fact.' He laughs. It's the old laugh, just as it was the old joke: a young laugh transplanted into this aged body. 'Anyway, she was more interested in the lowlife in London than in following me out to Cyprus. Probably not a bad thing, when all's said and done. She might have got in the way. Never the most discreet woman, Guppy. Might have mucked up the business something frightful.'

'What did you do in Cyprus?' Thomas asks. 'I remember Father saying something about a bank.'

'A bank?' Geoffrey pauses, as though trying to remember, as though he might have forgotten what his job was all those years ago. 'Oh, yes, there *was* a bank at the time. Levant Investment Bank. Long since deceased, like the whole bloody

Levant. Occasionally we actually did business, in fact – the odd investment, the occasional transfer of funds from one dubious account into another – but that wasn't really what we were about.'

'So what were you about?'

A sly smile, a rogue's smile, the smile of a man who's about to sell you something counterfeit, but you mustn't take it hard. It's just a game, for God's sake, just a game. 'I worked for Six, old chap.'

'Six?'

'My, you are an innocent fellow, Tom. Everybody knows about it nowadays. Then, of course, it was the job that dare not speak its name. MI6. SIS, whatever you want to call it. The Firm.'

Thomas laughs. It is a complicated laugh, an awkward mixture of amusement and nervousness and embarrassment. As though he should have known. As though Geoffrey is telling a funny story and he'd been led along thinking it was serious, and he has only just got the joke. 'The Firm? Did people really call it that? It sounds like a bad thriller.'

'It *was* a thriller at times, and sometimes it was a bloody bad one. Look at Philby and his crew. Look at the awful Burgess, for Christ's sake. But we had our moments in my neck of the woods, even though we never got old Grievous himself.'

'You were hunting Grivas?'

'Who else, old boy? He was the big fish, wasn't he? And we damned near got him as well.'

'My parents never said anything about all this.'

He roars with laughter. 'I should hope they didn't. In fact, I don't imagine your father even knew.'

'Do you mean my mother did?'

Geoffrey sips gin, purses his lips thoughtfully, as though looking for a way out of this awkward question. 'Well, she knew something. If she put two and two together.'

Thomas hesitates, watching this small man with the liverish skin and the bright, inquisitive eyes, and thinking of that woman leaning against the side of the car on a hot and dusty Limassol street, the woman who skipped through his memory of the harbour of Kyrenia, taking Geoffrey's hand and laughing as she never laughed with his father. While Guppy remained drink-sodden in London. 'You were always around her, weren't you? Sometimes it was only you, wasn't it?' he says. 'Often my father wasn't there, I mean.'

'Eddie? What a good bloke he was. A good, loyal, solid chap. The kind that founded the British Empire, and then, when the time came, bloody well went and did his duty and dissolved it. I was so upset when I heard of his death.'

Thomas isn't going to be deflected by discussion of his father. He asks, 'Were you in love with her, Geoffrey?'

And now Geoffrey laughs that uproarious laugh, the one that haunted Thomas' childhood. 'I loved her dearly,' he says eventually, through the laughter. 'I loved her; but in love? No, I don't think so.' He struggles to recover from his amusement, apologizing and wiping his eyes. 'I'm sorry, old boy. I think perhaps you've misunderstood. I mean, by that time . . .' He is about to add something, but whatever it is is lost, for the front door to the flat opens and closes and someone comes into the sitting room. 'We're out on the terrace, drinking gin,' Geoffrey calls. 'Come and meet Tom. You'll like him.'

A middle-aged man appears at the french windows, smiling and looking faintly embarrassed at seeing the two of them out there. He is Asian – perhaps Thai. His face is smooth and boyish, making him seem younger than his real age; Thomas guesses him to be about fifty. The face might have a certain innocence about it, but his eyes are bright and black and know-ing.

'Gordon is my prop and staff,' Geoffrey explains. 'He teaches piano at the Conservatory, but he looks after me in his spare time. Not that I'm incapable on my own. I just need a hand every now and again, don't I?'

'Just a hand,' Gordon agrees. He goes and stands behind Geoffrey and rests a hand gently on the old man's shoulder, while Geoffrey raises his own to put it over Gordon's. And the whole image of Thomas' past shimmers and distorts, as though Geoffrey has just tossed a bloody big boulder into the placid reflection of memory.

'Tom and I,' Geoffrey says, looking up at his companion, 'were talking about his darling mother, how much I loved her.'

'You loved many women, it seems,' Gordon observes. 'Was she like Guppy?'

'Was she like Guppy! Perish the very thought. Dee was a mammal, warm and furry; Guppy was a scaly fish. But, I have to confess, Guppy was the more beautiful. A beautiful fish. A barracuda, perhaps. Are barracudas beautiful? I think Guppy was the most beautiful woman it has ever been my misfortune to know. Dee, on the other hand, was one of the most *attractive*.' He raises an eyebrow. 'Oh, yes, Tom. I find women attractive all right. I just don't find them desirable. It's a very different thing.'

Gordon slips back inside – 'I will prepare the lunch,' he says – and leaves the two of them talking on the terrace. Geoffrey does most of the talking. His reminiscences combine apparent openness with subtle evasion, good stories coupled with utmost reserve. It's like interviewing a senior civil servant about overspending in the public sector. He agrees with everything you say, old boy, except that it was anyone's fault.

'We worked on radio and telephone intercepts, tracking EOKA couriers, that kind of thing. Muscled in on the local Special Branch operation, and then spent much of our time stepping on the toes of the Office.'

'The office?'

'MI5, old chap. They claimed it was their territory, being a colony. But we had the Greek specialists, while all they had were pinheads from Oxbridge and rough boys from south London. Of course that kind of thing's all out in the public domain nowadays – that fellow Peter Wright blew the gaff, didn't he? And now there are dozens of others doing the same thing. Sometimes I wonder whether I shouldn't publish my own memoirs. They'd probably sell better than poems.'

'My mother knew about this?'

'Your father fell for the banker nonsense, but she could put two and two together and see that it didn't quite add up to four.'

'And what about Damien Braudel?' Thomas asks. 'What about him?'

'Ah.' The sound that Geoffrey makes is faintly climactic, as though he has been expecting to hear this name. He reaches out to pick up his glass. 'How do you know about him?'

'I found a newspaper cutting. The *Times of Cyprus*. Among my mother's things.'

Geoffrey nods. 'Damien Braudel was a most charming young fellow.'

'What happened?'

Geoffrey sips his drink and looks across the glass at Thomas. 'They shot him, of course. That's what EOKA did, shot people. We lost our grip that year. We'd had them within our grasp and the politicians buggered it up and EOKA cut loose in nineteen-fifty-eight. Young hoods, mostly. Nothing admirable about them. Shootings in the back. Civilians as well as military. It was a bloody business at times. And Braudel was one of the victims. In Limassol, from what I remember. Actually I was out of the island at the time. I only heard about it second-hand.'

'Did they ever get his killer?'

Geoffrey shrugs, sips his gin, glances out over the railings of the terrace. 'I've no idea. I don't expect so. He's probably a respected politician now.'

'And what about his relationship with my mother?'

'That, my dear boy, is something that only he or she could tell you about.'

'They're both dead.'

'Aren't we all, sooner or later?'

Thomas takes a photograph out of his jacket and holds it up for Geoffrey to see. *Nick*, it says on the back. 'What about him?'

Geoffrey laughs. 'The Teddy boy.'

'Do you know who he is?'

'I remember him vaguely. A taxi driver. Nick the Cyprian, that was his name, I think. Kyprianou. He used to drive your mother quite a bit. She sort of adopted him. She used to adopt people less fortunate than herself. She adopted me.'

'Was he a member of EOKA?'

Geoffrey laughs. ' You know what the Mayor of Nicosia said at the time? "We are *all* members of EOKA."'

'So he was?'

'No idea, old son. Even if he was, he wasn't on my radar.'

'I found a letter from you among her papers.'

'Did you now? And did you read it?'

'What happened, Geoffrey? Between the two of you?'

Geoffrey smiles. There's a patronizing quality about the expression, as though he's amused by Thomas' attempts, and equally amused by the fact that he is not going to give anything away. 'I think Gordon must have lunch ready by now, don't you?' he says, lifting himself carefully to his feet. He gestures to Thomas to go through into the sitting room.

'What did you quarrel about, Geoffrey?'

The man is going. He has abandoned the attempt to let Thomas pass through the french window first and he is determined to lead the way. 'What does anyone quarrel about?' he says as he makes his way inside. 'Love and loyalty. Jealousy and envy. Those kinds of things. You know the trouble with spying, Thomas? The usual rules of evidence don't apply. You can be condemned just by being in the wrong place at the wrong time.'

'The same thing applies to history.'

'I suppose it does. You know, you have a very unhealthy interest in these things – your mother's past and all that.'

'Do you think I'm spying on her?'

'It does begin to look like it, doesn't it? I loved her, Thomas. Do you know that? I loved her. I wonder whether you did.'

'How did it go?' Kale asks.

They are sitting on a bench near the Palace Pier, with the crowds drifting past and a busker playing the guitar and singing that there 'Ain't No Sunshine', which is an accurate but unnecessary gloss on the day. Emma is chasing the pigeons. She has been on a couple of fairground rides, and played some games, but it's much more fun chasing pigeons. They flap and hop and never expend more energy than is absolutely necessary to evade the little girl. It is part of their lives, the price they have to pay for a life of ease.

'Let them be, Emms,' Kale calls. 'They've got as much right to be here as you. More. This is their home.'

'Do they have homes?'

'Course they do. Nests or something.'

'Are they cosy?'

'I expect they're very cosy.'

'Like our flat?'

'Very like our flat, I expect. About the same size.'

Emma goes back to her work. Kale turns to Thomas and repeats her question. 'So how did it go?'

He shakes his head. 'It was like playing poker or something, poker against a card-sharp. I got the impression that when he wasn't lying he was evading the truth.'

'Is he guilty?'

'Guilty of what?'

'Of having stuffed your mother.'

'I never said—'

'Oh, come off it! That's what you thought. I can read you like a textbook, Thomas, like one of those bloody books you're so surprised we haven't already read. You thought this – what's his name? Geoff? – you thought he was the one that did the dirty on your dad.'

Thomas laughs. 'He's an old queen.'

'He's a what?'

'A queen. Gay.'

She looks at him with laughter and amazement. 'He's a ginger? I don't believe it.'

'Ginger?'

Kale explodes with laughter. 'Ginger beer.'

Emma pauses in her chase of pigeons and looks round. 'Why's Mum laughing?'

' 'Cos Mum's just heard a funny joke.'

'Tell me.'

'You wouldn't understand, love.' She turns back to Thomas. 'So your little ideas, your accusations against your poor dead mum, are just a load of old rubbish.'

'They're not accusations. Anyway, there's more than that.'

'More?'

He pauses, momentarily embarrassed by what seems so unlikely now, sitting here on the esplanade at Brighton, surrounded by agitated pigeons, with a suggestion of rain in the air. 'He claims that he was working for the Secret Service.'

'He *what*? A spy? You gotta be kidding. James bloody Bond?'

'More like John le Carré. Sort of elegant seediness. He's got a boyfriend called Gordon—'

'Gordon Bennett!' she says, and laughs. It's a silly, girl's laugh and it's wonderful to see it, the light that comes to her eyes, the flash of teeth and glimpse of tongue, the bright lifting of her features. All too often she seems drawn and tired. He laughs with her, happy to forget Geoffrey Crozier. He has this weekend with Kale and her child, this ephemeral illusion of family life, and he wants to forget the shark-like Crozier, the card-sharp Crozier, the queer with the sleek white hair and self-satisfied superiority. He catches her hand and holds it to his lips. 'Has anyone told you that you're beautiful?'

'You have.'

'Well you are. And I want to make love to you.'

'You'll have to wait. If we do it here we'll get arrested and Emma will be embarrassed and all sorts of stuff.'

'What if I can't wait?'

'Then you'll have to go to the public toilets and have a wank, and be careful not to catch anything from the seat.'

'Why are you laughing?' Emma asks. 'You're always laughing.'

'It's Thomas,' she tells her daughter. 'He's so silly.'

The hotel is nothing fancy, but it has a restaurant, which means there is the prospect of putting Emma to bed and dining together on their own. Thomas watches Kale undress her child and give her a bath. Memories of Phil at the same age come flooding back – the same laughter, the same slippery little androgynous body splashing around in the water. Emma screws up her eyes against the soap and seems to find the discomfort funny. 'Is Thomas going to sleep with us?' she asks.

'Of course he is,' her mother replies.

'Is he like Steve?'

'What do you mean by that?'

Emma giggles, half hiding her face. 'Do you cuddle in bed?'

'Of course we do. Now stop being silly and let me dry you.'

'Does he put his willy inside you?'

'Does he do what? Who gave you that idea?'

'That's what ladies and men do, isn't it? But I don't want to do it. Billy Eccles tried to do it to me at school, but I told him to go fuck himself.'

'Emma!'

'Well *you* say that.'

'Mum can say what she likes. But little girls like you can't.' Kale turns to Thomas as though to high authority. He knows that he mustn't smile. He remembers the expression of moral rectitude that one has to maintain when the child is watching.

'Thomas doesn't find that funny, do you? Emma is going to promise me that she won't say words like that again, aren't you, Emms?'

Emma promises, but Thomas senses that she knows all the tricks, the adult evasion and dissembling. She watches him with those bright, knowing eyes as her mother rubs her dry and bundles her into well-worn pyjamas. When finally she is tucked up in her bed she calls for Thomas to come and kiss her goodnight. Confronted with this knowing six-year-old, he feels like an awkward teenager. He bends towards the little face. There is the warm smell of talcum powder and something else, baby pheromones presumably, designed to enmesh an independent adult in the snares of childcare. And as his face approaches her cheek she suddenly turns her head and catches his mouth full on her lips. There is a moment of wetness, and a giggle, and she has turned away.

'I think we're overexcited,' Kale says. The plural is appealing. We. The mother–daughter complex. 'Maybe Thomas should go down to the bar while we read a story.'

'I want Thomas to stay. Thomas can read me a story.'

Thomas obeys Kale, although the temptation is to obey her daughter. He goes down to the bar and orders a Scotch, and only when the deed has been done and Emma is asleep does Kale join him. She has changed. She is wearing one of those dresses that fit all over, a tight tube of sprung cotton, the colour just the purple side of black. The material clings to her as though it is wet. She seems to have nothing whatsoever on underneath – you can see the loose movement of her breasts and the nub of her nipples, you can follow the curve of her belly and thighs. Her stockings are a kind of mesh, for catching minnows. The eyes of the other guests follow her as she perches on a stool at the bar.

'Wow,' he tells her.

'Wow what?'

'Wow, please. That dress. You'd look more decent if you were stark naked.'

'You don't like it?'

'We love it. All of us. Everyone in the bar.'

'It's my special,' she says.

That night they undress quietly, with the silent, sleeping figure of Emma in the folding bed over by the window. 'No noise,' Kale whispers as they move together beneath the sheets. 'Silent as mice,' he assures her. So they make love in the dark, very quietly, while Emma sleeps. And Thomas feels all kinds of things – amorous, perverted, paternal. Those three, and probably others. Fearful, fumbling, fascinated. Fascinated, he knows, is something to do with snakes. Eve was fascinated, snared by a snake.

Twelve

Spring on the island wasn't like the grudging spring of the Peak District. This spring was a startling eruption of nature – Persephone's spring. Suddenly the sun was hot on the face and there were flowers growing in every scrap of dirt. Insects sounded in the vegetation, crickets and cicadas whirring and buzzing like small mechanical devices.

She sat in the garden, writing a letter to Tom.

Darling Tom
I hope the football match went well. I try and imagine you
running round the field in the rain – when here it is bright
sunshine and really very hot . . .

The radio sounded through the open french windows behind her – the radio always seemed to be on in this blessed island – and the new Governor was explaining to the people that we must build bridges of trust between the different communities. His hopes seemed at variance with the facts, for with spring had come the violence. It was only small bombs, targeting things, not people, but you could never be sure. You'd hear the concussion sounding flatly across the city, like a door being slammed. Pigeons would clatter panic-stricken into the sky and people would pause in their work, and then shrug their shoulders and get on with things. There would be a matter-of-fact report on the radio – a sewage plant damaged, a pump-house door blown open, a NAAFI warehouse on fire – and the engineers would set to work and put the damage right. But once again private life was circumscribed by fear and uncertainty. Families living outside the cantonments had been advised to lay in stocks of food to last them for a minimum of two weeks. Tins; no perishables. Prepare for siege. Curfews were often in force, confining people to their houses after dusk. Once more Edward carried a gun when they went anywhere. The wisdom was that when the killing began again women would not be targeted, but men off duty might be. 'It'll get worse before it gets better,' he said, sounding like an old sailor talking of a squall at sea.

Dee didn't write to Tom about all this, of course. She wrote about the chameleon that Paula had found, and cicadas, about Daddy and the visit they'd made to the ruins of Salamis and the votive objects they'd found at Curium – *Nick even came with us and did some digging himself, although I don't think he was very happy about it.* The letter was one of those wordy missives that she put together in the hope – a vain hope? – that when he read it he would hear her talking, feel his mother there beside him, jollying him along and trying to keep her presence in his mind when her bodily presence was so distant and in such a different place. Nothing about bombs and curfews.

Geoffrey is taking us to Umm Haram today. Isn't that a silly name? It's meant to be the tomb of Muhammad's aunt, and apparently there's this large stone that floats over the place, only they've had to prop it up with pillars so that pilgrims aren't frightened. That's what they say, anyway. We'll all go again when you get here for the holidays. Geoffrey says you should still be able to see the flamingos. Not long now, darling Tom. Paula sends her love, and so does Daddy, and so, of course, do I.

She signed off – *With all my love, Mummy* – and sealed the letter. Edward would post it tomorrow. Then she sat for a moment watching Paula searching the bushes, that strange, aimless search of the very young, where they look but never see. 'Maybe it's changed colour,' she called. 'That's what they do. It can't have gone far. Just keep looking.'

Umm Haram

(Muhammad's aunt – some say his foster-mother – who, coming to a place by the Salt Lake of Larnaca, fell from her mule, broke her pellucid neck, and died. *Umm Haram* literally means 'Sacred Mother'.)

Umm Haram came to Kition
In Caliph Othman's reign;
She took a fall and broke her neck
And never went home again.

The Prophet's aunt, probably;
A formidable woman,
Sitting on her mule and giving orders this way and that
Like a memsahib.

What did she think of the place?

A crayon line of pink
As in a child's sketch.
Seascape and landscape touched in lead
By a pencil propped against the sky.

What did she think of the place?

Heat and light polish the water,
And make a covenant of salt
Between God and Man.
The air shivers, like salt on the tongue.

What did she think of the place?

A stumble of the hoof, a sudden lurch,
Engendered there the minaret, mosque and tomb
And pilgrimage and reverence.

Did she think that, in this perfumed grove,
The thin gauze between life and death
Would soon be torn aside,
The covenant redeemed?

Meanings danced on the surface of her mind, settling for an instant before darting out of reach. Was there a solution to the poem? Was it like a puzzle, with a right answer? A covenant of salt seemed strange, and rather frightening. *The air shivers, like salt on the tongue,* she thought, shivering in sympathy, seeing a slug sprinkled with salt, like her mother used to do in the garden at home.

She listened for the sound of Geoffrey's Volkswagen. It was

just her and Paula going with him. She had tried to persuade Edward to come but he had already fixed up some sailing. 'Anyway, I'm not really sure you ought to be going at a time like this. Not with the security situation as it is.'

'The security situation,' she had repeated in careful mockery, 'would be better if you came as well.'

He had shrugged. 'I'm afraid I can't let people down.'

'You're letting me and Paula down.'

'Just be careful, that's all.'

'Geoffrey can look after us. He's been out here long enough.'

'I only hope you're right.'

So it was just the three of them that drove out of Limassol along the coast road towards Larnaca later that morning. 'D'you hear the Governor speaking on the radio?' Geoffrey asked. Away to their right the sea glinted like steel. Ahead of them the peak of Stavrovouni, the Mount of the Holy Cross, rose up from the surrounding hills.

'The man always seems to be pleading,' she said. 'At least Harding told people directly what he thought.'

'Harding was a soldier – this one's a politician. That's the difference. The government think they can work a settlement, so they've got to have a politician in place.'

'And can they?'

'Who knows? The Greeks want union with Greece and the Turks want independence and partition. It's not going to be easy to reconcile those two aspirations. Especially as both parties have the same fall-back position.'

'What's that?'

'Shooting at each other. Hey, have you heard this one? You know the EOKA ban on the use of English lettering? Well apparently the Roxy Cabaret in Nicosia has had to change its sign to Greek lettering. So what's it become? POXY.' Dee laughed. 'It's true,' he said. 'I've seen it myself.

People are queuing up to have a look. Taking photos standing under it.'

'What's poxy mean?' Paula asked from the back. 'What's funny about that?'

'Poxy's rude,' Geoffrey assured her.

'As rude as attitude?'

He gave a shriek of appalled laughter. 'Don't,' he cried. 'Don't!'

The countryside sped past, the landscape green with the spring growth and painted with flowers. There were poppies and marigolds and catchfly, and wild gladioli, and orchids, dozens of different orchids. They passed through villages with slogans painted on the walls, and roadblocks where they had to edge round steel stanchions under the eyes of soldiers touting Lee-Enfield rifles. Beyond Stavrovouni, the crumpled edges of the Troödos massif were ironed out into the plain cloth of the coast. Dull flats under a bright sky. They turned off the main road and followed narrow tracks through grasses and reeds, and then, quite suddenly, there was the surface of the salt lake, glinting like beaten pewter. Geoffrey stopped the car and they got out. The air was heavy with salt, as though salt could be vapour as well as a solute – salt on the skin, salt sticky on the palms of the hands, salt tangible on the lips and tongue. A covenant of salt. Across half a mile of water was the sanctuary of Umm Haram – a cluster of domes like knuckles clenched around the single finger of a pointing minaret. And in the distance there was a faint smudge of pink across the surface of the lake. Flamingos.

'It's like looking at the poem,' Dee said. 'How does it go – a crayon line of pink? Is that it? I was reading it just before you came for us.'

'How flattering.'

'Tell me . . . what's a covenant of salt?'

'Many things.'

'It's biblical, isn't it?'

'Biblical, yes. Numbers, as far as I can remember. And Leviticus. An indissoluble covenant. In the Arab world you cannot do ill to someone who has shared your salt.' He laughed. 'Although salt is very soluble.'

'And what if it loses its savour?'

'What indeed?'

They drove round to the *tekke*. There was no one there, no cars in the rough car park, no pilgrims, no other visitors. A path led through olives and tamarisks to the entrance of the mosque where an ablution fountain dribbled water into the still air. An old man, turbaned and swathed in black and grey, nodded and grinned through a barricade of rotten teeth. Geoffrey gave him some piastres. They left their shoes in the vaulted entrance porch and tiptoed in. Paula giggled at going barefoot – 'like a paddling pool,' she said.

Dee hushed her. 'It's like going into church.'

'Is there Jesus?'

'No, not Jesus. But there is God.'

Inside there was that strange emptiness that mosques possess – no altar, no pews or chairs, no clutter of statues or icons – as though the vaulted space had been left vacant in order to accommodate what cannot be seen: a sense of the numinous. There were just three worshippers: two old men in baggy black trousers and a youth wearing ordinary clothes. They took no notice of the intruders, but went about their business with the silent method of workmen at their craft, standing, bowing, kneeling, prostrating themselves to touch their foreheads to the ground. The air was soft and humid, thick with the smell of feet.

'They're saying their prayers,' Dee whispered to Paula.

'Do they believe in God?'

'Of course. They believe in their God.'

'Is he different from ours?'

Geoffrey led them round to the opposite side of the chamber, keeping to the wall as though leaving all the space to the worshippers. Behind the *mihrab* was the entrance to the domed mausoleum, and there, immersed in a stifling darkness, was the tomb itself. The upright pillars were draped in black velvet so that, to the believing eye, the massive cross-stone floated in the shadows four feet off the ground. Geoffrey leaned towards Dee and breathed in her ear. 'This is the very spot where the old dear broke her pellucid neck.'

Dee hushed him to silence, trying not to laugh, trying not to destroy the solemn nature of the place. They stood there for a long while in the silence, with only the scuffing of Paula's feet sounding in the tomb chamber, and the muttering of prayer coming through the doorway behind them. Dee was conscious of Geoffrey's presence just beside her, so close that she could feel the warmth of him and the touch of his arm.

For lunch they drove to a place that Geoffrey knew. It was down an unmade track that wound through the coastal flats and finally stopped at a sandy car park among the dunes. The taverna was little more than a shack, with a rickety wooden terrace built over the beach. There was no one else around. Geoffrey was greeted with laughter and much flashing of gold teeth by the ancient crone who ran the place. She clapped her hands in delight at the sight of Dee and Paula and pinched the little girl's cheek. '*Koukles,*' she cried. '*Koukles!*'

'She thinks you're both dolls,' Geoffrey explained. 'It's intended as a compliment.' A cool breeze rattled the cane chicks that sheltered the tables, but it was warm in the sunshine. Paula hurried through her food and ran down to the water. She hitched up her skirt, kicked her shoes off and paddled in the shallows, while the adults watched from their table. 'Thank you for being such a good guide,' Dee said.

'Did you enjoy it?'

'Umm Haram? Beautiful. Very strange.'

He lit a cigarette and blew a stream of smoke into the air. 'Can I ask you a question?'

Paula was coming out of the water, holding something in her hand. 'Look Mummy! Look!'

'What is it? What have you found?'

She came up the steps to their table, her feet leaving wet prints. She had found an oval shell, with a lucid brown pattern on the convex side, but as white and hard and polished as porcelain on the underside. A cowrie shell.

'Is it beautiful, Mummy?'

'It's very beautiful.'

The adults turned the shell over in their hands, looked at it with knowing eyes. The underside clearly resembled the female vulva.

'Can I keep it?'

'Of course you can. Go and see if there's another one.'

The little girl scampered away. Dee put the shell down on the table and looked up at Geoffrey. What, she wondered, was coming? Some personal confession? Was she about to be embarrassed? 'Go on.'

'It's about that taxi firm you use.'

'Taxi firm? What about it?'

'Phaedon Taxis, isn't it?'

It struck her how he pronounced the name, the d given the sound of th – 'phaethon'. 'What on earth are you talking about, Geoffrey?'

'What do you think of them?'

'They're all right. They seem safer than most of the others. Fewer dents. Why on earth do you ask?'

'What if I told you that the owner is an EOKA suspect?'

'Stavros? How on earth do you know that?'

'Things one hears.'

She didn't know whether to laugh. There was something absurd about Geoffrey, deliberately absurd, as though anything that might happen was, to him, some kind of joke. She had expected Guppy and marital crisis, maybe even some kind of confession, and she got Stavros and EOKA. 'I can't believe it. He's a rather unctuous little man, but quite harmless I'm sure.'

'Unctuous.' Geoffrey repeated the word with glee. 'Well, the story is that he is part of the oil that lubricates EOKA. So people tell me.'

'Who tells you?'

'Certain people.'

'How mysterious you're being, Geoffrey.'

'I'm being serious. That's a different thing. Could you keep what I'm going to say to yourself? I'd rather you didn't even tell Edward.'

'I can't keep secrets from my husband.'

He smiled. 'Oh yes you can. All wives can keep secrets, even if it's only the contents of their handbags.'

She blushed and reached for a cigarette as some kind of distraction. Paula was still splashing around in the water, trying to find another of her shells. The breeze had died away. 'Go on then,' she said quietly.

'Promise me?'

'I promise.'

He drew on his cigarette and stared out to sea.

'The year before last the Army more or less wrapped EOKA up in the mountains. You've heard all about that, haven't you? Operation Lucky Alphonse, and the forest fire.'

'People say it was started by the terrorists. It was a bit of a disaster, wasn't it? Nineteen British soldiers killed, half the Paphos Forest burned down.'

'That was a bit of a setback. In almost every other respect it was a victory – because it virtually destroyed the EOKA presence in Troödos. The only thing that took away from total victory was that old Grievous escaped. Somehow he was smuggled through the army lines—'

'Dressed as a woman, that's the story. Jennifer Powell told me.'

'Jennifer Powell doesn't know her arse from her elbow. What is more likely is that he was hidden in a car. We have information that unctuous Stavros Kyprianou did the driving.'

'Stavros?' She thought of the fat man and his little, twinkling feet. Somehow she'd always imagined him as a ballroom dancer, twirling his partner round, executing complex steps, his smile as fixed and smarmy as his Brylcreemed hair. 'That seems fantastic.'

Geoffrey turned towards her. 'If Kyprianou did do the driving, it means that he is trusted within the organization.'

'Even if it's true, what has it got to do with me?'

'You seem to know the family.'

She laughed. He *was* absurd. He was playing a joke, leading up to one of his punchlines. 'Hardly. I've only spoken to Stavros a few times. Once I was invited in for a coffee. You know the kind of thing. Glasses of water and lots of smiling and no real communication. They offered me those candied fruit . . .'

'*Glyká.*'

'His nephew Nicos translated for me, and that was that. You know I don't speak Greek, Geoffrey. I know less about them than you could get from chatting to Stavros in a bar. Oh yes, Nicos went to school in north London and he likes that rock and roll stuff. There you are, that's a useful bit of information.'

Geoffrey seemed indifferent to her sarcasm. He sipped his

coffee. 'Nicos. Yes, that's the lad's name. Nikolaos. "Victorious people", that's what it means, more or less. Nike was the goddess of victory.'

'You can't blame him for his name.'

'I'm not blaming him for anything, yet. Except for the fact that he seems to have taken quite a shine to you.'

'He reminds me vaguely of someone I once knew. An old boyfriend.' And then comprehension dawned. 'How do you know he's taken a shine to me, as you put it?'

'Isn't it true?'

'Maybe it is, but how do you know?'

He smiled. 'We have our ways.'

'We, Geoffrey? Who's "*we*"? Have people been watching me, Geoffrey? Is that it?'

'For your own sake,' he said. 'Lest you break your pellucid neck.'

The shock was palpable, like a blow in the abdomen. She imagined men in fawn raincoats, with cheap cigarettes and battered trilby hats. Something out of Graham Greene or Eric Ambler. And then she thought of Marjorie, plump, motherly Marjorie, and wondered whether she was the secret watcher, the whisperer of secrets. 'And now what are you suggesting?' she demanded.

He took a last drag on his cigarette and stubbed it out. 'We thought you might get to know him better. Get him into your confidence. Win him over. You know the kind of thing?'

'*We* thought, Geoffrey? Who is this "we"?'

'People I work with occasionally. You could help us, if you were willing to play a part.'

She should be angry. She should be telling him to get lost. But there was something ridiculous about the whole conversation, something implausible that just made her want to laugh. 'Who do you think I am? Mata Hari?'

'I think you are a tough and loyal Yorkshirewoman, actually. Someone who did her bit in the war and will do her bit now.'

Paula called, 'Mummy, I can't find any more. I've looked, but there aren't any.'

'You must come in now, darling. It's time to go.'

Her daughter hesitated, standing in the shallows with the water creaming around her ankles.

'If you don't come in now, you'll get cold.'

'Think about it,' Geoffrey said. 'Just mull it over.'

They were silent on the drive back. Dee was entirely bewildered by this conversation. She had thought of Geoffrey as a poet, a world-weary bank official, a *bon viveur*, a philhellene and classical scholar, and now he was presented to her in a startling new light. Spy? Secret agent? The very idea seemed nonsensical, the kind of idiocy that Geoffrey himself would have invented as a joke. Cloak and dagger. He had even – she recalled this with a small start of amusement – gone to the New Year's Eve fancy-dress party in the mess at Episkopi wearing a cloak and brandishing a dagger. Everyone had laughed at his antics. Good old Geoffrey, they'd said. Not like a civilian at all. Quite one of us.

'He's just a young boy, Geoffrey,' she said when they stopped outside the house. 'He's an innocent, an outsider dumped in this place just because he happens to have relatives here. I can't believe he'll have any knowledge that'll be useful.'

'Who's a young boy?' Paula asked.

'Nobody you know,' Dee told her. They waited while her daughter ran ahead of them up the path.

'You'd be surprised what's useful to us,' Geoffrey said. 'Often it's the innocent ones who are the best sources.' There was no pretence now. It was 'we' and 'us', not 'they' and 'them'. Who *was* Geoffrey Crozier? For whom did he work? 'Anyway, think it over. Give it some time and let me know. But please' – he smiled, his old beaming smile – 'please don't say anything to anyone. Let's keep everything secret, shall we? A covenant of salt.' He glanced at his watch. 'Is that the time? I really must be going.' He touched her on the arm. 'You'd only have to listen, Dee. Make him want to talk to you. Give him a shoulder to cry on.'

'How do you know he needs to cry on anyone's shoulder?'

'Don't all men?'

She hesitated. 'Do you, Geoffrey?'

He seemed to think for a moment, as though he were lost for words. Geoffrey was never lost for words. Then he leaned forward and kissed her on the cheek. 'More than most,' he said, and turned back to the car.

Dee watched him drive away. She watched the empty street long after his car had clattered out of sight. She sensed the whole island around her, Aphrodite's island, Saint Paul's and Saint Barnabas' island, Umm Haram's island, the island of hate and love, a fabric that could hold together for a while but would come apart sooner or later. She thought of EOKA fighters holed up in the mountains and hidden in the villages and towns; and British soldiers stalking them through the forests and the alleyways. She thought of Damien, and she thought of Nicos, each of them woven into this fabric for no particular reason other than the workings of spiteful chance. The noise of thought sounded in her head like a dozen voices all talking to her at once: Edward, Paula with her trusting innocence, and strange, remote Tom, who came into the family during the holidays with his pedantic manner and thoughtful way of looking at adults, as though he were storing things away in his mind like a miser with a cache of coins. Children had been all she had ever wanted, motherhood all she had ever aspired to; and now there were other things.

The taxi threaded its way through the traffic by the bus station, behind donkey carts and ramshackle buses and battered cars. Nowadays taking a taxi wasn't a luxury, it was a necessity – you were advised against taking public transport and going out alone. A taxi was the only solution.

She watched the back of Nicos' head as he drove – the oiled hair, the careful sculpting. 'Duck's tail' was what they called the style; 'duck's arse', the soldiers said. Sometimes his eyes would catch hers in the rear-view mirror and hold her gaze, for a fraction longer than one might expect. What was he thinking? Marjorie had said that he was soft on her, and warned her off; Geoffrey wanted her to exploit that very weakness and draw him closer to her, give him a shoulder to cry on, or a lap to lie in, or whatever it might be. What, she wondered, did *he* want?

The vehicle came to a halt. 'Something up ahead,' Nicos said. There were cars and trucks and people milling around. An army Land-Rover drove past and then a ten-tonner, loaded with soldiers. With the windows down you could hear a distant noise, like an insensate sea sound, roaring and crashing. Along the street shopkeepers were slamming down their shutters.

'What's going on?'

'Demonstration.' Nicos looked round to see if he could turn the car, but they were pinned in the traffic. There was a bus directly behind them, its driver craning to see. 'We'll just have to sit it out,' he said. 'Best stay in the car.'

Youths ran past, like kids running out of school, darting and jumping, laughing and shouting. Some carried banners, crudely painted. There were English words: FOOT NO, HARDING YES! and the single word TAXIM. People pressed around them. There was the sudden smash of breaking glass from the bus. One of the youths was throwing stones.

'Who is it? What sort of demonstration?'

'Turks,' Nicos said. The very name 'Turk' carried with it a threat. It went with 'Hun' and 'Vandal' and bore in its sound the sharp plosives of violence. Dee felt panic welling up. *Turks.* Someone hammered on the roof, a great concussion battering on her head, like thunder discharged from a dark cloud.

'Hey!'

Was it Nicos who shouted? The car rocked like a boat in a storm. He twisted round and leaned over the seat and grabbed her hand. 'You're all right,' he said. 'I'll look after you.' People were all around the car now, a great scrum of people, dark faces staring in at the windows. A woman screamed, and then an amplified voice called over the hubbub in words that were Greek or Turkish, Dee couldn't tell which. Then the crowd had gone, like a squall passing by, and there was a kind of stillness.

'You all right, Mrs D?' Nicos released her hand. It was sore where he had grabbed it, but his grasp had been a comfort, as though just by holding her he might have protected her in some way. It was difficult to read his look – his expression was pinched and pale, perhaps with fear, perhaps with anger. 'You OK?' he asked.

'More or less. Where are the police?'

His laugh was laden with sarcasm. 'The Turks *are* the police, Mrs D.'

'Can't we get moving? Can't we get out of here?'

'It's all blocked.'

Now there were soldiers coming past, wearing helmets and carrying shields made of chicken wire. They had pickaxe handles in their hands. A group of them wore gas masks. These looked inhuman, like amphibians of some kind, frogs thrown down from the sky by the passing storm. But they were only the lads who visited Marjorie's canteen, the youths from Birmingham or Manchester or Liverpool, National Servicemen measuring out their time in the colonies.

Then she saw Damien. He was walking along beside an army Land-Rover following the soldiers. There was a sergeant in the vehicle and a corporal driver at the wheel, but Damien was walking. He was in uniform and wearing a beret. At his waist was a webbing pistol holster and tucked beneath his right arm was an officer's cane – what they called a swagger stick. But he was not swaggering. He was walking briskly, as though to an appointment, looking around him with interest, talking to the sergeant occasionally. In the back of the Land-Rover was a signaller with a radio. The whip aerial swayed above the vehicle like the antenna of a cockroach.

She wound down the window. 'Damien!' she cried. And then, an instinctive sense of propriety taking over: 'Major Braudel!'

He turned, frowning.

'Over here!' she called.

He said something to the sergeant, then hurried across the street. There was that brisk, military manner, the slick transfer of his cane from right arm to left, the snapping of a salute. It seemed comical to be saluted, especially by him. He leaned in at the window. 'Dee, what the hell are you doing in the middle of all this?'

'I was at Marjorie's.'

'Didn't you know there was going to be some trouble? Do you need help? Are you OK?' He noticed the driver and laughed. 'Can't the Teddy boy get you home safely?'

Dee felt angry and defensive. 'He's been marvellous.'

'I can look after Mrs D all right,' Nicos said.

Damien seemed amused. 'Jolly good fellow. Look, I'm afraid I can't stay chatting like this. I'll try and send someone round to see that you're safely home. OK?'

He smiled, and touched his beret in a mockery of a salute. She noticed the cap badge, a bugle-horn hanging from ribbons, like a toy. 'Must go,' he said. And then he had returned to the Land-Rover and was talking to the sergeant again.

Nicos began to manoeuvre the car, screwing round to look out of the back window. The engine roared. He spun the wheel, jerked the car back and forth in the narrow street, and suddenly they were free of the jam and going back the way they had come. 'This ought to get us out of here,' he said, turning down a side street. And sure enough they had cleared the traffic and were driving through narrow back streets, and then the empty suburbs, the deserts of waste ground and building sites that formed a shifting hinterland around the core of the city. Nicos caught her eye and grinned. She began to recognize landmarks – the fire station, the police barracks, and then Demetris' corner shop and the sign saying 16TH OF JUNE STREET.

The road was deserted. No inhabitant in any garden, no customer in Demetris' shop, no one sitting in the cars parked against the kerb. In the silent suburban street only lizards moved. The riot, demonstration, whatever it was, seemed to have taken place in another world.

'Here we are, Mrs D. Home sweet home. Did you think we wouldn't never make it?' *Fink*, he said.

'You did very well, Nicos.' She felt she should make up for Damien's mockery. 'Why don't you come in for a cup of tea or something, after all that excitement?'

'That's real decent of you, Mrs D. Real nice.' He leaped out to hold the door open for her. 'If I can just make a phone call. Tell 'em where I am.'

'Of course.'

She led him inside – 'There's the phone' – and went into the kitchen. She could hear him dialling and then talking rapidly in

Greek. Foreign, staccato sounds, surprisingly alien. Not like French or Italian, where you could pick out words even if you couldn't speak the language. There was something disconcerting about having him here in the house. No longer a youth; an adult, male, taller than her and stronger.

A moment later he appeared at the kitchen door. There was that glance of amusement, that uncertain reflection of Charteris, just as soon vanished as noticed. She put the kettle on. 'Make yourself at home. Do you want tea or coffee? It's only Nescafé, I'm afraid.'

'Nescaff's fine.'

'So what's going to happen now?' she asked as she bent to get the cups out of the cupboard. She sensed him eyeing her. She felt disturbingly vulnerable, and yet the sensation was not unpleasant. It was like someone stroking the palm of her hand, evoking a shiver of delight.

'Happen?'

'In Limassol. Now the Turks have had their riot, what's EOKA going to do?'

'Why do you ask me about EOKA, Mrs D?'

She turned. 'Don't you know? Doesn't every Greek Cypriot know what's going to happen? EOKA's like an endemic disease, isn't it? Everyone's infected.'

He watched her, puzzled. 'What's endemic mean?'

'It's Greek, so you ought to know. And you're evading the question.'

'Well, what do you want me to say?'

'The truth. About how you feel.'

'There's a truth for yourself and a truth for others, isn't there?'

'Is there? What's that supposed to mean? You say one thing to one person and another thing to someone else?'

'More or less. You smile and say polite things to the British, but inside you want EOKA to win because at least it's Greek. At least it's us, rather than a bunch of snotty-nosed toffs from Eton or wherever.'

'And that's what you do with me, say polite things to my face while thinking something else?' The kettle came to the boil. She spooned the brown dust, poured water, stirred. To her surprise her hands were shaking. Maybe it was the aftershock of the demonstration. Maybe it was this conversation with Nicos, quite unlike any they had had before.

'Why do you want to know what I think, anyway?' Nicos asked.

'Because I like you and I want to understand you. And EOKA. I want to understand EOKA. No one else seems to, none of the people I meet.' She put the cup of coffee on the table. The question of EOKA lay between them, dangerous and ugly like a weapon – like the Sterling submachine gun that had lain on the front seat of the car taking her and Tom to the airport. 'You don't have to say anything if you don't want to. This isn't a court of law. But you can't pretend it doesn't matter.'

'What if I did say what I think? Where would it get me?'

'I'd listen.'

'Fat lot of good that'd do. You British can never understand.' He sipped his coffee, blew across the surface to cool it. 'Sorry,' he said, and suddenly she was reminded of Charteris again: the same sharp anger, the same wry apology. And a sheepish grin. 'I shouldn't have said that. You're different.'

She laughed. 'Am I? I hope I am.' She offered him a cigarette – you couldn't get Players on the open market any longer, not since the EOKA ban on British goods – and he accepted eagerly, cocking his head on one side as he lit it. It was a practised gesture that smacked of James Dean or Frank Sinatra, one of those Americans he idolized. 'So tell me. Tell me what you think.'

He drew in the smoke and then let it out in a thin stream, watching her all the time. 'OK. I believe in an idea, see? The idea's called democracy and it means rule by the people and it was invented by the Greeks two and a half thousand years ago. And ever since then the Greek people of Cyprus have been denied it – by the Romans, by the Turks and now by the British. Now I believe it's time for us to take it back, and unite with our brothers and sisters in Greece itself. OK? When I was in Enfield I used to get into trouble – you know, picking fights, that kind of stuff. About nothing. Just for the sake of it. Bloody silly when you think about it. But here . . .' he hesitated, smiled nervously, '. . . well here I reckon there's something worth getting into a fight over.'

'Against us?'

'It's not against the British. We love the British, don't you see that?' His tone was urgent, willing her to believe him. 'The British fought with us when the Germans came. They were on our side. And they did the same when we were fighting for freedom from the Turks. The British are our friends. Here in Cyprus, we're not fighting against the British. Believe me, Mrs D. What we are fighting is the people who are occupying our land.' He looked embarrassed, as though aware he had transgressed some invisible barrier. 'I'm sorry. I should've shut up.'

'I asked you.'

'Yeah, but it's dangerous to say what you feel. Especially knowing what I know.'

'What do you know?'

He laughed – a sharp, ironic sound. 'I know things they'd kill me for, if they knew I was talking to you like this.'

'Don't be silly, Nicos.'

'I'm not being silly, either.'

'So what do you know that's so dangerous?'

He looked up at her standing there at the sink. 'I know that I'm in love with you,' he said.

She blushed. 'Don't be silly.'

'You asked me and I've said it.'

She turned away and looked out of the window on to the dusty garden. This foreign world, of sudden violence, of sun and heat and passion, disturbed her. It wasn't fear she felt. She had mistaken it for fear at first, but now she knew it was something different – a sense of elation, a feeling of being alive more acutely because of the very closeness of death.

The palm tree rattled in the breeze. A lizard darted along the windowsill. Behind her she heard the scrape of his chair being pushed back. She knew, of course. Without turning she could interpret the sounds and the things that were more than sound – a movement, a perception of presence, the faint exhalation of breath just behind her. When she turned he was there, standing over her, mere inches away.

She tried to read his face: the eyes with their wide pupils, the tightening of his jaw, the sudden, lizard dart of his tongue. His Adam's apple bobbed as he swallowed. Men had prominent Adam's apples, women did not, as a rule. Why was that? Something to do with glands, the thyroid maybe. Or the parathyroid. How did she know things like that? How could she think of them at a moment like this?

'Nicos, what are you doing?' He was close enough for the warmth of his body to be perceptible, and she put up her hand and placed it against his chest. His heart was beating rapidly, like an animal trapped there beneath her palm. He closed his hand over hers and kept it there. This, she guessed, was what he did with the girls in the dance halls, the shallow girls with beehive hairstyles and over-made-up faces. 'Please, Nicos,' she whispered. 'Don't do anything silly.'

He laughed faintly, that dry, sarcastic sound. 'You like me, don't you?'

'Of course I like you . . .'

'There you are, then.' He leaned forward. She held herself very still. One of his hands was in the small of her back, pulling her against him, and she was conscious of the thinness of her dress, the only thing between her and him, a mere scrap of cotton. His eyes watched hers carefully, as though he was looking for something there.

'Nicos,' she said.

'What is it, Mrs D?'

'We shouldn't be doing this.'

A breath of amusement. He wasn't stupid. He'd noticed. *We.* 'D'you want us to stop?' he asked.

'Please.' The word was equivocal, everything was equivocal. He moved forward and she could feel his breath, not bad but strange: the cigarette he had smoked and the coffee he had drunk, and something else that was him alone. Then he touched his lips on hers. Just fractionally she opened her mouth. His tongue slipped inside, like a thief in the night, moving here and there as though looking to see what there was to steal. She pulled away, turned her head aside, swallowing the saliva that was there. His and hers, presumably.

'Oh, God,' she whispered. 'Please don't.' She felt a terrifying shortage of breath, as though his mere presence might suffocate her.

Slowly he relaxed his grip. 'There, you see,' he said, as though by letting her go he was demonstrating something – trustworthiness perhaps, honour, decency, all those qualities that people pay lip service to.

She extricated herself from his grasp and went over to her handbag. 'What do I see? What am I meant to see, Nicos?' She took out a cigarette and lit it with trembling hands.

'You see that I'd never hurt you. That I'd never do anything you don't want me to.'

She tried a laugh. 'I'm not sure I wanted you to kiss me.'

'You didn't stop me, though.'

She drew on her cigarette, felt the smoke calm her. 'Perhaps you'd better go. Cool down a bit.'

'I thought you liked me,' he said.

'I do. Of course I do.'

'I mean, *really* liked me. You know what I mean. You look at me sometimes . . . and I think, you know . . .'

'What do you think?'

'That if it wasn't like it is, it'd be different.'

'Well that's obvious. A tautology.'

He shook his head. 'I haven't got a chance with someone like you, have I? Me talking like I do and not knowing half of what you know an' all. It's me that's wrong, isn't it? Too young, although it's only a few years, and I can't talk posh like you, and I'm a Cyp. I mean, if I were like that officer bloke it'd be all right.'

'What on earth are you talking about?'

'You know what I mean. The one that was there today. The one you met in the bar.'

She didn't know what to say really. There was something comic and strangely moving about him, both at the same time. 'Major Braudel is just a friend.'

The boy grinned. 'That's what they all say. Just good friends, like Princess Margaret and that group-captain fellow. I'm not stupid, you know. But don't worry. I'm not going to tell on you. Your secret's safe with me—'

'There is no secret.'

'—just as my secret is safe with you. We're obligated to one another, aren't we?'

'What do you mean, obligated?' She wasn't even sure whether

the word existed. Obliged? The thought almost made her smile, almost brought laughter, which would have been dreadful. He would have thought she was laughing at him.

'We both got secrets, haven't we? What I said is true. They'd kill me if they knew I was with you like this. Dangerous, see? Knowledge.' His expression was difficult to interpret. There was a look of imprecation about it, as though he were risking everything in this one throw.

'*Kill* you? Who'd kill you?'

He nodded. 'I told you: I know things.'

She drew on her cigarette, cast around for some way out. 'Look, really it'd be better if you went. And forget that this business ever happened.'

He seemed to take breath, as though summoning up his courage. 'I know where Dighenis is hiding.'

At that moment the doorbell rang. The sound rattled through the house, shrill and frenetic. There was sudden panic in the boy's face. Dee looked round, startled. 'I'd better get it.' She stubbed out her cigarette and hurried to the front door. Her hands were still shaking as she struggled with the handle. The door opened on to the bright light of the veranda, and there was Damien. His Land-Rover was parked on the far side of the road with the sergeant watching from the driver's seat.

He grinned. 'I said someone would drop by. Everything OK? You got home safely?' Something must have shown in her expression. 'What's happened?'

'Nothing.'

He came forward. 'Dee, are you all right?'

'I'm quite all right.'

Nicos appeared in the hallway behind her. 'I'd better be off,' he said. He pushed past and headed down the path.

'What's up?' Damien asked. 'What's been going on?'

'It doesn't matter. Really.'

'Hey, you!' he called out.

The sergeant moved. Nicos had reached the gate and the soldier had left the Land-Rover and was crossing the road towards him, his Sterling levelled at the youth's stomach. Dee screamed, 'No! Let him be.'

Nicos stopped and glanced back, his expression smudged with fear. There was a moment of stillness, the two men standing there in the road in the spring sunshine, military khaki against civilian white and grey. Dee noticed other things: a Morris van down at the corner shop; a bird, some brilliantly coloured species, scratching in one of the palm trees in the garden; a dog barking from a neighbour's plot. 'For God's sake let him go,' she said to Damien. 'He's done nothing.'

Damien hesitated. 'It's all right, Sarn't,' he called out. 'You can let the lad go.'

Cautiously the sergeant lowered his weapon. Nicos said something, but they couldn't catch the words. The sergeant's reply was clear: 'Just push off, lad, and don't make any trouble.'

They watched Nicos get into his car and start the engine. He glanced round at Dee, directly at Dee, and then drove away, accelerating hard so that stones skittered out from under the tyres. Damien called, 'Sergeant Borthwick, just give me a minute or two, will you?' and took Dee's elbow to steer her inside. 'What's going on? Tell me what happened.'

She stopped in the shadows of the hallway. She wanted to appear composed and collected, but somehow she was trembling. 'Nothing.'

He turned her to face him, put his hands on her shoulders. 'Nothing happened, my foot. Tell me what's up. Do you want me to phone Edward?'

'No, no don't do that.' She put her hand up to stop him,

placed it on his chest just as she had with Nicos. 'I'll be all right. It's just . . . He's mixed up, that's all. We were talking.'

'You want to be careful, talking to the natives. If it gets you upset.'

'Why must you talk about them like that? Why must you always put them down? They're people, just like us.'

'It was meant to be a joke.'

'The joke wears thin at times. Look, I'm sorry, Damien. I feel confused, that's all. It's been a bit of a morning, what with the riot and everything. Can I get you something, a cup of tea perhaps? Do you want to get your sergeant in?'

'He can wait a few minutes.' He followed her into the kitchen. 'You know we pulled your friend in the other day?'

She turned, alarmed. 'What do you mean?'

'Your Teddy boy. A couple of my lads pulled him in for questioning.'

'They did what?'

He was smiling. 'Took him in on suspicion. Something that came through from our intelligence officer. I shouldn't be telling you this, but it's for your own good. They gave him a going over.'

'What does that mean? What's a "going over" for God's sake? Did they hurt him? He never said a word to me—'

'Oh, come on, Dee. We're fighting terrorists here. People expect to be picked up and interrogated. They know the score—'

'Score? So it's a game, is it? Well it's not to him. It's his country and his people . . .'

He was still smiling, that placid, patronizing smile. 'If I didn't know you better, Dee, I'd be wondering about the two of you.'

The moment seemed suspended, like a breath held. She felt herself redden. 'You don't know me at all, Damien,' she said.

His smile faded. 'Maybe I don't. Look, forget the tea, eh? I'd better be going. There's a war out there to fight.'

'A war?'

'Another joke.' He turned and made for the front door. 'I'll be in touch. Keep out of the town, if I were you. The next few days . . .'

She opened the door to let the light flood in.

Damien put his beret on and turned to her. 'It's you,' he said quietly. 'You're the problem. It makes it difficult getting things right.' Then he went out into the daylight and down the path towards the waiting Land-Rover.

She watched as the vehicle drove away, down past the corner shop owned by Stavros' cousin and round on to the main road. The Morris van was still by the shop. It had Greek writing on the side. ΑΦΡΟΔΙΤΗ, it said: APHRODITE. It was always Aphrodite on this bloody island. She watched for a while but no one appeared. Then she went inside and closed the door, and stood in the silence of the hall. The frightening thing was the muddle of emotion that she felt, the very plurality of it, the vivid, crowding sensation of paradox – desire and loathing, love and hate, attraction and repulsion, the first of each dyad directed at him, the second at herself.

'You know I got caught up in that Turkish demonstration in town?' She mentioned it casually, as though it didn't matter.

Edward looked up from his plate. 'You what?'

'It was nothing. I'd been down to Marjorie's and on the way back we drove into it. It soon dispersed. The troops were there.'

'It's bloody ridiculous, you going round on your own like that.'

'I wasn't on my own. I took a taxi. That lad Nicos – you know the one. Damien Braudel's unit was there in the middle of the whole thing, poor fellow. It was all over in a moment and no harm done. But it was pretty scary at the time.'

'Well, I really think you ought to be more sensible about going into town these days.'

'But I was being sensible. I took a taxi, didn't I? I always take a car. And what are the police and the Army for, if not to keep civilians safe? Do you know they arrested Nicos the other day? That's what Damien told me. They took him in for questioning. Isn't it incredible?'

'Is it? Any Greek under the age of eighty seems a good enough suspect these days.'

'But what about principles? I mean, just dragging someone off the street.'

'How do you know what their reason was? You can't just apply your half-baked socialist ideas to a situation like this.' He turned back to his food. 'We never did invite Braudel and his wife round to dinner. Didn't you want to?'

'I can't believe he'd hurt anyone.'

'Who, Braudel?'

'No. Nicos. He goes out of his way to help.'

'If I know taxi drivers, I'd guess he goes out of his way in order to earn a bigger fare.'

She got up from the table and began clearing the dishes. 'Shall I give him a ring then?'

'Who, your taxi driver?'

'Don't be daft. Damien Braudel. We haven't had Binty and Douglas round for ages, and perhaps we could invite the Frindles. But we'd need another female. That's the trouble here – there are so few single women you can invite.'

'I thought he'd got a wife.'

'She'll be back in England by now.'

'What about Marjorie?'

She laughed. 'What a pair they'd make.'

The next day there was a coffee morning at Episkopi. She didn't have to go, of course. She'd often turned such invitations down, but she didn't want to gain a reputation of being standoffish. And Binty wasn't going, which meant that she couldn't get a lift from her. So she was left with no alternative.

She prepared breakfast for Edward and Paula and saw them off in the car, and then went inside to busy herself round the house. There were things to get ready for Tom's return for the Easter holidays – his clothes to go through, his room to sort out. '*Paidi mou erchetai*,' she explained to the maid. '*Se treis imeres*.' Voula laughed, as though the idea of Tom's imminent arrival was a mild but harmless delusion. And all the time there was this sensation in her chest, behind her breastbone, her state of mind rendered physical. Was it fear? Anxiety, yes; and embarrassment. But was there fear among the confusion? She couldn't tell, that was the absurd thing – she couldn't recognize her own feelings. But the physical manifestation was there surely enough: an unsteadiness in her chest, a sensation that seemed localized in the front of her neck where the collarbones came within an inch of one another and there was a smooth hollow like the imprint of a thumb: a fluttering of anticipation.

When finally she picked up the phone, it was something of a relief that Stavros' voice answered. 'I need a car,' she told him. 'As soon as possible, please. I'm sorry, I should have rung earlier, but—'

'Of course, my lady. I send Nicos.' The upward intonation in his voice seemed to make it a question. A small cloud of suspicion gathered.

'Can't you do it yourself?'

'I'm sorry, my lady. There are businesses for me to do. But don't worry. Five minutes, a car is there. Nicos, he won't drive you through a demonstration this time. This time he go the safe way.' It was a joke. They laughed at either end of the line, separated by more than mere distance. 'The Turks,' he added, 'are great trouble.'

So, she thought, are the Greeks. She went back to Tom's room. There was his little collection of archaeological relics to be dusted, things they had found at Curium when they had gone with Nicos the previous year. They'd dug with a trowel, illicitly, among the dust and stones to discover bits of votive objects – a bull's head, a crude female torso – and pot handles and potsherds and an enigmatic fragment of painted plaster. Cleaning them was a task that she couldn't entrust to the clumsy Voula.

A few minutes later she heard the sound of a car drawing up outside and Voula answering the door. She recognized Nicos' voice, and the phrase '*Kyria* Denham'. 'I'm coming,' she called. 'I won't be a minute.'

She paused, then picked up the pride of Tom's collection – a tear bottle. The glass was opalescent, tainted green and blue, shining like sunlight reflected from the surface of the sea. She dusted it carefully, as though it mattered, then returned it to its precise place and went out to get her things.

Nicos didn't look her in the eye as she appeared. He was leaning against the wing of the taxi and as she came near he just opened the door for her, waited while she climbed in, then slid behind the wheel to start the engine.

'Miss Marjorie's, is it?' he asked. His eyes avoided hers.

'Episkopi. There's a coffee morning.' Why did she offer that information? What did it matter to him?

'OK,' he said. 'Episkopi.'

*

The road traipsed westwards out of the city. Signs announced Coca-Cola and Keo beer and Hellas cigarettes. They passed through the pungent stench of a carob factory, and then the buildings gave way to the dense green of orange groves. The surprising, perfect cube of Kolossi Castle appeared above the trees, looking like some kind of geometrical puzzle that you might disassemble into a bewildering collection of irregular pieces and never find the way to put back together. They slowed behind a donkey cart as an army lorry passed by on the opposite side. For an instant Nicos' eyes met hers in the reflection of the mirror.

'I didn't think you'd call me again,' he said.

'I didn't, I just called for a car.'

'I'm sorry,' he said. 'About what happened yesterday.'

'It's all right. There's nothing to apologize for.'

'You're angry.'

'No, I'm not. Not angry.'

'What, then?'

'Upset,' she said.

'What d'you mean by upset?'

'Many things. Unhappy, miserable, confused, disappointed. Many things.'

His eyes were there for a moment. 'Which of those?'

'Most of them.'

The citrus groves gave way to scrub and the road began to climb. He changed down through the gears as the car snaked upwards through cistus and carob and dry white limestone, a tortured landscape of twisted ravines and pillars. The story was that this had been caused by an earthquake, the same earthquake that destroyed the ancient city of Curium up ahead on the ridge. That's what Geoffrey had told her. She sat in the oily interior of the car and watched the countryside pass. 'Can you stop, please?' she asked. 'I'm not feeling well.'

'I can't stop here, Mrs D.' He glanced round. 'I'll pull over when we get to the top, if that's all right.'

'Please.'

At the summit there was a rough turning to the left where a battered sign announced the authority of the Cyprus Department of Antiquities. ANCIENT CITY OF CURIUM, it said. NO ENTRY. NO PARKING. Someone had discharged a shotgun into the centre of the notice, creating a nebula of rust spots. They pulled off the road and Dee opened the door and climbed out. There was a warm, southerly breeze and she stood there breathing deeply for a while, with her face into the wind.

Nicos got out on the far side of the car and looked across the roof at her. 'Are you OK?'

'Just a bit carsick.'

'I've got some water.'

'I'll be all right.'

'Look,' he said. 'I said things—'

'It doesn't matter. It doesn't matter what you said. Really. Forgive and forget.'

He shook his head. 'There are some things that I don't want you to forget.'

'Don't you want me to forgive them either?'

'They don't need forgiving.'

She turned away. 'I'm not sure about that.'

'You *let* me,' he said. His tone was almost indignant. 'You *let* me, Dee.'

It wasn't sickness, it was fear. She was afraid. She walked away from the car as though she might be able to walk away from her fear. 'Where you going?' he called after her, but she ignored him and went on, past the barrier and over the uneven ground of the excavation site. The wind buffeted her. The wreckage of Curium lay all around, a wasteland of stone and dust and rock with occasional pieces – columns, bits of mosaic, fragments of frieze – poking up through the soil like shards of bone protruding from a complex compound fracture. Somewhere beneath, as yet unexplored, was the whole skeleton of the place.

His voice called after her, faint against the wind: 'Hey!'

She ignored him and walked on. There were anemones and asphodel beside the rough path. Anemone was the wind flower: *anemos*, wind. Geoffrey had told her that, and it was there in the poem he had dedicated to her, the one called 'Persephone'. 'Anemone, the wind flower,/Is blown away by gales.' That's how it went. Maybe she'd be blown away by this gale. It flattened her dress against her body. She could feel it pressing between her thighs like a hand.

'Mrs D!'

She stumbled over the rocks, her feet slipping. At one point she put her hand down to steady herself. There were thorn bushes and a few derelict carob trees, their dried husks hanging in the wind. Ahead was the edge of the escarpment, the edge of the whole world. She stopped at the brink. Before her the sea unravelled to the horizon, like a sheet of blue silk flung out into the distance by the pale arm of the Akrotiri peninsula over to the left. At her feet the land dropped away suddenly, dizzyingly, down hundreds of feet to the wide expanse of shingle beach far below.

She remembered Charteris. You are your memory, she thought: there is nothing else, just memory piled on memory, a fragile pyramid of record and remembrance that rises up to this summit that is you. She remembered walking with him across the Kinder Plateau, to the very edge of the Downfall where you could stand like this on the lip of the cliff. They had looked out over the waterfall and the valley below, and the wind had blown in their faces and carried with it a breath of water, and there had been just the same mingling of exhilaration and fear, with the void mere inches from their feet, and Charteris saying, 'I hope you're not thinking of jumping.'

'Flying,' she had replied. 'I'm thinking of flying.'

He had stood close behind her, his hands on her waist as though to hold her safe. 'You'd only fall.'

She turned. 'But you don't feel that, do you? You feel that you could step off and just fly, like one of those dreams.' She was serious. She didn't smile, and neither did he. 'Do you have flying dreams? I do. I step up and up and up and it's obvious really, easy, just a matter of doing it. Walking on air, I mean.'

'And then you wake up.'

'Of course. You always wake up.'

There was a moment of hesitation. The wind battered against them, the sound of it in her ears like a voice arguing with her, insisting on its point of view, never giving her pause to think. Then he kissed her very softly, as though frightened that even now she might pull away. And she said his name. Just that – his name.

They picked their way back through the excavation site to the car. The doors slammed the wind out and hurled them back to the present, to the fact of a coffee morning, to the dull and the quotidian. He was about to turn the key in the ignition when she stopped him. 'Wait.'

He looked round. 'You'll be late.'

'It doesn't matter. I'm already late, and anyway there's something I've got to tell you.'

He was smiling. His smile did that thing to her, undermined her resolve, pulled away the supports of decency and rectitude. 'Nick, this is serious.' She frowned, to make it so. 'What you said yesterday. What you said about EOKA.'

His expression shifted from amusement to caution, a subtle thing of changing light and dark. 'What about it?'

'People know about it. At least, they know that you're involved in some way.'

'What d'you mean people know about it? Who's "people"?' His voice had risen. 'Did you tell someone? Christ, did you tell?'

'I didn't tell anyone. Believe me. It was someone I talked to. He works for them.' *Them* and *they*. It seemed ridiculous, a kind of child's fantasy.

'It's that major, isn't it? What's his name? Brawdle, something like that.' He reached over the seat and grabbed her hand. 'You know they pulled me in for questioning, his soldiers—'

'It's not him. He told me about that, but it's not him. Really, Nick.'

'He's always around you, isn't he? He's a bastard, a typical English bastard.'

'I said it wasn't him.'

His grip relaxed fractionally. 'Then who was it?'

'Someone more important than that. We meet lots of different people, people involved in all sorts of things. Police, security, that kind of thing. Look, I shouldn't be telling you this, but I am, so listen to what I say.' She paused, watching him, willing him to believe her. The wind pummelled the car, rocking it on its suspension. 'I think they've been watching you. Us, even: watching *us*.' The idea brought a sly thrill, that they had some kind of collective identity, the two of them together.

'Watching us? Fucking hell! Who's been watching us?' He looked confused. It was as though someone had drawn a finger through his portrait, distorting the eyes, turning down the mouth, smudging the cheeks with white. 'Why didn't you tell me all this earlier? And why are you telling me now? Is this some kind of trap? Get him talking to you and then along come the soldiers and arrest him? Something like that?' He looked round, as though there might be watchers hiding behind the thorn bushes, crouching behind the rocks. But there was no one: just the bare hillside and the sky, and beyond the edge of land the smudged blue of the sea.

'Of course it's not a trap. I've been trying to find the right moment to tell you, and now I realize there is no right moment.'

He was examining her face, as though something there might betray the truth, some evasion in her eyes, some flicker of amusement in the mouth.

'You must believe me, Nick. For your own good.'

He looked round. There was the sound of a vehicle on the road below and as he turned an army ten-tonner ground up the hill into view, the canvas sides tied up and a row of pallid English faces looking down on them. She heard his sharp intake of breath, saw the movement of his Adam's apple as he swallowed. Then the vehicle passed by and headed on up the road and Nicos breathed out slowly. He gave a fleeting smile, as though merely seeing them go past was some kind of triumph. 'So what do you expect me to do?' he asked. 'Run away from them? You must be joking.'

There was that absurd bravado about him. Like Charteris. 'I'll swim to you,' he had boasted to her. 'If they sink the ship under me, I'll swim all the way back to you.'

'I just want you to be safe.'

'Safely out of the way, more like.'

'Don't be daft.'

He smiled. 'I love the way you say "daft". Northern, like.'

They drove back to Limassol. It was too late for the coffee morning now, too late for many things. 'I'll have to ring,' she said, thinking of the flock of wives gathered in a sitting room in one of the married quarters in the midst of a housing estate called Kensington or Gibraltar Village or something. She could hear the noise of gossip and the percussion of cups and saucers, and imagine the shock that would go through them if they knew – the flutter, the scattering of feathers, the shrill alarm calls.

Nicos turned in his seat to look at her. 'What do we do now?'

'I don't know,' she said. 'Nick, I just don't know.'

Thirteen

Marjorie is a memory. She is a torso and a memory. There seem to be few other functions. The torso is crab-like and immobile, seated in a special chair beside the window of her room in Peace Haven, the Home for Distressed Gentlefolk in which she lives. The window looks out from the front of the house, so that she can see the main road. It's not a busy road but it's better than nothing.

'They offered me a garden view at the back. They said, "Ooh, you're a lucky one: a Back Room has just become available." But I told them to stuff it. Well, I didn't quite say that. Distressed Gentlefolk don't say that kind of thing. But I told them I was quite happy with a Front Room.' You can hear the capital letters in her discourse. Her large, moon face lights up and her mouth grabs hold of the words with gusto. 'That way I can see what's going on. Watch the milkman rather than just watching sparrows and blackbirds. Sparrows and blackbirds are all very well, but they aren't Life, are they? They're alive, but they aren't Life.'

'Is the milkman?'

'I'll bet the women on his milk round think he is.' She laughs uproariously, as though at a joke of universal dimensions. She has to be levered out of bed in the morning and placed in her chair so that she can see out. Her legs don't work, that's the problem. Neither do her hands, although she does retain some control over a few fingers. 'I've got a kind of electric buggy, and I do get out a bit. But I'm very happy here.'

Shame crawls through Thomas' mind as he watches her: he is repelled by her condition, yet fascinated. Like looking at a road accident, or someone with a hideous physical deformity. 'What is it?' he asks. 'Your problem, I mean.'

'My neurones. That's what they tell me. Of course they haven't really got the foggiest idea what it is. They've got a name for it, but no idea how to treat it. It gets steadily worse. Six months ago I could walk around perfectly well. Stumbled a bit, but only what you do with too much gin in you. And now look at me.'

'You're doing very well, as far as I can see.'

'Very well, my foot. Or my hand, come to that. They're neither of them any good.' She hoots with laughter, or perhaps with despite; or perhaps with both. Her limbs don't work, but her memory does. She remembers. She plays with her memory as a child might play with a toy, twisting it this way and that, opening it up, pulling it to pieces, examining the component parts and then finding that it can no longer be reassembled. 'Paula was the little monkey, wasn't she? Dear little monkey. But you were a rather solemn little boy. He's going to be a Policeman or a Lawyer, that's what I thought. She'll be a Dancer, but he'll be a Lawyer. Was I right?'

'Not quite.'

She dimples and laughs. 'I rarely am, Tom, I rarely am. So what did the two of you become?'

'Journalist and historian.'

'Which is which?'

'She's the journalist.'

'Ah, so you're a historian.' She looks triumphant. 'Not far off, was I? Historian is a rather Solemn Undertaking, isn't it? Just like a lawyer. All those dusty Facts sifted through your fingers, and then the final, grim Judgement. I don't like History, I like Memories. Quite a different thing, you know. No judgement and precious few facts. And is the historian married with a nice, cosy family?'

'A fifteen-year-old son. The marriage didn't last. She's with someone else now.'

'Oh dear. And what about you? Is Tom with someone else? Quite an opportunity, I'd have thought, finding out about someone else when you might have expected boredom and familiarity for the remainder of your life.'

He wonders whether to tell her about Kale, and decides not. 'There have been some girlfriends. Nothing serious.'

'At least you've got your son. I never found anyone who would put up with me and now all I've got left are memories. Apart from the road outside the front door, that is, and the milkman. The wonderful thing about memory is that it dies with you. I remember your mother telling me that. Ephemeral. I like that word. Ephemeral. You know in spring I found mayflies in the room. Where do you think they came from? The park? They're beautiful. Little delicate things. Anyway, they are Ephemera, did you know that? Do you know what Ephemera means?'

'Something that doesn't last long?'

'Worse than that. Something that only lasts One Day. And *we* only last one day, don't we, in the Great Scheme of Things? A mere blink of God's Eye.' The capital letters are laid down with the pleasure of a wine buff laying down bottles. The Great Scheme of Things. God's Eye. 'Don't you feel like God himself when you remember the past? You hold it in your Mind. It's yours alone. History you share with others, but Memory is yours alone. Gosh, how philosophical.'

'Will you share yours with me?' Thomas asks.

'Maybe.' She watches him thoughtfully. 'It all depends on what you want me to remember.'

There's a knock on the door and a woman puts her head into the room. 'Oh, you've got a visitor. How nice. Do you need anything?'

'We're fine, thank you. This is Tom who was once rather solemn and is now rather curious.'

The woman smiles at him. 'Hello, Tom. Just ring if you want anything, won't you?' The head vanishes and the door closes softly. Suddenly, and for no particular reason, he thinks of Kale, and wishes she were here. She'd be better able to deal with Marjorie. She'd just be herself. Being himself is something that Thomas has never been good at. 'I want you to remember *her*.'

'Who? Your mother? Oh, but I do, Tom, I do. Often. I was so sorry not to have been able to make the funeral, but you can see why. Darling, darling Dee. You know she came to visit me here? Hadn't changed. Still a Breath of Fresh Air just as she was when I first knew her. And we didn't always get fresh air down by the harbour, I can tell you.' The laugh again, too jolly by far. 'I can see her now, sleeves rolled up to the elbows – well, maybe not sleeves; you didn't actually wear long sleeves very much out there, but you know what I mean – and her hands in the soap suds and just mucking in. And the laughs we had. And the teasing with the soldiers – lovely boys they were, quite bewildered a lot of the time. Never been out of England, mostly. It wasn't like it is nowadays, what with all these package tours and everything. Nowadays they're all off to the Seychelles or Mauritius, and they think they've travelled. But in those days . . .'

Her voice fades. She turns her head towards the window and seems to be looking out, but presumably she is actually looking through her memories, as though flicking rapidly through a series of files and extracting details as needed. Thomas seizes the moment. He reaches into his jacket pocket and takes out an envelope. 'I've got some photos. Maybe you can help me identify them? I found them in her papers.'

She turns her head. 'It's no use *handing* it to me, darling.'

'Of course. I'm sorry – I wasn't thinking.' He holds the photo up, like a conjuror showing a card to someone he is about to bamboozle with sleight of hand. The name *Nick* looks back at him from the obverse.

'Ah!' she says.

'You know him?'

'Of course I know him. That's the boy who used to drive her. He was quite a charmer. A Rough Diamond. Used to come into the canteen quite a bit and sit and talk to her. They claimed he was teaching her Greek.'

'And what *were* they doing?'

A faint stir of the fingers. 'Oh, chatting. This and that. I think your father didn't listen to her enough, that was the problem, and Nicos was a sympathetic ear. Nicos, that's what we used to call him.'

'It says "Nick".'

'Nicos, Nick. He'd lived in London, you see. Spoke good English. Well, not good English; not educated. He spoke with a broad London accent, actually. But it was more like speaking to one of the soldiers than to a Cypriot, if you see what I mean.'

'So they were friends?'

'I suppose you could say that. I think he had a bit of a Crush on your mother, really. And she maybe rather fancied him a bit. Used to get quite hot under the collar when I warned her off him. Never know what's going to happen when you flirt with someone, do you?'

'And she flirted with Nick?'

'Just a little, darling. Just a teeny-weeny bit.'

'I've always thought of her as a bit strait-laced.'

'You know what they say don't you? Straight laces are easiest undone.' She laughs again. It could annoy, that laughter.

'And what about him?' He shows the newspaper cutting, the brown paper, crisp with age, the photograph of a young and hopeful soldier.

Marjorie's expression changes. For once the laughter dies. 'Oh my goodness, I'd forgotten all about him. Braudel. Major Braudel. He was another friend of Dee's. Yes, of course he was. How could I forget?' She pauses, considers the past, frowns at matters of contingency and coincidence. 'Yes, that's right. He was killed.'

'How was he killed? Do you remember?'

'Yes, now I think about it, of course I do. I remember the very day.' She turns her head and looks once more out of the window. 'It was springtime, wasn't it? Nineteen-fifty-seven, fifty-eight.'

'May nineteen-fifty-eight. That's what it says in the newspaper story.'

'And I was at the canteen, on my own. Not that we had many of the lads in. It was just an ordinary day. And we heard something, a gunshot maybe, and then the sirens. It happened all the time. Bombs occasionally, sometimes guns. They blew up the sewage works and the place stank for days. Pooh! You got used to it, you see. Not the smell, the attacks. So the lads in the canteen didn't do much more than glance up and catch each other's eyes, and then go back to whatever they were doing – playing cards probably. Rules didn't allow proper gambling. They used to play for mils, which weren't real money. Then after a while a corporal came in and said something about returning to barracks. There'd been an incident. That's the term they used: an "incident". The soldiers got up cursing and swearing. "We'll have none of that," I used to tell them. "The only foul language I'll allow here is 'duck'. Not the other one." That's what I used to tell them. Foul and fowl, you see. A joke. And they always apologized. They were good lads in those days, not like nowadays. Punks and all that. They need a spell of National Service, that's what I think. Put them in uniform and send them off somewhere the other side of the world. Anyway, they got up from their game and went away, leaving me all alone. I was used to being alone. I mean, why should I be at risk? Who'd want to attack me? Although people did say that I should take more precautions. But I used to tell them, no one would turn a hair if I was bumped off. And then the door opened and there she was.'

'My mother?'

'Yes. I was just finishing the till – my bosses in London were most particular about keeping the accounts accurate. They didn't want any funny business, and quite right if you ask me. And the door opened and there she was. I remember her standing there, silhouetted against the daylight. I couldn't really see her face, just the shape of her, and all that brightness. She looked like an angel or something. Really lovely. She was wearing this lovely summer frock, full-skirted. Pale blue. "Marjorie," she said, "they've shot Damien." Just that. "Marjorie, they've shot Damien." Then she came in and sat down at one of the tables, and that was that. Just sat and stared. Shock, I suppose.'

Marjorie moves her head, as though trying to see whether the muscles are still working. 'I went to the funeral, do you know that? Major Braudel's funeral.'

'Did you?'

'I went with Dee. She said she wanted me for moral support. They buried him at the military cemetery in Nicosia. Wayne's Keep, it was called. Now I remember. Good Lord, isn't it amazing how things come back? A rather bleak place outside Nicosia. Eucalyptus trees, I remember that. The major's wife flew out. She looked ever so lovely, standing by the grave all in black. Oh dear, they were very upsetting things, the military funerals. Rest on your arms reversed, they used to do. All in slow motion. And then the salute over the grave, the crash of rifles. And the Last Post. There were lots of tears. But not Dee. She just stood there. It was a bit frightening, really. She just stared. Like someone locked in, you know what I mean. I think she was rather fond of him.'

'Who did it? Did they find out?'

'EOKA, of course. Young thugs.'

'But did they find out who the killer was?'

She moves her head. 'I've no idea. Perhaps they did, perhaps they didn't. People sheltered them, you know. The killers, I mean. They were frightened to death, the ordinary people. It wasn't a very happy time, really. And of course it only got worse. But what can you expect?'

'And my mother? How was she after that?'

'Oh, she came round to help out in the canteen a few more times, but very soon a married quarter came available at Episkopi and she and your father moved in there. I hardly ever saw her after that.'

'I remember that. I remember the move.'

'I suppose you were at boarding school most of the time.'

'I remember bits,' he says. 'Nothing coherent. Just glimpses. It's like . . .' What is it like? It's like a landscape lit up by flashes of distant lightning – a scene here, a scene there, and all around, darkness.

'Funny, isn't it?'

'What is?' Nothing seems very funny, not in her condition.

She smiles indulgently. 'You never know what really happened, do you? Not to other people. You know, I wonder whether she wasn't a tiny bit in love with Major Braudel. She never spoke much about him, but I sensed something there.'

He leaves soon after that, apologizing for deserting her. 'Someone is picking me up and I can't be late.'

'Will I see you again?' she asks; the words of a woman to a fickle lover.

'I'll try.'

'Please. Please do. It's so nice having someone to talk to like this.'

In the entrance hall the nurse repeats the plea. 'Do come to see her again. She doesn't have many visitors. She's got no relatives at all, in fact. There was a lady who came once or twice, but Marjorie tells me that she died.'

'That was my mother.'

'Oh, I'm so sorry. Marjorie was most upset when she heard. How kind of you to keep up the good work. I do hope you'll be back.'

She's expecting a reply.

'I'll try.'

She smiles. When she put her head round the door to Marjorie's room her smile had seemed bright and optimistic. Now Thomas sees the resignation behind it, and the weariness. 'I know it's a burden,' she says, 'but it won't be for very long.'

Kale is waiting for him across the road when he comes out. She has picked up his car from the garage and collected Emma from school and she says she's OK when he asks if she wants him to take over. But she drives nervously, chain-smoking, glancing in the mirror too often, braking too sharply, accelerating too rapidly. Whenever they come to a halt at traffic lights, she taps her fingers on the wheel and glances round at the vehicles packed around them.

'You seem uptight,' Thomas says.

'It's this trip, isn't it?'

'It's just a weekend. Just family, nothing more.'

'That's the whole point. I'm not family. Me and Emms and my mum, we're our own family, just about. I'm not inviting you to a do with her, so why am I invited to this?'

'Because I want to be with you. Both of you. You know that, Kale. You know what I mean.'

'But there'll be your sister.'

'She wants to meet you.'

'She'll talk about her bloody journalism or whatever it is and make me feel crummy and inadequate.'

'She'll talk about her journalism and you won't be crummy and inadequate. You'll be what you are. That's more than good enough for me; and her.'

She glances in the mirror at her daughter in the back seat. 'A weekend in the countryside, Emms. What do you think of that?'

Emma tries to decide. 'Will there be . . .? Will there be . . .?'

'Will there be what, Emms?'

'Cows,' the little girl decides finally. 'Will there be cows?'

'Horses,' her mother says. 'More likely there'll be horses.'

They make their way through the suburban sprawl south of the city. Terraced houses and office blocks give way to rows of semis. 'How was she, that Marjorie woman?' Kale asks.

'Remarkable, considering. A lesson in hopeless optimism.'

She glances at him. She's looking older than her years today. A good thirty, her features shadowed, as though sketched in with charcoal. 'Aren't we all?' she says.

Paula's house is imposing, almost daunting. Built of Kentish ragstone sometime in the seventeenth century, it has gables and mullioned windows and chimneystacks that would look good as pillars in a medieval cloister. 'Christ, what's this?' Kale cries as they approach. 'A hotel? I told you we shouldn't have come. It looks like a palace, Emms. You'll have to wear your crown.'

'But I haven't got a crown.'

'Thomas'll buy you one.' She brings the car to a halt on the expanse of gravel at the front of the house. 'What do we do? Wait for footmen to appear?' But when the front door opens it is only Paula and the children who emerge, with the latest au pair hovering in the background.

Kale flinches at the sight of Thomas' sister. 'She looks like your mum.'

Thomas can never see the resemblance, but that's what people say. For him she is just Paula, who has always been there, more or less, who is part of his life whether present or absent, whom he loves in the indifferent way that siblings have – the kind of love that will only really manifest itself when it's too late. They greet each other with casual familiarity, while the children execute that strange dance that children employ when encountering someone new: part enthusiasm, part reserve, like cats greeting each other.

Paula gives the smile that she uses when trying to put inter-viewees at their ease. 'You must be Kale. Lovely to have you here.'

Kale looks doubtful. 'Thanks for inviting me.'

Paula bends towards Emma. 'And your name is . . .?'

'Emma.'

'Hello, Emma.'

Emma considers her thoughtfully. 'Have you got a crown?'

'A crown? Not exactly. But I have got a tiara.'

'What's a tiara?'

'Sort of half-a-crown.'

'Can I see it?'

So Paula sends her off in the care of the au pair, to rummage through the dressing-up trunk in one of the bedrooms. When they come back Emma is wearing a plastic tiara that once did duty in a school production of *Sleeping Beauty*: she wears it with the sublime acceptance of a child, for whom such artificial things may correspond with reality.

'We're going to play in the pond,' Paula's son announces when she reappears in her regal splendour. 'Have you brought your boots?'

Emma squints at him. ''Ave I?'

'*I* don't know.' Christopher has the manner of a prep-school pupil, who knows exactly what he possesses and where every item is at all times. 'You should know. They're your boots, after all.'

'Emma doesn't have any boots,' says her mother.

'No wellies? How can she get by without wellies?'

'She walks on concrete.'

Paula intervenes. 'I'm sure we can lend Emma some boots. Birgit will show you where.'

So Kale and the au pair take Emma off on the search for boots while Thomas and his sister go through to the garden. Graham isn't there, which is a relief. He is away on some business trip, in the US, due back tomorrow. Thomas recalls Paula's evasion when they discussed the possibility of their mother having an affair, and he wonders now about the two of them, Graham and Paula, and how they fit together when they spend so much of their time apart. Maybe Graham is screwing someone in New York, while Paula is screwing someone else in London. Who knows?

'Is it serious?' Paula asks. 'The two of you, I mean.'

'I told you, didn't I?'

'You always say it is. But it never turns out to be. Has she met Phil?'

'No. No, she hasn't.'

'Is she going to?'

'Of course.'

'She's a bit sharp, isn't she?'

'She's nervous.'

'About what?'

'You. All this. It's a bit of a contrast to what she's used to.' He doesn't want to admit the fact, not even to himself, but Paula's approval of Kale is what he seeks.

'The house? It's a millstone round our necks.'

'For God's sake don't tell her that.'

Kale comes out on to the terrace, with Emma now clumping along in rather oversized boots. The older children are already down the end of the garden, beyond the box hedge. Kale watches her daughter run clumsily down the lawn towards them. 'You be careful, now,' she calls. 'I don't want you getting wet.'

'Chris will look after her. He's very good like that.'

'This,' Kale says, meaning the garden, the entire property, the lawns and the flowerbeds and the trees, the summer-house down by the tennis court, the pond with golden carp, the three-port garage with Paula's car in it, and the motor mower and the children's bikes, the whole damn lot in fact, 'is it all yours?' She tries in vain to get the note of incredulity out of her voice. She knows it is all Paula's. Her intelligence tells her so; it is her instinct that says different. 'I mean, you don't share it with anyone or anything like that?'

'All ours. As far as the wall.' Paula seems embarrassed. 'Well, we share it with a few dozen rabbits, and the odd fox and things like that. Anything that can get in from the forest. Don't you have—?'

'A garden? You're joking. The nearest thing's Loughborough Park.'

'Isn't that Camberwell?'

'Someone who's heard of it! More like Brixton.'

Brixton. The name is still redolent of racial antagonism, of barricades in the street and cars burning. Paula can smell 'story', some heartening fable of working-class pluck in the face of adversity. 'Is that where you live?'

'Off Coldharbour Lane.'

'What have you got?'

'Got?'

'A flat? A house?'

Kale laughs; a small exhalation of derision. 'Oh that. A room. Just a room at the moment. In my mum's flat. Overlooking the railway. I did share a flat, but we've just moved in with her.'

They talk for a while about life in Brixton, about looking after Emma, about Income Support and Child Benefit. It's an awkward, fitful conversation. You can tell that Paula wants to ask about Emma's father but that seems a bit tactless, even for her. So she asks about the history course that Kale has signed up to, and for once Kale isn't defensive, but talks with enthusiasm and intelligence, that native wit that her schooling never managed to feed.

'I think it's quite inspiring,' Paula observes, 'to find someone like you going into further education. Makes me realize how easy I had it.'

Kale looks at her with something approaching contempt. 'What do you mean, "someone like you"?'

In the afternoon Paula suggests an expedition to feed the ducks. Emma didn't know there were ducks. 'Where are the ducks?' she asks. 'Where are the ducks?' Ducks seem too good to be true, better even than a real plastic tiara.

'They're in the forest.'

'Where's the forest?'

'Through the gate at the bottom of the garden.'

'Is it a secret gate?' Emma is at that age when the questions all have answers of some kind. Thomas wonders whether that's what growing up means: it's when you start asking questions that have no answers.

'It is a secret gate,' Paula assures her, 'but we know the spell to open it.'

The secret gate opens on to a small copse of beech and rhododendron. Beyond the trees there's open heath. They venture out, the children running ahead.

The forest isn't a forest, really. It's a British sort of forest, distinguished mainly by the absence of trees. There is a sandy car park with wooden picnic benches and notices that admonish lighters of fires and scatterers of litter. The place is an Area of Outstanding Natural Beauty, the notices announce, in case the fact isn't clear. Apparently, if you look carefully, you may find bog asphodel and sundew and things like that. Beyond the lake the slope is wooded, but you can see the roofs of houses among the trees. For all the bog asphodel, this is a tame landscape, a forest in nothing but name.

At the water the ducks converge on the children, hustling them for pieces of bread. There are patches of light on the far trees, scudding fast in the wind. The sun shines after a fashion. Once the supplies of bread are exhausted they all return to the house, straggling up the hill from the lake with the ducks complaining at their departure.

'Where's Emms?' Kale asks when they reach the back door.

The question goes unheard at first. 'Where's Emms?' just gets lost in the general hubbub as Paula's children take off their boots. 'Where's Emma gone?' she repeats. 'Birgit, where's Emma?'

'She was outside.' The German girl's voice rises in pitch as though she is questioning the very thing she is saying. Kale goes out to see. A moment later she is back.

'She's not there. Where's she gone?'

Impatience at first, of course. 'Paula, did you see Emma come in?'

She didn't.

'Christopher, where is she?'

Thomas goes back outside with Kale. They stand on the stone terrace looking out across the empty lawn, and feel only impatience. 'Emms, where are you?' Kale calls. 'Mum wants you!'

There is no sign of the little girl. Kale walks across the grass – 'Where the hell's she got to?' – and then suddenly she's running. 'The pond!' She runs through the gap in the hedge and down to the lower level, to the stone surround of the pond where large, mysterious carp float just below the surface. Thomas follows her, dreading what they might find. But there is nothing. No Emma, no figure floating face-down in the shallow water, nothing. 'Emms!' she shouts, looking round. Her voice echoes off the flint wall. The light is grey and the wind sweeps through the trees beyond the wall – a sea sound, like waves raking through a shingle beach.

'Emms!'

A small pulse of fear throbs in Thomas' throat.

'Emms, where are you?' Kale calls. Her face is pale, like the face of someone at the scene of a road accident: shock, disbelief, fear. 'Where the fuck's she gone?' she asks. She doesn't ask it of Thomas, she asks it of the garden around her, of the lawn and the bushes and the trees.

'Let's go and look through the gate.'

'Oh, Christ, she hasn't gone outside . . .'

They discover that the gate is open. There is nothing dramatic, no plastic tiara on the ground or anything like that; but the gate is open. They step out into the trees.

'Emms! Emms, Mum's looking for you!'

The trees are swaying and roaring in the wind. Fright metamorphoses into panic, and panic brings the suspension of time. From mere concern to desperation takes a second and it takes half an hour. Impossible to tell which. Time runs at lightning speed and it stops. Immeasurable, it becomes useless. They run, through the trees and out into the open heath. They run because they feel that every second counts; they run without knowing where to run.

'Wasn't there a van in the car park? A car, wasn't there a car? Fuck – there was a car.' She runs towards the car park, and then stops and looks round desperately, not knowing what to do or where to go. The car park is empty. There are tyre marks in the gravel, and a chocolate bar wrapper blown against the base of the litter bin.

'Emms! Emma!' The name is pitched against the wind, but the little girl doesn't answer. They run down to the lake, and pause there at the water's edge and listen to the ducks chuckling quietly to themselves. It's quite a good laugh really, a practical joke on the grand scale, with the adults panicking and running this way and that, calling and arguing and feeling the flood of irrationality that comes with fear; and the little girl squatting on the edge of the lake quite happily, talking to the ducks.

'Emms! What the hell are you doing?'

Emma looks round. She is still wearing the tiara, although it's a little lopsided now. 'Listen to the ducks laughing.'

Kale runs to her and snatches her up into her arms. One of the little girl's boots falls off. Kale is weeping, from relief, from misery, fear and despair overcome. 'Emms, what the hell did you go off like that for? Why didn't you tell Mummy? You mustn't just go off on your own.'

Emma clings to her mother, grabs on to her like a monkey. 'I hadn't finished talking to the ducks.'

Kale is weeping and laughing at the same time, and burying her face in her daughter's neck; and Thomas understands that he will never ever again be loved like that, never completely and convulsively, never with the whole being. He feels dispersed, separated from Kale in her happiness, lost among the sound of the trees in the wind, the swaying of the branches and the seething of the leaves.

Fourteen

There was the usual rigmarole of the airport, the coils of barbed wire, the soldiers in their sand-coloured uniform. She stood with Edward and Paula and watched a phalanx of passengers cross the concrete apron towards the customs shed. Over by the perimeter fence was the charred wreck of an airliner – a Handley-Page Hermes, destroyed months earlier by an EOKA bomb just minutes before it was due to take off for Britain, left now as a warning and a reproach.

Hermes was the Greek deity who conducted the souls of the dead to Hades. Tom knows this. He knows the type of aircraft; he knows the god. He watches and finds out, listens, reads, notes. Facts and ideas stick to his mind like flies to a flypaper. He doesn't know what to make of this gift. It goes with school reports that accuse him of wasted talents, of much intelligence but no diligence. A diligence is a kind of horse-drawn carriage. Intelligence is the ability to unravel knowledge, but it is also the knowledge itself. The language coils around like a snake, words meaning things, things meaning words. As he walks across the concrete apron he hears a cry, far out on the edge of his awareness. 'Tom!' the voice cries. 'Tom!'

The small figure turned and looked, and raised one hand in a salute. 'There he is!' She waved. 'It's Tom!' She felt tears – of joy, of relief, of shame. 'Tom! Tom!'

Permitted to wave, they were not permitted to touch. There were documents to present, suitcases to be examined by sweating customs officers, chalk marks to be made on suitcases, queues to be followed before his arrival at the gate where Turkish policemen stood guard. It was half an hour until he was there before them, small and serious, distant despite his proximity.

His mother's soft pliancy, her smell of earth and spice. Orange blossom, perhaps. Jasmine, maybe. He isn't sure. Smells and words go poorly together. And his father proffering a tough hand for him to shake. And Paula watching with hostile eyes from behind his mother's ice-blue skirt. But for the moment his mother is everything, the all-consuming love, the love that dare not speak its name because there is no word for it.

'Tom. Darling, darling Tom.'

'My ears are popping.'

'Your ears are always popping. You'll get over it. Aren't you happy to be home?'

'Of course I am.' But he looked uncertain about it. Was it home?

The road climbed upwards into the hills. The fields were painted in the spring colours of a million flowers. He deflected questions about school, about his friends, about his other world. There was this world and there was that world. Explorers of one rarely spoke about it to the inhabitants of the other. They passed through the villages, each with its mosque and its church, each with its donkeys and its curious villagers who turned and stared at passing cars. ΖΗΤΩ ΕΟΚΑ was daubed in blue on one of the walls. There were army trucks on the road, and Land-Rovers with steel bars sticking out from their bonnets like the claws of some giant raptor – a protection against wires strung across the road. Tom explained to Paula how this trap would work – heads spinning across the tarmac, blood spurting, vehicles plunging out of control. 'Don't be so gruesome,' Dee protested.

'But it's true, Mummy. It's true.'

'It may be true but you don't have to talk about it.'

And then the car breasted a rise in the road and they could see the sea for the first time, the blue of the Mediterranean, bluer by far than her dress. There was a field of poppies, red against the blue.

'Oh, do look!' she called out. 'Can we stop? Edward, can't we stop for a moment?'

'Better if we keep going.'

'Oh, for goodness' sake!'

Reluctantly he slowed the car and pulled off the road. 'This isn't very sensible.'

'Don't be ridiculous. There's no one around.'

'You seem to think there's no danger.'

'I'm realistic, that's all. And I know that most Cypriots wouldn't hurt a fly.'

'They kill birds happily enough, never mind flies.'

'Don't be so literal. You know what I mean.'

She flung the door open. There was a place where the rubble wall had fallen away. Hitching up her skirt, she negotiated the stones. 'Come on, Tom, help Paula.' They walked through the field holding her hands, Tom and Paula knee-deep in blood, her skirt sweeping the flowers. 'Take a photo,' she called. 'Get the camera.'

They turned to pose, Persephone with her children among the spring flowers. 'Do get a move on, Edward.'

She wished it were him. She wished it were Charteris. Tears stung her eyes. Edward stood at the breach in the wall, with his eye to the camera. 'Smile,' he called.

No one did.

A warm evening. The french windows were open on to the garden and you could hear the sound of crickets, a soft, patient trilling. The diners smoked and drank, and argued.

'We're on a bloody seesaw,' Damien said. 'We move one way – in favour of the Turks, say – and the Greeks are up in arms. We shift the other way and the Turks start complaining. One side demands partition and the other side refuses to countenance it.' His voice was quiet and insistent. They listened to him carefully because they knew that he lived on the front line. He walked the streets with his soldiers. He confronted the youths of both sides face to face. 'They need their heads banging together, that's the truth of it. And I'm afraid that Foot isn't the man to do it.'

'Was Harding any better?' Johnny Frindle asked. 'When he was in charge we were fighting a military battle, but really this is a political issue. I mean, Britain doesn't really want to be fighting either the Greeks or the Turks. We damn well ought to be concentrating on the Soviet Union. Mustn't take our eye off the ball. That's what we're here for.'

Dee excused herself for a moment and went to check that

the children were asleep. When she came back the debate was still going on, the bloody politics of Aphrodite's island being pulled this way and that. 'Keeping the Turks happy, that's the problem,' Edward was saying. 'We've got to keep the Turks happy.'

She began to clear away the dishes. Damien stood to help her and she gestured that he should stay in his seat – 'No, really, Damien' – but he followed her into the kitchen just the same, carrying a couple of plates. At the sink he brushed against her, his hand touching her arm. 'Please,' she said. Her tone was uncertain, hung between admonishment and entreaty.

'I've got to see you alone,' he said. 'I can't bear this.'

She could hear the loud expostulations of Douglas sounding through the closed door from the dining room – 'These people don't know what's good for them,' he was saying.

'But we've got to do something.'

'We can't do anything.'

Out in the hall the telephone rang. The dining-room door opened and Edward came out. She felt Damien move away as Edward picked up the phone. The passage of time, seemingly halted for an instant, moved on.

Tom is lying in bed, asleep.

He's not asleep, but he's meant to be asleep.

He's lying in bed, and when his mother comes in to check, he's asleep, and when she doesn't, he's awake. Is this behaviour forbidden? Sort of. 'Go to sleep' is an injunction with a degree of compulsion behind it, as though you can induce sleep merely by willing it. But sleep just happens. You wait, and it happens. Or not. In the dormitory at school he lies awake for as long as he can because in the dormitory, after lights-out, he is free . . .

There are guests to dinner, and he's listening to the laughter, to the murmur of conversation, to the rise and fall of words. Some phrases he can hear, some voices he can recognize. Douglas', of course. Binty's laughter. Others he doesn't know.

Paula is next door, and she's asleep. But then she's younger and oblivious to the delights of eavesdropping. Sometimes when there are guests he creeps out of bed and goes to the dining-room door to listen. He's a spy. Spies do these things. Spies watch and listen and note things down. Spies construct stories from the small hints that people drop.

He's lying in bed awake. He can hear someone going to the kitchen. He recognizes his mother's footsteps. Other steps follow. Then the telephone rings and there's a burst of volume, and then the dining-room door closes and all he can hear is the rise and fall of his father's voice on the telephone. The words are blurred by the inter-vening wall but you can sense things from the tone. Insistence. Shock. The undulations of concern and distress. Something has happened.

Sleep. He's lying in bed asleep. Then he's awake, and his father is talking on the telephone again, this time with a certain author-ity, as though he knows what he is doing. Talking to someone of a lesser rank. His words cut through the wall, cut through the door, cut through Tom's sleep: 'I want to get on the flight tomorrow. Supplementary crew. Yes, that's right. My father has just died and I've got to get back to the UK.'

Tom is lying in bed, asleep.

Next morning his father has gone. 'Grandpapa's ill,' his mother tells the two of them over breakfast. 'Daddy's had to go and help Grandmamma.'

'Help her do what?' Paula asks.

'Help her look after Grandpapa, of course.'

He has never caught his mother out in a lie before. But perhaps she's not telling a lie. Perhaps Grandpapa is ill. Perhaps he's alive and dead at the same time. Perhaps two contradictory truths can coexist.

'How would you like to go to Binty's tomorrow? There are things I've got to do.' She smiles brightly, as though to encourage them, as

though this might help Grandpapa on the road to recovery or resurrection.

'I don't want to go to Binty's,' Paula says. 'I want to be with you.'

'You'll be with Tom. Tom doesn't mind going to Binty's, does he?'

He doesn't. Tom is hardened to dislocation.

The day vanishes from memory. Days can have that evanescent quality, like the colours in spring: there so vividly, just as soon bleached out by the summer sun. The next morning he wakes early and goes to his parents' room where his mother is still in bed, half asleep. He climbs in beside her, into the warmth and the smell of familiarity and family, a smell that other homes and, presumably, other beds do not possess; a unique, territorial smell. He cuddles against her and feels the soft masses of her breasts through the cotton of her nightdress.

'How is Grandpapa?' he asks.

She considers the question and her answer for a few moments. 'I'm afraid Grandpapa's dead, darling,' she tells him.

After careful thought he admits that he already knows.

'You know?'

'I heard Daddy talking on the phone.'

'You've known all the time?'

'Yes.'

She holds him close. 'Don't tell Paula yet, will you? It would upset her too much.'

He hasn't the heart to tell her that Paula won't care. Death is something that adults feel, not children. That is the thought that has been worrying him. Why can't he feel any emotion over his grandfather's death? That jovial, amiable man whom he knew well and loved. Why doesn't he cry, as he suspects his mother has been doing? Why is he merely curious about what has happened? Not upset; curious. What's it like, being dead? What's it like being absent from everything and everyone? What do you become? You become your remembrance.

B inty looked at her quizzically. 'Are you all right, darling?' Dee smiled. 'I'm fine.' Walking on the edge of a precipice, she thought, thinking of flying.

'Are you sure you don't want to come with us? Have a talk, get things off your chest?'

'I'd love to, but I can't really desert Marjorie. She's all on her own and what with the disturbances there are lots of customers these days. I'm sorry to dump you with the children.'

'Oh, they'll be all right. We'll go for a swim first and then I'll take them home. They'll entertain each other. I'll bring them back at about six, if that's OK? How's Edward getting on? Has he phoned?'

'Yesterday. It's not that easy getting through. I expect I'll hear from him this evening. He seemed OK.'

She kissed the children and waved as they drove away, then went back inside to change. She put on the full-skirted frock, the one with blue and white stripes. It suited her. Edward always said so. And then she could only wait, washing the breakfast things – she had given Voula the day off – pottering around the house, tidying some of the children's toys away. She felt a variety of emotions – anticipation, anxiety, a strange abstraction from reality, as though she were in a dream state of some kind, as though all the mundane things around her were abnormal, and the only reality was within her mind. She opened the french windows and went out into the garden. The air was laden with the perfumes of spring, the scent of jasmine almost overpowering in its intensity. She wandered along the dry paths. There was no grass. It wasn't like England. Nothing was like England. Here, growing out of dry earth, were hibiscus and pomegranate and oleander, plants that she had never seen, barely even imagined, until she came out here. Oranges, of course, and myrtle and bougainvillaea. It was only two days ago that Tom had found another chameleon in one of the trees; or maybe the same one. How on earth could one tell? The animal had watched them impassively through the barrels of its armoured eyes, grasping its branch with slow thumbs and, when Tom picked it up – Paula had screamed – and moved it to another place, delicately changing its colour to suit its background. Dee had felt a curious affinity with the animal. One colour in Sheffield, another here; one for Edward, one for Damien, another for Tom and Paula, another for Nicos.

On one of the paths she discovered Paula's tricycle. The children were always leaving their stuff outside. Lying beneath a hibiscus bush was a football that Tom had been given for his last birthday. She warned them that anyone could climb into the garden and take things, some child from the gypsy camp perhaps. It would be their own fault if their toys disappeared.

She was about to take the things in when she heard the car. The sound was distinctive, like a familiar voice. Trying not to hurry, she picked up the tricycle and strolled round to the front. The car was parked outside the gate, and there he was, climbing out. He smiled awkwardly, anxiety in his eyes. 'Hello,' he said. 'You look great. That dress.'

She wondered how often she had worn it before that he might have seen. Her wardrobe wasn't extensive. 'It's an old one.'

'It's lovely.' He looked round, standing just outside the gate as though waiting to be asked in. 'What about the kids?'

She showed him the trike. 'Tidying up after them. They've gone swimming with Mrs Paxton. And Voula's got the day off.' Why did she tell him that? To make things clear? They stood looking at one another for a moment. 'Do you want to come in for a moment? A cup of coffee or something?'

He opened the gate. 'If that's all right. I don't want . . .' But he never said what he didn't want. From behind his back he produced a flower, a single cyclamen of intense magenta, and held it out to her. He blushed slightly. 'Found it on the road-side, underneath some trees. Not exactly a bouquet of red roses, but it's something.'

She accepted the flower with elaborate solemnity, as though this were a tradition in a strange country where she had never been before. That was how she felt: a traveller in a land whose customs she could only guess at. 'It's beautiful.'

He followed her up the steps to the front door. Inside was a kind of sanctuary, away from strangers' eyes. She put the trike down and closed the door. 'Come through. Make yourself comfortable. What would you like? Coffee? Shall I make a cup of coffee? Before we go?'

He followed her into the sitting room. There was a photograph of the children on a side table, Tom in his school uniform, Paula wearing a pretty frock with smocking across the front. She watched him pick it up. 'Lovely kids,' he said. 'She's a right terror, isn't she?'

Dee laughed. 'I'll just put this in some water. Otherwise it'll die.'

'It'll die anyway.'

'Maybe I'll press it. I used to press flowers when I was at school. Between sheets of blotting paper. You know?'

He didn't.

'They last for ever,' she told him. 'Almost.'

The beach is called Lady's Mile because a British officer used to exercise his horse, a mare called Lady, here. When? Some time ago, before the war. Tom has found this out by asking people. He finds things out, like a detective, or a spy. So it's Lady's Mile, not Ladies' Mile, not lots of women sunbathing. Those were the days when you could name a part of the world after your pet horse, if you were an Englishman. The beach is a long stretch of grey sand in the western arm of Limassol Bay. To the left lies the city, the line of buildings along the seafront, the warehouses and the water towers; beyond it the coast curves round towards the east and fades into the haze of distance. There are ships anchored out in the roads, unloading into lighters. Behind the beach is the Salt Lake with its birds, the sly pink flush of flamingos.

'Tom forgot his football,' says Neil.

'Too late now.' They're unpacking their things from the back of the car. Alexandra is inside a large towel, changing into her swimming costume. Tom watches her.

'We wanted to play,' Neil says.

'We're here to swim. I thought that's what you wanted, a swim.'

'But after. We want to play when we get home.'

'There are other things to do.'

'We wanted to play football.'

Alexandra completes her changing without letting anything slip. She looks back at Tom as though claiming some kind of victory. Her body is just acquiring the shapes of womanhood, a narrowing of the waist, tiny breast buds beneath her costume. Does she have hair between her legs? he wonders. She turns and runs across the sand towards the edge of the water. 'It's freezing!' she cries from the shallows.

'Don't be silly. It'll be fine once you're in.'

'Can we go back for it?'

'Back for what?'

'Tom's football.'

'Oh, for goodness' sake.'

'Please!'

'It's all right,' Tom says. 'It doesn't matter.'

'But we want to play football.'

In the kitchen he stood beside her, watching. She could hear the gentle whisper of his breathing, his head close to hers as he bent to see. She had opened a book – that account by Durrell of life on the island – and laid a sheet of tissue paper on the right-hand page. Carefully she positioned the flower on the bed of tissue and laid a second sheet over it, like a winding-sheet on a corpse. You could see the faint shadow of the flower beneath, the sinuous stalk, the curved magenta petals. Then she closed the book shut and pressed down on it with all her weight. 'As simple as that,' she said. 'You need to keep it pressed for a while. A week or two. At home I've got a special press, but this'll work just as well.'

When she turned she found him in the way. He put out a hand to stop her but she laughed and slipped past, taking the book through into the bedroom. The shutters were closed and the room was deep in shadow. She put the book on a side table and looked around for something heavy to place on top – a glass bowl containing pebbles that Paula had collected on the beach. When she turned round he was there at the doorway, silhouetted against the daylight from the sitting room.

'I've been thinking about what you said.'

'And what have you decided?'

'It depends on you.'

He came forward until they were facing each other in the middle of the room, awkwardly, like casual acquaintances suddenly thrown together in an unexpected closeness. That's what they were, really, strangers meeting in a foreign country and uncertain of the norms of behaviour. She reached up and touched his face, just faintly with the tips of her fingers, along the line of his jaw. 'What's it got to do with me?'

'It's got lots to do with you. With what you want.'

'I don't know what I want.'

He took hold of her hand. She watched as he turned it over and lowered his head to touch his tongue, soft and moist, against her open palm. The dampness glistened like a snail's trail across the lines of life and head and heart. 'I'm in a bit of a muddle, really. Liquorice Allsorts, Aunt Vera says. All of a muddle.'

'Aunt Vera?'

'My mother's sister. Her husband was a master cutler.'

'What the hell's a master cutler?'

'Very important. In Sheffield.'

'We're not in Sheffield now. You can have different ideas.'

'Oh, I do. Many different ideas, most of them impossible and all improbable.'

He smiled. 'That's you, isn't it? All that difficult stuff. You want to keep things simple.'

'But what if they are complicated? This is complicated.'

'No it's not, Mrs D, it's easy.' And as if to demonstrate the simple fact of it he eased her towards him and bent down and touched his mouth on hers. 'See?'

She swallowed. There was a feeling of panic, something inside her throat cutting off her breathing. Like looking over the edge of the precipice, daring to step off.

'You've been wanting that, haven't you?' he said.

'Have I? How can you tell? All those girls you've had?'

He shrugged. 'Not so many.'

'But some . . .'

'One or two.' Then he kissed her again, and this time his tongue moved between her lips. She spoke against his mouth. 'Please,' she said, and he laughed.

'Please what?' His hands were lifting her dress, touching the bare flesh above her stockings, and her own fingers were scrabbling at the buttons of his shirt, and going inside and finding the hard corrugations of his ribs. And then the fragile barricades of propriety and rectitude, of inhibition and restraint, broke and there wasn't anything else, nothing articulate, nothing rational. 'Nick,' she said. 'Nick.' Just the sound of his name repeated like a mantra as he lifted her dress and pulled it off over her head and she stood almost naked before him in the shuttered bedroom, beside the sly yellow reflections of a beaten brass side table that she and Edward had bought on a visit to the Turkish quarter of Nicosia.

He lifted her. That was the ridiculous thing. He lifted her up like a child, picked her up off the ground and carried her to the bed, and laid her down. No one had ever done that with her before. And then he was pulling at her underthings and she was undoing his trousers and the two things were happening together, an awkward, breathless scrabbling at each other, all shame cast aside. No speaking, just a breathless doing.

Goats in the road, and long-tailed, ragged sheep. What the British call shoats because, so the story goes, they are a hybrid between the two species. The shepherd wears knee-high black boots and baggy black trousers. A Turk. The trousers are because when the Prophet comes to earth again he will be born of man rather than woman, and so the men wear these trousers, just in case. That's what Geoffrey says, anyway.

'Geoffrey says all sorts of things,' says Binty. She taps her fingers on the steering wheel as the sheep mill around, this way and that, and the shepherd shouts at them and swats with a branch he has pulled off a bush. Over there are some houses, the outermost houses of the town, battered and decaying. And the minaret of a mosque.

'You said it would only be a few minutes out of our way, and here we are stuck in a traffic jam,' Binty complains.

'Animal jam,' says Tom. 'Not traffic jam.'

Binty recites: 'Mother dear, what see I here/That looks like strawberry jam?/Hush, hush, my love, it is Papa/Run over by a tram.'

In the back seat the boys laugh and push each other while the sheep swirl and complain round the car. One of them is on its hind legs, pulling at the leaves of an olive tree growing at the roadside.

Udders like the bladders of a football. The boys giggle and push at the back of Alexandra's seat. 'Tits,' they whisper. 'Tits.'

A faint breeze crept with stealthy fingers across her belly. She rolled away from him and sat up, lifting up her hair to cool her neck, looking back at him where he lay. He hadn't much hair on his chest – less than Edward's. His nipples were smooth and dark, like damsons. Everything was different, each little detail. His limbs were sinewed – only the arms suntanned. His cock lay limp against his thigh, its glistening head now hidden within a monk's cowl. She had never seen an uncircumcised penis before, not on an adult. Why was it called a cock? As in hens and chickens, pecking at you? Or taps, faucets, spigots? Or pistols? She'd wanted to kiss it. When he put his tongue in her mouth, she'd wanted his cock in there. She'd never felt that before, neither with Edward nor with Charteris. The idea disgusted her; and yet she wanted it. There were so many things she wanted.

At that moment – precise in memory – there was a movement beyond the doorway, a sound. She gave a small cry of surprise.

He sat up. 'What's up?'

'Something, someone.' Panic rose in her like gall. Grabbing up her dress, she got up from the bed. In the sitting room across the hall the french windows were still open. The curtains rose and fell. Sunlight was smeared across the floor and one of the walls, and beyond the french windows was the luminous green of the garden.

Her heart was beating fast. What had she thought? An intruder or something. But there was nobody, just something lying on the tiles, a chased-brass bowl, another piece they had bought in Nicosia at that market. She picked it up and put it back in place. Exterior sounds came in from the outside world –

birdsong, insect noise, the barking of some dog shut away in a nearby farm, the noise of a car. 'I left the windows open.'

He had appeared at the door, anxious.

'I thought someone was in the house,' she said.

'Cats, maybe.'

Cats, of course. Or just the wind catching the curtains. Anemone, the wind flower. She went over to close the french windows. How far had the sun moved since he had come? It was like a sundial. She remembered a sundial on a church wall. Eyam village, St Lawrence's Church in Eyam. She and Charteris had discovered it. Fancy remembering that. 'You need an equation of time to read it accurately,' he had said. An equation of time. She needed an equation of time, in which the solution could be zero, time suspended, so that this moment, alone and naked with him, could become for ever. Like something preserved in the golden amber of sunlight. That was it. A poetic conceit.

But there was the swell of panic inside her. 'You'd better get dressed,' she said.

'What time is it?'

She found her watch. 'It's nearly midday.' With a small stir of anger she thought of Edward, as though this situation was his fault. He would be ringing this evening and she might have to explain her day. And Binty would be coming back with the children later in the afternoon. She would have to construct her alibi, just in case. She needed to be back among the normal, to consign this moment to a secret, private past. 'Are you in some kind of a pickle, darling?' Marjorie would enquire when she asked for her support. And she'd reply, 'Just a bit,' and the admission would be enough to get Marjorie on her side. She would be like a criminal. She *was* a criminal, almost. What she had just done was a criminal act until – when? Not long ago. And it was still morally reprehensible, wasn't it? And for a moment she hadn't cared. Everything had seemed justified.

In the bathroom she washed between her legs, towelled herself dry, fixed her make-up. When she came out she found him in the sitting room examining the framed photograph of Paula and Tom that stood on a side table, the two children watching the adults with solemn, well-behaved faces. She wanted their gaze to be elsewhere, but still they watched as Nicos returned them to the table and took hold of her instead. He had rights over her now, rights of memory if nothing else. Things could not be undone.

Something must have shown in her face, for he frowned and touched her cheek. 'Are you all right?'

Was she all right? The question suddenly seemed an interesting one. Know thyself. But she didn't know herself, couldn't read her own feelings. Love, yes, absurd and irrational. But other things besides, that blend of disparate emotions, insidious and deceptive and disguising themselves in chameleon ways – anger, laughter, depression, elation. And pure physical desire, the need to have him there inside her, a sensation that both shamed and exalted.

'I'm as right as I'll ever be. Come on,' she said, putting his hands aside. 'We've got to go.'

'You want to get rid of me.'

'I don't. I don't ever want to get rid of you. But there's nothing we can do, is there? You'd best not come in when we get to Marjorie's. You know what she's like. Just drop me and go.'

'And then what?'

She looked at him. 'I don't know, Nick. I don't know what we do then. I've got no idea at all.'

The road rises gently out of the coastal plain, through olive groves and derelict fields. Tom watches out of the window while Binty talks. He is not really listening. He's thinking, watching and wondering, consigning things to memory.

'What do you think, Tom?' Binty is asking.

What does he think? They've been to Lady's Mile, swimming, and now they're going to the Paxtons' house for lunch. This much is certain. They pass a farmyard where a donkey walks round and round a well, turning some ancient contraption designed to draw water to the surface.

What does he think? He thinks there are things you see and things that are hidden; things that you talk about and things that remain forever unsaid. Things that become secrets, like death itself. He holds his football tightly, in case anyone should try and take it from him.

Later they play pelmanism, on the floor of the Paxtons' sitting room. Binty has joined them. Tom is kneeling on the floor, and Paula is complaining that she never wins. Alexandra is wearing a frock with smocking on the front. She sits cross-legged. If he leans forward, Tom can see her knickers. He mustn't be obvious about it. He must be calm and casual. Is she old enough to have hair?

Neil reaches out and turns a card. The Jack of Clubs. He pauses, considering the uniform backs of the cards, their collective anonymity.

Alexandra giggles excitedly. She knows, she knows.

Neil stretches and turns another card face-up. The Queen of Hearts.

His sister breathes out in relief, waits for Neil to turn the cards face-down again, and then pounces. There! Jack of Clubs and Jack of Clubs. A pair, snatched away and stored on the carpet by her side. She reaches for another. Ace and Ace, of Diamonds. And pauses, with her skirt stretched tight from knee to knee and the warm triangle of white cotton visible to Tom's eager eye.

'This is a silly game,' Neil says. 'Let's go and play football.'

Alexandra protests. 'That's because I'm winning.'

'It's because you can't play football.'

Against her protests they abandon the cards and go out into the garden.

She felt quite calm, that was the astonishing thing. She walked into the canteen and apologized for being late, and she felt quite calm. 'Sorry I'm late,' she said.

'Where's Nick?' Marjorie asked. 'Aren't you going to bring him in?' She was making sandwiches. She had a large pot of some kind of filling made of mayonnaise and chopped vegetables that she called 'Saturday-night vomit'. The label claimed it as sandwich spread.

'I thought it better not. Not after that trouble.'

'Oh, come on. That was nothing. A silly misunderstanding.'

'Was it? Did you know that some of Damien Braudel's men took him in for questioning the other day? I think it's appalling that they can do that kind of thing, without any grounds, without any reason. It's like the Gestapo.'

'That's what we've come to, I'm afraid. Who can blame them really, what with the bombs and everything?'

'But why should they be suspicious of Nick? He wouldn't hurt a fly.'

'I'll take your word for it, my dear. Now come on, roll your sleeves up and do something useful.'

Nick laid his hands on her memory as she worked. 'Marjorie,' she said, 'did you talk to Geoffrey about Nick? About him and me, I mean. Did you?'

Was there a fractional hesitation on the older woman's part? 'Geoffrey? Who's Geoffrey?'

'You know perfectly well. Geoffrey Crozier.'

Marjorie frowned, looking over the pot of sandwich spread, her knife poised like a weapon. 'Is he that bank manager fellow?

Why do you ask? Is something going on? Are you in a bit of a pickle, darling?'

'Of course not. I just wondered. Something Geoffrey said. He seemed to know about . . .' About what? Was she about to protest too much? 'That we were friends, Nick and me. It really doesn't matter.'

'Doesn't it?'

'No. No, it doesn't.' She let the moment die.

'How is Edward?'

She shrugged. 'His usual impervious self.'

Fifteen

'It's her business,' Paula insists. 'You've no right.'

They're in the sitting room, an expansive place of low sofas and armchairs with french windows looking out on to the dark terrace. Thomas stands in front of the fire, a glass of Graham's cognac in his hand, looking at the two women. Kale is curled up into the corner of one of the sofas, her legs folded beneath her like a gull's wings. Her own drink is something as brightly coloured as a boiled sweet, a liqueur Paula and Graham brought back from the West Indies. 'It's nothing to do with rights,' he says.

'Tommo, she's dead. You can't exhume her. It's indecent.'

He sips his brandy. They've consumed two bottles of wine during dinner and he is feeling the elation that comes with alcohol. 'I'm not exhuming her. I'm creating a historical discourse.'

'That's just jargon.'

'My whole job is jargon. Words, words, fucking words. I think I hated her, do you know that? As a child, I think I hated her.'

'Oh, Tommo, no! How the hell can you say something like that?'

Kale gives a bitter little laugh. 'Christ, if I'd hated my mum because of every man she'd fucked . . . So what if it did happen? What the hell's it got to do with you? It's her business, isn't it? And now she's dead and you should just leave her alone.'

'I was always pleased to go back to school, you know that? Pleased to get away from her. I hated boarding school and yet it was better than her. It was the worst kind of hate: the kind that's nurtured in love.' He searches for an example. He wants to educate them in this, something that he has only now understood for the very first time. 'Think . . . I don't know . . .' He looks at Kale. 'Think of Steve.'

Paula asks, 'Who's Steve?' but gets no reply.

'I don't hate Steve.'

'Well, someone you have loved who then betrays you. The Janus face of love. Who said that?'

'I've no fucking idea. Anyway, your mum didn't betray you. From what you and Paula say, she seems to have been a loving mother. If she betrayed anyone, she betrayed your old man, and he's dead.'

Momentarily the two women seem to be allied against him. He shakes his head. 'It's obvious. She's there in Cyprus on her own and she's bored. Imagine it. Father was away at work for most of the day and there she was, stuck at home. And she found someone else. You know what he said to me once? "I had to persuade your mother to marry me." It was she who needed convincing, you see.'

'Ridiculous,' Paula says. 'Anyway we'd have known about it, wouldn't we?'

'Would we? Would we have read the signs right? Remember how they used to fight? What was that all about? We were just kids. You were little more than a baby.'

'But she just wasn't that kind of woman.'

'Who the hell isn't that kind of woman? People have affairs all the time. Always have, always will. What else could stay with her for over three decades, to ambush her with guilt when she was dying?'

Paula laughs derisively. 'Women have a million things to feel guilty about if they try. How about, not having another child? How about not loving us enough?'

'She adored us.'

'But it's not something you measure on a scale. Maybe she adored us and yet still felt it wasn't enough. Who knows? How about feeling guilt about abandoning you to boarding school, or not doing the same with me? How about not loving Dad enough? With women, it's usually something like that – not loving enough, not doing enough, not being enough. Men feel guilt about excess, women about paucity.'

'Very clever.'

'Anyway, you're just making suppositions. You've no real evidence whatever.'

He considers this, considers evidence, considers the present and the past, neither of them certain, the one ephemeral and random and bound by perspective, the other imperfectly perceived, like a dream recalled the morning after – something devoid of continuity or sense, and imbued with significance merely by virtue of being recalled at all. He sips his brandy. 'Yes I have,' he says. 'I was there.'

There is a silence. Like so many silences, it is relative. There's noise on the periphery: the fire in the grate, the television in the next room where the children are watching a game show with Birgit – there's the muffled, incoherent sound of audience participation that conveys the idea of what's going on but not the specifics. But between the three adults there is silence.

'You were there? What the hell do you mean, you were there?'

He frowns. Suddenly he feels like a child put under some kind of sharp, adult interrogation, his eyes blistering with something that may be tears, the muscles round his mouth turning down under the weight of emotion. How to distract from this ridiculous weakness? He raises the brandy glass to his lips again and coughs with the sudden harshness of the liquor at the back of his throat. It gives him an excuse to get out his handkerchief. 'I think so. I don't know, really. I have this . . . dream, memory, I don't really know what it is.'

'What on earth are you talking about, Tommo?'

'It's like looking at a picture, really. There's nothing else around it, no context or anything. No, not a picture. It's more like standing in the wings of a theatre and watching what's happening on stage. But just a scene, not the whole play. Just a scene. And . . .' He tries a smile. 'And it's badly lit.'

'What the hell are you saying?'

'It's always been there. Memory of a memory, perhaps. That's the problem, isn't it? Remembering becomes part of the memory. Or maybe it's a dream, I don't know. But I can see her; I've always been able to see her.' He gestures, as though Dee might be there, if they only have eyes to see. 'She's there in the shadows. I'm in the light and they're in the shadows, and I'm watching them.'

'"Them"?'

'I can't see him. I don't know who it is. When they've finished, she sits up and looks at me.'

'Finished what? They were screwing? Who? Where is all this? Tommo, are you quite all right?'

Kale unfolds her legs and sits up. 'Tom,' she says. She's never called him Tom before. 'Let's go to bed. You're tired.'

'Let him finish.'

Kale looks at Paula, her face clenched in anger. 'Can't you see how stupid all this is? She's dead, your mum. She's fucking dead! She doesn't have to stand trial in front of you two.'

'It's not really your business, is it?'

'It's my fucking business if I have to sit and listen to it.'

'I wish you wouldn't speak like that in my home.'

He looks from his sister to Kale. He's not oblivious to the argument between them; he just doesn't feel it matters. 'I don't know where it is, nor when it is. I'm just standing there, looking. There's bright light behind me, and a breeze.' He laughs faintly and without conviction. 'And I'm holding a football. Strange, that. A football. I don't even like fucking football.'

A hot, dark room, ransacked by shadows. In the room there is a bed, strewn with sheets. Among the sheets, on the bed, two figures, naked, glazed with sweat, limbs locked together. Their movement is violent and staccato, with no beauty to it. There is sound, a rough grunting, neither male nor female, barely even human. He walks over to watch. The man is a shadow. He wants to see his face but can't. Of the woman's face there is no doubt: it is Kale's, his mother's, Gilda's, his mother's again. No doubt about any of them. And there's more than just her face, the whole naked length of her in fact, her slopped breasts and splayed legs, the open mouth, the cave where he longs to hide, does hide, curled up like a foetus in the warmth.

And then abruptly he is standing by the bed again and the two figures part, and lie for a moment side by side among the ruin of the sheets and still he cannot see the face of the man.

She sits, running her fingers under her hair so that she is lifting it up in a cloud – an uncharacteristic gesture he has never seen before. One of her legs hangs off the bed; the other is up, the knee bent. Her lap is a deep shadow that crawls part way up her belly.

She turns and speaks to him. 'Tom, you're here—'

Thomas wakes from nightmare. There's no one beside him in the bed and when he turns he sees her standing naked at the window, a pale, ghostly presence moulded out of light and dark. Through the windowpane in front of her is a wet, monochrome day, all colour leached out by drizzle.

'What's up?'

'It's raining.'

'I can see it's raining. Come back to bed.'

She glances round. 'You were pissed last night.'

'Not pissed. Eloquent.'

'Eloquent my arse.' She returns to her contemplation of the raindrops that are chasing each other down the pane, and the wet garden, and the woods on the far side of the garden wall. 'I want to leave,' she says.

'What the hell are you talking about?'

'Were you so pissed you didn't hear? What was it she said? "Please don't speak like that in my home."' She has put a dreadful accent on, an exaggerated imitation of Paula's. 'Emma and I just don't fit in here, do we? So I want to go.'

'For God's sake, Kale—'

'For *my* sake, thank you. Nobody else's. You can keep your bloody sister, OK? And her house that's like a bleeding palace, and her questions like she was a social worker or something. The way she stares at me, as though I'm some kind of freak. I feel like something on day-release from the zoo. She's got everything and yet she's so possessive. Won't let anyone else in, won't let you go, and you won't let your mum go. Your bloody family, always clinging on to each other.'

'That's what families do, isn't it?'

She stares pointedly out of the window. 'I wouldn't know, would I?'

Down in the kitchen everyone is already up and sitting round the breakfast table. Despite the weather, the mood is one of high excitement. Graham is due back that morning from the States, and the children are eager to see him. Birgit and Paula are organizing them, and Christopher is explaining things to Emma, how far away America is, how much money his father makes there, how clever he is. 'What about your father?'

'He's very clever too,' Emma says.

She has her tiara on. 'All night she is wearing it. All night,' Birgit insists. 'She is a princess.'

'If I'm a princess,' Emma explains to Christopher, 'that means my father's a king. So there.'

'No he's not.'

'Yes he is.'

'Did you mean all that stuff you said last night?' Paula asks Thomas. She's talking *sotto voce*, so that the kids won't hear.

'What stuff did I say?'

'About catching Mummy at it. About hating her.'

'I was pissed.'

'You mean you didn't mean it?'

'I mean I shouldn't have said it.'

'But hating her . . .'

'Childish, isn't it? But sometimes it's the only defence a child has. I mean . . .' What *does* he mean? His whole working life has been about meaning, the meaning of history; and all the time there's that feeling in the background that he's chasing a phantom – there is no meaning, no sense at all, just contingent events piling one on top of the other, driven by nothing more than the mechanics of chaos. 'I mean, I suppose Phil hates me at times. He probably hates me all the time. Parents aren't very fashionable these days, are they? Nowadays you don't understand them, you just blame them. Maybe when he grows up he'll come to understand.'

'I'm sure he doesn't hate you, Tommo. Just adolescent angst.

But I'd be careful about introducing him to Kale. He'll either loathe her or lust after her. Or both.'

A moment later Kale appears in the doorway. She's barefoot and wearing only a short nightdress. The image of her body is visible like a ghost behind the thin material – her breasts like teardrops, the curve of her hips, the smudged shadow nestled between her thighs. There is a palpable intake of breath from Birgit, a small exhalation of annoyance from Paula. Christopher blushes.

'Just coffee,' she says when Paula asks. 'I just want coffee. Instant'll be fine.'

'We don't have instant.' Paula is tight-lipped. 'Well, maybe we've got some somewhere. I'll have a look.'

'Don't bother. Whatever. Whatever's the easiest.'

In the sober light of the morning it's as though the gloss has been stripped from the two women, exposing the bare foundation of antagonism. Kale glances at Thomas. 'I feel shitty,' she says and takes her mug of coffee to go back upstairs. Christopher giggles uncertainly.

When breakfast comes to an awkward and silent end, Birgit takes the children to clean their teeth while Thomas and Paula clear the table. 'She doesn't have to parade around stark naked in front of everyone,' she complains.

'She didn't even realize.'

'Didn't realize, my foot. Miss Kale knows exactly what she's doing. She was pretty obnoxious last night. Is she going to apologize?'

'I think she expects *you* to.'

'When she was effing and blasting in my house?' She rinses plates and bowls and stacks them in the dishwasher. Milk and butter go into the fridge, one of those double-door American ones big enough to hold a corpse.

'I'm afraid she wants to go this morning. She's pretty pissed off.'

'Oh dear, Tommo. Is it all coming to pieces?' There's amusement in her expression, and a poor attempt at disappointment. 'She's really got you by the foreskin, hasn't she?'

'I don't have a foreskin, Paula. They cut it off long ago.'

At least she laughs. 'I'll give her a hug and tell her she's very sweet and mustn't take me too seriously. Is that what you want?'

'I think that would be the worst thing possible.'

That's the moment when Kale appears again. She's wearing a T-shirt and a short denim skirt now, with no more than a narrow smile of midriff to greet strangers. 'You talking about me?' she asks. 'I don't like being talked about behind my back.'

Paula tries a placating smile. 'Tommo was telling me you have to go. What a shame. Graham will be so disappointed.'

Kale shrugs. 'I'm sure he'll be all right.'

'I expect he will, my dear. That's not quite what I meant.'

The two women face each other across the kitchen, protagonists in an obscure, undeclared cold war. Kale shrugs. 'Anyway, thanks for having me and Emms to stay.'

Paula smiles her thin, acid smile, the one she uses with obnoxious interviewees. 'It was a pleasure. Maybe we'll see you again.' The words are not posed as a question.

'I wanted to stay with Linda,' Emma says from the back of the car as they pull away from the house. In the mirror Thomas can see Paula with her two children waving, and the clumping Birgit standing beside them.

Kale lights a cigarette and winds the window down. 'Shut up, Emms. You've got no choice.'

'But I was having fun.'

'You can't have fun all the time.'

284

'Why not?'

'Because.'

It's Sunday morning and the traffic into the city is light. They pass quickly from the countryside into the outer, twentieth-century purlieus – the semi-detached houses, the shopping malls, the plate-glass office blocks. In the back Emma sleeps, her head lolling from side to side. The journey takes them further into the city, into an inner circle of concrete flats and brick terraces where railways ride above the road, the arches boarded up or turned into lock-up stores and makeshift cafés. Torn posters announce raves that have long since passed, demonstrations that have long ago dispersed, sales that are over. Sometimes, like a fossil preserved amidst the accretions of the twentieth century, there's a stretch of Victorian terrace.

'I'm sorry,' Kale says at last. 'For fucking up like this.'

'It's all right. You haven't fucked up.'

'I just felt I was being used.'

'By whom?'

'By you. A trophy of some kind. "Look, I can still pull young women." You know the kind of thing.'

They have paused at traffic lights while a train rattles and shudders on an iron bridge overhead. Disconsolate figures shuffle along the pavements, mouthing things to people who aren't there. Thomas wonders whether that's what he has been doing as well, mouthing words to someone who isn't there. 'I'm not using you, Kale,' he says. 'I love you. It's different.'

She doesn't respond, just looks out of the window at walls scrawled with lurid slogans and indecipherable tags, daubed with fists and faces. 'It's not so bad, you know. This place, I mean. It's all right.'

'I never said it wasn't.'

'It's genuine, the people are genuine.'

'Genuine what?'

She shrugs. 'Genuine poor.' The lights change and they move on. 'Is that bathos? I read that word "bathos", but couldn't really get it.'

'It'll do.'

She nods and lights another cigarette. 'Good to know I'm making progress.'

They slow down to pass a street market – clothes mainly, racks of dresses shrouded in polythene – where people stare in through the windows of the car as though they are intruders from another continent. A woman recognizes Kale and waves. 'Just a friend,' she explains, as though it might have been an enemy. Beyond the market they turn past a newsagent and an Afro-Carib restaurant, past a pub with graffiti on its walls and last night's vomit on the pavement, and finally they reach an anonymous road of jerry-built housing from the nineteen-fifties. He parks the car where Kale indicates, in front of a block of flats with balconies and steel-framed windows overlooking the road. There are no doors. The doors are all inside, through tunnels, up staircases, like a medieval fortress barricaded against the world.

Kale gets out of the car. Thomas has a feeling of loss, the understanding that if he does let her slip away she will be back in this strange world for ever, like an animal returned to the wild. 'What about next weekend?' he asks. 'I tell you what – we could go to my mother's house.' He turns to Emma, who is emerging from her sleep, her face crumpled and unsmiling. 'Emma would like that, wouldn't you?'

'Will Linda be there?'

'Just the three of us, at the seaside. There are boats and sea-gulls and things.'

'I don't want it if Linda's not there.'

He turns back to Kale, as though for adjudication. 'What about it?'

'Maybe.' She looks at him thoughtfully, her mouth twisted. He knows the answer now: can you feel the little shreds of skin where she has nibbled? You can't. It's all painless, without any damage. 'What you said back there. Did you mean it?'

'Of course I did.'

She nods. 'Puts me in a sort of awkward position, doesn't it?'

'And me.'

She turns to undo Emma's seatbelt and help her out of the car. 'Come on, Emms. Let's go and see how Gran is.'

'Will you be in college this week?' he asks.

She glances round. 'Of course I will.'

From a third-floor window a face peers out through grimy net curtains as though to view the progress of their conversation. Is that Kale's mother? The word 'mother' means two things to him – other people's mothers, mere pieces of biology; and his own mother, on whom he was once some kind of parasite and who now lives, parasitically, in his own mind. What would she have thought of this place, of this mother called Kale and her child, now crossing the turd-littered grass into the shadows of a urine-scented archway? Her short skirt and pale legs, her jacket with GLAMOUR across the shoulders. What would she have thought of his confession of love?

'See you,' Kale calls.

Has she gone for good? Part of him poses the question objectively, as a point of academic interest as he drives across the city back to his flat; another part of him feels that dreadful sickening of loss, something akin to bereavement, anguish and misery coupled with anger. She loves him or she does not love him. The choice is hers. Or rather, it is not even a matter of choice but of some subtle work of chemistry and circumstance. Certainly it is beyond his powers of influence.

He opens the street door to his apartment. There's the familiar smell of disinfectant and damp in the hallway, the familiar sight of the bicycle belonging to number 2A propped against the wall and the pram from number 3A tucked under the stairs. The light switch fires a relay and sends current up the stairwell to dim and dusty light bulbs on each floor. Climbing the stairs, he thinks of his mother and of Kale, of memory and forgetting and the fragile borderline between the two. In the future will Emma remember him as he may or may not have remembered Nicos? Will he stay lodged in her adult memory and will she try to make sense of his presence there? Or will he just be consigned to a scrap heap of forgetfulness, along with dozens of other men who have lain, briefly, with her mother?

On the fourth floor he struggles with his keys and discovers, with surprise, that his front door, armoured and reinforced, with bolts that sink into lintels and jamb, opens on the first turn of the main key. He pushes the door open cautiously, Kale momentarily forgotten. Did he forget to lock the place up properly? Or has someone broken in? He steps in, fearing the chaos of a break-in, doors flung open, clothes strewn all over, cupboards emptied, drawers tossed on the floor, electronic equipment vanished. There's noise coming from the living room. Someone's there. Tapping, and the sound of footsteps and music. He turns the handle and opens the door, prepared for flight or fight, or anything in between.

'Is that you, Dad?'

Phil. It's Phil, sitting on the sofa with his back to the door and his computer plugged like a parasite into the television across the room.

'What the hell are you doing here?'

'Been here since yesterday.'

'Yesterday?'

'Yes, yesterday.' There's a little man on the screen, a cartoon figurine moving back and forth through a maze of tunnels and caverns. For the moment there's no way out. The word PAUSE appears and the figure freezes. The boy turns with that wary, belligerent look. 'It was my weekend with you, Dad.'

Thomas closes his eyes and sits heavily on the sofa beside his son. 'Oh Jesus. I'm sorry, mate.'

Phil shrugs. 'It doesn't matter. Forget it.' PAUSE vanishes. The little figure on the screen goes back to searching, his feet splashing through puddles, the inane repetitive music following him round on his quest.

'I'm really sorry, Phil.'

'Forget it, Dad. I'm concentrating.'

'Why didn't you ring?'

'I didn't know where you were, did I?'

'I was at Aunt Paula's.'

'How was I to know that?'

'Well, you could have tried her number.'

The manikin has found a hidden lever. Along the bottom of the screen it says 'walk to', 'push', 'pull', 'give' and half a dozen other functions you need for life. There's even 'talk to', but there's no one to speak with at the moment and so that option is conveniently greyed out. 'Pull' is the command that Phil selects for the lever, and immediately the wall of the cave opens. Some mechanism inside the computer whirrs and clicks. The manikin is no longer in the cave but in an open room where there's a single window, a single table and a single exit. Nothing else. A pistol lies on the table. 'Yeah!' the boy exclaims.

'Why didn't you phone your mother?'

'She'd have gone ballistic, Dad. You know that.'

'Yes, but here all by yourself—'

'It's all right. Really.'

'What have you been doing all the time?'

'Playing.'

'What did you eat? Did you find things? Tell you what.' He moves closer to his son and makes an attempt to put an arm round his shoulders. 'Hey, can I join you? We'll get a Chinese, have some fun.'

'You get bored, Dad, you know that. And I had a Chinese last night. Oh yeah, I said you'd pay them later so you'd better not forget *that*.' The manikin has picked up the gun. 'Pistol' it says at the bottom of the screen, to go along with 'old book' and 'whip' and other arcane possessions. 'You were with a girl, weren't you?'

Thomas hesitates. 'Yes, I was. She's called Kale.'

'And is she the real thing?'

'I think so, yes.'

The manikin has begun searching for the way out of the room. He could try the door, but the window looks more attractive. 'You always say that,' says Phil.

The class is discussing interpretations of history – the Whig interpretation, the Marxist interpretation, modernist and post-modernist interpretations. They are all there, the motley collection of androgynous youth, the jeans and the trainers, the sloganed T-shirts and the glowing shalwar-kameez, and, next to that, Kale in her tight denim skirt and the jacket that says GLAMOUR across the shoulders. 'What d'you mean, "interpretation"?' Eric asks, in that nasal way he has. 'Isn't there just what happened?'

Thomas catches Kale's eye. She holds his gaze for a moment before glancing down at her notes. 'There are differing views of what history means,' he explains. 'Historians try to understand what went on as well as just record the events.'

'I don't think it means anything. I think it just was. Chaos, like. History's just the pattern we make out of things after they've happened.'

'That,' Thomas says with a little smile of triumph, 'is precisely what I mean. It's an artificial construct developed after the event in order to explain what happened.'

She stays behind after the class breaks up, sorting things in her bag, waiting while the others leave. She seems smaller than he remembers. How ridiculous, that memory can be so deceptive, even giving someone physical stature they do not in fact possess.

'What you said on Sunday,' she says, looking up at him. 'Do you still mean it?'

'Of course.'

She nods. 'I've been thinking. Maybe love is like history. Maybe it's an artificial construct developed after the event in order to explain what happened.'

He can't help but laugh. 'It's more real than that. It changes things. History never changed anything.'

'Changes for better or worse?'

'How do I know? That depends on your response.'

'Difficult, isn't it? Confusing.'

'How about some lunch? Maybe we can sort it out.'

' 'Fraid I can't. I've got to get back.' She picks up her bag and slings it over her shoulder, making for the door.

'What about next weekend . . .?'

She pauses in the doorway. 'I'm not sure . . .'

'Like I said, I thought we could go to my mother's house. Just the three of us. Emma'll enjoy it. You know she will.'

'I'll give you a ring,' she says. 'Let you know.'

From his office window he looks down on the grey concourse and the bright figure crossing it. Even at that distance he can see the shape of her legs, the sway of her hips, the slight toss of her head as she acknowledges something said to her by the man on the gate.

He watches her on to the traffic island in the centre of the road, willing her to look the correct way, left, the word spelled out there in white letters at her feet. How absurd that a portion of his whole well-being is invested in that small figure out there among the traffic and the anonymous crowds, travelling to a part of the city that he doesn't understand, has barely visited, thinks of as a foreign country. She appeared one day in his class, and smiled at him, and said, 'Cognate with cabbage, you're thinking,' a phrase that seemed witty and perceptive at the time, and she slept with him speculatively, as they do these days, and now she hesitates on the kerb, like Persephone pausing on the edge of the upper world before stepping into the unknown. She glances left, pauses for a double-decker bus to rush past, then crosses safely to the other side. The contingent event avoided.

Never get yourself on the wrong side of an unequal relationship, that's what his father warned him. But you can't legislate about it. You can't choose your moment of fall.

Sitting at his desk, he tries to replace her image with quotidian tasks, checking over some lecture notes, giving a desultory glance at a pile of student essays, going through his mail. There are a dozen letters, from journals, from acquaintances, an invitation to attend a conference in Bratislava in the autumn, a call for papers for another the following year. And one with a Cyprus stamp and postmark.

Dear Professor Denham.
Thank you for your letter inquiring for informations concerning a certain Nicos or Nikolaos Kyprianou. After exhaustive enquiries in a number of archives (I append detail), I am confirming that a man of the same name and occupation (a former taxi driver, resident in

Limassol) was a member of the EOKA
organization from at least 1958. It seems that
he spent some time in British detention in
that year for possession of firearms, but was
released in the amnesty that followed the
settlement of 1959. Records show that he was
afterwards killed in action against Turkish
irregular forces (TMT) in the Kokkina enclave
in August 1964. There is some evidence that he
was killed in air strikes by aircraft of the
Turkish Air Force. I enclose a document that I
found in the national archive which relates to
the man in question that may be of interest. I
hope these informations are of use to you, and
take the opportunity to convey my greetings
and assurance that I am at your disposition
for any further works in this or related
areas.

Yours faithfully,

Costas Nicolaides, Professor.
Department of History,
University of Cyprus.

enc.

The enclosure is a photocopy of a military document: '147
Field Security Section', it says at the top, with the date 12th
May 1958. The title is in bold: SUSPECTS, EOKA, LIMASSOL AREA,
and across one corner there is a faint stamp: the single word
RESTRICTED. Below the title are photographs of three men, each
with a brief biographical sketch. One of the photos shows

Nicos – it's a mug shot that might have been taken for a passport, but it's clearly recognizable as the youth posing beside his mother in that photograph. *Nikolaos Kyprianou*, it says beneath. *Part educated in England and speaks English almost like a native. Strong London accent.*

Thomas shrugs. So what? So nothing. Just a fact. The man called Nick, the man in the snapshot with his mother, the man called Kyprianou, the Cyprian, the man he vaguely recalls for the hollowness of his cheeks and the slicked quiff of his hair, was a member of EOKA. What does that mean? Maybe it matters, maybe it doesn't. History is full of that kind of thing, facts that you give weight to, incidents that you blow out of all significance.

What was it Voltaire said? History is a bag of tricks played on the dead by the living. Something like that.

Sixteen

Nothing happened, that was the strange thing. Life went on. The sun shone, with that alien insistence that it had out there in the eastern Mediterranean, and nothing had changed. Binty organized a picnic at Aphrodite's Rock, with Geoffrey and the Frindles and another couple who had only recently come out from England. The newcomers were as white as larvae in their swimming things, as though they had lived in the dark for years. Moonburn, Geoffrey called it. He stood with the great rock as a backdrop and, despite Binty's objections, gave them his spiel: 'It was here,' he told them: 'the most momentous event in the history of mankind – Aphrodite arrives in the world. How does she do it? Well, it's not your usual epiphany, I can tell you that. Uranus, if you'll forgive the expression, was her father, see? His son, Cronos, cuts off Daddy's private parts and tosses them into the sea, and out of the foam – his semen, really, and not the kind you find in ships – comes the goddess of love herself.'

Binty was shocked. 'I really think you could moderate your language in front of the children, Geoffrey.'

He considered her protest with mock seriousness. 'Which bit don't you like, old thing? Uranus?'

The children went swimming. They dived and swam and splashed one another, while Dee sat detached from the group, gazing out to sea and smoking. The water was still, as calm as a jelly. No foam today, no sperm. Geoffrey came and sat beside her. 'When does Edward get back?' he asked. 'Haven't seen him for ages.'

'Tomorrow. Binty and Douglas are taking us to the airfield.'

'How are things with you? Been managing on your own? You look rather unhappy.'

'I'm all right,' she assured him. 'Just fine.'

He watched her carefully. 'Tell me something.'

One of the boys was swimming far out, way out of his depth. He was older than Neil and Tom, more self-assured. She watched him, the strong confidence of his strokes. 'Tell you about what?'

'About your taxi driver.'

She drew on her cigarette and held the smoke in her lungs for a few moments, then expelled it in a careful stream. Her hand, the hand that took the cigarette from her mouth, was unsteady. 'There's nothing to tell, Geoffrey.'

'It's just that he's gone.'

She looked round at him sitting in his deckchair. 'Gone?'

'It's all right, you don't need to raise your voice. He's vanished, my dear. No longer found in his usual haunts. I thought you might know something.'

'Nothing at all.'

He sipped his beer, staring out to sea as though the goddess herself might suddenly rise up out of the water. 'You saw him the day before he did a bunk, didn't you? He drove you down to the SSAFA canteen.'

She felt a small pulse of fear. 'Perhaps he did. He used to drive me down there most days. Tuesdays and Thursdays, at any rate. Him or his uncle. I don't remember.'

'Oh, you remember all right, Mrs Denham. He turned up in the morning and you invited him in.' Geoffrey was smiling, watching her through the haze of his cigarette smoke, and smiling. 'You spent a couple of hours together, didn't you? What were you doing all that time, I wonder? Discussing the weather?'

'Were you spying on me?' Her voice rose in pitch. She hoped it sounded angry. 'Are your nasty little men watching me? He was trying to teach me Greek, Geoffrey. *O kairos einai kalós.* The accent's not very good, but you get the meaning, I'm sure. He's a friend. Maybe the idea is strange to you. That nonsense you talked about his being a member of EOKA or whatever – he's what I said, just a young man a bit out of place here, and eager to have a chat with someone from England. He's more English than Greek and the soldiers he meets are suspicious of him, of course they are, and so he's befriended me. What's politics got to do with it?'

'But his Greek friends are murderers. Maybe he's one himself.'

She gave a cry of some kind – disbelief, protest, horror, it wasn't clear. 'How can you say such a thing?'

'It's not difficult, you know, not when you move in that sort of world. The creed justifies the means, doesn't it? It always seems easy to kill in the name of a belief.' He sipped his beer, glanced across at her. 'I think you warned him off, didn't you? Is that it? Did you betray our little covenant of salt?'

She got up from the deckchair. Where was Tom? Paula was splashing around in the shallows, but where was Tom? 'There was no understanding, Geoffrey,' she said flatly. 'None at all.'

*

There's another boy, a newcomer called Stephen. He's older. Fourteen, perhaps fifteen. A strong swimmer. He goes out, way out of his depth, swimming freestyle. And Tom follows. There is a moment when he detaches from land. It's almost a boundary crossed, some invisible but real borderline on the languid surface of the sea. Up to that point you are swimming with the others, turning and calling and waving to them to show them how it's done; and then you've crossed the border and suddenly you are at sea, and they are mere figures on the shore, barely distinguishable for sex or age, their sound coming to you from far away and long ago.

Never has he been out so far. Never has he been out of his depth like this. He pauses, treading water and looking down through translucent layers to the seabed far beneath. He's flying. It's like one of those flying dreams he has, where you can just step up into the air and all is easy and all is possible. Fish pass below him, cautious about the shadow overhead. Stephen is still further out. Tom is all alone here, in the midst of the ocean, Aphrodite's ocean, where the goddess drifted towards the shore and began to play havoc in the lives of men and women.

'Tom!'

The sound doesn't intrude. It's from another world.

'Tom!'

Someone is swimming out towards him from the shore – a mere head floating on the surface, hair plastered. His mother. 'Tom!' she cries and then sinks back into the flurry of disturbance that she has made for herself. 'Tom!' She hasn't crossed the border yet into this distant world of the ocean where Tom floats. She is shouting and trying to raise herself out of the water, attempting to rise above the surface, waving her hand and calling – 'Tom!' – and falling back and swimming on. He hangs, suspended. Time seems suspended. He can see his own shadow, far below him on the seabed.

'Tom, come in,' she cries, and suddenly she is there close to him,

swimming up to him, her limbs flexing beneath the surface. 'For God's sake, you're right out of your depth.'

'Look,' he says to her, pointing downwards at their shadows moving together on the seabed far below. 'It's like flying.'

She looks; and panics. 'Oh, God!' Her cry is almost a prayer. 'Oh God, no!' Panic comes from somewhere else, from the darkness and the shadows deep inside her; it wells up out of the depths, floods through the fragile constructs of sanity and self-composure, sweeping everything before it. Her arms thrash around. The placid skin of water is ruptured and torn, ripped apart as though with a knife. Her legs writhe. There is a moment when she seems about to go under, and he watches her, wondering whether this will be the moment when she dies. Absurd, that: he wonders whether she is going to drown there before him, and all the time she can fly just like him.

It takes talk and calm to get her back to shore. Binty sees her flailing arms, hears her cries and swims out. They talk to her, calm her, persuade her to lie still, not to look down, to remember that she can swim as easily as they. Slowly the seabed rises towards them, the gap between their floating bodies and the black frogs of their shadows diminishing, until they can put down a foot and touch. She wades out of the water and sits, shaking as though with cold, on a towel. He looks down at the two women, Binty with her comforting arms around his mother, his mother shivering.

'Don't ever do that again,' Binty snaps at Tom, as though he just might, as though he might deliberately swim out there in order to drown his mother. That is the idiocy of adults, he thinks.

'It's all right,' his mother says. 'I'm quite all right.'

But she's not, is she? She's shaking, and she's in tears. He has never seen her in tears before, not really in tears. He stands there looking down on them, then wanders away to entertain himself.

Like a family welcoming their hero back from war they stood in a group on the perimeter track and watched as the Comet approached. The aircraft bucked and twisted in the hot spring air as it came in over the coastal flats, touching down with a puff of blue smoke from its tyres and a small sigh of relief from the watchers. It roared down the runway past them, then slowed and turned in the distance.

'Is Daddy inside?' Paula asked. 'Is he waving to us?'

'Of course he is.'

The aircraft was coming back at them now, like a threatening wading-bird, its legs reflected in shining pools of mirage. It turned broadside to them and the engines died. Vague shapes swam behind the Perspex bowls of the windows. 'I can't see him,' she cried, 'I can't see him!'

They watched while the stairs were manoeuvred into place and the passengers filed down to the concrete, their faces screwed against the heat and the light, their clothes crumpled. He appeared with the crew, after everyone had disembarked. Paula jumped up at him and shouted 'Daddy, Daddy!' while Dee kissed him and Tom stood aside and watched. Edward reached out and tousled his son's hair and called him 'old boy'. They walked across the apron towards the car, and all seemed normal. 'How did your mother take it?' Dee asked. She felt that she was searching for the right things to say, the correct phrases, the usual platitudes.

'You know how she is. Tough. There's a sort of fatalism about her.'

'I hope you sent her my love.'

'Of course I did. So how have you all been without me?'

She shrugged and looked away. 'Fine. We've been fine.'

'What have you been up to?'

They climbed into the car, the children pushing and shoving in the back seat. 'Up to?'

'What have you been doing with yourselves?'

She looked away out of the window across the airfield. 'This and that. Nothing much.' Out there in the middle of the dry grass there was a hut painted with red and white stripes. On its roof a radar scanner went round and round, seeking things out, sensing messages that were invisible and inaudible but there nevertheless, projected intangibly through the warm spring air.

'Are you all right, Dee?'

She looked round, and almost didn't recognize him sitting there, his hand on the ignition key, his foot just ready to touch the accelerator as the engine came to life. 'Of course I'm all right. Why shouldn't I be?'

'You don't look well.'

Perhaps it was his question, his faint air of concern, that breached her defences, for quite unexpectedly she was weeping, sitting there in the car beside Edward with the children shocked to silence in the back seat, and weeping uncontrollably, convulsively, like someone struggling for air, like someone drowning. He reached out and put his arm round her and patted her on the back. 'It's all right, darling,' he said. 'It's all right. I know it's all been a bit of a strain, but now it's all right.'

And then, as the convulsions abated, she told him: the swimming, the going out of her depth – 'It wasn't Tom's fault, don't blame Tom' – that awful space beneath her and the panic welling up inside. 'I thought I was going to drown. I thought I was going to drown. I still feel that I'm going to drown.'

'Still feel it? But you're safe. I'm back and you're safe.' He held her awkwardly, as though he had just rescued her and didn't quite know what to do next. 'You're on dry land. You're here and now and I'm back with you.' He patted her shoulder and carefully eased her upright in her seat, and turned the key in the ignition. The engine started. 'Let's all go home and you can have a rest, and the children will be especially quiet and good. All right?'

She swam, out of her depth, throughout the night, and woke in the early morning when it was still dark. Edward was beside her in the bed, turned on his side and facing away, breathing deeply. She lay there sweating beneath the sheet and clinging to her secret memory like a drowning woman clinging to a lifebelt. Her hand moved between her legs, evoking a thin, impoverished flood of sensation that washed over her and, in the first light of dawn, cast her up on dry land. When Edward awoke she had already been up two hours. 'I couldn't sleep,' she said as he appeared at the kitchen door. 'I haven't been sleeping well. Not in the last few days.'

He came over and embraced her. His hands on her hips were somehow repellent. 'Please,' she whispered against his neck. 'Not now.'

Later that morning – Edward had gone to work, Voula was hoovering in the sitting room – the phone rang. But when she hurried into the hall to answer it there was no one on the other end, just a thin rush of sound like a chill wind blowing through the wires. 'Hello? Hello?'

The receiver whispered its hollow, electronic silence back at her.

'Hello?' she said. 'Who's there?' Then softer, dangerously, she asked, 'Is that you? Where are you?'

When she phoned Phaedon Taxis it was Stavros who replied. Nicos had gone, he told her. If she wanted a taxi, he would drive. Where had he gone? The line was silent for a moment. 'He's a grown man,' he said. 'He do what he like.' And the phone went down.

She's standing in the garden, by the hibiscus bush. 'Tom,' she says. He looks up from what he's doing, which is pursuing a scorpion into a crevice among the stones. Paula's somewhere else, doing whatever stupid thing keeps her amused, digging.

'Yes?'

'What are you doing?'

'Nothing.'

'Binty's coming to take you for a swim.'

'I'm busy.'

'You said you were doing nothing. Anyway, I thought you liked going with Neil.' *For a moment she stands watching him.* 'Tom,' *she says.*

'Yes, what?'

'The last time, when you went with Binty. To Lady's Mile.'

'Yes?'

She tries to smile. It's a half-smile, with half the face, just the bottom part. 'You came back after swimming, didn't you? You came back for your ball.'

He shrugs and returns to the scorpion, which has backed into the hole and sits there with its claws raised, like an armoured car or a tank backed into a narrow defile. Chelae, *the claws are called. It's from the Greek. He knows that. He knows words.*

'Didn't you?'

'Maybe. I don't remember.'

'Did you come in?'

If you taunt a scorpion lots, it'll sting itself. If you surround them with fire, they'll sting themselves. He's been trying to test these things scientifically. He wants to see whether it's an old wives' tale. How old do wives have to be before they tell tales?

'Did you? Come into the house, I mean?'

'I don't remember. I don't remember anything.'

She stands there watching, irresolute, scuffing at the ground with one toe, like Paula does when she doesn't know what else to do. She says, 'I love you all very much, you know that, don't you? I love you and I love Paula and I love Daddy. You know that?'

She's never said anything like that before. Does that make it an old wives' tale? He shrugs, prods, watches the scorpion watching him with black scorpion eyes, armoured against the world.

The killings began. The British read about them in the *Times of Cyprus*, heard about them on the wireless, discussed them at cocktail parties and on the beach. Threadbare, squalid incidents: a Turk shot in a café, a Greek informer gunned down in his house in front of his wife and children, an off-duty soldier dying on a pavement in Nicosia, two military policemen shot in a street in Famagusta. Occasionally there would be a photograph, a grainy rectangle of newsprint showing limbs in postures that they never would have adopted in life – a foot twisted, an arm bent round, a head turned in the opposite direction from the body.

'You really ought to be in married quarters,' Binty told Dee. 'You can't be safe stuck out there in the town.'

'In June,' she said. 'They've promised June.'

'And that canteen where you help out. It's really not safe.'

'Of course it's safe. It's inside the port. There are guards.'

She felt detached from the world around her – from Edward, and Binty and Douglas and the others, detached from their fears and concerns. It had been like this when Charteris had gone. She had heard nothing for months and the life of the grimy city had continued around her, but all the while she had felt herself dispersed on a cold and distant ocean that she had never seen but which raged, icily, in her mind.

Stavros drove her down to the canteen. He was sullen and suspicious, but he was her only link. 'What's he doing?' she would ask. 'Tell me what he's doing.' His eyes, watching her in the mirror, evaded hers whenever she looked. 'Is he doing anything dangerous? You can tell me, you know you can tell me.'

'Look, I not know anything, understand? I tell you that.'

'The fighting that's going on, the Turks and the Greeks. Is he tied up in that? Please tell me.'

'I know nothing, lady.'

They drove through the narrow streets, with the domes of the cathedral on one side and the minaret of the Djami Kebir mosque on the other. 'This is not a good area, lady. The Turks.'

'You're as bad as Nicos.'

Her laughter made him bridle. 'What do you mean, "bad as Nicos"?'

'A joke.'

He shrugged. 'Jokes, always jokes, you English. I only warn, that is all. Better we go somewhere else.'

'Well, I want to go this way.'

He drove on in sullen silence until she offered a sacrificial apology. 'I'm sorry,' she said. 'I'm sorry I snapped. *Signomi.*'

He glanced in the mirror. 'Nicos say that you are a lady with, how do you say? – *pnevma.* Spirit. I like that.'

It seemed that for a moment his defence was down. 'Have you . . .' she hesitated in case the question would conjure up its own denial, 'have you heard from him?'

He made a gesture with his hands, taking them from the wheel and opening them momentarily to the sky. 'Maybe, maybe not.'

'Tell me. Don't talk in riddles.'

'He tell to me to look after you. That is why I am not happy you go through this area.'

'What else did he say?'

Another silence.

'Did he say if I can see him?'

They were past the Castle and down by the waterfront where

the sea unravelled to the horizon, towards Egypt. There were the old godowns, the storehouses, the harbour gate with its armed guard. He drew in to the kerb, and in a moment was there at the door, opening it to let her out. 'Perhaps,' he said as she climbed out. 'Be ready if I phone.'

'What do you mean, be ready?' Her heart, her perception of time itself, had stopped. 'You're talking riddles again.'

'I don't know riddles.'

'Stories. You're telling stories.'

'I tell nothing. I just say to be ready for if I call. And you tell no one. You understand? Tell no one.'

'I won't. Of course I won't.'

'He trusts you,' he said. 'I do not.'

S he sat with Marjorie, smoking, waiting for custom. The canteen was in danger of closing. With the outbreak of violence had come curfews, usually in the evening, sometimes throughout the whole day. Often the men were confined to camp, shut in their lines of sweltering tents out in the hinterland, behind barbed wire and sandbags and the impenetrable barriers of military routine. 'I don't know whether we should strike the flag,' Marjorie said. 'Not the kind of thing I want to do, but it all depends on the powers that be.'

But for the moment they soldiered on. That phrase, of course, was Marjorie's. 'I suppose you won't be able to help out once you move into a married quarter?' she asked. 'I don't know if I'll be able to carry on alone.'

'They ought to send someone else out from England.'

'That's the trouble. They might, if there was still demand, but in the present circumstances . . .' Marjorie looked at her sideways. She had a way of looking at you, as though she was peering over spectacles that she didn't, in fact, possess. 'By the way, where has your Nick gone? I haven't seen him for days.'

'I've told you, he's not "my Nick". And I don't see why everyone is so interested.'

'It sounds as though you're missing him, darling.'

At that moment the phone rang, as startling and intrusive as a stone thrown through a window. Marjorie went to answer it, then looked across to Dee. 'It's for you.'

Dee took the receiver. 'Hello? Who is it?' There was the crackle of interference on the line. Somewhere far away a voice twittered, some distant, unintelligible conversation.

'Hello? Who is this?'

For a moment she thought it might be him. But another voice spoke: 'I thought I might find you there, hidden dreamer. I rang you at home but there was only the maid, gibbering at me in Greek. I haven't seen you for ages.'

'Oh. It's you.'

'Well, don't sound so enthusiastic. Look, can't we meet, at least for a chat? I'm at that bar on the seafront. Aphrodite's. I won't say anything embarrassing. Promise. Just a social chat, like old times.'

'Old times weren't like that.'

'No, I suppose they weren't. New times, then. I'll be on my best behaviour. Nothing that anyone could gossip about.'

'Look—'

He talked over her: 'No, don't say it. Don't say anything. I'm there right now. Try and get away if you can. Just a few minutes.'

'I told you, I can't. I don't think it's—'

'Don't think, just do it.'

'Damien . . .' And then the click of the receiver on the far end, and the buzz of the dialling tone. She looked up at

Marjorie. 'Damien Braudel,' she said. 'Apparently he's at a bar near by. Do you mind if I nip out to say hello? Just for a few minutes?'

It was a fine morning. The heat had not yet blurred the air and the sky still possessed that intensity of blue that you never saw in England, as though it were a solid medium, not transparent. Before her was the cool expanse of the sea, ruffled by the morning breeze. There were a few couples strolling in the sunshine, some hopeful fishermen standing by the sea wall. A radio blared from a café. Was she being watched? She felt like an animal, a mouse or something, scurrying along beneath the watching eyes of carnivores – Geoffrey's watchers in their anonymous vans, their neutral cars, their fawn raincoats and shop-soiled lightweight suits. Were they watching her now? She had no answer to the question. Once you think you are being watched, you are.

Cleopatra Street was bisected by sunlight, as though cut by a knife, the buildings on the right in shadow, the ones on the left in the glare. A grocery shop erupted across the pavement with crates of vegetables and fruit. Among the cars jammed along the pavement was a white coupé with the maker's name, Borgward, in chrome letters. The Café Aphrodite was almost unchanged – only the name, in accordance with the EOKA edict, had been replaced by Greek lettering: ΑΦΡΟΔΙΤΗ. Otherwise there were the same dusty bottles in the window, the same half a dozen Formica-topped tables out on the pavement, the same feeling that the place still hoped for a clientele that had never materialized. Damien was sitting at the same table as before, nursing a similar brandy sour. He half rose as she approached. 'Long time, no see.'

There was an awkward greeting, a fumbled handshake combined with a chaste kiss, cheek to cheek. Precisely which cheek was determined by a kind of lottery, a self-conscious bobbing of heads, a fumbling avoidance of mouths, a clumsy apology. She sat down across the table from him and tried to compose herself. 'I'm afraid I've got to be quick. Marjorie's expecting me. She's all on her own.'

'Can't we get some lunch somewhere?'

'I'm sorry, there just isn't time.'

Waiting for her order – she wanted tea, with fresh milk, not that terrible evaporated stuff – they constructed some kind of a conversation out of whatever there was to hand: the children, their spouses, the situation on the island. 'I think they may ship all the families home,' Damien said. 'This place is a tinderbox at the moment.'

'Douglas says there's a settlement in the pipeline.'

He laughed. 'Fat lot people like Douglas know about it. I'm in the front line. They sit cosily in the Club drinking gin and tonic and reading *The Times* and the *Telegraph*. They should get off their backsides and experience a bit of reality.'

The tea came. She sipped, and smiled vaguely and glanced round. They seemed out of place sitting there on the pavement, under the eyes of passers-by. Dee looked away, towards the promenade and the sea, out towards the hairline of the horizon that divided the soft blue of the water from the hard, turquoise sky.

'You know your taxi driver fellow?' Damien said.

She felt a small shock, like the sensation you might get from touching an appliance that hasn't been properly earthed, a sharp tingling of pain and suspicion. 'What about him? Have your men beaten him up again?'

'It was hardly as bad as that. They gave him a bit of a going over perhaps.'

'There's a difference?'

'Sure there's a difference.' He reached inside his jacket, took out a folded sheet of paper and handed it across the table. 'Anyway, it seems that we weren't altogether off the mark. Don't wave it around, for heaven's sake. There'd be a hell of a stink if anyone knew I'd shown it to a civilian.'

The document originated from 147 Field Security Section, whatever that might be. The word 'RESTRICTED' was stamped in red ink across one corner. 'What is this?'

'Just read it. It's obvious enough.'

SUSPECTS, EOKA, LIMASSOL AREA, the title proclaimed. Below were photographs of three men, each with a brief biographical sketch. One of the photos, she realized with a start of fear, showed Nicos – a younger, bland Nicos posing for the kind of snapshot that might have been used for a passport, but certainly Nicos. *Nikolaos Kyprianou. Part educated in England and speaks English almost like a native*, it said. *Strong London accent.*

Her mind trembled. For a moment she wondered whether something in the unsteady fabric might give way, whether she might break down there and then in front of Damien, with people walking past and watching them in the curious manner of the Greeks.

'It seems he's rather deeper in it than we might have thought.'

'Why should I care?'

He was smiling at her. 'Oh, but you do, don't you, Dee?'

There was sweat on her forehead, sweat trickling beneath her arms. 'Of course I don't.' She pushed the paper back across the table to him. 'I haven't seen him for days. His uncle has been doing the driving recently. That's all I know.'

'There's quite a flap on about him.'

'And I don't believe he can be involved in anything of this sort. It's you, it's the Army and the government, it's the situation they find themselves in.' Anger grew inside her, anger and fear grafted together. 'Why can't you all just leave this bloody island alone? Tell me that. What's the place got to do with you?'

He returned the sheet to the inside pocket of his jacket. 'What's it got to do with you, Dee?'

'Nothing. I'm as much a foreigner here as you are. An invader.'

'We're getting the socialist sermon now, are we?'

She pushed her chair back and stood over him, oblivious to anyone who might have been watching, suddenly possessed by an anger that had never been given expression until this moment in the spring sunshine of Cleopatra Street. 'It's not a sermon, it's just common sense. Our presence here makes criminals of the innocent. That's all.'

'The day of the riot . . .'

She paused, about to turn away. 'What about it?'

He smiled up at her. 'What went on between the two of you? Something had happened when I turned up. You looked as frightened as hell and he ran off like a kid that has been caught stealing apples. It wasn't politics, that's for sure. What was it, Dee?'

She managed a shrug. 'Nothing. He had a bit of a crush on me, I've told you that. He said things. *You've* said things, haven't you? People say things that they don't always mean.'

'I meant them.'

'Maybe he meant them as well.'

He looked up at her. He was no longer sitting back in his chair with his legs casually crossed. Now he was leaning forward across the table, willing her to listen to him. 'There was something between you, wasn't there?'

'Don't be stupid. We're friends, that's all. I used to get cigarettes for him, that sort of thing. And he used to teach me Greek. I bet I can do better than you. *Parakaló, mia oka portokália?* See?'

'What's that?'

'Please can I have an *oka* of oranges.' She picked up her handbag and moved away, then paused and turned back. It was suddenly clear. Like the sea water beneath her trembling limbs – clear all the way down to the depths. 'Who put you up to this, Damien?' she asked.

'What on earth do you mean?'

'Who suggested that you contact me and ask me these questions? Was it Geoffrey?'

He looked puzzled. 'Who the hell's Geoffrey? What on earth are you going on about, Dee?'

She stood over him for a moment, trying to sort things out, trying to understand whether he was telling the truth and whether it was possible that he didn't know Geoffrey, trying to work out whether it was possible that Nicos was a terrorist, whether it was possible that she was here, on Cleopatra Street in Limassol, involved in this little altercation, with passers-by staring. 'Marjorie's expecting me, Damien. I'm going.'

He stood. Perhaps he meant to lean forward and give her a kiss, but she didn't allow him the opportunity, just turned from the table and walked away. She knew he would be watching her, but she didn't look back. She walked briskly along on the sunny side of the street towards the seafront and only at the corner did she glance back. Damien was standing at the table, watching. He waved but she didn't acknowledge his salute. She turned and set off along the esplanade.

Nothing had changed. The houses with their peeling plaster, the bar with its empty tables. The wireless blaring out, something from Athens Radio. The waiter at the bar called out to her: 'You want a drink, lady?', something like that. They could spot her as English, of course. She shook her head and walked on, wondering about Nicos, wondering what she felt and why she felt it, trying to fit Edward into the terms of the complex little equation that described who she was and what she was doing on this sunny late morning in the spring of 1958 with the British Empire crumbling around her.

There was a sharp report, like a car backfiring. Then another. Pigeons clattered into the air. She hesitated. The fisherman glanced up from his task on the sea wall. Someone came out from the bar, wiping his hands on a towel and saying something in Greek, perhaps to someone still inside.

She stopped. People were staring from doorways. There was noise. Difficult to be precise, really. Disembodied and incoherent noise. Someone ran along the esplanade, or perhaps that had nothing to do with it. Just a boy on an errand. Edward said that cars were always backfiring because they didn't maintain them properly. It was unburned fuel igniting in the exhaust pipe, that's what he said. She looked round. Shutters were going up all along the seafront. People were scurrying around as though a storm were expected, carrying chairs and tables in from outside the bars, rolling up sunshades, slamming doors.

She turned and began to retrace her steps, walking purposefully, hurrying now, nearly running. A sort of skipping. It seemed almost light-hearted, but she felt something else, a small, hidden stir of disquiet whose origin was in her mind but which manifested itself somewhere behind her breastbone, and lower down in the sickening depths of her abdomen.

She turned the corner back into Cleopatra Street. There was noise coming from the crossroads at the far end of the street, like the sea booming in a cave. A small crowd had gathered. At the Café Aphrodite the waiter was carrying tables inside. A siren wailed, the sound of wartime. She could see a blue police Land-Rover and some uniforms.

Disquiet swelled and became anxiety. Anxiety is fear spread out thin. Where had she heard that? Anxiety coagulated into fear. She hurried up the street. People were running past her in the opposite direction, scattering into the open space of the esplanade, young boys, perhaps from a school. Shutters were going down on the shops. Vegetables were being carried hastily inside. Someone, a Greek woman, was wailing – a sound tinged with the discordant tones of the Middle East – and at the cross-roads people were shifting round the edge of something, as though they were standing on the lip of a precipice and looking over. There was no coherent talk, just the muttering of imprecations, like in church, and the wailing.

An army Land-Rover drove up. Uniforms multiplied, soldiers as well as policemen. A British voice was giving orders. Dee pushed forward. 'What's going on?' she asked. 'What is it? What's happened?' Someone grabbed at her but she slipped out of his grasp and dived forward through the loose circle of onlookers.

There was an arena, an open space such as a crowd might make round a fight. You almost expected to see two men squared up against each other, fists raised. But there was just a young army officer standing there, and at his feet, half on the pavement and half on the roadway, was a heap of clothing – trousers, shirt, jacket. A twisted foot, shoeless, protruded from one end. The shoe was there as well, standing apart in the road. A polished brown brogue with the shoelace still tied. There was something absurd about the sight. A shoe on its own.

'Who is it?' she cried. 'Who is it?'

A hand grabbed her shoulder and held her tight. 'Come on, ma'am.'

She looked round and saw an English face, white, blotched with red. A red military cap with the peak pulled down. A military policeman. 'Who is it?' she asked. 'What happened?'

'I think you'd best stand back,' the MP said.

'What happened?' Her voice rose in panic. 'I just left some-one here. A friend. What happened?'

'Someone's hurt. Now why don't you—'

The officer came over. He was a captain of the Ox. and Bucks. Dee recognized the regimental badge on his beret, the hunting horn on its ribbons looking like a trinket, the kind of thing you might find in a Christmas cracker. The muscles of his face were taut. He frowned at her. Perhaps there was some kind of recognition. Perhaps he had seen her before, at that Christmas party at the garrison headquarters. 'Did you see anything?' he asked.

'Who is it? Do you know who it is? I was just having a drink – a friend—'

He turned away impatiently. 'Sergeant,' he called. 'Get a couple of dozen men off their arses and go through these houses.' He waved his hand at the buildings. 'Round up anyone who looks suspicious. And get on to battalion HQ. Get some more men over here in a hurry. We're not going to take this kind of thing lying down.'

'What are we looking for, sir?'

'Any able-bodied Greek males. Round the whole fucking lot up, do you understand? The whole lot. Anyone under the age of sixty. Where's that fucking blood wagon got to?'

He looked back at Dee. 'Why don't you get the hell out of here? This is no place for civilians.'

'Is it Damien? Is it Damien Braudel?' Her voice rose. She could hear it going out of control, climbing the register. Something moved – the pavement, the kerb, maybe the whole street – like a deep seismic disturbance beneath her. The officer grabbed her. She heard his voice calling, and hands holding her, and then her limbs lost all strength and she sat down on the pavement, her legs bent and useless. She was icy cold and sweating, as though she were ill. But she wasn't ill. There was nothing wrong with her at all. She would just wait a moment and then get up and go back to Marjorie's and everything would be all right.

'Come on, darling,' a voice said. 'Let's get you away from here.'

Hands grabbed her, strong, male hands. There was a shop near by, a tobacconist selling cigarettes and pipes and things like that, and they carried her in there, into the warm, comforting smell. A Greek woman escorted her to the bathroom at the back, where there was a threadbare towel and some pink soap and the smell of drains. '*Endaxi*,' she kept saying, '*Endaxi*.' All right, all right. Dee leaned over the basin and vomited, nothing much coming up, just acid slime and stuff, while the woman held her hair back. *Endaxi*, she said. *Endaxi, endaxi*.

After a time – how long? What happened to time? What determined its pace, its thrust? – other hands were helping her up and shuffling her out of the narrow confines of the bathroom and she was back in the shop. *Karekla*, someone said, and they produced a chair for her. Someone else came with a glass of water. They ministered to her, and she said that she was all right and please leave her alone, but still they fussed. There was a uniformed police constable, a big mustachioed Turk, standing at the doorway, and a British police officer who came over and introduced himself. 'Detective Sergeant Higham, ma'am.' And then there was someone else, a civilian coming forward and crouching down to look into her face, as though she were a patient and he a doctor.

'What are you doing here, Geoffrey?'

He didn't answer her.

'Geoffrey, why are you here?'

There was something in his expression, a dead look, as though the laughter was over and he didn't have anything else to put in its place. 'I've come to see if you are all right.'

'They killed Damien, Geoffrey.'

'I know.'

'Of course you know. There's nothing you don't know, is there?'

'There are a lot of things I don't know, Dee. Maybe there are things that you know that I don't.'

Why was he talking in riddles? 'Shall we go?' he suggested. 'I've got a car outside. I don't really think we can talk here.'

'But I don't want to talk. I want to know why you're here.'

'Don't be silly.' He put a hand on her arm but she shook him off.

'I'm not being silly. I want to know.'

There was a streak of embarrassment in his expression. Someone produced another chair and he sat down close to her. He patted his pockets and produced a packet of cigarettes. Players. That's what she had given Nicos. Players Navy Cut. 'Would you like one?'

'Yes, please.'

'They're not tipped, I'm afraid.'

'I don't like tipped. You know I don't like tipped.'

'Of course you don't.'

She noticed that his fingers were stained yellow with nicotine. Had she noticed that before? His poet's fingers were stained from all the smoking he did. The fact seemed significant, a clue of some kind. He tapped a cigarette on the packet and then carefully put it between her lips, as though she had lost the ability to do such things for herself. There was the little ritual with his cigarette lighter, the flint sparking, the wick catching a flame. She drew smoke deep into her lungs. It calmed her. 'That's better,' she said, which wasn't true but went some way to describing her state of mind now the nicotine was flowing through her blood. She looked at Geoffrey. His skin was coarse, the texture of the skin of a citrus fruit almost. There was a thin sheen of sweat. And crawling across his upper lip that narrow caterpillar of a moustache.

'What happened?' she asked, thinking about Damien, who had been and now wasn't. Was that possible? Could someone be snatched through the thin fabric of existence quite so suddenly? Could one just *be* one second, and then *not be* the next? 'What happened?' She knew that Geoffrey knew. He knew everything, so surely he knew this.

'Just wait for a bit, finish your cigarette and then we'll go and talk.'

'I'm not going anywhere to talk, Geoffrey. I'm going to Marjorie's.'

'I'll take you there.'

'I'm perfectly capable of walking. It's no distance.'

There was the noise of a vehicle outside. She craned round to see but there were too many people in the way – policemen, a few civilians. She heard the engine roaring and a clash of gears. 'It's all right,' Geoffrey said. He was trying to distract her, like a doctor trying to take a patient's mind of something that was unpleasant and a bit painful. But she knew what they were doing. They were lifting him up on a stretcher and manhandling him into the back of the ambulance. She waited, almost as though she was watching from outside, seeing this woman sitting on the straight-backed chair in the middle of the shadowy tobacconist's, with the man sitting just beside her, his chair set precisely at right-angles to hers. And the people standing watching, and the squat, ugly vehicle manoeuvring in the street outside. The white panels on its sides with the bright red crosses. Blood wagons, that's what they were known as.

'The children,' he said. 'Are they all right?'

'For the moment.'

'When does Binty bring them back?'

She drew on her cigarette and tapped the ash into the ashtray that he was holding for her. 'How do you know they're with Binty?'

People rallied round. That was the expression used. There was a military flavour to it, as though they might be rallying round the colours or something: Binty and Douglas were at her side, and Betty Frindle came round and spent a day with her. And there was Marjorie, of course. A shoulder to cry on, that was how she described herself. 'How simply ghastly for you, darling. How dreadful.' The epithets of sympathy, as though Dee had suffered a personal bereavement.

Edward seemed distracted, almost indifferent towards her, until the time when he summoned up courage to confront the issue. 'Were you having an affair with Braudel?' he asked.

'Don't be absurd, darling.' She felt almost happy to be able to tell the truth. 'He was a close friend, that's all. I could speak to him.'

'You can speak to me.'

'Of course I can. You're my husband.' He seemed puzzled by that response, as though there was a step missing in the argument but he couldn't quite see what it was.

They drove to Nicosia for the funeral. The interment was at the military cemetery at Wayne's Keep, a bleak place outside the city, a wasteland of dust and rock and eucalyptus trees. The officers of Damien's regiment were among the mourners and the burial party was chosen from his company. The soldiers performed their strange, slow-motion drill, like dancers performing an underwater ballet. And then, after the coffin had been lowered into the ground and riflemen had aimed their rifles at the sky and fired a salute, a lone bugler played the Last Post. Damien's wife and daughters stood at the graveside as motionless as sentries as the mournful notes rose like ghosts into the hot air.

Dee went over to her when it was all over. 'We met last Christmas,' she said.

The woman looked at her and smiled bleakly. 'Of course. Deirdre, isn't it?'

'Dee, yes.' She touched the woman's arm. 'I'm so very, very sorry.'

Sarah raised her pale eyebrows. 'What do you have to be sorry about?' she asked. 'Did you do something wrong?'

It was two days later that Geoffrey came round. Tom was in his room and Paula was outside in the garden. As they sat in the living room sipping coffee, the adults could hear the little girl talking to some animal she had discovered among the bushes, explaining how it should behave if it was to be a good boy. She collected beetles, assembling them into families, giving them names, ascribing to them human follies and human desires.

'He's not tried to get in touch?' he asked.

Dee fiddled with a packet of cigarettes, took one out and lit it with a trembling flame. 'Why should he?'

'We're not playing games, Dee. You were having an affair with him, weren't you?'

She felt the sting of blood in her cheeks. 'Where do you get that idea from?'

'Why can't you just answer me straight? For God's sake, Damien Braudel is dead, murdered in cold blood by EOKA. You were one of the first people at the scene and for all we know the killer may be the man who you've been fucking!'

'How dare you speak like that!'

'Dare? I dare all right. I'll continue to dare until I get some sense from you. Remember the day when he came round here, the day before he disappeared. Remember that?'

'Of course I remember.'

'He was here for over two hours. We know that. We know something else, as well. There was another visitor that morning.'

'Another visitor? What are you talking about, Geoffrey? Why

320

are you talking in riddles? Why is everyone talking in riddles?'

'There's no riddle, Dee. There was another visitor. He came in a civilian car driven by an Englishwoman. I've checked the number plate. Douglas Paxton's. It pulls up by the gate and a young boy gets out. The others wait in the car, while he goes through the gate and round the side of the house. A few minutes later he comes back. Carrying a football.' He paused, watching her closely. 'Did you know that?'

'I don't know what you are talking about. Do you mean Tom? Is that what you mean? Don't be ridiculous.'

'Perhaps I should have a word with him. Perhaps I should go in and have a little chat with him. As a family friend. Dear old Uncle Geoffrey. What exactly happened that day when you went to get your football? What did you see, old fella? Did you see your mummy fucking the taxi driver?'

'Don't you dare do such a thing!'

'I'm just saying things as they are, Dee. The games are over. Now it's serious. Can't you get that into your stupid little head?'

The phone rang. Every time it rang she felt a small pulse of fear. The silent calls seemed to be more frequent now. The phone would sound through the house and she would grab the receiver up and there would be nothing. 'Hello,' she would say, 'hello?' And then, sometimes, dangerously, 'Is that you?' And the line would hiss back at her, and she wouldn't know whether it was him or not, whether he was on the other end listening to her hesitant, anxious voice, or whether he had forgotten all about her and the call was nothing more than a wrong number, a random mechanical error at some unknown exchange. But this time as she snatched up the receiver there was a voice.

'Good-morning.' It seemed oiled, like a well-kept knife blade. 'Is that lady Denham?'

'It's Mrs Denham, yes.'

'Ah, Mrs Denham. This is Stavros Kyprianou. That car you ordered, lady. It will be there in ten minutes. Is that right?'

She tried to swallow, but the obstruction in her throat wouldn't go down.

'Lady? Are you there?'

'Yes,' she said. 'Yes, I'm here. Yes, that's right. The car—'

'That you ordered. It is there in ten minutes.'

'Yes.'

She put the phone down and stood there, almost as though the power of movement had deserted her. How should she prepare? She found no answer to the question. There was no way to prepare, no special clothes to wear, nothing to take with her, no way to stiffen her resolve. She opened the front door and glanced outside. There was the row of anonymous houses, the strip of potholed tarmac leading down to the shop at the corner with the delivery van parked near by. ΑΦΡΟΔΙΤΗ, it said on its side. The shop belonged to Stavros' cousin. It was where she had gone on her first exploration of the world outside the house, the place where she had been offered a chair – *karekla*, the owner had called it – and Paula had been given a glass of orange juice. But the shop wasn't called Aphrodite. She realized that now. Almost everything else in this cursed island was called Aphrodite, but not that shop. General Stores, or something.

She went back inside. 'I'm going shopping,' she told Voula. *Pao yia psonia.* The girl nodded and grinned, as she always did when Dee attempted anything in Greek. 'Back in the afternoon. *Apoghevma.*'

Ten minutes later Stavros was there exactly as he said – the Opel

Kapitan, with its familiar splashes of undercoat, idling outside the gate and he himself standing at the passenger door awaiting her arrival, just as usual. She settled into the oily interior, feeling sick with apprehension. 'All right, lady?' They pulled away from the kerb. She had expected to head out into the countryside, but instead Stavros followed the familiar road towards the town centre, past the fire station and the police compound. 'Where are we going?' she asked.

His eyes watched her in the mirror. 'You think I tell you where we are going? Of course I don't tell you.'

She glanced out through the window, bewildered. Not only 'where are we going?', but also 'what the hell am I doing here?' She looked round to see if anyone was following, but there was just the usual traffic milling around behind them, the buses, the trucks, the battered cars, the donkey carts.

'Nicos is stupid, lady,' Stavros said. 'I tell to him, he is stupid to do this. *Palavos*, I say him. Stupid.'

'Say to him,' she said.

'Say to him what?'

'No, that's what you say. Say to him. Not "say him". And "tell him", not "tell to him".'

A glance in the mirror, his eyes narrow. 'Look, lady, I not correct your Greek, you not correct my English. OK?'

'I'm sorry,' she said. '*Signomi*. I'm sorry. Is that right?'

He shrugged. 'Maybe it is, maybe it isn't.'

They came to a halt behind a bus. Old women climbed on board. There were sacks on the roof, produce for market. Stavros tapped his fingers on the steering wheel and hooted impatiently. 'I say him that he should not trust an Englishwoman, but he say me that you are his friend. What kind of friend? I ask. Just a friend, he say.' Again the eyes, watching, questioning. She looked away, out of the window at the passing traffic and the dilapidated buildings.

She shouldn't have asked about *signomi*. She knew it was correct. Nicos had taught her.

The bus moved away, trailing a cloud of black smoke. Stavros drew out after it. They passed a market, stalls with fruit and vegetables spilling out over the pavement. A cyclist teetered across in front of the car and Stavros rammed his fist on to the horn, shouting something out of the window. Then without warning he braked and swung the car down a side street. It happened in an instant – a sudden deceleration, a squeal of rubber on the hardened asphalt, the centripetal force flinging her against the door – and they were off the main road. The side street was barely wide enough for one car to pass. A pedestrian pressed back against the wall and shouted abuse. A couple of old ladies retreated into a doorway. Glancing back Dee saw a donkey cart jammed across the road behind them, with the driver climbing down to see about something. Perhaps it was the cyclist. Maybe they'd hit him. Cars hooted in anger. There was a couple of men arguing and gesticulating. And then she understood – it was something about Stavros' manner, a small laugh, a glance of satisfaction in the mirror – that what she had just seen had been deliberate, that any following vehicle was irrecoverably stuck on the far side of that little street incident, that they were now on their own. He slowed and turned the car again and the scene vanished. Now there was only a succession of narrow streets, little more than alleyways, with shops and bars and a patch of wasteland where a building had apparently been pulled down or was being rebuilt, or perhaps both of those things at the same time.

The car slowed to a halt. On the right there was a garage door, an open mouth between two shuttered façades. He swung the wheel over and the car lurched on to the pavement and eased into the narrow entrance. They stopped. The door rumbled down behind them and darkness fell.

'Where are we?'

'No matter, lady, where we are.' He climbed out and opened the rear door of the car to take her arm. 'You come. Please.'

There was the smell of oil about the place, and in the shadows a vague suggestion of bits of machinery. A door opened on to a narrow corridor. There was a flight of concrete stairs lit by a dusty window. He ushered her up to a landing and a bare, whitewashed room with a table and two chairs and a picture of Makarios on the wall. There was always a picture of Makarios.

'You stay,' he said, and was gone.

She waited. A single window overlooked a high-walled courtyard where sparrows scratched in the dust. Pigeons were strutting along the top of the wall, chests puffed out in the vain hope that that kind of thing would impress the females. And it did, for a moment. She could hear cooing and burbling and a rapid clatter of wings. Easy for pigeons, she thought.

A footfall on the landing made her turn. The door opened and he stood there in the doorway.

'Nicos.'

He was unshaven, the dark hair on his upper lip already making the beginnings of a moustache. His hair was no longer Brylcreemed into a quiff but had been left rough and disordered. He seemed older, as though she had found him halfway through some kind of metamorphosis, a transformation from fragile, vulnerable larva to tough, carapaced adult. There was a pistol – she didn't know the type but it looked like one of those army revolvers – stuffed into his waistband.

He came in and closed the door. 'It's good to see you,' he said. 'Bit of a surprise, really.'

'Is it?'

'Well, you know. Things have changed a bit, 'aven't they?' The London slant to his voice, the glottal stops, the dropped Hs – it was somehow surprising to find them all in place. They looked at each other with the same suppressed awkwardness as before, but then there had only been a narrow gap to cross; now it seemed to have become a gulf. 'What are you doing, Nicos?' she asked. 'What on earth have you been doing?'

He sniffed, glanced round the room, then pulled the revolver out of his waistband and placed it on the table. 'I can't tell you that, can I?'

'What's that thing?'

'What d'you think it is?'

Anger rose inside her. 'This is damned silly.'

'Look, we've only got a few minutes. Let's not argue, eh?'

She looked away from him but there wasn't much to look at – just the bare room with its single light bulb hanging from the ceiling, and the dusty window and the bright light outside; and the pistol, like a great black arachnid, a glistening scorpion, lying on the table. Her eyes stung with tears. 'What happened?' she said, not knowing what to say. 'Between us, I mean. If only—'

'If what?'

She shrugged. 'Things had been different. If we'd met in England or something. God, I don't know . . . If I'd met you in London, before I'd got married . . .' She shook her head. 'I don't know, Nicos. I just don't know.'

He laughed. It wasn't a forced laugh like Geoffrey's. It was dry and rough and natural, devoid of artifice. 'I'd just have been a Ted, wouldn't I? You might have passed me by in the street and thought yuck or something. You wouldn't even have talked to me.'

'I'm talking to you now.'

He came nearer, turned her face gently towards him. She wanted him to kiss her again. She wanted his tongue inside her mouth, and other things that she dared not even imagine. That dreadful compulsion. Was it love? 'Do you remember that time when I took you to the airport?' he asked.

'Of course. Of course I do.'

'And you were in tears and I thought you were the most beautiful thing in the world, do you remember that?'

'I remember the tears. I don't remember the last bit.'

'Well that's what I thought. I thought, if I could have this woman my life would be complete.'

'So you've had your wish, haven't you? And is it complete?'

'It was a only few minutes. Is that enough to last a lifetime? That's the question. Difficult calculation, in't it?' He stood there looking at her with almost no expression, as though she should provide the answer.

She nodded towards the pistol. It pointed diagonally across the table and she could see the bullets in its chambers, like seeds in a pod. 'What are you going to do with that thing?'

'Whatever's needed.'

'Isn't that killing? Isn't that what they do?'

'It's a war, isn't it? Killing happens. But it needn't happen, not if the British get out and leave the island to its people.'

'And the Turks?'

'The real war is with the Turks.' His tone suggested that she was stupid not to have seen this obvious truth. 'We're not fighting the British, Dee. We are fighting the Turks.'

'The Turks are just people, like the Greeks, like you and me.' She felt disgust, and anger and impatience. 'Like Damien Braudel. You know about Damien, don't you? You know what happened?'

He gave a dismissive laugh. It was an expression from the dance halls of Tottenham. So what? it said. Who cares? Who gives a fuck?

'Was it you?'

He smiled. 'Is that what they say?'

'He was at that café. You know where. That place near the seafront.'

'You said you didn't care about him.'

'That's not the point, is it?'

'I s'pose not.' He shrugged. 'Do you think I'd do something like that?'

It was stuffy in the room and she was sweating, the thin rivulets of sweat running down from her armpits. She pulled away from him and went over to the window. 'I don't know. I didn't think you'd be able to do something like *this*.' Outside, the pigeons were still going through their absurd little rituals, pumping and preening at one another along the top of the wall.

'Did he mean anything to you?' he asked.

'He was a friend. A human being.' She looked down. There was a movement down there in the courtyard, someone moving out of sight. 'Where's your uncle?' she asked.

'He's waiting downstairs.'

She opened the window and let the exterior sounds come in, the absurd burbling and the cooing of the birds and behind that the sound of the town – traffic, the honking of car horns, a ship's siren somewhere in the distance, near at hand a woman's voice calling.

'Close it,' Nicos said.

'I want a breath of fresh air.' But the air was only ever fresh up in the mountains, never down here on the coast.

'Close it, I said.' His tone had a new quality to it, a sharp edge of command. He crossed the room. 'Close the fucking thing.'

'All right, I'll close it.' As she reached out for the handle, a man appeared in the yard below. Khaki overalls and plimsolls, like a builder. He looked up for an instant, then moved out of sight. 'There's someone down there,' she said, leaning out to look down.

'What?'

'Someone.'

There was a patter of sound. Nicos grabbed her waist and pulled her back. Someone shouted. It was impossible to say what, what language even. Just a shout, then another shout and a sudden noise outside the room, the sound of people running up the stairs. Nicos swung her away from the window just as the door slammed open and two men erupted through the doorway.

There was a chaos of movement and shouting. 'Let the woman go! Let her go!'

'Don't shoot!'

'Let her go!'

And then stillness: a strange, static geometry with the two intruders at either corner of the room, and Nicos and Dee at the apex, at the window. He held her motionless, his left arm tight across her chest. She could feel his breath just behind her, hot and sharp. With sudden clarity she noticed that the pistol had gone from the table.

'Don't be a silly bugger,' one of the men said. They held submachine guns, the weapons levelled directly at Dee's abdomen. 'Let 'er go.'

A third man appeared at the doorway, a police officer with the familiar black cap and khaki shirt, an Englishman, pale and sweating. His shirtsleeves were rolled up and perfectly pressed but there were dark stains under the arms. 'Come on, lad, let the lady go,' he said.

Nicos spoke quietly just behind her head. The words were for her alone, breathed in her ear. 'You brought them here,' he said.

She tried to turn but he wouldn't let her, kept her facing the guns. The barrels pointed – small round mouths of surprise. At her back she could feel Nicos trembling. There was something hard and accusing against the side of her head. 'I didn't, Nicos. I didn't.'

'You fucking brought them here.'

'I didn't,' she repeated. 'I promise.'

'Come on, lad,' said the officer. He had a serious expression on his face, as though a solecism had just been committed and he was really rather shocked. 'Just take it easy. There's no point in messing about with guns. Someone could get hurt.'

Faintly, as you might sense someone fall asleep, she felt Nicos relax his grip.

'Put the gun down, son.'

'Don't hurt him,' she said. 'Please don't hurt him.'

'Of course we won't hurt him.'

Still she didn't move. His arm had gone from across her front but she stayed pressed against him. 'I love him,' she said softly, as though love might be a mitigation.

'I'm sure you do, ma'am. We all do. A jolly good chap. Now just come over here and we'll all be happy.'

She turned and looked up at Nicos. There was bewilderment in his eyes, and fear, and loathing. The gun was there in his right hand, no longer against her head but close to her cheek. She could smell the oil and the scent of its metal, like the smell of blood. 'Put the gun down, Nicos. Please.'

'Don't drop the fucking thing,' one of the soldiers cried. 'The fucker might go off.'

'Just put it down, lad,' the policeman said. 'Just put it down on the floor.'

Slowly, watching the soldiers, Nicos crouched down and laid the weapon on the tiles.

'There's a good chap,' the policeman said. He held his hand out towards Dee. His eyes were blue, the lashes so pale as to be almost invisible. He smiled at her, as though to assure her of the wonderful things he had to offer – a return to normality, to family and friends, to Edward and Tom and Paula, to hearth and home. 'Now come over to me, love. Just come slowly towards me. You'll be quite all right, won't she, Nick? She'll be quite all right.'

330

She looked round and raised her hand to touch Nicos' cheek, as though to assure herself of its reality. It was difficult to read his face, the tightness of the muscles, the rapid shallow breathing, the pupils dilated as they had been when they made love. Perhaps touching him would give some clue. Her fingers traced the line of his jaw, scraped against the roughness of his beard, touched his lips which were soft and fragile, almost feminine. She wanted to kneel down before him. It seemed absurd. She wanted to kneel down before him and feel his hand on her head in some kind of benediction. 'You must believe me,' she said quietly. 'I never knew they were coming.'

'Come on, love,' the policeman repeated.

She moved minutely away, smiling up at Nicos. Then she turned and walked towards the door.

As soon as she reached him the police officer grabbed her and flung her out of the room. Outside on the landing there were other hands to take hold of her, other voices, other accents. Behind her was a sound, difficult to interpret, a rush of noise, a scuffle and a cry. There was a shout, Nicos' voice crying something. And then the shouting died. 'It's OK!' a voice called. 'It's OK. All under control.'

She tried to turn back but hands held her and a couple of soldiers grabbed her and hurried her down the stairs. At the bottom of the stairwell were two Turkish policemen. Outside there was staring white sunlight and faces peering through windows and doorways. Suddenly she was shaking. Her legs almost gave way beneath her but there were always hands to bear her up, soldiers all around her. She saw that the street had been cordoned off and there were civilians crowded at one end. Barricades were being pulled into place. Policemen, dark-skinned Turks with heavy moustaches, were standing beside their vehicles and there was an army lorry as well, and an army blood wagon. That's what they'd been expecting. Blood. They'd been expecting everything.

Geoffrey stepped forward from among a group of policemen. 'Are you all right?'

'I'm fine.'

'Do you need a doctor or shall we go? I've got my car here. I don't really think we can talk on the pavement.'

He put a hand on her arm but she shook him off. 'I'm fine,' she said.

He smiled reproachfully and stood aside for her to go out first. His car was parked against the kerb a few yards down, the Volkswagen that she knew so well. He handed her into the back, then went round to the other side and climbed in beside her.

'I don't want to talk, Geoffrey.'

'Don't be silly. Cigarette?'

'Please.' He fiddled with his lighter and there was the spurt of flame. She drew smoke into her lungs and stared away, out of the window. Some civilians had come out of a nearby block of flats to watch the drama, fat women in slack cotton dresses, men in white shirts and grey trousers, the uniform. There were children. A couple of boys began to shout something. '*Enosi*,' they shouted '*Enosi!*' Dee craned round to see but there were too many people in the way – policemen, a few civilians. And then they brought out Nicos. They'd handcuffed and hooded him, but it was obvious who it was. Pushing and shoving, they led him towards the police van. She watched as they opened the rear door and lifted him in like baggage. Two policemen followed, and then the doors slammed shut. There were two little windows high up in the doors, with wire grilles. 'You're a bastard, Geoffrey, do you know that?'

'It goes with the job, Dee.'

'What'll happen to him?'

There was a silence. He smoked, watching her. 'Depends what charges they bring. And that depends in part on you . . .'

The engine of the police van roared. There was a clash of gears. She drew on her cigarette and tapped the ash into the ashtray, and looked at Geoffrey. She attempted a smile. It felt like someone trying a difficult manoeuvre that they haven't quite perfected, a cartwheel or a handstand or something. But she pulled it off. A smile. 'I have nothing to say to you, Geoffrey. Nothing at all.'

Seventeen

Nothing has changed. The furniture is still in place, the pictures and the clutter of possessions that she accumulated over the years. Yet everything has changed: every object, every surface, every plane and every vertical. All has lost its gloss of recent handling and acquired instead a micron depth of dust, a grey bloom that might have been the brushwork of time itself, blurring memory and recall. This place is not the past, is certainly not the future. It is some kind of limbo, occupied by grey shades: Persephone's kingdom.

Thomas closes the door behind him, picks up mail from the doormat – circulars, bills, letters from the bank and the solicitor – and takes it through into the kitchen. Sitting at the table he tears open envelopes and glances over the motley contents. One of them is a handwritten letter of condolence – 'We were abroad and we've only just heard . . .' – another comes from some charity, suggesting that the loss of a loved one is the perfect moment to consider making a donation. There are, it makes clear, tax advantages to be had. Then there is a new bank statement, sent despite the fact that the account has been frozen, and a letter from the building society explaining how much money can be made available prior to a grant of probate, and one from the solicitor dithering over some technicality: 'There appears to be a slight problem with one of your mother's bank accounts. I think we would be best advised to meet personally in order to clarify this issue.'

Searching in the cupboard beneath the kitchen sink he finds old copies of *The Times* neatly folded like laundry, and a packet, half opened and half used, of firelighters. It isn't a cold day – an ordinary day of intermittent cloud and sunshine, the rain, when it comes, a fine drizzle, the sun, when it shines, something pale and glistening like a reflection – but still he takes these things through into the sitting room and prepares a fire in the grate: the firelighter, loosely bunched pages of the newspaper, a small pyramid of kindling wood from the basket that is still there beside the fireplace, some pieces of coal laid carefully on the timber construction. He waits for the wood to take, then puts the guard in place and goes quietly upstairs to his mother's bedroom.

There is the painted wardrobe, the photograph of his father, the watercolour of Hope village, all the mementoes, the possessions, the *things* that are all that remain. There is also that dress, hanging in the wardrobe. He takes it out and carefully lays it, empty, a mere skin, on the bed. His mind plays over the memory of Kale standing there in the centre of the room, incongruous in the fashion of the nineteen-fifties, posing with a clumsy grace and twirling round so that the skirt flared out; then sitting suddenly on the bed for him to remove her shoes. And lying back as he lifted the skirt. Her expression of puzzlement. 'What are you up to, Thomas?' The rough scribble of her hair, the closed mouth, the subtle shades of cream and ivory, and then the deep pink, like the throat of an exotic flower. Her smell and taste.

He picks up the phone and dials her number. A woman's voice answers.

'Is that Mrs Macintosh?'

'Who's this?' The tone is guarded, as though he might do violence to her down the telephone line.

'It's Thomas again. Thomas Denham. You remember? I rang before.'

'Oh. Yeah, that history teacher.'

'Something like that. Is Kale there?'

There's a pause, as though for thought. 'Hang on and I'll get her.'

He waits. There are sounds off, like talking overheard from the next room, and then the noise of the receiver being picked up and Kale's voice loud in his ear: 'Yeah?'

'It's Tom.'

'Where are you?'

'At the house. I've got someone coming round to take stuff away. Look, I was wondering if you were still coming. You were meant to ring to confirm.'

'I've been busy.'

'You're always busy. How's Emma?'

'She's great.' The word lacks the last consonant. 'Grey,' she seemed to say.

'So you're coming?'

She hesitates. 'I dunno. Emms has still got a bit of a cold—'

'You just said she was great.'

'Well, she's all right. You know what I mean.'

'The sea air will be good for her. Better than Coldharbour Lane air, that's for sure. She'll love the boats and the seagulls, and the river. You'll enjoy it, both of you.'

'It's just—'

What is it just?

'I don't know what the point is.'

'The point is to enjoy yourselves, the two of you. Nothing more. No pressure, no relatives. I told you, just the three of us.'

'I s'pose.'

What the hell does that mean? There's a silence. He hates talking on the phone, hates the single dimension of it, the conversations without depth or colour. Like reading a play without seeing the performance. 'You do what you think best,' he says, dangerously.

'OK, I'll do what I think best.'

'There's a train at five to one. I'll be at the station to meet it.'

'Right.'

He wants to say other things. He wants to say that she means everything to him, that he wants to spend the rest of his life with her, that he loves her; but he dare not say any of them. 'See you' is all he manages, before he cuts the line and turns back to the wardrobe. Methodically he gets the other clothes out – the dresses, the skirts, the slacks – and lays them on the bed, neatly in rows, like laying out so many corpses. Then he begins to empty her drawers – underwear, sweaters, blouses, the whole mass of garments tossed on to the bed along with the other things, and then everything stuffed into black plastic bin bags. Like evidence being taken away from the scene of a crime, evidence of a life being consigned to the limbo of forgetting. He humps the bags downstairs to the hallway. There is a dozen of them by the end.

He glances at his watch. In his imagination Kale and Emma take the Underground away from the land of concrete and graffiti and waste. He pictures the train rattling in its tube deep beneath the river, with Kale clutching her daughter's hand and staring at the black window, while strap-hanging

337

men jolt speculatively against her. He imagines the pair of them standing on the escalator as it slides them up from the depths at Liverpool Street, Persephone and her daughter returning to the upper world from Hades.

In the sitting room the fire has taken, the coals cracking in the heat and glowing a dull red. A faint, luminous flame hovers over them. There are other things to do. He goes up to the study and with care he assembles the evidence: the letter from Geoffrey, the envelope of *Oddments* with its burden of ship's menu and its few typewritten sheets, the newspaper cutting, the two poems, the circumstantial photograph. *Nick.*

He carries his little bundle down to the sitting room, moves the fireguard aside, then crouches down and feeds the pieces of paper, one by one, into the flames. Each sheet curls and wrinkles and browns before flaring into brief and intense life. The black skeletons float in the hot air for a moment, as fragile as memories, before shattering against the firebricks. He watches the small holocausts of incident and memory, until finally only the photograph remains. This is made of sterner stuff than the rest and it takes longer to burn. It curls, the emulsion cracking and charring, the two figures staring out at him like bodies in a cremation while the circle of black constricts around them. Then the flames billow, consuming everything.

If there is no evidence, there is no history.

The doorbell rings. It's the man from Oxfam, complete with the white van that he has borrowed, so he says, from a mate. Together they hump the bags into the back, and Thomas hands over a tenner for his trouble. He stands and watches as the van draws away before turning back to the house.

The place seems different now. Void, empty of something fundamental. He goes through into the kitchen to get something together for lunch. Will Kale come? He hopes, imagines, doesn't dare to doubt that she is even now standing beneath the departures board at Liverpool Street Station, looking up at the letters and numbers flickering over, the dominoes falling; with Emma beside her, clinging to her hand.

He's about to start eating when the doorbell interrupts him again, but this time when he opens it he discovers Janet Burford on the doorstep. She stands there blinking, her feet planted wide as though she's on a deck and not going to be put off by any rocking of the boat. 'I'm sorry,' she says. 'I hope you don't mind, but I saw you clearing things out earlier and I thought I'd drop in.' She looks over his shoulder. 'Are you alone? Do you think I could have a word?'

'I was just starting lunch. I've got to meet someone at the station.' Is Kale even now sitting in the train with Emma beside her, the pair of them watching the dull Essex flats pass by the window?

'Just a sec. Please.'

'Can't we make it some other time?'

'I'd rather not.' There's a blunt stubbornness about her presence, as though she has made up her mind about this and is determined not to be put off. Reluctantly Thomas steps aside to let her pass. He follows her into the sitting room and watches as she looks round as though to see what's missing. Then her eyes light on the only tangible thing that Kale and he share, the piece of pottery that she gave them, that sits now, like a gynae-cological specimen, on a shelf beside the fireplace. She picks it up and runs her hands over it fondly, as she did with the piece of Meissen that stood there before.

'You and Kale. Are you still together?'

'She's meant to be coming this afternoon. With her daughter.'

Her eyelids flicker. 'How nice. I'd love to see her again. She's such a lovely young woman. Strong, isn't she? Lots of guts. And I'd love to meet her little girl. Maybe you can come round. Would you like to? This evening if you want.'

He shrugs. 'Look—'

'I love children. But somehow I didn't dare have them when I was married. I thought I might destroy them if I did.'

'Why are you so special? Every parent risks that.'

'Because I almost destroyed myself?' The upward lilt, as though she isn't quite sure about the destruction and wants reassurance on the point. 'And now I'm too old even if I wanted them. So whose responsibility was that? Mine, I suppose. I don't know. Who's responsible for someone being what they are? That's what I mean about being a parent. And I was adopted, so there were other factors, weren't there? But you can't blame my adoptive parents. They tried their best . . .' Her voice trails away. She seems close to tears.

'Look, can I get you something – a cup of tea or coffee perhaps? And then I'm afraid I must ask—'

'No, it's all right. I'm fine, really, Tom, I'm fine. I don't want to put you to any trouble.'

Tom? He's not Tom. He's never been Tom, not since leaving school. He's always been Thomas. Tom only to his mother, and now Kale sometimes. But not this woman, who is looking at him now with something approaching fear, as though the distress she has shown is his fault. What was it Kale said about her? She's damaged.

'Then perhaps—'

'Have you heard of a man called Charteris?' she asks. The question has nothing to do with what she has been saying – it's a symptom of the erratic way her mind works, like that bloody blinking. 'Charteris,' she insists. 'Didn't Dee ever mention him?'

'Look, I've really got things to do . . .' He moves as though to show her the door.

'*Tom* Charteris?'

Thomas stops. 'Yes, she did. He was an old boyfriend of hers, back home in Sheffield. Killed in the war.' A pause. 'But I never knew his name was Tom.'

'There's a lot you don't know. You see, Tom Charteris was my father.'

And Thomas *can* see. Suddenly, fleetingly, he can see the resemblance. It's like a familiar face recognized in a blurred photograph – something about the cast of her eyes and the set of her cheek and jaw. He sits down heavily in the other armchair, the one that was his mother's. He's no longer inclined to try and stop her. In fact he's bound to hear her through to the end: it's his duty, more or less. 'Go on.'

She opens her hands. They have been clenched tight and now that she relaxes them there are the marks of her nails in the palms, and the scar tissue on her wrists that Kale noticed. 'Where do I start? With me as a little girl, wondering about them? You do, of course, once you've been told the truth.' Her face works in that convulsive manner, as though the machinery beneath the skin, the delicate articulation of nerve and muscle and tendon, has broken. 'As a child I used to lie in bed and imagine them coming to rescue me. How was I to know that he was dead? Of course I wasn't. But my mother was still alive, and she never came looking either. Never at all. Well, she wouldn't have, would she? She'd barely even seen me. I was hardly even a memory.'

'And then?'

'You come to terms with it after a fashion. You get on with your life and make of it what you can. Which in my case wasn't a great deal. A failed marriage, work of sorts – a bit of sculpting and pottery. I even taught for a few years at an art college. And then, some time after the break-up of my marriage, I decided to find out for myself. It was me who went looking for her.'

She pauses, as though to leave him space to speak. But he hasn't anything to say. All those words have come to nothing.

'I made enquiries – the local council, the birth records, forms to fill, interviews, pleading, pleading. It's weird, distressing, like your own past is someone else's secret and they're not letting you in on it. And then, of course, if you do find out, you have to make contact indirectly in case the other person doesn't want to know. You can't plead, you can't persuade. All you can do is ask a plain question, through a third party. "Do you want to meet me?" It's like appealing to a jury and waiting for the verdict. Guilty or not guilty? Nothing in between. But she agreed to a meeting.' Janet makes a sound. It might be a cough, might be the sound of choking. Tears have gathered in her eyes once more. 'So here I am, Tom. Here I am.'

And it's there again as she stares back at him, that familial likeness, the shadow of a past cast forward into the future. He shakes his head, searching for something coherent to say. 'There were things she said. I thought . . . I don't know what I thought, really. I had this idea she had betrayed my father. All those years ago in Cyprus.'

Janet smiles. 'She never betrayed your father, Tom. Or you, or Paula. She betrayed me.'

The station is little more than a halt – a single platform with a small shelter and a single track coming to a single pair of buffers. The end of the line. He waits, looking down the rails, where they converge in the distance amidst trees and grass banks and the low grey sky. There is a single gantry with one of those old mechanical signals on it, the arm slanting upwards.

He waits.

A voice crackles out into the still air announcing, barely intelligibly, the arrival of the 12.55 train from Liverpool Street Station. Apparently as a result of the announcement, as though words can conjure up events, the train itself appears, at first no more than the idea of a train, a mere spot at the distant apex of perspective.

Thomas watches it grow larger. Of course, it's only the illusion of perspective that makes it grow, just as the perspective of memory throws things into different proportion according to how you see them; and everything is larger in a child's world.

And then the train rolls over some subtle boundary and it is no longer there in the distance, but here, present, a steel and aluminium tube sliding alongside the platform, groaning and grinding as the brakes go on, a sealed capsule painted and daubed, with windows and doors and lives inside, the present lives of however many people there are who have come out to the far reaches of estuarine Essex on an afternoon of one Friday in early summer.

The doors bang open. Passengers climb down on to the platform and look around in that uncertain way they have when they arrive at their destination.

He waits, watching for a slender, pale woman and her little girl.